Christmas
Cards from the
Edge

JENNIFER ASHLEY

LISA CACH

NAOMI NEALE

LOVE SPELL

NEW YORK CITY

LOVE SPELL®

October 2005

Published by

Dorchester Publishing Co., Inc.
200 Madison Avenue
New York, NY 10016

ISBN 0-505-52657-3

Visit us on the web at www.dorchesterpub.com.

Christmas Cards from the Edge

TABLE OF CONTENTS

Return to Sender

by

LISA CACH

To my nephew Wade,
who has an eye for finer things.

Chapter One

Seattle, Washington

A hand on my shoulder jolted me out of sleep, breaking my erotic dream of being forced into a steel-boned corset by five naked footmen with powdered wigs on their heads. I squinted against the bright light, raised my head off the kitchen table, and discovered that my right arm was dead to the world. My mouth had that dry, fuzzy feel that tells you you've been sleeping with your mouth open.

"It's two A.M., Tessa," my housemate, Lauren, said, her voice stabbing me through my fog of sleepy, drunken confusion.

"Murrr," I grunted, and swung my arm around, growing alarmed as my hand flopped and swayed, as lifeless as a corpse. The rubbery limb hit my wineglass, knocking it over and spilling its remnants of cheap merlot all over the Christmas cards I'd been writing. I stumbled out of my chair a moment too late to keep the rivulets of red from running over the edge of the table and onto the lap of my bathrobe, the blue chenille sucking it in as eagerly as a sailor at a dockside bar, leaving no drop to hit the floor.

"Oh, jeez," Lauren said, and grabbed a rag to mop up the spill on the table.

Feeling marginally more awake, I dragged myself over to the kitchen sink and hoisted a wad of my robe over the rim, prepared to wring out the drippiest bit.

"Don't wring it!" a male voice ordered.

I froze, not recognizing the voice, and knowing that my hoisted robe was giving the man a clear view of my granny panties and the pale thighs and butt that went with them.

"Pour white wine on it, or club soda, then soak it in cold water," he continued, and I heard the lilt of a Scottish accent.

"I *know* how to treat stains," I said, embarrassed, dropping my robe back over my legs and turning to face the intruder. "Of course I know better than to wring it, but does a girl have to do the right thing all the time?"

The man grinned at me, his teeth white and straight in his handsome narrow face with its five-o'clock shadow. "I should hope to God not."

"Tessa, this is my cousin Ian, from London," Lauren said. "Well, from Scotland originally. Never call a Scotsman an Englishman, if you value your life. Ian, my housemate, Tessa."

"It's a very real pleasure to meet you, Tessa," he said, coming forward, his hand rising just enough from his side for me to realize that he was waiting—very properly—for me to extend my hand to him first.

But I was staring at him like I was a squirrel in the middle of the road waiting for a delivery truck to squish me flat. A blush burned my face, and I hunched down into the sheltering thickness of my robe collar, stupidly hoping that the truck would veer off at the last moment. I gaped and blinked and considered hiding under the kitchen sink. It's a pathological reaction I have to a good-looking man near my own age. I'm not proud of it, but neither can I help it: men like that scare the bejeebers out of me.

"Pleased to meet you," I finally mumbled, dropping my gaze from his roughly beautiful face and his gorgeous dark

4

blue eyes. My shy gaze was now resting on the expanse of his chest, covered in a straight black leather jacket and a fine-gauge dark green sweater that looked to my expert eye suspiciously like cashmere. Its slim lines flowed smoothly from broad chest to narrow hips, flattering his lithe frame.

"Lauren tells me you know more about costume history than anyone she's ever met," he said, his warm hand gripping mine. His skin was dry, his strong hand engulfing my small, damp squirrel paw. A hand like his promised protection and strength and pure, undiluted *male.* A twinge of longing pierced my heart, and as he released my hand I scrunched even lower into my robe and tucked my freed hand into its sleeve, the fist closed tight as if holding on to the feel of his touch.

"Lauren's getting a Ph.D. in chemical engineering—she doesn't know any other costume historians," I said, and then wanted to kick myself for sounding so ungracious. It was the shyness doing it to me.

Lauren made a rude noise. "Don't listen to her, Ian! You should see the things she has in her workroom upstairs, and just get her started on a discussion of historic textiles—"

"I'm going to bed," I mumbled, embarrassed, and shuffled over to the table to scoop up my soggy Christmas cards. Why on earth was she telling her cousin about my work?

From the corner of my eye I saw Lauren shrug and make a helpless face, a silent communication with her cousin. "I offered Ian the use of the futon," she said aloud. "He's only in town for the night, and I'm driving him to the airport in the morning."

"Okay." I risked another glance at the divine Ian and made myself smile, although I must have looked like a sickly stray dog begging for attention. "Have a nice flight. I hope you don't have any delays heading home."

He laughed, the corners of his eyes crinkling. "I'll be out of your house before you know it. Sleep well."

"I didn't mean—" I started to say in alarm, but then thought discretion the better part of valor and scooted out of there. I escaped through the dining room and down a short hall to the haven of the bathroom. I could hear the murmur of their lowered voices and quiet laughter, and my face heated anew at the thought of what a terrible impression I must have made on Ian. I dumped the ruined Christmas cards into the trash and looked at myself in the mirror.

Oh, lord.

My long, dark hair was flat and stringy, desperately in need of washing; my pale face was mottled with pink creases where I had lain on the table and cards; mascara was smudged under my bloodshot brown eyes; and worst of all, my chapped lips were stained purple by the wine I'd been drinking. I smiled and saw that my teeth were tinted the same creepy shade.

I brushed my teeth and took a quick shower. I thought better of filling the tub and soaking the robe, since *he* might want a shower in the morning. Instead, I sat on the lid of the toilet and ran water over the wine stain, grateful for the sound of the running water and the fan overhead, the white noise making me feel like I was in my own steamy little cocoon of privacy. A girl could be herself in the bathroom.

I picked a Christmas card out of the trash—not one of the cards I'd been writing, but one of those that my old college friend Rachel had sent, and to which I'd been responding. The cover was a paper-framed photo of her and her husband cheek-to-cheek, arms around each other, grinning with delirious happiness. They wore leis and bathing suits, the blue skies of Hawaii overhead. The note said the photo was taken on their third anniversary, and my friend's bare tummy showed the bulge of her first child growing inside.

It had been this card that had encouraged me to open the bottle of wine. I was happy for my friend—happy for all my friends who had sent me cards filled with husbands and young children to go with their degrees and careers—but it did remind me that my last relationship had expired eight months ago, turning slowly unhealthy, like an aging tub of cottage cheese. I still thought that my ex, Alan, had been the closest I'd ever gotten to Mr. Right, and there were many days when I wondered if I should have fought harder to keep the relationship going.

The truth was, though, that I had a secret suspicion that I'd never really loved Alan. Sadder still, I'd never been with *any* man I deeply loved, loved past reason or self-preservation. I'd never been with anyone with whom I could joyfully, without doubt or a creeping sense of future unhappiness, contemplate spending the rest of my life. I was thirty years old and losing hope that I would find that mythical *he* who could erase all the questions and fears from my mind.

Maybe I was too strange a person to find a match, or maybe there was something wrong with me that made me incapable of loving. Maybe it was my fate to end up the eccentric professor whom students laughed at behind her back and told anecdotes about. I'd tell my female students that you didn't need a husband or a family to be happy; that books and travel and friends and creativity were more than enough. I'd probably *be* happy, too—except for that part of me that still wept for the broken dream, and still looked to find it in the face of every man I met.

I felt tears well in my eyes as I looked again at the photo of Rachel in the encompassing embrace of the man she'd married.

I wanted my own husband to love, who would fold me in his arms at night as we slept, the warmth of his body sheltering me against the cold and promising his companionship until the end of our days.

I don't know how long I'd been asleep in my bed when Lauren's hand once again shook me awake. She clicked on my bedside lamp and I groaned and turned away. "What?" I asked. "*What?*"

"Tessa! Do me a huge favor? My sister just went into labor. I'm driving up to Bellingham to be with her. Can you drive Ian to the airport in the morning?"

I rolled back over and squinted one eye open just enough to read the clock. Three thirty A.M. "What time does he have to be there?"

"His flight's at eight. It's international, so he has to be there two hours early. . . ." She paused to think, which was good, as I was beyond figuring timetables. "So you should leave here by five thirty."

I pulled the covers over my eyes. "Set my alarm for five, would you?" I didn't want to face handsome Ian again, but at the moment I was less interested in protesting than I was in slipping back into sleep and a dream filled with dancing men in tights.

"Thank you! I'll wash all the dishes for a month." The light was back off and the door half-shut when it creaked back open again. "Oh, and wake up Ian when you get up! He doesn't have an alarm clock."

"Mmm," I said, already asleep again.

Chapter Two

I hit my snooze button yet another time, then woke enough to remember that I didn't have to go to work today. I flipped the alarm all the way off.

It was over an hour later that my eyes suddenly flew open, some dreg of memory working its way up through my cozy dozing to remind me that I was supposed to drive Ian to the airport. A panicked glance at the clock showed the time in glowing, accusatory red: six fifty-five A.M.

Aieeee!

I sprang out of bed and out of my room, careening around the corner and into the living room. The futon had been unfolded into a bed, and Ian was sprawled across it, one arm flung above his head, feet dangling over the edge, the sheet and blanket in a wrinkled heap over his legs and groin but leaving his dark-haired chest uncovered. He was snoring softly in the dim gray light of morning, his thick black lashes shadowing the delicate skin under his eyes.

"Ian!"

The snoring continued.

"Ian! Wake up! We're late!" I shook the edge of the stiff

mattress and made not a ripple. *Damn futon.* I reached out to touch him, but my hands hovered over his bare chest; they didn't have the guts to settle on that exposed skin. They drifted down over his thigh, but that was all too close to his privates. I whimpered and flapped my hands helplessly, then moved to the end of the makeshift bed and, using thumb and forefinger, gingerly grasped the hand he'd flung above his head. I waggled it back and forth. "Ian!"

His hand turned and gripped mine and began to pull. His eyes opened halfway and met mine, and my heart began to pound in my chest. The pull on my arm continued, and I leaned forward, ready to topple down across him. *Yes, yes, pull me into bed with you. I won't fight; I won't say no. . . . Lie on top of me and press me against the mattress with your whole glorious, manly length. . . .*

Recognition filtered into his eyes, and a frown drew down his brows. "Sorry!" he said, releasing my hand.

Dammit.

He sat up and rubbed his face, the covers pooling across his loins. There was a narrow trail of black, silky hair from his navel down into the shadows of the sheet. What I wouldn't give to trail my fingers down it. "What time is it?" he asked.

The question recalled me suddenly to myself. "Seven!" I shouted. "Seven! We've got to go *now!*" I dashed back to my room and threw on the clothes closest to hand, then made an unavoidable pit stop in the bathroom. A glance in the mirror while I did a quick brush of my teeth revealed horrors of rat's-nest hair and, despite my shower, smudges of mascara still lodged like smashed spiders under my eyes. I grabbed a washcloth, but before I could so much as wet it, Ian was rapping on the bathroom door.

"Are you ready?"

I squeaked and gave up, tossing the washcloth into the sink. Interesting him in me was hopeless to begin with, and the man was leaving town. All he wanted me to do for him was get him to the airport *on time.*

10

I opened the door and rushed past him and through the house to the foyer, stepped sockless into a pair of beat-to-death running shoes, grabbed my purse and keys, and reached for the front door. He beat me to it, his hand grasping the knob a moment before my own. I felt the warmth and movement of him in the air, catching a faint scent of something spicy and deliciously masculine. When I caught my breath I took a moment to look at him.

The dark scruffiness of his one-day beard and his bed-head hair looked intentional, as if he were modeling for a sultry black-and-white cologne ad, perhaps with a diamond-encrusted blonde pawing his naked chest. How old was he? Thirty? Forty? He had a few creases on his brow, beside his eyes, and at the sides of his nose, but they could as easily be from weather or laughter as age. He had a black leather garment bag in his left hand, and nodded to me to go first through the door. There was a faint hint of a smile on his lips, and I scowled as I wondered if he was laughing at me.

"Go ahead; I have to lock up," I said. "It's the blue Wagoneer at the curb."

I locked the door and followed him down the steep cement stairs to the sidewalk. My 1975 Jeep Wagoneer had the soft blue-gray patina that only age can bring, and which I personally feel it would be a shame to destroy with something so crass as regular cleanings and polish. I opened a back door for him to toss in his garment bag.

"Why is there white felt all over?" he asked as he put his bag on the lumpy back of a folded-down bench seat. The entire back of the Wagoneer was coated in felt, the felt in turn covered with tiny snippets of abandoned thread, stray pins, a stack of tissue paper, a few paper garment boxes, and drifts of filmy plastic dry cleaning bags.

"I don't know how much Lauren told you," I said as I unlocked the front passenger door for him, all the while feeling the ticking of the clock and mentally planning the best route to take to the airport. "I'm an assistant professor in

11

the theater department at the University of Washington. I teach costume history and I design the costumes for the school's theater productions, which means I sometimes transport a lot of expensive fabrics and costumes. I'm a little obsessive about keeping them clean."

"So you really *did* know not to wring your robe," he said, shutting the back door and opening the front one.

"Yes." I jogged around to the driver's side, getting in and slamming the old heavy door with a clang that probably woke the neighbors. The Jeep started with a roar and we were off. "If traffic is clear we might make it," I said with forced cheerfulness. "Might," I repeated more quietly, and turned on the radio just in time to hear that Interstate 5 was a mess. *"Damn."*

"Is that going to affect us?"

I muttered a few curses against the traffic gods, then tossed Ian a bright smile and took the Jeep into a sharp turn, the centrifugal force knocking him against his door. "Oh, no, don't worry. I have my ways."

"Do you then," he said, his voice rising half an octave as I barreled down the street, his face going still and his eyes intent on the road in front of us in that way frightened passengers have. I took another corner and he reached for the assist strap above the door. Unfortunately for him, all that was left of it was a three-inch stub of plastic. Our family dog had chewed it off when I was a kid.

I got onto Highway 99 south and began to pick up speed. The wing windows started to whistle, then to howl. Ian said something, but it was lost under the roar of wind and motor.

"What was that you said?" I shouted. Fat splats of rain hit the windshield, and I turned on the wipers, adding their screech and thwack to the tumult. The highway took us onto a high, long bridge, the gray waters of the Lake Washington ship canal far below. Up ahead I could see the bright red flares of brakelights on unmoving cars. I muttered another dark imprecation as we slowed to a crawl, and then to a stop. We were about twenty feet from reaching the end of the bridge.

"I asked you what drew you to costuming."

I tapped my fingers on the steering wheel, eyeing the cars ahead and looking for possible escape routes from the traffic jam. "I love beautiful clothes."

"Do you."

I glanced at him and caught his gaze flickering over my outfit. I was wearing a baggy gray sweater with frayed ribbing at the cuffs and a cotton broomstick skirt of the ten-dollar variety. "Yes, I do. Not that my wardrobe is any indication," I admitted.

"You love beautiful clothes, your work revolves around beautiful, creative clothes, you know the history of beautiful clothes, and yet you don't wear them."

I heard the implied question, crouching in his words like a hungry psychologist. "Because I don't have the time. Besides," I added before he could comment further, "it's historical clothing I really love, not contemporary. Contemporary clothing is too utilitarian."

"All historical clothes were contemporary at one point. All were utilitarian to some degree; all served some purpose."

"But I wasn't living then, so they still have magic for me." I sought further words to describe the feeling that an embroidered apron from the eighteenth century or a pair of hand sewn leather boots from the fourteenth gave to me: the sense of touching another period of time, of touching the lives of people who had been gone for centuries. That magical sense held true even if the garment itself was nothing more than a theatrical reproduction. Time put a gloss of romance on the past—a romance that I had always felt sorely lacking in my own existence.

"Is it the magic of the inaccessible?" he asked, breaking into my reverie.

I was surprised by his perception. "Yes, the magic of a

time and a life that I will never have." I frowned at him. Who was this Ian? Why would he be sensitive to such things? "What is it that you do, Ian? For a living, I mean."

"My business cards call me a purveyor of luxury goods," he said with a wry smile.

"Sounds shady, 'purveyor.' Do the goods fall off a truck?"

"We'd have a higher profit margin if they did." He shrugged. "It's so inelegant to say I'm just a shopkeeper. Accurate, but inelegant."

"And you're an elegant guy?"

"I pretend to be."

"Can elegance truly ever be faked?"

"I count on it."

But before I could follow up on that intriguing line of thought, the car in front of me inched forward and I spotted my escape route. I eyed the narrow distance between the lane of cars and the high curb. "Hold on," I said.

I put the Jeep in gear and veered half off the road, carefully riding the right-side tires up onto the tall sidewalk. Ian grasped the handle on the door, trying and mostly failing to keep from sliding across the bench seat into my lap. His leg hit mine, and I struggled to keep my foot on the gas as I myself fell against the driver's side door. The Jeep was canted at what felt like a forty-five-degree angle.

"How far am I from the bridge rail?" I asked.

He struggled to peer out his side window. "A few inches! What in God's name are you doing?"

"Trying to get you to the airport!" I eased the Jeep along the tall sidewalk, checking out my own window to be sure I didn't take off anyone's side mirror. Passengers in the cars I passed gaped at me: a woman jerked and spilled her Starbucks in her lap; a teenage boy's sullen expression turned to sly joy; a small child in the midst of a red-faced, screaming temper tantrum went suddenly silent, her round, tear-filled eyes staring as we slid by.

"It's not worth getting in a wreck!"

14

"Oh, pish. I'm not going to get in a wreck. I have an off-road vehicle, so I can take it off the road!"

"Maybe *you* should be taken off the road."

"What was that you said?" I asked as we came to the end of the bridge and the sidewalk disappeared. The Jeep thumped down onto the gravel and mud beside the road, and I stepped on the gas, shooting us twenty feet to the turnoff to go up Queen Anne Hill.

"God in heaven . . ."

I realized I was enjoying myself. He'd seen my granny panties; he'd seen me drunk and covered with wine. This was my revenge. He might not ever find me attractive, but at least he'd find me memorable. "I learned to drive on dirt logging roads. Don't worry; we'll be fine."

" 'Don't worry' she says again. . . ."

I grinned and glanced at him and saw that his hand was still affixed in a death grip to the door handle. There was a grimace of fear tugging on the corner of his mouth. He caught me looking and widened his eyes, gesturing with his chin back toward the road. He must think I should watch where I was going.

A stop sign popped up out of nowhere—was that there before?—and I slammed on the brakes, squealing a nice smear of rubber onto the road. "No problem," I said.

He grunted and tightened the seat belt over his hips.

Back on pavement we made good time going up the hill and over, passing by some of the grander houses in Seattle and catching a few ghostly views of the city and Elliott Bay, covered in a thin fog.

"Rain and fog together. It's like Scotland," he said.

"Maybe the fog will delay your flight. Do you have a cell phone? You could call and check."

He perked up. "Good idea." He took his phone out of the inside breast pocket of his leather coat and started pushing buttons. He put it to his ear, listened, pressed another series of buttons, then did it all again. Listen, push buttons, listen, push buttons, the jabs at the buttons becoming fiercer each time. He must be stuck in his airline's phone system.

He suddenly said a very bad word, his button-punching finger bouncing up as if it had been singed. "Three, not two! Three! I wanted option three!" A few more bad words followed and then he settled down with the phone to his ear, a grim, bleakly accepting look on his face, like a prisoner awaiting execution. I could hear the spillover of McLean's "American Pie" coming from the receiver.

I felt a surge of regret for having suggested the phone to him. I'd gotten my fun with the wild ride; putting him in an airline's phone system was kicking a man while he was down. "So what brought you to the States?" I asked by way of making amends as I pulled back onto Highway 99, the traffic flowing smoothly here. "Was it just to visit family?"

"Business, mostly. We want to expand into the U.S. market. I had a meeting here in Seattle and took the chance to see Lauren."

"So why is she American while you're Scottish? What's the relationship?"

"Her father fell in love with an American girl and moved out here to be with her and raise a family. I'd never met any of them until Lauren and her family spent a summer in Scotland with us when she and I were teenagers. We've kept in touch ever since."

A tinge of my Christmas card sadness came back. What a romantic life Lauren's mother must have had, her Scotsman leaving his world behind to be with her. I didn't want to hear any more about it. "So how big is this luxury goods emporium you work for?"

"I—" he started, then cut himself off as the music ended and a tinny voice spoke into his ear. "Hello, yes, I need to check if my flight is leaving on time. . . ."

A minute later he hung up. "It's delayed ten minutes."

"We only have another fifteen minutes, tops, until we get there," I said, feeling a surge of hope. "You might still catch it!"

I felt a burst of adrenaline. We really might make it! "There's only one thing that could stop us now."

"A speeding ticket?"

"It only feels like we're going too fast because the ride is rough." I glanced at the speedometer: seventy-five. Could he see it from the passenger seat? "No, the only thing that could stop us . . ." I trailed off as I saw my nemesis up ahead: the drawbridge over the Duwamish Waterway.

"Yes?"

"Is that. Dammit!" Up ahead, the warning lights beside the bridge began to flash and the black-and-white gate to come down. There was no one ahead of us, and I knew that it would actually be another minute before the drawbridge began to come up. Flashes of movies came to mind, cars flying off the rising section of road as if trying to jump a row of school buses. For a moment, my foot pressed down on the accelerator.

"*No!*" Ian shouted in such a firm and commanding tone that my foot immediately came off the pedal. "You will not!" There was no question in his voice, no pleading, just the demand of someone who would not be opposed.

I put my foot on the brake and glided to a long and easy stop several feet before the barrier gate. My heart was pounding, and I felt a tremor in my hands. There was part of me that had been ready to take the risk. "I wouldn't have," I said. "That's not the type of thing I do."

He didn't answer. I looked at him and found him staring at me, examining me as if he were an entomologist who had come across an unknown form of beetle.

I didn't know who I was myself at the moment, either. My friends occasionally said I was eccentric, especially when I became obsessed with research and design for a theater production and could talk about nothing else, but I'd never been a spontaneous or unpredictable person outside of that. And I'd never been a physical risk taker.

Was I that desperate for some male attention?

The bridge slowly began to rise. The seconds ticked past,

and then minutes as a barge moved slowly through the gap. A sailboat came after it, motoring sedately, its mast bare of sails.

"We're not going to make it," I said quietly, feeling a wash of shame. This was my fault for hitting the snooze button.

"They might be able to get me on another flight. I doubt I'll be trapped here over Christmas."

Christmas. *Oh, jeez.* He might have to spend it alone in a hotel room because of me.

The bridge finally lowered and I gunned the engine as the gates came back up. I was across the bridge in a shot, my hands tight on the wheel and my gaze scanning the road for all possible obstacles. Ian was silent, and a quick glance his way showed me a man lost in internal thoughts and calculations. He didn't look happy.

We finally made it to the airport, and I dropped him at the curb in front of his airline. "Good luck!" I called to him as he took his bag out of the back.

"Thanks for the lift. Have a merry Christmas, Tessa. It was a pleasure meeting you."

"It was a pleasure meeting you, too," I mumbled as he shut the door. He headed toward the sliding glass doors but turned once, giving me a smile and a wave. I waved back, and felt my heart sink as he disappeared through the glass.

Gone.

I put the Jeep in gear and pulled away from the curb, the days ahead suddenly looking bleaker and emptier than they had a day ago, not counting my drunken sobbing over the Christmas cards. School was out and I'd filed the grades for my classes; I had nothing to do but finish making a few presents, debate attending a party I'd been invited to on the twenty-third but which I knew I'd chicken out of at the last minute, write uninspired Christmas cards to my friends, and spend Christmas Day in nearby Snohomish with my family, deflecting the pitying looks of sisters-in-law who thought it a shame I couldn't catch a husband.

The only intriguing element of the whole week was presently checking in for a flight out of here.

Or was he?

I saw the turnoff for the parking structure and on impulse took it. Ian might not catch his flight, after all, I told myself as I drove around and around the upward-spiraling ramp. He might be delayed several hours. Maybe I could buy him breakfast as an apology for making him miss his plane.

I parked and headed for the terminal, a nervous sweat breaking out under my arms as I hurried through the sky-bridge. What if I didn't catch him before he went through security? I'd have to page him, and I didn't even know his last name. They'd make the announcement on speakers throughout the terminal: "Scottish Ian, cousin to Lauren Gold, please go to a white courtesy telephone for a message from the sex-starved maniac who drove you to the airport."

All right, so they'd leave out the maniac bit. Still, he'd think I was insane. Worst of all, would he suspect I did it because I wanted a few more minutes in which to bask in the glow of a lusciously handsome man?

Nah, probably not. Experience told me that men were obtuse about a woman being interested in them. Even if you did your best impression of a lick-lipping porn star while making meaningful eye contact, he'd only suspect that you had a salivary disorder and offer you a napkin. A truth unhappily proven to me at a college party I'd attended at age nineteen.

I spotted the sign for his airline and jogged toward the ticket counter, scanning the people in line. No Ian . . . no Ian . . . Ian! He was talking to the man behind the counter under the BUSINESS CLASS sign.

I stopped in my tracks, overcome by shyness. Now that I knew I could still talk to him, I wasn't sure I wanted to. He might have to run to his gate, and have no time for dealing with me; or even if he was on a later flight and had a few hours to kill, he might be annoyed by my return, wrinkling

19

his nose at me in dismayed surprise as if I were a burp after a garlicky meal.

I crept toward him, as hesitant as a stray dog unsure of its welcome. The ticket agent was busy typing and messing with unseen items on his counter, and then he handed a ticket folder to Ian. I stopped a foot behind Ian and stared at his back, trying to gather the courage to tap him on the shoulder.

He picked up his garment bag and turned around, the movement so sudden that I didn't have time to back away. Bag and shoulder collided with me and I stumbled, his free hand reaching out to steady me, apologies tumbling from his lips in that lovely Scottish lilt. "Terribly sorry, excuse me, are you all right . . . ?" The apologies came to a halt. "Tessa?"

"Hi." I waved hello, knowing I looked like an idiot. "I felt bad dumping you at the curb like that, and wanted to come make sure that you caught your flight."

He led me a few feet away from the ticket counter, the look of surprise lingering on his features. "That was kind of you. Unfortunately, they've given my seat to a standby passenger. Everything is booked solid, so they've rescheduled me for a flight on Christmas Eve."

"Oh. Oh, dear. You can't get a standby seat?" My stomach fell, guilt sinking it to the ground.

"Trying would mean spending the next three days here at the airport. No, I'd rather stay in a hotel downtown and take the Christmas Eve flight."

I perked up a bit. "So the airline is paying for a room? Where? I hope it's someplace nice."

"It's out of my own pocket, I'm afraid. Do you have any suggestions on where I should stay?"

I stared at him in sick shame, my lips parted but saying nothing. Not only had my oversleeping caused him to lose three days, but he was going to be out several hundred dollars on top of whatever the airline had charged him for changing his flight.

"Tessa?"

"You can stay with me," I blurted.

His eyebrows rose.

"In Lauren's room," I added. "I'm sure she won't mind. You can't stay in a hotel, not when there's room for you in our house. It's the very least I can do, when it's my fault that you're in this mess."

His brows drew down and he studied me. I wondered if he was thinking it would be torture to spend three days under the same roof.

I tried to look innocent and hopeful, although I myself was suddenly wishing he would say no. What would I do with him for three days? I'd be a mass of nerves, unable to relax. "Please?"

Some mysterious thought apparently crossed his mind at that moment, for he cocked an eyebrow, tilted his head, grinned, and said, "Why not? But I want you to clear it with Lauren first." He took out his cell phone, dialed, and handed it to me.

I took it, the plastic warm from his body, a faint scent of aftershave tickling my nose as I held it up to my ear. I turned half away from Ian and plugged my other ear with a finger, blocking out the noise of the airport.

The phone rang half a dozen times before Lauren picked up. "Ian?"

"No, it's Tessa, on Ian's phone. Ian missed his plane."

"What?" A few choice swear words followed.

"I offered him the use of your room until the next available flight, on Christmas Eve. Is that okay?"

She was silent for a long moment.

"Did your sister have her baby? Are you coming back today?" I asked, thinking that she might need her room.

"No, it's looking to be a long labor. I'll probably just stay through the holiday."

I lowered my voice, stepping several feet away from Ian. "I could give him my room instead, if you don't want him in yours for some reason."

"He doesn't have cooties," she said with a laugh. "No, it's nothing like that. I just . . ."

21

"Rapist? Drug addict?"

"No!"

"For heaven's sake, tell me! I'm getting frightened."

"It's just that . . ." Lauren paused again, then sighed. "Ian loves women, and he knows how to say all the right things."

I snorted.

"No, really, Tessa. I remember him as a teenager, sweet-talking the panties off of girls, and from the sounds of it he's only polished his moves since then."

"I seriously doubt I'm in any danger from him. I don't think I'm his type." I imagined he went for women with bleached hair and long fingernails, high heels, tight jeans, and a lot of cleavage.

"You're pretty and you're single. That makes you his type."

"I'll be the only deer in the rifle sight, you mean, if he's at the house. If that's really your only concern, then will you please tell Ian that it's okay if he stays with me? I feel terrible for not getting him to the airport on time."

When she didn't answer I added, "And I promise to keep my defenses up against his charms."

"Okay, put him on."

I came back and handed the phone to Ian. "Lauren."

I couldn't discern much from Ian's end of the conversation, although when he laughed I suspected that it was at some admonition by Lauren to keep his hands off me.

I pondered the possibility of his hands taking liberties with my pale and obscenely yearning body, and where such liberties might lead. I wasn't sure I'd have a problem with it.

At least, I didn't have a problem with it in my imagination, which was where such acts were going to stay. I'd never had a one-night stand, and I didn't want one now . . . even if an evening of wild sex with a handsome Scotsman might be just the type of Christmas present a lonely single girl could wish for.

"I swear it!" Ian was saying into the phone. "On my

mother's soul, I swear it! Now go back to your sister and give her a kiss from me. Yes, please let me know when the baby's born. Bye, love." He flipped the phone closed and smiled at me. "Ready, then?"

Oh, yes.

Chapter Three

I finished the final seam on a princess dress for my niece and snipped the threads. Vivaldi was playing softly on my CD player, filling my attic workroom with the energetic strains of a violin. It was good music to work to, although it didn't keep me from trying to hear every noise Ian made on the main floor below in order to track his movements.

Upon our return to the house I'd given him a tour of the facilities and then offered him Cocoa Puffs for breakfast. Apparently he wasn't a connoisseur of the all-time best breakfast cereal. He'd even disdained a secondary offering of holiday-colored Crunch Berries. He said he would make his own breakfast, if that was all right.

I'd left him to settle in and retreated to the safety of my attic. As I sewed I heard him shower, get dressed, unpack, run a load of laundry, and for the last few minutes he'd been making mischief in the kitchen.

A buttery, herb-filled scent drifted up the stairs, riding atop the comforting smell of toast. My stomach gurgled. I'd been too embarrassed to sit down in front of him and eat a bowl of Cocoa Puffs, so I'd gone without breakfast. And now I couldn't muster the nerve to go downstairs and beg a bit of whatever he was making. A perverse shyness trapped me in my aerie.

I had lured the male into my lair, but I had no idea what to do next. If I were a spider or a praying mantis, I could have sex with him and then eat him. At least the bugs had a standard way of dealing with these things.

I heard a footstep on the creaky bottom stair. "Tessa?" Ian called up to me.

"Yes!" I squeaked, and jumped to my feet as if called to attention.

There were a few more footsteps on the stairs, his voice coming closer. "Is it all right if I come up?"

"Sure!" My eyes darted around the room. *Oh, lord.* Fabric was everywhere, spilling out of under-eave cupboards and boxes and piled on the floor and tables. Machines for steaming and pressing and hemming and overlocking; mannequins and tables; racks of thread and scissors and pattern-making tools; costume drawings tacked to the slanted ceiling; shelf after shelf of costume history books, fashion magazines, and piled paper patterns; half-finished garments hanging from a portable rack, from the window frames, from the top of the door, from any nook or cranny that would hold the end of a hanger.

Ian appeared in the doorway, a plate of food in one hand and a mug in the other. His eyes widened as he took in the multicolored chaos. It took a moment for him to locate me in the midst of it all, standing as motionless as one of my mannequins. He smiled, a hint of uncertainty revealing itself in the corners of his mouth. "I know you missed breakfast, so I made up a plate for you."

He probably thought I was as insane as Hannibal the Cannibal, standing stiffly in his prison cell. Only not as tidy. "Thank you."

He looked around. "Shall I set this down somewhere?"

I shoved aside some material on my sewing table. "Here's fine."

He brought my breakfast over and set it down, then fingered the hem of the princess dress. "A costume for work?"

I felt my mouth crook upward. "It would be a very small production." I refrained from chortling at my witticism, especially as he was still looking at me with a question in his eyes. "It's a Christmas present for my niece." I picked up another costume folded up on a table and shook it out. "Superhero duds for my nephew." I put it back and touched a pile of silky quilted material. "Bathrobe for Mom." I pointed to a dark green felt hat on a Styrofoam head. "Hat for Dad."

"You even make hats?" He sounded impressed.

I shrugged, trying to hide my pleasure, and watched as he wandered slowly around my workroom. He stopped at a half-finished red silk dress on a hanger. "This is gorgeous. It looks like a dress Jean Harlow would have worn. Who's it for?"

"Uhh . . ."

He raised his brows.

"Well . . ."

"Is it for you?"

I wrinkled my face, embarrassed. "Yes." I came over and stood protectively next to it, softly touching the side seam with its pins, as if I could make the dress feel better about being in pieces and ignored. "I was going to wear it to a Christmas party, but I don't really feel like going."

"Why not?"

I shrugged, but when he kept waiting for an answer I spilled it out. "My ex-boyfriend is going to be there—which I knew—but I just heard that he's bringing a date."

Ian's face cleared. "Ah. So you don't want him to see you there alone and think you haven't been able to move on."

"I'm more pathetic than that," I confessed, his easy understanding encouraging me to spill more. "I don't want him to think that he was the better catch on the dating market than me. He's been snapped up, while I'm still standing around like day-old fish." I grimaced as I realized what I'd just said to this man I found so physically attractive. *Way to sell yourself, Tessa*, I silently scolded. *Day-old fish. Charming.*

"So, when you started making the dress and didn't know about the girlfriend, you were thinking, 'Ha-ha! Let—' What's his name?"

"Alan."

" 'Let Alan see me in this, and he'll be sorry he ever let me go.' "

"Something like that," I mumbled.

"Did he break up with you, or you with him?"

"He broke up with me. He said he didn't feel anything for me anymore." I shrugged. "I thought at the time that he was more interested in his career than in having a relationship. Guess I was wrong; he just didn't want that relationship to be with *me*."

"So now you are frightened by the girlfriend. She must be prettier than you—more charming, more entertaining. That's what you're thinking, isn't it? What if everyone adores her and privately thinks that Alan made the right choice when he dumped you and got her?"

"Yes!" I snapped, horrified at his piercingly accurate perception. "That's exactly what I've been thinking, and it sucks! It makes me feel about as appealing as canned dog food!" I went back over to my plate of food and picked up the fork, moving the scrambled eggs around the plate. They were flecked with green: herbs, most likely. Why hadn't I ever thought to put herbs in my eggs?

I tensed as I heard him approach. The hairs on the back of my neck stood up, a tingle running down my spine as I felt the air move and knew he was but inches behind me. My annoyance and embarrassment of a moment before were submerged in a wave of anticipation. Would he touch me?

His hand lightly stroked down the back of my head, sliding over my hair and setting my nerve endings tingling. He moved his hand over to my shoulder and rested it there. "I'm sorry. I only said so much because I've been there myself."

Pleasure at his touch rippled through me. I peeped over my shoulder at him. His dark blue eyes met mine with an intimate understanding that unnerved me. I turned back to the less-threatening plate of food and he removed his hand, my shoulder feeling cold without it. "What did you do?" I asked.

"Went to the party and made an ass of myself."

I turned fully around, and this time he was the one who stepped away, fingertips sliding into his pockets as he rested his arms akimbo. He had a wry smile on his lips as he shook his head. "I drank too much, hit on every woman there, and even sang karaoke, for God's sake."

My mouth crooked into a smile. "What song?"

" 'Copacabana.' "

I giggled.

" 'Her name was Lola; she was a showgirl'," he sang off-key, bobbing his head and dancing with the awkward stiffness of a thirteen-year-old suburban boy.

I choked and covered my mouth. "Oh, dear."

He shrugged and smiled. "Are you going to eat your eggs? They must be cold by now."

I picked up the plate and the mug and headed toward the door. "I'll nuke 'em."

Two minutes later I was sitting across the kitchen table from Ian, self-consciously eating the breakfast he'd made for me. The shyness of stuffing food in my mouth while he sat back and sipped coffee warred with the desire not to offend by showing insufficient enthusiasm for the food. Hunger and truly excellent eggs won out. "Delicious," I said around a mouthful.

"Thanks."

I saw his own dishes and the frying pan in the dish drainer, already clean. "Do they raise men differently in Scotland?"

"What do you mean?"

I gestured at the food and at the dishes. "You know how to take care of things."

"I can darn socks, too."

I frowned at him, not sure if he was joking.

"Truly." He shrugged. "It was expected that boys learn the basics."

"These eggs aren't basic."

"Why be satisfied with mediocre? Life's too short. Everything around you should be beautiful, your food should be delicious, your clothes should fit well and feel good against your body, you should have fresh flowers on your table and perfumed soap in your bath."

"Who has the time or money for all that?"

"Who has a life to waste, living in unpleasant surroundings and eating bad food? All that we have of life are the pleasures of today."

"That sounds like the philosophy of a hedonist."

He shrugged, unoffended. "And if so?"

"There's a lot more to life than physical pleasure. There's friends and family, work that's interesting, creativity, learning new things. . . ." I trailed off as I realized I was giving my old maid speech.

He set his coffee mug down and leaned forward, arms on the table, his dark blue eyes locking with mine. His voice lowered. "But we do need tactile pleasures; pleasures of the senses of touch and taste. Pleasures of vision. Like richly colored soft fabrics sliding against your naked skin. Candlelight, and exquisite food fed to you by a man who adores you. You need to catch sight of yourself in the mirror and smile at the way the silk of your dress follows your body, the way your high heels make your gorgeous legs look long. You need the pleasure of knowing that the man you want will be unable to keep his hands off you."

I started to tingle. *Touch me, touch me, crawl across the table and smother me, reach your hand down my panties and . . .* "You think I have gorgeous legs?" I croaked.

He slowly smiled. "And a nice ass." The smile turned sardonic. "Terrible taste in underwear, though."

"They're comfortable," I mumbled, looking down at my plate and nudging my toast with a fingertip.

"So is silk."

"I've always *wanted* silk underwear," I confessed pathetically, aware that I was trying to please him. "Well, fancy underwear, anyway, with ribbons and lace."

"Of course you want that."

"And a garter belt. And a corset that would push my breasts up to my collarbone," I added, getting excited as I recounted my fantasy underwear vision. "And maybe a pretty white riding crop with feathers at the end, that I'd slap against my—" I cut myself off, wondering if I'd said too much.

His eyes sparkled, watching me. "Why haven't you bought them?"

I met and held his gaze, imagining him running his hand over my bare butt cheek, its white skin pinkened from the crop. His comment was clearly a come-on. "I've had no one to wear them for."

"Now you see, that's exactly what I've been talking about!" he exclaimed, slapping the table.

I blinked, taken aback by his enthusiasm. I couldn't detect any sign of lust in it. Did he need a clearer hint that there was no toll on this highway? Had I been too subtle?

"You're saying I've been too long without a man," I tried, and lowered my voice until it reached a Lauren Bacall huskiness. "You're right; I'm more than ready for someone to toss me onto the bed and make love to me."

He frowned. "Are you coming down with something?"

A croaking noise of humiliation came out of my throat.

He got up and poured a glass of water, then handed it to me, watching while I drank it. I smiled sickly at him and put the glass down.

It was the lip-licking bar scene from my youth, lived again in full color.

"You've wanted luxurious lingerie, but never given it to

yourself because there was no man to see it," Ian said, sitting down. "It's as if your own pleasure isn't worth the effort, and you can only have something nice if it benefits someone else. What about *you?*"

I'd been *trying* to get something nice for myself just now. The hint I'd dropped had been pretty broad, and given what Lauren had said about Ian's womanizing, I doubted he'd missed the hint. Which meant he'd chosen to ignore it.

Ay-yi. I shouldn't try to flirt with men. All I ever did was embarrass myself.

I picked up my plate and went to the sink, stuffing the toast down the disposal with more violence than it deserved, feeling a volcano's worth of sexual frustration bubbling inside me. Moments ago my body had been molten with aroused desire; now I had wet toast. "What *about* me?" I said, using my fork to mangle the helpless bread. "I have rent to pay. I can't spend hundreds of dollars on lingerie that no one will see."

"Even if you were the only one who knew you were wearing it, it would change you. It would make your life better."

I snorted and flipped the switch to the disposal, reveling in its growl that drowned out the possibility of conversation. *Wish I could shove you down there, Ian. Sexist pig.*

"If you felt sexy, you'd act sexy," he said as soon as I shut the disposal off.

I flipped it back on for a second, pretending there was more to grind. *Rrrrrrr!* When I shut it off there was silence. For a moment.

"And if you acted sexy, you might attract a lover."

I turned around and leaned against the counter, arms crossed over my chest. "Do you realize how insulting that is?"

He raised a brow, all innocence. "Why?"

I spluttered. *Because it means that you don't find me sexy,* was what I was thinking, but I couldn't say that. "Because! Because it suggests that no man will be interested in me just for myself; that being smart and educated and independent aren't important. That being a good person or having a

31

sense of humor doesn't matter. That sex appeal is all that counts." *That sex appeal is all that matters to you, and that you've clearly found me lacking.*

"Are you saying that you didn't know this?"

I gaped at him.

"We are talking about attracting men, after all," he said.

"What *type* of men?! Not a type that any self-respecting woman would want!"

He waved away my protest. "It's true of all men. A man has to find something sexy about a woman to be interested in her. And there's nothing sexier than a woman who *feels* sexy. She could be the Hound of the Baskervilles, but she'd have a pack of men following her anyway if she walked with a sway that said she knew how to ride a man, and enjoyed it."

"You're sick."

He took a sip of his coffee, unperturbed. "You're only making such a fuss because you know it's true."

"It's what's wrong with male-female relations."

"I'd say it's what's exactly right. I should think you'd applaud such a statement," he said, a twinkle in his eye.

I was too incensed to let that twinkle sidetrack me. "*Applaud* it? *Applaud* such a shallow, sex-obsessed viewpoint?"

"Yes, applaud it. It means that every woman can be beautiful, whatever her size or features. I thought that that's what women had been complaining about for the past few decades: impossible standards of beauty. I'm saying that the beauty comes from within, from the confidence with which a woman carries herself, and from her acceptance of her own desires and her willingness to explore them."

I suddenly felt as stiff and prim and awkward as a Victorian spinster. No wonder he didn't find me sexy. I had none of that. "So to get back to where this conversation started, that must mean that the secret to loving one's body lies in buying lingerie," I said dryly, trying to regain ground in this losing battle. "I don't think so."

"Have you tried it?"

"I don't always wear granny panties, you know. I do own a thong." Not that I ever wore it. "Although why anyone would find sexy a piece of elastic running through a woman's private parts, I'll never know." I remembered the sight of myself in the thong, and scowled. "Foul, useless thing," I muttered.

"Mm," was his only comment.

An awkward silence stretched between us. I heard a car going up the hill outside. The neighbor's terrier barked madly at it, the barking cut off by an irate shout from the dog's owner. The sounds were so mundane, and my conversation with Ian had been so outlandish by comparison, I suddenly chuckled and rolled my eyes, as much at myself as at Ian. "I don't want to spend the day discussing underpants. Is there anything you'd like to do to pass the time? I have a bunch of novels, if you'd like to read. There are some shops you could walk to, or you could walk around Green Lake. You could take the bus downtown." I hoped he'd take one of those last options, just to get him out of the house. I wasn't going to be able to relax with him here.

"What are you going to be doing?" he asked.

"Me? Oh, this and that. Hanging around, mostly." I tried to make my day sound boring. I'd just realized that I needed to go to the bathroom, and I'd prefer to wait until he was out of earshot and wouldn't be aware of how long I was in there. Which meant he had to be out of the house.

"No plans?"

I shrugged. "Not really. More sewing. Writing some Christmas cards."

"Excellent! Then you can give me a tour of your fair city."

I didn't answer at first, my brain having trouble taking in this proposition. When would I go to the bathroom?

It was a slow shift of gears to change from thinking I'd have a slobby, stay-at-home sort of day with bathroom privacy to having a "tool around Seattle with Scottish *über*-hottie who makes me nervous" sort of day.

But as my brain wrapped itself around the idea of giving Ian a tour, my sweatshirt began to feel like an unflattering sack, and my feet in their oversize socks were suddenly itching to be confined to shoes and carrying me about in the brisk December air. It might be nice to clean myself up a bit and go downtown. It would be fun to soak in some of the Christmas hubbub and good cheer.

I could always run the water in the tub to mask any noises I made in the bathroom.

"Sure, a tour sounds like fun," I said. I'd show Ian that I could act normal and be charming.

I could be normal, couldn't I?

Chapter Four

"Is that the Space Needle?" Ian asked with a betraying hint of boyish enthusiasm at odds with his suavely elegant appearance.

I didn't have to look out the bus window at the tall, narrow tower with its flying saucer–shaped restaurant on top in order to answer. "Yes."

"Are we going—"

"No," I said as the transit bus continued past an empty parking lot where visitors on a better day might have left their cars as they visited the Space Needle or the multicolored, lumpish building at its base that was the Experience Music Project and Science Fiction Museum.

"Why not?"

"I'm sorry," I said, patting his knee as if soothing a child, "but it's a code amongst the natives of the city. Only tourists are allowed to go to the Space Needle. It's a mark of shame for a resident like myself to notice its existence."

"But it's the most recognizable landmark in the city."

"And Elvis made a movie there."

"No."

I cocked an eyebrow, amused. "Yes. Unfortunately. *It Happened at the World's Fair*. Not one of his better efforts."

Ian frowned.

"What?" I asked.

"I'm trying to think of an Elvis song to sing, to persuade you to go to the Space Needle with me."

"Oh dear. We don't want a repeat of the 'Copacabana' incident." I affected a mighty sigh. "Maybe on the way home."

He put his arm around my shoulders and pulled me against his side, used his hand to tilt my head toward him, and planted a quick kiss on top of my hair. I was too surprised to enjoy it, and then his arm was gone and I was sitting silent and stunned, already missing the weight and warmth of his arm.

It was less than five minutes later that we were getting off the bus in Pioneer Square, the historic old town part of Seattle. I'd insisted we take the bus in order to avoid the madness of trying to park downtown on one of the last shopping days before Christmas.

"This is historic Seattle," I said as we cleared the small crowd of fellow bus riders and made our way down the sidewalk. It was a district of dark brick buildings occupied by art galleries, rug dealers, and antique shops, the sidewalks punctuated by leafless trees wearing their winter gear of white fairy lights. "I know that our history is painfully short compared to Scotland's or England's, but if you want to hear about Native Americans, or miners preparing to head north to the Yukon gold rush, we have that."

Instead of answering, he grabbed my arm and pulled me after him into a gallery of handblown glass. "Beautiful," he said. "Look at these colors."

I held my arms close to my side, afraid of bumping into any of the vases or bowls perched atop white stands and shelves. The colors made a kaleidoscope of the gallery, and above us hung dozens of blown-glass shades illuminated by bulbs within.

"We need to sell something like this," he said, reaching up and touching a golden glass chandelier.

"We?"

"My company."

I reached up and tapped the dangling price tag until it spun around. "Your company sells three thousand dollar chandeliers?"

He met my eyes and grinned. "We sell three hundred pound knockoffs of three thousand dollar chandeliers."

"So not the real thing."

" 'Real' is a relative term. It's real enough to the middle-class flat owner who can never hope to afford the original."

I gave him a questioning look.

"We all want a little better than we have or can afford," Ian explained. "We all want to take our lives a step up from where they are. We want to be a little richer, a little smarter, a little more talented or more beautiful, or possessed of greater taste and discernment than we deep down know ourselves to have. My company lets people indulge the illusion that they are rich, cultured, and possessed of the finer sensibilities."

"It sounds like you cater to their vanity."

"Of course! Oh, don't look at me that way," he chided, putting his arm around my shoulders and leading me back out the door. "Every business caters to vanity of one sort or another; to how people want to think of themselves. We're helping people to feel good about themselves. We put their hearts' desires just beyond their financial reach, then put it on sale. They grab it, and then every time they look at their bargain chandelier over their dining table, or their seven hundred-thread-count sheets, or their lead-crystal stemware, they feel like life's pretty good, they're pretty clever, and they're doing all right in this world, after all."

I shrugged off his arm as we reached the sidewalk. "I've never heard anything so depressing and empty."

"But true." His gaze searched over my face, as if trying to find some secret hidden there. "Most of life is a game of facades."

I shook my head. "No."

"Your entire career is based upon pretending."

"But everyone agrees to take part in the illusion of a play, for the sake of fun. There's no deception in it."

"And yet you love that deception more than you love your own life. You said yourself that the clothes of another era are magical to you in a way that today's clothes are not. We all need our illusions, our make-believe, to make life more bearable."

I shook my head again, refusing to agree. "Life doesn't need to be that way. There is joy in it simply as it is. Friendship. Love. Those are real things. *Real*, not make-believe."

"But even with those we love we hide parts of ourselves. We try to appear better than we are, afraid of losing them if they see what sorry creatures we truly are."

I shook my head again, even as I felt the dart of truth hit home. Hadn't I always felt compelled to hide part of myself in every relationship I'd had with a man? I'd never been so trusting of a man's affection that I could lay my soul bare before him. "You've never had a truly loving romantic relationship," I said. I suddenly knew it was true; knew it only because it was true of myself, and I could see that same lack of trust hiding behind the perfection of Ian's clothes and the handsome angles of his features. He wanted people to believe the facade, and not question too closely what it was that lay beneath.

"I've been in love before. I even thought of marrying once or twice," he said lightly.

"No, that's not what I meant," I said, and resumed walking with him at my side. "I meant that you've never been with a woman you've felt would always be there for you; someone who would take you for richer or poorer, in sickness and in health, come hell or high water—"

"Is that in the vows?"

"Should be. But do you see what I mean?"

"You've never found that either. You'd be married if you

had. Maybe some of us aren't made to have a 'happily ever after.'"

"Don't say that," I said softly. His words struck too close to my own fears.

"I didn't mean *you*. I meant myself."

"You! You're not weird. You should be able to find someone."

"I haven't."

"I'll bet you've been looking at entirely the wrong sort."

He gave me a look. "Why do you say that?"

I rolled my eyes. "Oh, come on. Handsome men go for beautiful women. And you've already said how much sex appeal means to you. It hardly seems like the basis for a solid relationship."

"I'd like to see the relationship that survived *without* a good dose of sexual attraction."

"I'm not going back to our underpants discussion."

"Do you know, I think you're a bit of a snob, Tessa."

"*What?*"

"An anti-sex snob. You think that sexy people have inferior characters."

"I do not!"

"Which is ironic, as you yourself have a certain smoldering sexiness, under those hideous clothes."

I gaped at him, feeling both gratified and insulted. "I don't think sexy people are inferior," was all I could think to say.

"Then why else would you assume that any sexy woman I pursued would by definition make a poor mate? Would you make a poor mate?"

"I'm not sexy," I grumbled, hoping he'd argue the point. I *wanted* to be sexy. "I'm pretty sometimes, but not sexy. But that's not what I meant in the first place! I meant that the women you probably pursued were party girls, out to have fun."

"Ah. So now we see where the true snobbery lies."

"No!"

"Yes, my darling Tessa. Women who drink and dance and have sex do not make good mates. No matter that they may be smart and accomplished; if they go out and have fun, they're bad. I knew this was a puritan country, but—"

"No! I meant . . ." But I didn't know anymore *what* I'd meant. I had a sour suspicion that my words had been based on the secret resentment that the nerdy like me have of those who are exuberantly social and know how to let loose and have a good time. I was, I had to admit, jealous even of women who could have a fling with a man and not hate themselves for it in the morning. "I only meant that perhaps the women you've pursued are not ready yet to settle down," I said weakly.

He shrugged and grinned. His arm went around my shoulders again and he pulled me against him in a quick sideways hug. "I shouldn't have given you such a hard time. Yes, there were a lot of party girls; yes, some of them were not the sort to bring home to Mother; but there were several who were charming and intelligent, and who left me to marry another within a year."

"Why did they leave you? Besides your argumentativeness, that is."

He dropped his arm off my shoulders and gave me a light, flirtatious pat on the butt.

"Hey!" I said, and hoped he'd do it again.

"Naughty chit," he said, mock scowling, a smile pulling at the corner of his mouth.

"Spank me!" I pleaded.

His eyes widened.

My own widened, and I could feel a horrible false grin stretch across my mouth. Had I really said that aloud?

"You like that, do you?"

"Kidding! Just kidding!"

He raised one brow. "Were you?"

I felt a warming in my loins. "Of course! I'm not into violence!"

"It's not violent when it's done correctly. The idea isn't to hurt; it's to arouse."

"You mean you've done it?" Some of my embarrassment gave way to intrigue.

"The *Kama Sutra* has pages and pages on the different ways to bite and spank and scratch for pleasure."

"I don't want to be bitten." But to be bent over the edge of the bed, his bare hand on my ass, his palm almost touching my sex each time he lightly swatted me . . . *Oh, good lord.* I could feel myself getting damp. I swallowed and squeaked out, "You didn't answer my question. Why did the women leave you?"

His eyes swept briefly over my chest. My jacket was unzipped, my hardened nipples visible under my T-shirt. *Please let him think it's the cold doing it.*

He put his hands in his pockets. "I couldn't give them what they wanted."

"Which was?"

He shrugged. "Commitment. A house and children. The rest of my life."

I felt something sink inside me. Some small, burgeoning seed of hope that Ian might . . . that I might . . . But no.

He must have seen the look on my face. "You would have left me, too," he said.

I smiled weakly. "I would never have gotten involved with you to begin with. If there's no prospect at all of a future with a man, then what's the point?"

"A good time. The pleasure of each other's company."

It was said nonchalantly, but I examined his expression, looking for some hint of whether he meant that as an invitation to me. I could see no sign of it. "Then why not promise forever?" I asked.

He was silent for half a block. "I don't know," he finally admitted, sounding surprised at his own answer. "Isn't that strange? I truly don't know why I never could take that final step. I had reasons at the time, but it was never anything insurmountable. Fear, maybe?"

"Fear of what?"

"Of making the wrong choice. Of meeting someone a year later and realizing that *she* was the one I should have waited for."

"Then maybe you've never met the right person."

"Maybe I have," he said softly, and my heart skipped a beat. "But maybe I was too blind to recognize her, and let her go."

Well, he obviously wasn't talking about *me*, then. "Then I suppose you're doomed to live a sad life of degenerate bachelorhood," I said lightly. "You'll grow a paunch and take to wearing Brylcreem, open-necked shirts, and a tan, and spend your vacations seducing wealthy old women on the Riviera."

He laughed. "I'm not going to be a gigolo. No, I'll be a grouchy old man who pinches the bottoms of young women and gets slapped for the effort."

"As well you should!" I said, laughing.

"Here's a shop for you," Ian said, pulling me to a stop in front of a window.

We'd come a fair distance during our conversation and were now in the heart of the city, the brick buildings of Pioneer Square having given way to larger, newer buildings that at street level housed clothing stores and jewelers and small restaurants. The window we'd stopped in front of had a mannequin dressed in a white Edwardian dress. A pair of white boots with a dozen buttons sat at the base of the mannequin, along with a beaded purse and a silver flask. "Ohhhh . . ." I moaned, and pushed through the front door without saying a coherent word. I could hear him chuckling, but then I was inside and everything else faded from my awareness.

It was a cozy shop with deep red carpets and a small selection of fine clothing. My fingers danced lightly over the dresses and velvet coats hung so carefully on their padded hangers. "They should never be worn," I said quietly, hearing Ian come up behind me. "They should be lying flat, in acid-free paper, away from the light. I shouldn't even be touching them with my bare hands." I pulled my paws back to my chest, tucking them there to resist the temptation to touch, touch, touch.

Most of the gowns were silk evening gowns from the first half of the twentieth century; not so very old or so very valuable, but someday they would be. They were waiting to become treasured history, but would never get the chance if a modern body squeezed itself inside, splitting seams and sweating on fragile fabric.

"May I help you?" a young woman asked. "Are you looking for a dress for a special occasion?"

I shook my head mutely and turned away from the temptation. I wanted to squeeze myself inside one of those beautiful dreams from another era. When I turned I saw the glass display counter of jewelry and small decorative objects. On a middle shelf, calling to me like a pirate's treasure, lay a three-strand garnet necklace with a large garnet-studded pendant. "Ohhh . . ." I moaned, and went to it, pressing my fingertips to the glass and staring at the necklace as if I had PMS and it was a five pound chocolate bar.

"Can you take it out?" Ian asked the shop clerk.

"Sure," she said, and although I didn't take my eyes off the necklace to look and confirm, I could hear in her voice the simper directed at Ian.

A rattle of a keychain and a sliding glass door later, and she was lifting the necklace off the shelf and laying it down on a piece of velvet on top of the display counter. I touched it, then started to pick it up, checking the clerk's expression for permission first. She looked away from Ian long enough to nod.

It was heavy, the garnets clicking against one another like rosary beads. When I turned the pendant over I saw a panel of glass attached to the back. "It's a locket," I said. "She would have kept a lock of hair in it."

"Whose hair?" Ian asked.

"Someone she loved. Maybe someone who had died."

"Do you like it?"

"Of course!"

He looked at it doubtfully. "It's a bit gaudy, don't you think?"

"I *love* it. Look at the color in these garnets." I held up a strand so that he could see the light through them. "Can't you imagine a nineteenth-century woman wearing this over a bodice with a neckline that went almost all the way up to her ears? Or maybe a younger woman wearing it on her bare skin, her ball gown low-cut and this pendant shielding the bit of cleavage that showed?" I found the small price tag tied to the clasp and turned it over.

Fourteen hundred dollars!

I grimaced and put the necklace carefully back onto the velvet.

Ian took out his wallet.

"What are you doing?!"

"I'm buying it for you. A thank-you for my tour of the city."

"Ian! No!" I stepped closer to him and said between gritted teeth, "It's fourteen hundred dollars."

His eyebrows went up. "For that?"

"Yes, for that."

"I thought it would be more."

I gaped at him, not sure if he was joking or being serious. "Even if it were only a tenth as much, I couldn't let you buy it for me," I said uncertainly.

"Propriety? Not accepting jewelry from a man not your fiancé?"

"I'm not *that* old-fashioned. No, I mean because this meager tour is the least that I can do for you, since it's my fault you're stuck in town to begin with."

"Then perhaps I could buy it for you simply for the pleasure it would bring you," he said lightly, his tone only half-serious. "It's good to have things we enjoy."

I hesitated, still not sure that he was serious. He *couldn't* be serious, not when the necklace cost fourteen hundred dollars! "I don't need to own it to enjoy it," I said carefully. "Having seen it and held it has given me as much pleasure as I can get from a piece of jewelry."

He laughed. "I don't know of many women who share your philosophy."

I shrugged, relaxing now that I saw his wallet hand lowering, the threat of an emerging credit card apparently gone. "I know the necklace exists, and now it exists in my imagination, as well as in reality. Maybe I'll use a copy of it in one of my costume designs. That's more than enough for me. I don't need to own it. I don't even *want* to own it," I added, and knew as the words left my mouth that I'd gone too far. I might be content to have seen and held the necklace, but part of me *did* want it. I only told myself I didn't because I was used to denying my desires for almost everything: fatty foods, expensive furnishings and clothes, sex. . . . "It's easier not to want it," I said softly.

I looked back at the garnet necklace, its deep red hue and heavy strands calling to the ravenously greedy pirate deep inside me. I wanted my own treasure chest overflowing with jewels that I could sift through at my leisure, admiring and gloating and decking myself in strands upon strands of pearls and shining stones, a gem-encrusted tiara on my head and heavy rings on my fingers.

"What would I ever do with such a necklace, anyway?" I asked, my eyes still fixed on the beautiful thing. "It would sit in my jewelry box." I smiled wryly, meeting his gaze. "No, even if it were affordable, it's better that someone else should have it. Someone who would wear it."

"You're sure you don't want it?"

"It's fourteen hundred dollars. I don't deserve a necklace worth fourteen hundred dollars."

He looked about to say something, but then he shrugged and put the wallet back in his pocket.

We left the shop and headed down to the waterfront to find a place to eat where we could watch the boats and ferries. I chatted about the city as we walked, but in the back of my mind I wondered: had he already guessed how much the necklace would cost before he offered to buy it for me? I remembered Lauren's warning: that he would try to get into my panties.

Had Ian set his seductive sights on me?

No. He'd already proven not. If he'd wanted me, we would be at my house right now, in my bed.

Ian was just being nice by offering to buy the necklace, and couldn't have suspected how much the necklace cost. How could an employee of a fake-luxury-goods company afford to buy such a thing, anyway? He couldn't, and was probably relieved that I'd saved him the embarrassment of admitting it. If he had that type of money to throw away, he never would have slept on our futon that first night, nor agreed to stay in Lauren's room for two nights instead of getting a room at the Four Seasons. For fourteen hundred dollars, he probably could have upgraded to business class and gotten a flight home!

The cabernet reds of the necklace shone in my mind. Yes, memory was enough, especially when I could remember that once upon a time a handsome Scottish man had wished to buy me such a beautiful thing.

Chapter Five

Lunch was a couple buckets of steamer clams in a restaurant on a pier, washed down with a local microbrew. I quizzed Ian about growing up in Scotland and was surprised by how much our childhoods had in common. His family had been lower middle-class like my own, and he, too, had spent a goodly amount of time outdoors. His expression was bright and excited as he recounted the fun he and his friends had had improvising fishing poles and trying to catch trout, or digging up pieces of glass and metal and pretending to themselves that the bits of trash were artifacts of incalculable value. I told him about playing hide-'n'-seek in the woods, and in summertime riding an inner tube down a river.

"If I ever have kids, I hope I can give them a childhood like mine," I said.

"You wouldn't raise them in the city?"

I shook my head. "Not if I had the choice. Those are some of my best memories, running around in the field and woods. When they got older I might move back to the city, but for kids . . . it's hard to beat the fun of being a wild savage." I toyed with an empty clamshell. "What about you? What do you want for your children?"

He took a sip of his beer. "I haven't thought about it."

"Do you want kids?"

"Someday. But there are a lot of steps between where I am now and being a father."

"You have to find a wife," I said.

"I'm not going to get married just to have children."

"I wasn't suggesting—"

He cut me off. "No, I know you weren't, but it's something a guy starts to feel from women when they reach a certain age."

I raised my brows. "Care to explain?"

"You feel them looking at you as a potential father to their future children."

"What's wrong with that? Of course they do!"

He shook his head. "No, I mean they look at you as meeting their checklist of minimum requirements: has a job, no chemical addictions, looks all right, seems like a decent fellow, we get on well. He's not what I dreamt of, but he's good enough. Let's get married!"

I felt a grimace of a smile pulling at the corner of my mouth, knowing that I and several of my girlfriends had spent evenings hashing out just such trains of thought. "I think everyone wants more than that. No one wants to settle for 'good enough.' It just becomes tempting when even 'good enough' seems so hard to find."

His dark blue eyes locked with mine, his expression intense. "I want to know that a woman wants me, Ian McLaughlin. Not just that I'm the right age and have the right income, and treat my mother well. I want to feel that a woman's world would not be complete without me; that I gave her something that no one else in the world could. That she found something in me that made her feel that she had come home after a long journey through a cold and lonely winter, and that she could never find exactly that same feeling with anyone else."

I didn't answer. I *couldn't* answer; there was something

too raw and honest and powerful in what he'd said, and it was something I'd never even considered before. I hadn't known that a man could need to be needed in that way.

For so many years I'd heard it said that when a man was finally ready to marry, he married whomever he was with at the time. I'd thought that men were easier to please than women were, when it came to choosing a mate. I'd thought, somehow, that they didn't really care how well a woman knew them.

Ian smiled wryly. "It makes me sound insecure, doesn't it? Needing to be needed like that."

I shook my head, still dazed. " 'Need' is part of love. I sometimes wonder if it isn't impossible to fall hopelessly in love unless you have an empty space in your heart that needs to be filled." It was my turn to make a wry face as I listened to my own words. "That doesn't sound like a foundation for a healthy relationship, does it?"

He laughed away my protest. "Any psychologist will tell you that being in love is a form of insanity." He raised his glass. "Here's to losing our minds, if we're lucky enough."

I clinked my glass with his, smiling, but I felt a tremor inside. His words of wanting to be needed by a woman had struck deep into my heart. I wanted to be that woman for a man; wanted to be that woman for Ian. I wanted to be the only woman he'd ever truly loved; I wanted him to feel like he'd found in me an acceptance and an understanding and an adoration that no other woman could ever offer.

Don't let me fall for him, I silently pleaded to whatever God might be listening. *Don't let me lose my heart to someone who is leaving in two days, and who is not going to love me back.*

After lunch we stood outside in the chill air, leaning on the rail at the end of the pier and watching the ferries and boats ply the bay, the seagulls begging for scraps from the few hardy tourists out in the cold with us. We stood together in silence for several minutes, our elbows touching. I stole a glance at him, trying to guess what he might be thinking. He caught me looking, and smiled.

I smiled back, and the moment stretched between us. The wind lifted a strand of my hair, blowing it across my chin, and I saw his gaze lower to my mouth. He shifted, turning more toward me, his body blocking the breeze and creating a cocoon of warmth. His eyes met mine, the smile fading from his face, and I could feel the possibility of a kiss hanging in the air. My heartbeat quickened. Maybe there *was* possibility here, after all.

I reached up and pulled the strand of hair away from my mouth, my hand shaking. A small, quick frown pulled between Ian's brows, and then he looked away from me. His stance changed from that of someone relaxed to that of someone who has had enough of a place and is ready to go, his hands going into his pockets and his chin rising. Although he had not moved away, I felt the chill of the winter air sweep between us.

"Ready to go?" I asked, trying not to let my disappointment soak through into my voice. Stupid, stupid me, getting my hopes up *again* for something that was not going to happen! I was an idiot.

He nodded. "Where next?"

"Pike Place Market."

I led the way back to land, and then under the two-storied Alaskan Way Viaduct that carried the highway we had taken on our failed journey to the airport. The city sloped steeply upward from the water at this point, and we had several flights of stairs to take to climb our way up to the bottom floor of Pike Place Market. The market was built along the side of a hill, its top floor at street level, its long lower floors layered down the hillside.

I was getting a headache by the time we had wandered half of the serpentine lower halls of the market, the air stuffy from the heat of too many bodies and infused with the smells of moldering antiques, incense from the import shops, and cheap synthetic-leather goods. The top floor that opened onto the street had more air and was where the fresh produce and seafood stalls were, along with flowers and handicrafts and about eight people per square foot moving through the clogged corridor between the stalls at the pace of a heavy meal through an intestine.

"Is it always this crowded?" Ian half shouted near my ear, trying to be heard over the din as we inched past a stall selling an assortment of winter squash.

"A lot of the time. Christmas doesn't help!"

A foot-traffic blockage stopped us completely, and I realized we were in front of Pike Place Fish. "Oh! You have to see this," I hollered to Ian, and grabbed his arm as I wormed us through the crowd to where we could get a better view of the seafood counter. "This is where they throw the fish!"

"What?"

"Throw fish!"

"Why?"

I shrugged. "Because it draws a crowd?" I wasn't feeling like much of a tour guide, between the headache and the lingering sense that I had embarrassed myself on the pier. Ian had been quiet during our window-shopping in the market, and the dismal suspicion had lodged in my brain that he had seen how open I was to a kiss and was now distancing himself, not wanting to encourage a crush.

The crowd waited in tense anticipation for the fish-tossing show to start, and then there was an unintelligible shout from a single fishmonger behind the counter, echoed by the same shout from all the fishmongers in unison and an "Ahhh!" from the crowd. A large, shiny silver-black fish sailed through the air behind the counter and was caught neatly in a piece of butcher paper by another of the Pike Place Fish employees.

"Salmon?" Ian asked.

I nodded. "I assume so."

"Do they ever miss?"

I shrugged. "Don't know!"

"What type of crab are those?" he asked, nodding toward the fat orange crustaceans on display on a bed of ice.

"Dungeness. When I was kid we used to take a boat out into the sound and catch them in pots," I half shouted over the noise. "Never eat them now, though—too expensive!"

There was another series of shouts from the fishmongers, another roar from the crowd as another fish took flight. Ian moved closer to the fish counter, clearly more interested in the assortment of oysters, clams, crabs, and fish than in the tossing. I used his diverted attention as a chance to dig around in my purse, looking for some aspirin.

Jeez, Louise, my head hurt. Hadn't I seen some little travel envelopes of aspirin or ibuprofen sloshing around in the bottom of my bag? I shouldn't have had the beer. I always felt a little queasy after drinking. *Dammit!* Where the hell had those aspirin gone?

I was only dimly aware of the crowd, dimly aware of the shout behind the counter, dimly aware of an extra-loud noise from the crowd, the people pulling away from me like a receding tide. I looked up only when I heard Ian's frantic shout, "Tessa!"

Something dark was flying through the air toward me; something long and silvery black. I thought I saw an open mouth on it and a dull, evil eye glinting in the light, large and flat and dead. I was too stunned to move, too stunned to do more than start to lift my arms to shield myself from the missile. Before my arm was halfway up, though, Ian tackled me from the side, throwing me out of harm's way.

We went down together, he rolling to his back as we fell so that I landed on top of him. He let out an "Oof" as I smooshed him to the cement.

Something soft hit my shoulder and flopped to the ground. I didn't look at it; I was too concerned about Ian, lying beneath me.

"Oh, God, you didn't break something, did you?"

He opened his mouth but was as silent as a fish, his eyes wide.

"Ian?" I rolled off him and put my hand on his chest. He wasn't breathing! "Ian!"

His face showed the strain as he tried to speak. His lips moved in what looked like a *W* sound.

"'What'? Is that what you're trying to say? Oh, God, you've broken something, haven't you?"

He shook his head and moved his lips again in the *W* shape.

I'd killed him. He was going to be rushed to the hospital with internal bleeding, a crushed spleen or lungs, or broken shoulder blades, or a fractured hip. Look what he got for spending time with me: Major injuries! Internal damage! "I'm sorry, Ian, I'm so sorry! We'll get you to an operating room; they'll patch you up, really! Don't worry!"

His eyes widened in alarm, a look of horror on his face.

A young man spoke from the crowd. "Hey, lady, I think you knocked his wind out."

"Wind!" Ian suddenly wheezed, then gulped air like a suffocating fish. "Just"—*gulp* "lost"—*gulp*—"my wind!"

"Oh." Relief washed through me, and I got up on my knees and helped him to sit up.

A Pike Place Fish employee came over and squatted down beside us, a look of deep concern on the young man's face. "Are you okay?" he asked.

Ian nodded, then his eyes went to the flying missile that had caused the problem. I turned as well, seeking out the thing that had hit my shoulder with such surprising softness.

It was a fish, all right: a fake fish, obviously different from the ones the employees usually threw.

The fishmonger picked it up, the stuffed fish sagging in his grasp. "Sorry about that. It's part of the show."

"Quite all right," Ian gasped, and let the young man help him to his feet. I got up, too, aware that the crowd had edged in a little closer, watching the drama with interest.

"Let us treat you to dinner," the young man said. "Choose whatever you want."

"Really, it's not necessary; I'm quite all right," Ian said as the man led him toward the case.

I started to follow, but then someone tugged on my

sleeve. I turned and saw a teenage girl grinning madly. "Hey, I caught a picture, if you want to see!" She turned her camera phone toward me. "I was trying for a picture of the fish in the air."

It took me a moment to make sense of what she was saying, and then to tilt the screen so I could clearly see the photo. But there it was: my face in profile, mouth open in a silent scream; the edge of Ian's face looking harshly determined as he lifted me off my feet, and the dark photographic smear of a fake flying fish.

"Cute guy," the girl said, chomping gum. "Wish I had someone to save me from a fish." She grinned again. "Want me to send the picture to you?"

My heart leaped. "Could you?"

"Sure! What's your e-mail address?"

I spelled it out to her as she worked the buttons of her phone, and a minute later the picture had been sent. I knew it wasn't free to do that, so I dug in my purse and found a five-dollar bill. "Here, treat yourself to a latte."

She waved away the money. "Nah, it's Christmas. Just give him a kiss for me."

"If he holds still long enough, I will," I said.

I rejoined Ian just as the Pike Place Fish man was handing him a bag. They shook hands and laughed, and exchanged the sort of male-bonding words and noises that seemed required.

"Thanks for saving me from the fish," I said as we left Pike Place Fish.

"I'm a real hero," he said, laughing. "But at least I got us dinner."

"What'd you get?"

"You'll have to wait and see. Is that a wine shop?" he asked, pointing to a glass door.

"Gourmet imported foods and wine. Want to go in?"

He nodded and opened the door for me. He seemed to know exactly what he was looking for, quickly tossing jars into a plastic shopping basket and then going to survey the meats and cheeses in the case. I caught sight of some imported chocolates and wandered over, intent on a few minutes of private worship.

"Tessa?" a woman said, as I debated the merits of Toblerone versus Lindt.

I blinked in surprise, then grinned. "Carolyn! And baby Gracie!" I held my arms out to eighteen-month-old Grace, a cheerful, outgoing little mite. She recognized me, and easily released her mother and settled on my hip, tugging at my hair and pounding her fist on me in happiness. Carolyn was a good friend in the theater department, and I'd spent many lunches with her and Gracie.

"Are you getting your last-minute Christmas shopping done?" Carolyn asked.

"No, I'm playing tour guide." I briefly explained the situation, and pointed out Ian over at the cheese counter. His back was to us, but then his head turned slightly, displaying his profile.

Carolyn's eyes widened. "Poor you, stuck with *him* for three days! You have all the luck. Hey, if you get tired of playing tour guide, I'll trade you Grace for him for a night."

"What will Mike think of that?" I asked, laughing.

She waved away the issue of her husband. "I'll tell him he can stay up all night playing online poker. He won't hear a thing." She looked again at Ian, then leaned closer to me, lowering her voice. "So is anything going on between you two?"

"I've only known him for half a day!"

"Long enough to know if you're interested."

I rolled my eyes, but felt the heat of my cheeks betraying the truth.

"Ha-ha!" she said, sounding like a movie villain discovering the enemy's secret flaw. But then she wrinkled her nose. "Doesn't make much sense, though, considering the guy is flying out of your life in a couple days."

I raised a questioning brow. "I thought you'd say I should lock him in my bedroom and make the best use of the time available."

"I would, except I have someone I want you to meet; someone who actually lives in town: Mike's cousin Kevin. I think I told you about him before? Thirty-five, good-looking, owns his own house over in Magnolia. Sweet guy."

"Oh, that's right," I said, and remembering as well that there had been something that turned me off of meeting him. "What does he do again?"

"Mortgage broker."

"Ah." That was it.

"Don't say 'ah.' It's a good career. And he doesn't have a salesman's personality, if that's what you're afraid of."

I shook my head. "It's not that. I just think I'd get along better with someone more . . . intellectual. Less business, more arts."

"That's been your problem all along," Carolyn said, exasperation creeping into her voice. "You choose 'intellectual' sticks-in-the-mud like Alan, then wonder why they don't excite you."

I looked down at Gracie and walked my fingers up her arm, her wide hazel eyes watching them in anticipation. When they got to the top I made animal noises and tickled her, and she screamed in delight.

"Tessa," Carolyn said, either scolding me to respond or scolding me for getting Gracie wound up.

I looked up at her. "I'm just trying to find a good match. I thought that Alan was going to be the one for me. He seemed to have everything I was looking for."

"Ah, sweetie." She sighed. "Everyone you've dated looks good on paper, but you need to start listening to what your heart has to say. Does he make you laugh? Does he make you feel special? Would you trust him with your life?"

I felt a smile pull at the corner of my mouth. Ian had taken a fish for me.

"Come to the party," Carolyn implored.

I made a face. "Alan will be there."

"Alan." She made a rude noise. "He shouldn't keep you

from having a good time now; he did enough of that while you were together."

I shrugged. "I just don't feel like going. I can meet Kevin after the holidays."

"Going where?" Ian asked, joining us. "And who is Kevin?"

"Ian! This is my friend Carolyn, and this little cutie pie is her daughter, Grace." I turned so that he could get a clear sight of her. Grace stared at him with the wide-eyed uncertainty of a baby for a stranger, then suddenly broke out in a grin and a gurgle. I caught Ian making a contorted monkey face, and started giggling myself.

"She's a heartbreaker," Ian said to Carolyn. "It's a pleasure to meet you." He held out his hand.

Carolyn shook it, then made a face at me as if to say, *Not bad!*

I turned my attention back to Grace, the safest companion of the three.

"You have to talk Tessa into going to the party tomorrow night," Carolyn said to Ian. "There's a man I want her to meet. I think they're meant for each other."

"Indeed?" He sounded nonplussed. "Ah, but Tessa would rather stay home with me tomorrow night," he said, recovering. "She's promised to give me a pedicure, and I'm very much looking forward to it."

I gaped at him. "I promised no such thing!"

"You aren't going to do it?" he asked.

"I'm sure your feet are beautiful, but I'm not trimming your toenails for you."

"No? Then you mean you're not busy tomorrow night?"

I scowled at him, and then at Carolyn, who was looking far more amused than a good friend should. "He knows perfectly well why I don't want to go," I said to her.

"Alan was never right for Tessa," Carolyn said to Ian. "All her friends know it, but we're not sure she's ever believed it herself."

I rolled my eyes and talked to Gracie in cooing tones.

"What nonsense are they spouting, huh, pumpkin? Your mommy's being silly. A silly goose, yes, she is!"

"Na-na-na-na!" Gracie said.

I looked up just then and caught Ian watching me. He had lost his smile, and his dark blue eyes looked almost black. For a moment there was an illusion of utter stillness about him as he looked at me, the noise and color of the busy shop around us becoming but a river passing by a silent stone. I couldn't fathom what he was thinking, but knew I was at the center of it.

"Do you want to hold Gracie?" I asked.

The question seemed to shake him from his reverie. "Thank you, but I think I'd best go find a wine for dinner tonight." He gave me a quick, preoccupied smile and then extended his hand again to Carolyn. "It was a pleasure to meet you."

"It was a pleasure to meet you, too."

When he was gone Carolyn pretended to mop sweat off her brow. "Phew! Now *there's* a man! Are you going to sleep with him?"

"Carolyn!"

"I don't know, Tessa, maybe it would be worth it. Kevin can wait a week. No, I'm joking. Joking!" she said as I gaped at her.

"I should hope so."

"He looks like he's considering sleeping with *you*, though. He seemed pretty unhappy when I mentioned Kevin."

I shook my head. "It doesn't mean anything. Lauren warned me that he's a womanizer. And he told me himself that he's never committed to anyone. He wouldn't care if I hooked up with someone else. Probably be happy for me."

"I'm not so sure."

"Gracie, your mommy is kooky. Kooky!" I kissed the little girl on top of her head and handed her back to Carolyn. "I'd better go keep an eye on him."

She put her hand on my arm. "Ian may be exciting, but

that's not the type of excitement I'd wish for you. I don't want you getting hurt."

"Nothing's going to happen. I'll save myself for Kevin, I promise!"

She laughed and waved me away. "See you tomorrow night! And dress up! I want Kevin to see how pretty you really are."

"For the last time, I'm not going! We'll meet some other time!" But even as I said it I had the feeling that I was going to end up at the party. Somehow Ian was going to talk me into it.

Chapter Six

"Oh, my God," I moaned in ecstasy. "What are you doing to me?"

"Feeding you as you deserve to be fed," Ian said, serving me another section of Dungeness crab that had been roasted in a rich butter sauce flavored with herbs, red pepper, and orange juice. "Do you know that all you had left in your refrigerator was a half-eaten packet of soy sausages, one pickle floating in brine, and nonfat cheese?"

"I needed to go shopping. And the pickle belongs to Lauren." I was too engrossed in sucking dripping butter sauce and succulent crabmeat off my fingers to be offended by his disapproval of my pantry. I took a piece of crusty French bread and dabbed at the flavorful mess on my plate. Ian had also made a salad of field greens with a tarragon vinaigrette, and there were chocolate pots de crème waiting for dessert. Heaven.

"Soy sausages are a crime against cuisine. And people say the British are the ones who serve bad food! At least we know our sausages."

"Sausages," I said, giggling, and took another sip of the

crisp pinot grigio he'd bought to go with dinner. It was a vast improvement over the Two Buck Chuck I usually bought at Trader Joe's.

He raised a brow. "Sausages, yes. What's so funny about sausages?"

"Men are obsessed with them. Every man loves his sausage!"

Ian looked at me askance, as if unsure of my meaning. "Well, er . . ."

I realized the possible misinterpretation of my words, and started to laugh. "No, I didn't mean that! I only meant that men like them more than women do."

He widened his eyes in mock shock.

Still laughing, I waved my hands at him as if to blow away such a thought. "And it's the word. 'Sausages!' It makes me laugh. Something about the sound."

"Sausages?"

I giggled.

"You're an easy drunk, aren't you?" he asked, smiling.

"I'm not drunk. I'm naturally silly."

He laughed. "You *are* drunk."

I shook my head, smiling, knowing that at most I was a wee bit tipsy. It was the pleasant evening that had lowered my guard and let my normal goofy self show through. Although Ian had been in charge of dinner, I'd helped by chopping and dicing and whisking, and setting the table. It had made for a lovely hour of working together, free of the mutual "you're doing it wrong!" tension I'd experienced with other men.

Come to think of it, except for forbidding me to jump the Jeep over the opening drawbridge and lodging protests— quite reasonable that he should, really—about my driving on the sidewalk, Ian hadn't commented on my driving, either. He didn't tell me to give more time between signaling and changing lanes, or advise me to use my rearview mirror more. He didn't suggest that he himself should take over the driving.

Not a bad guy, Ian.

I dug the last bit of crabmeat out of a claw and dropped the empty shell on top of the rest of the crab's remains in a big bowl on the center of the table. "I can't eat another bite," I said, and sighed in contentment.

"Shall we wait on dessert?"

I nodded, and together we cleared the table and cleaned up the worst of the mess.

Ian opened a second bottle of the wine and filled clean glasses, and in silent consent we retired to the living room. The futon was back in its couch form, and I sat down at the end closest to the dark fireplace, leaving for Ian the padded rocking chair that was the best seat in the house.

"Does the fireplace work?" he asked.

I nodded. "But I almost never use it. It's pretty and cozy once it gets going, but it's such a lot of work."

"Do you have wood?"

"There's a stack in the backyard."

It was all he needed to know. Ten minutes later a fire was crackling happily, sending heat and an amber glow into the room. He found the sound system, tuned the radio to a station playing Christmas carols, and turned the volume down low. The first flutter of a nervous tremor went through me as he then started turning off all the lights in the room. He left a single dim table lamp lit in the corner, then ignored the vacant rocking chair and sat down beside me, his weight making the cheap futon creak, his body beside me large and warm. He stretched his arm over the back of the futon, his fingertips draping down to brush my shoulder.

Half-lit room. Wine. Fire. Quiet music. Couch. The classic setup for a smooth slide from conversation to kissing to petting and to that moment when he drew back with a question in his eyes, wanting to know if tonight meant sex.

My mind leaped ahead to that final question, and my nervousness grew. I didn't know what the answer was in the real world. In fantasy, I was willing to do just about anything with him, including hanging upside down from a chandelier and singing "You Are My Sunshine" while he took me from behind.

In reality, I didn't know if I could do so much as bare my breast to a man I'd known only one day. He was too unfamiliar: I trusted him only with that same doglike trust I had in anyone who was friendly toward me. I didn't know his intentions beyond physical gratification; I didn't know how hurt or how angry with myself I'd be if he patted me on the thigh afterward, said, "Thanks, babe," and left.

But oh, he did smell so very good. And I did so want to lay my hand against that broad chest, then let it slide down to the crotch of his pants, feeling the stiff folds of the bunched fabric and wondering if the bulge under my palm was just his zipper forced upward into an arch, or something far more interesting. My eyes fell to that bulge, and I tried to imagine what he looked like when naked and aroused.

He lightly, almost absentmindedly stroked my shoulder. I felt a shiver run down my body and straight to my loins, all my attention focusing on those slight, careless movements of his fingertips.

I'd been wrong so many times today about Ian's attraction to me. If he wanted me, I wished he'd say it in clear English. I parted my lips to ask point-blank, but cowardice held back the words. "We forgot to stop at the Space Needle," I said instead.

" 'Forgot'?"

"I didn't skip it on purpose," I said in something approaching the truth.

"I have two more days here. We're going to the top of the Space Needle on one of them."

"Mmm." I nodded as if I were only humoring him.

"You're a little devil, Tessa," he said, reaching over with his other hand and tickling my stomach.

Laughing, I contracted around his touch as if I were a house cat taken by surprise, batting at his arm and pulling up my legs, curling into a ball as his fingers kept at me. His other arm came down over my shoulders and he pulled me toward him, the better to keep torturing me. Still laughing, I found myself falling into his lap. "Stop, stop!" I pleaded. "I'm full of dinner!"

He stopped and held me in an embrace across his chest as I caught my breath. "A little devil, but a ticklish one," he said, smiling.

I grinned, still breathing heavily from my laughter and struggles. The grin turned to a small shriek as I felt his supporting arm give way, and I slid down onto his lap, my head and shoulders across his thighs. I put my bare feet on the arm of the futon, a zing of anticipation coursing through me as I lay vulnerable before him.

Ian stroked my hair back from my face and then ran his fingertips through my hair, setting shivers of pleasure sparking along my scalp. "Purr," I said. "Purr, purr."

He smiled and tangled his hand in my hair, wrapping a thick lock of it around his palm. He tugged gently, the sensation strangely pleasurable even as it sent the faintest touch of fear through me. If he wanted, he could hold me trapped by my hair. He could keep me at his mercy while he explored me as he wished.

My nipples tightened.

His other hand lighted on my belly, two fingertips touching the sliver of bare skin where my shirt had ridden up. They brushed over that soft bit of flesh, stroking along the hem of my T-shirt, playing there, teasing as he traced a route across my torso and down my side. My nerve endings tingled with expectation, my breasts and my sex urging him onward. *Enough with the belly! Go up! Go down! Get to the good parts!*

He pushed up the fabric enough to lay his whole warm hand against me. He rubbed me gently, then slid his hand up to the edge of my rib cage, running his thumb along it, his fingers a few short inches from my breast. His thumb slid up under the center of my bra, pressing against my sternum and barely touching the sides of my breasts. The movement forced my contoured bra to slide over my breasts, creating a caress all its own. He slid his thumb up and down, still firm against my sternum, arousing me in a manner I had never known was possible.

His other hand still tangled in my hair, he raised my head and bent his own down. I watched wide-eyed as his face came closer, then could watch no longer and closed my eyes, waiting for the touch of his lips against mine.

I felt the warmth of his breath, and then the soft brush of his lips against mine. His kissed me again, featherlight, a sliding touch of his lips. His hand on my ribs went down to my waist, curved around it, then slipped behind me and went down my jeans. At the same time, his lips came more firmly down on mine, moving to part them slightly and then, taking the edge of my lower lip between his, nipping at it, sliding it between the caress of his own lips and massaging its fullness with the tip of his tongue.

His hand on my buttock stroked me, then moved down yet lower, barely finding space within the confines of my jeans to go down to where his fingertip could barely touch the edge of my heat and dampness. His kiss grew more vigorous, playing more quickly on my lips, his hand behind my head holding me more firmly. I kissed him back, my own lips embracing his by turn, copying him by stroking their smooth length with the tip of my tongue.

His fingertip below stroked over my opening. I moaned into his mouth.

He brought his hand out of my jeans and slid it up my back, unhooking my bra with a dexterous twist of his fingers. Then he was shifting on the futon, lowering me down onto it as he stretched out on top of me, releasing my hair and holding up his weight with a knee and elbow. The top of one thigh was against my sex, tempting me to rub against it.

His lips still on mine, his hand slid up my chest and under the free-floating bra, the warm roughness of his palm against my breast making me shiver in pleasure. He explored the shape of it, tracing an outline of the base and a swirling path up toward the peak, stopping just short of the waiting pinnacle.

"I want to see you," he said, and tugged lightly at my shirt. I raised my arms and let him pull it and my bra off me. I lay back down beneath him and was glad to be half-naked. Glad to have him see me and touch me, as "White Christmas" played softly on the radio and the fire crackled and popped.

He raised himself high enough that he could see me, his eyes gazing upon my breasts until I began again to feel vulnerable, the slight drafts of the room touching upon my skin. "They're beautiful," he said, his voice hushed as if he were in a church. "Perfect."

He looked me in the eye then, locking gazes with me for a long moment. "You're beautiful. You're like a woman in a Renaissance painting."

He must have seen my self-conscious doubt, because he touched the side of my face and went on: "Beautiful pale skin. Beautiful dark eyes. Beautiful long hair. And your body has the proportions of a work of art. You are beautiful, Tessa."

"No," I said softly.

"I'll prove it to you." He slid down my body and lowered his mouth to my breast, taking my nipple into the damp warmth and playing it with his tongue. I arched beneath him, my hand going to the back of his head, his tongue catching my body between a tickle and a bolt of sheer sexual pleasure. I wanted him to stop, and wanted him to go harder and faster.

He seemed to know he was torturing me, flicking his tongue against me and then with a long suck letting my nipple slide from his lips. It was dark pink and tight, the wetness upon it making it feel even chillier as it pointed upward, feeling suddenly alone in the dim darkness. His mouth moved to my other breast to repeat the treatment.

His hand moved down my side to the top of my jeans, following the waistband around to the center front. He lifted off me enough that he could reach between us and flick open the button, then unzip me.

My wiser, more cautious self came awake, distracted from the pleasure of what he was doing to my breast. My heartbeat quickened, a spurt of fear contaminating my pleasure. *Too fast, he's going too fast, I'm not ready for sex. . . .*

His hand slid into the top of my jeans and to my hip, cupping it and then forcing my jeans down a few inches.

"Ian," I said, touching his cheek and making him look up at me. "Wait, there are questions we—"

I was interrupted by the muffled, pulsing tones of a ringing cell phone, *brr-rrr-rrr!* It sounded like it was coming from his leather jacket, hanging over one of the chairs in the kitchen.

His hand stopped pushing down my jeans, but his thumb stroked my skin as he asked, "Questions?"

Brrr-rrr-rrr!

"I think that's your phone."

"It can wait. Which questions?"

Brrr-rrr-rrr!

"You know, the health questions we have to ask," I said, as the ringing of the phone started draining away what was left of my sexual excitement. *And the question about whether I'm ready to do this at all,* I added silently.

"I'm all right. Clean bill of health," he said.

Brrr-rrr-rrr!

"Me too." I grimaced as the phone kept ringing. "Are you sure you shouldn't get that? It might be important."

"Voice mail will pick it up."

I waited for the next ring, and it didn't come. "Ian, I'm not ready for this."

"I have protection, if you want to go that far," he said,

misunderstanding me. "But what I was planning on doing was just for your enjoyment. No risk." He smiled.

I felt a melting sensation in my loins. Did he mean he was going to go down on me? Oh, God, yes, let that be it! The thought of those lips and that warm mouth and tongue working the same magic down below as he'd done for my lips and breasts was bringing me halfway to orgasm.

Brrr-rrr-rrr! Brrr-rrr-rrr!

"Aagh!" I cried. "It's making me crazy! Please, just answer it!"

He looked at me with a question in his eyes, then climbed off me and went to fetch his phone.

I sat up, found my T-shirt and pulled it on, then made a dash for the bathroom. If he was going south, I wanted to be sure that I was fresh and clean.

As I washed up I could hear his voice out in the kitchen, deep and businesslike, the tones different from the ones he'd used when we talked together. He sounded almost like another person. The conversation went on, and then his voice started getting closer to the bathroom. I got myself squared away and opened the door just as he was about to knock.

"Tessa, do you have a fax machine?" he asked, the mouthpiece of the phone held against his chest.

I shook my head. "Not here." I had one in my office at the university, but that was no help to him now.

"Damn. Is there a twenty-four-hour place where I can receive a fax?"

"Kinko's. There's one a few blocks away."

"Thanks." He lifted the phone back to his ear. "I'll call you back in fifteen minutes."

"Work?" I asked when he hung up. I'd done the time-zone math, and guessed it was morning in Britain.

"Yes." He seemed agitated. Distracted.

"It's okay; you can go get your fax," I said lightly, trying not to sound disappointed. I felt it, though; felt the letdown and the sudden loneliness.

He frowned at me, then put his hands on my shoulders.

"No, it's not all right. I started something and I intend to finish it. You *deserve* to have it finished."

I made a face. "It sounds like a chore."

He stepped closer to me and slid his hands up my neck, tilting my face so that he could bend his down close. "I *want* to finish," he said a hair breadth from my lips. "I want to feel you against my mouth." He laid his lips against mine and used his tongue to paint a slow caress across the seam of my lips. With another stroke of his tongue he parted my lips and coaxed open my mouth, delving inside to rub against my tongue, telling me clearly what it was he would do to me down below.

My legs went weak and my sex pulsed.

He broke the kiss and looked at me. "You'll wait up for me?" he asked.

It took a minute for me to understand that he was still going out. "Uh . . . yeah." My mind regained a trace of rationality. "Don't I need to drive you?"

"It's only a few blocks, I thought you said?"

I nodded.

"I'll walk."

"I'll go with you."

He shook his head. "No, stay here by the fire. I want to think of you here, waiting for me."

How could I argue with that? "Okay," I said helplessly, and gave him directions to Kinko's. Even if he was back in twenty minutes, it was going to feel like an eternity.

Chapter Seven

After forty-five minutes, Ian still hadn't returned. I'd used the time to frantically search through my underwear drawer for something pretty. The only sexy item I had was the thong, so I'd swapped my granny panties for it and now was suffering the annoyance of a string up my crack.

I'd brushed my teeth. Spruced up my makeup. Done a quickie shave job on my underarms and then, when he still hadn't returned, my legs. I'd changed the sheets on my bed.

Still no Ian.

My eagerness was fading, a tinge of annoyance creeping in. He hadn't been gone very long, really, but it was longer than I'd expected. I scolded myself for getting ticked off at him for not following my imaginary time schedule, and looked for something to distract me.

The dining room of the house had been turned into a shared office for me and Lauren. My computer was there. I sat down at my desk and turned it on, thinking of that photo the girl at Pike Place Market had sent to me.

It was there, and even funnier than it had looked on the small screen of her phone. I looked utterly surprised, and

Ian looked like a superhero in black, swooping in to save the day. The fish was still a blur, but there were a few faces in the background that showed surprised fear as they, too, thought that a real fish was flying into the crowd.

It was a great picture.

A mischievous thought struck me, and I giggled. I played with my photo program, and a few minutes later was printing out multiple copies of the picture. As my printer was running I fetched my Christmas cards. I took one out of the box, opened the blank card, and began to write:

Dear Candice,

Merry Christmas! It was so good to hear from you, and I'm glad to see that you and Jared are so happy. Life here in Seattle has its own excitements, though—like being tackled by a Scotsman at Pike Place Market! Actually, his name is Ian, and he's staying with me for a few days before heading back to London, where he works. The photo is of him "saving" me from an airborne salmon. It's not a long-term thing between us, but sometimes the shortest affairs can be the sweetest.

Hoping you get everything you want for Christmas,

Tessa

Heh, heh! I might not have a husband nor any hope of a family on the horizon, but at least I could look like I was having fun with my life. I reached for another card.

Five cards later, a glance at the clock showed that Ian had been gone for an hour and a half. I scowled and went to the kitchen to fetch a spoon and one of the chocolate pots de crème that had been set aside for dessert, hoping that food would calm my rising tide of anxiety and impatience and a sick feeling of abandonment. That fax had better turn out to be life-and-death serious.

I sat back down at my desk and ate the chocolate while reading over my latest composition. The flying-fish story

71

had evolved into something a little more dramatic, and a little farther away from the truth:

> *Dear Rachel,*
>
> *Do you remember how, when we were teenagers, we used to make up goofy stories of how we'd meet handsome men who would sweep us off our feet and treat us like princesses? Well, I never expected that a Scotsman would do just that, and at Pike Place Market, no less! He thought he was saving me from a renegade flying salmon. As you can see in the photo, he literally swept me off my feet. Next thing I knew, I was lying on top of him on the ground, and it was like one of those moments in the movies where you look into each other's eyes and think,* Yes, this is someone I will love. *I invited him to stay at my house for a couple days and now he's spoiling me rotten, cooking for me and buying me jewelry and . . . Well, let's just say that he knows how to make a woman happy. He's flying home to London in a couple days, so we're making the very most of his short time here in Seattle. I'll probably have to wait until spring break to go to London, but that's not so far away.*
>
> *I never thought I'd get a gift this good for Christmas.*
>
>

Love ya,
Tessa

I bit my lip, wondering if I'd gone too far. Nothing I'd written was a through-and-through lie, but there was plenty of distortion of the truth. I didn't want to lie to my friends. Worse yet, sending the card would mean that at some later date I'd have to answer the question, "What ever happened to that Scottish guy you were so excited about?"

On the other hand, Rachel and I were mostly Christmas-card correspondents, falling out of touch for the rest of the year. She'd get a kick out of the story—a kick, too, out of hearing in next year's card that I no longer was with the Scotsman.

I shrugged and picked up another blank card. I'd write the cards, but wait until tomorrow before deciding whether to seal up my white lies and send them to my friends.

It was two thirty by the time I finished writing them and finished off Ian's share of dessert, as well. It was with more than a little angry fierceness that I scooped the last bits of creamy chocolate out of the bottom of the glass. Where the heck was he? Couldn't he at least call me and tell me when he'd be back?

Didn't he care about coming back and taking advantage of me?

I set the glass down with an angry clatter of the spoon. Lauren had warned me that he could talk the panties off a girl. Maybe, once he'd more or less achieved that, he lost interest. Maybe he hadn't been interested to begin with; as I'd said to Lauren, I was the only deer in the sights. What else was he going to do with me all evening, other than try to get into my pants?

Wasn't I worth coming back for? something small and hurt inside me asked. When he'd told me I was beautiful, I'd almost believed that I was.

"Dammit," I said aloud, my voice cracking with tears. I sniffed them back. "Dammit, dammit! I'm not going to cry about him!"

I got up, stomped over to the fireplace and put the screen up over the embers, turned out all the lights but the one over the kitchen sink, and then went to my room and changed into my most raggedy flannel nightgown. I crawled under my covers and pulled them up tight under my chin.

I felt a tear seep out and pool on the side of my nose. I wouldn't be crying if I hadn't allowed my heart to get involved. I'd started believe my own Christmas card lies: I'd started to fall in love with him.

Dammit!

Chapter Eight

It was a crush that I had on Ian; that was all. A stupid, juvenile crush. It would go away the moment I met a man I could have a future with—a man who lived here in Seattle, and who kept his word.

Someone who found no sport in talking the panties off of women.

I finished pinning a piece of the red silk charmeuse into place and moved over to my sewing machine. I was going to finish the red dress and go to the party tonight. I'd ignore Alan and his new girlfriend—or better yet, be impeccably civil and as coolly aloof as the iceberg that had sunk the *Titanic*—and I'd charm Carolyn's cousin-in-law Kevin, sweeping him off his feet and convincing him he'd found the woman of his dreams.

Ian could come along if he liked. It made no difference to me.

I sewed the piece of fabric into place and checked for puckers in the silk. None. It was coming together beautifully.

I imagined myself in the dress, my hair in a new, fashionable cut, my makeup sultry, my nipples making small beads under the fabric. The cut of the dress wouldn't allow a bra: it would be only a silken coating of red between my breasts and the open air. I imagined myself in the dress, drop-dead sexy and sultry as Mata Hari, and imagined the look on Ian's face.

He never had seen me at my best. He didn't know the magic I could work with a bit of satin and my sewing machine. Talk about illusions—ha! He knew nothing of illusions. I knew how to fit a dress so that every asset was magnified and every flaw ceased to exist. I knew how to make short legs look long, a small bust big, a thick waist thin. I could turn a dumpy woman into a siren, an awkward gnome into a graceful fairy, a fat domestic duck into a wild black swan.

Ian would see me in my red dress and be sorry for last night—sorry he'd lost his one chance to touch me. He'd be sorry about it for the rest of his life. He'd go home to London and wonder forever after if *I* had been the magical *one* with whom he would have been happiest.

I didn't know what time he'd finally gotten home. The last time I'd looked at my clock it had been four fifteen, and when I'd awoken at ten I found the door to Lauren's room closed and the light in the kitchen off. So he'd come home, but hadn't thought to let me know.

He hadn't thought to sit down on the edge of my bed and gently nudge me awake, apologizing and explaining, and persuading me to let him come under the covers with me.

I tightened my lips against the hurt of it, and then silently scolded myself. *No, no, no!* Carolyn was right. I needed someone who would be here for me; someone who lived in the same city. Someone ready to settle down.

The last thing I needed was a womanizer who lived in London.

I did need a fresh cup of coffee, though.

The house was still quiet, and I guessed that Ian was still asleep. I padded down the stairs in my stocking feet and made a beeline to the coffeemaker. I filled my cup and started to raise it to my lips.

"Is this you and me?" Ian asked.

I yelped in surprise, then yelped again as I sloshed hot coffee on my hand, dropping the mug and yelping a third time as it shattered and coffee splashed on my dancing feet.

"Tessa! Are you all right?" Ian appeared out of the dining room and rushed toward me, grabbing a dish towel on his way. He crouched down and dabbed at my feet, shoving aside the pieces of broken coffee mug. He was unshaven, his hair unkempt, and looked like he was wearing the same clothes as last night. He looked good with his perfection rumpled; he looked vulnerable.

"You scared me!" I said, trying to hide how much I wanted to take his face between my hands and cover it in kisses.

"Sorry, sorry!"

I squatted and started picking up shards.

"Let me do that," he said, gently nudging my hand away. "I don't want you cutting yourself."

I made a noise, reaching for another shard. "I'm capable of cleaning up broken crockery without hurting myself."

I could feel him looking at me, but I kept my gaze on the mess on the floor, biting the inside of my lip to keep from asking him the half dozen questions that had plagued me for the past ten hours. He helped me pick up the rest of the pieces in silence and we both stood and dumped them in the trash.

"I'm sorry about last night," he said.

I hesitated, then shrugged, turning on the water and washing my hands. Was he sorry he hadn't come back, or sorry he'd touched me at all? "It was business. I understand." I dried my hands and looked at him, my "brave" face firmly in place. "It's for the best, really. I'd had too much wine and wasn't thinking clearly. I shouldn't have let things go so far between us." I said it almost as a challenge, daring him to contradict me. *Wishing* he'd contradict me and say that last night had been more than wine-induced passion and the convenience of the moment, that it had meant something to him.

Instead, he said nothing. I couldn't read the expression on his face, or what thoughts were behind his beautiful dark blue eyes. A muscle twitched in his jaw. The silence stretched.

I felt myself swaying toward him. I wanted to lean against his chest and feel his arms around me, I wanted to hear him murmur soothing sounds against my ear. I wanted to press my lips into the crook of his neck, against that tender bend of flesh.

"So did everything work out with the fax?" I asked suddenly, brightly, trying to break the tension and forcing myself to walk past him toward the dining room. Embarrassment began creeping up my neck as I belatedly remembered the pile of photos I'd printed out. They were a giveaway that I was not as indifferent as I was pretending. A girl didn't print out a dozen photos of a man unless she cared about him.

"I got it, yes," he said, following me.

"Was it a crisis in the company?" I looked down at my desk and saw the last Christmas card I'd written wide open, my exaggerated story of the flying fish right there for anyone to read. I quickly flipped the card shut and looked at him. How long had he stood here at my desk? Had he read it?

"Not a crisis. A crossroads, though, and coming much sooner than I'd expected." He came to the desk and picked up one of the photos, ignoring the Christmas cards. "This *is* you and me, at the market. How ever did you get it?"

I explained about the girl with the camera phone.

"Can I have a copy?"

I shrugged. "Sure." Why did he want a copy? My obsessive girl brain worked the question over, looking for some hint of his motivation. An interest in me? A wish to *appear* interested? A meaningless impulse? Or did he just want the picture of himself? "So what's the crossroads?"

He sighed and ran his hand through his rumpled hair. "I'm not allowed to discuss it."

77

"Your boss said you couldn't?"

He gave a startled laugh. "My boss? No. My legal counsel."

I frowned, not understanding, but didn't ask anything more.

"It's nothing bad or unsavory," he said.

"Well, that's good, I guess."

Another silence fell between us. I fidgeted.

"Lauren's sister had her baby," he offered. "Late last night. Lauren called while I was at Kinko's."

"Great!"

"A girl, Elspeth Miranda. All the fingers and toes, and apparently a pair of lungs that could wake the dead."

I smiled. "Quite a name. Lauren will make a terrific aunt."

"A fiercely protective one, I think." He smiled wryly. "She'll probably persuade her sister to send little Elspeth to a girls' school, far away from the pawing hands of boys."

"What makes you say that?"

His gaze met mine. "She looks out for those she cares about." Before I could question him on that he changed his tone, saying lightly, "I heard you sewing upstairs. I hope you're going to tell me that you're finishing the red dress and are going to that party tonight. It sounds like there's someone waiting to meet you."

He took the wind right out of my sails of spite. The little that was left of my "I'll show him!" defiance deflated and flapped in the breeze. He wasn't supposed to want me to go to the party and meet men. Where was the jealousy? Where was the possessiveness? I wanted anger, I wanted hurt, I wanted yearning and suffering, the pulling of hair and the rending of garments!

I didn't want, "I hope you go to the party and have sex in the middle of the carpet with half a dozen marriageable guys. I'll stay here and eat French cheese, thanks, and you can tell me all the details when you return."

"Yes, I thought it might be fun to go, after all," I said. "I can't let Alan scare me off from doing things." And I couldn't let a foolish wish to be with Ian keep me from meeting a man who might give me the type of relationship—and future—that I wanted. I was too old for crushes on inaccessible men. "Besides, maybe I can still make him sorry that he let me go."

"You don't want him back, do you?"

"No . . ." I said without total conviction. If Alan dumped his date and went after me, would I want him?

"Are you sure?"

"I think I can do better."

"That's my girl!" he said, and gave me a light, awkward punch on the shoulder.

"Chin up, stiff upper lip, what ho? Carry on, soldier, and please, may I have another?"

He laughed, but the examining look he gave me said that he wasn't sure of my resolve.

"You're welcome to come with me," I said in as neutral a voice as I could manage. I wanted him to see me shine. I wanted him to see that other men might find me irresistible. "The invitation said 'and guest.'"

"Thanks. I think I will, if it won't bother you."

"Why ever should it bother me?"

"Why ever indeed?"

Chapter Nine

I turned around once more in the mirror, making sure that there were no unseemly puckers in the red silk, or hints that I wore nothing but a half-slip under my gown. No bra, no panties.

The dress rippled over my curves like a crimson river. It was deceptively simple in front, with a V-neck and narrow straps, but the back had a *V* that went down to the small of my back. Double-sided fashion tape secured the straps to the tops of my shoulders. Without it I'd have been at risk of playing Amazon warrior and flashing a breast.

I checked my teeth for lipstick and arranged my newly cut bangs *just so* over my forehead. This afternoon I'd gotten a drop-in appointment at a salon a few blocks away, and for the first time in many years I had a stylish mane of hair. It was still long, but there were layers, shape, and movement to it now, and it shone like the impossible tresses in a Pantene commercial. I felt worthy of a blowing fan and a slow-motion camera.

This was as good as I was going to get, and I thought I looked pretty damn fabulous.

Didn't I?

A twinge of doubt pierced me, and I hoped I hadn't crossed the line from "beautiful and sexy" to "slutty and skanky."

Oh, well. Too late now, even if I had.

I heard Ian leave his room and go out into the living room. He must be ready to go. I'd spoken to him through my door an hour ago, but hadn't seen him since late this morning. He'd gone out, saying he had business to attend to, and had been gone all day.

My bedside clock said that the taxi should be here any minute. I'd decided it was the safer bet, considering that there would be alcohol consumed.

I opened my door and went out, my high heels loud on the wood floor. Ian was sitting in the rocker, reading a book. He looked up at the sound of my entrance, and slowly, slowly the paperback in his hand slipped out of his grip and fell to the floor.

"*Good Christ*," he swore softly, his eyes roving up and down over my body and then resting on my face as if he were looking at a stranger. He stood and continued to stare. "Tessa?"

"I do clean up well," I said lightly, struggling to keep my grin under control.

"You're friggin' gorgeous."

"Until midnight, anyway. At the stroke of twelve my silks turn back to sweats."

"Burn the sweats. It's a sin to put them on someone as beautiful as you."

"Do you think Alan will be sorry he let me go?" I asked, but the question was really meant for Ian. *Are you sorry you didn't come back last night? Are you sorry now that you lost your one chance to make love to me?*

"He'll shoot himself."

"Good. That's exactly what I wanted to hear."

* * *

81

"So you like hiking, too?" Kevin asked loudly, trying to be heard over the noise. "My friends and I take a weeklong trip in the Olympics every summer. . . ."

I listened with half an ear, my eye caught by Ian as he moved through my field of vision. He seemed at ease amongst all these strangers, many of whom were connected in one way or another with the university. I'd introduced him to several people, but then Carolyn had stolen me away and he'd been left to his own devices.

He apparently had plenty of devices. He was at this moment charming our hostess, a cheerful middle-aged professor in the art department who came from family money and liked to spend it. She'd rented out the private nightclub at El Gaucho, in downtown Seattle, and we now all mingled in the dim room and held drinks in our hands while a band on the low stage played jazzed-up Christmas carols and old standards. "Strangers in the Night" was playing now. Long buffet tables held a changing array of appetizers, main courses, and desserts, and guests·were keeping the bartenders busy at the long mahogany bar. A photographer maneuvered amongst the guests, her flashes catching people with their mouths full and drinks sloshing.

I turned my attention back to Kevin, who had just asked me whether I liked to ski. He was a decent-looking guy, a little under six feet, a bit beefy and probably going to get a lot beefier as the years progressed, and with ruddy skin made worse by his being flushed and nervous. There was a trickle of sweat on his temple, and he seemed afraid to look at me. "I like cross-country skiing," I said, "but downhill is a little too fast for me."

"Oh. I think I might like cross-country, if I gave it a chance. Maybe we should go sometime." He took a big swallow of his beer.

"That could be fun."

"Really?" he croaked, finally looking at me.

"Sure." Why not? He seemed like a nice enough guy. Normal. The type of guy who would have friends over to watch football, drink beer, and grill some bratwurst in the backyard. He seemed the polar opposite of intellectually pretentious Alan, who favored black turtlenecks as formal attire. Kevin had on a nice dark suit and a red-and-green Hawaiian tie with hula girls on it. We were struggling to find an easy area of conversation, but maybe that was due to the noise, and being forced to half shout every word. "I should give you my e-mail address."

"I'll find a pen," he said, and dashed away.

My eyes went again to Ian. Now he was talking to the waiter who was refilling one of the warming pans. They seemed to be getting on well. I tried to compare Ian to either Kevin or Alan, and failed. He was a creature apart. He was a playboy. A con man like any salesman. A charmer with the gift of gab.

I shouldn't like him. And I shouldn't have mistaken his occasional flashes of vulnerability for an open heart that wanted love. No, my own heart would be safer in the hands of someone like Kevin.

Speaking of which, what was taking him so long?

I stood abandoned in the sea of people, and then I saw Alan, black turtleneck and all. He was looking at my chest, even while his arm was around a woman I'd never seen before. She didn't notice, engrossed as she was in a conversation with another woman. His new girlfriend was cute and seemed a little funky, wearing a vintage dress. Her hair was cut in a short ragamuffin style, and I found myself liking her based on appearance alone.

I hadn't expected to like her. Nor had I expected the thought that now popped into my head: *Couldn't she find someone better to be with than Alan?*

I headed over to them. Alan's eyes widened as I approached, as if wondering whether I'd noticed where he was staring and was going to come punch him in the face for it. It took a moment for me to realize he didn't recognize me. He thought he'd been staring at a stranger's breasts.

Instead of the in-your-face triumph I'd expected to feel at

a moment like this, I felt instead a queasiness in my gut. Had he ogled other women while I'd been with him? I felt a sudden stab of pity for his new girlfriend.

"Merry Christmas, Alan," I said.

"Tessa?" His eyes bulged.

The girlfriend turned away from her conversation and looked me over in alarm, her eyes uncertain, then turned to Alan for support.

He ignored her, his arm dropping from around her waist. "I didn't recognize you! You look incredible!"

I smiled politely and held my hand out to the girl. "Hi, I'm Tessa."

She shook my hand, her grip damp and soft and weak. "I'm Amy. I've heard a lot about you," she said, and then winced at her own words. "Good things," she amended.

"Probably not all good," I said lightly. "I love your dress. I'd guess about 1965?"

Her brows rose in surprise. "Thanks! Oh, that's right, you're a costumer. Nineteen sixty-five, you think? The tag said 1950s."

"No, that neckline—"

Alan interrupted our girl talk. "Are you here alone?"

"Oh," I said, waving a hand airily, "yes and no. I'm not *with* anyone, if that's what you mean, but . . ." I saw Kevin approaching. "Kevin! I'd like you to meet a friend of mine." I made the introductions as Kevin panted beside me, sounding like he'd run three blocks to find the pen and scrap of paper in his hand.

The moment the introductions were complete, I felt a hand on my shoulder. "Tessa, darling, you've been ignoring me all night," Ian said.

I gaped at him, wondering what on earth he was doing.

"Hello, I'm Ian," he said, left hand still on my shoulder as he reached forward with his right toward Alan.

"Alan," Alan said, shaking his hand and looking bewildered, his gaze going from Ian to me to Kevin.

Ian leaned forward and reached across me to Kevin, shaking Kevin's hand and introducing himself.

I stood amidst them like a doe in a meadow of stags, not quite sure how I'd managed to go so quickly from dateless spinster to hot babe surrounded by males. Amy was staring at me as if wanting to know what magic perfume I was wearing, and where she could buy some.

"Ian is my housemate's cousin from London," I explained to my audience. "He's stuck in town for a few days, so I invited him to come with me to the party." Alan and Kevin started to relax at this news, but then Ian did his part to tense them up again.

"I'm staying at her house. She's been keeping me entertained so well that I don't want to leave." He put his arm around my shoulders and squeezed, then kissed the side of my head. "She's a treasure, this one is."

"Staying at your house?" Kevin echoed.

I lifted Ian's arm off my shoulders, but he dropped it to my waist. "He's staying in his cousin's room." I pried Ian's fingers from my side and he removed his hand—only to give my bottom a soft spank. "Ian!"

"Sorry, darling. I forget myself." He leaned toward Alan and said in a stage whisper, "But can you blame me?"

I rolled my eyes and turned to Kevin, reaching for the pen and paper. "He's plastered. Ignore him. Here, let me give you my e-mail address."

"Are you sure you should go home with him?" Kevin asked by my ear. "I don't like to think of you alone with a drunk with . . . well, with *that* on his mind."

"Don't worry; it's all talk. He'll pass out the moment we get home."

"I resent that!" Ian said loudly. "I can hold my liquor!" He swayed toward me, arms wide for an embrace. "Give me a kiss, will you?"

Everything that happened next was a series of brilliant flashes, the motions of Ian, Alan, and Kevin all caught in frozen snapshots of white light from the photographer's flash.

Ian lurched and puckered. Alan abandoned Amy and lunged for Ian, reaching for his arms. Kevin pulled me aside and put his fist in my place, in the path of Ian's face.

Fist connected with face. Hands grabbed arms.

A tangled mass of flying limbs as Ian fought back.

Alan on the floor. Amy holding back her skirts as if not wanting to soil them on him. Kevin bending over in pain.

All three on the floor.

Nightclub bouncers pulling the men apart.

The flashes stopped. The music stopped. Most of the conversation in the room stopped, except for whispering as those who had not seen the action told others what it was that was happening.

The bouncers dragged all three men up the stairs to the street level. I went to the coat check at the bottom of the stairs to retrieve my coat and Ian's, my body shaking and my mind focused only on getting out of there, finding Ian, and assessing the damage to his beautiful face. I could think of nothing else.

"Was that all over you?" Carolyn asked, appearing at my side. Her husband had already run up the stairs, following his evicted cousin. "What did you do to Kevin? I thought he was sweet-tempered as a lamb. A little loud if he drinks too much, but—"

"Men! Rutting stags!" I said, grabbing the coats and running up the stairs to find Ian. *Don't let him be hurt, please don't let him be hurt*, I prayed silently, and didn't pause to wonder why it mattered so much.

Chapter Ten

I sat in the back of the taxi with my arms crossed, fuming. "Kevin probably thinks I have weirdness like this happening around me all the time. He's not going to think I'm ready to marry and have kids."

"I was helping," Ian said. He was sitting beside me, and there wasn't a trace of alcohol on his breath. The man was stone-cold sober, and had been so the entire time. He thoroughly deserved the bloody nose that had just now stopped bleeding.

"Helping! How were you helping?"

"I was arousing his protective instincts. Encouraging him to action. He was standing there beside you like a frightened sheep, and needed a prod to act like a man."

"Getting into a brawl at a Christmas party is 'acting like a man'?"

"You'll see. He'll call you tomorrow to check up on you. You'll tell him that you're packing me off to the airport; you'll thank him for keeping me off of you and say how no one has ever looked out for you that way before; and then he'll ask you out and feel like a king when you say yes."

I grumbled sour nothings under my breath.

The taxi driver got into a turn lane to get off Denney, the street we'd been traveling down. I suddenly realized that we shouldn't have been on Denney to begin with—that we should have gotten on Highway 99 several blocks back. "What are we doing here?" I wondered aloud.

"I told him to come here, before we got in," Ian said.

"Here? Where's here?" I peered out the window and then saw it: Seattle Center, and the base of the Space Needle. "Oh, no. You don't think that after what you did . . ."

"It's open until midnight." He reached through the dividing window and paid the taxi driver, then opened his door.

I stayed in place, only leaning forward to give the driver my address. "The Scot can stay here. Take me to—"

"Tessa, *please*," Ian said, bending down and leaning into the cab. He held his hand out for me. "I'm sorry that I upset you. I'm sorry that I embarrassed you. Please come with me to the top. It won't mean anything if I go alone."

"It won't mean anything with *me* there, either."

"It will," he said quietly.

I sighed and took his hand and slid out of the cab. His entreaty had touched me, despite my being furious with him. He'd behaved stupidly, immaturely, and he shouldn't be rewarded for it, but if I was honest I could admit that there was a very small part of myself deep inside that was starting to giggle, thrilled to be the center of such a dramatic confrontation. Nothing like this had ever happened to me before.

Ian kept hold of my hand, tugging me along. There was no line for the elevator ride to the top, and a minute later Ian was twenty-six dollars poorer, and we were zipping upward at a stomach-dropping speed. The elevators rode the outside of the Needle, their glass fronts giving a panoramic view as we rose above the city like birds taking flight.

I was reluctant to show how much I was enjoying the ride and the view. "Was that really why you did it?" I asked.

"Why you pretended to be drunk? You wanted to give Kevin a chance to act the hero?"

"Maybe I just wanted to see what your weasel of an ex would do."

I cast him a glance and caught a wry smile on his lips. He bobbed his eyebrows at me with a twinkle of mischief in his eyes. I scowled, but felt a smile tug at my own lips, as well. "I think his girlfriend is going to break up with him."

"See, we've saved a woman from a terrible fate."

"You might have saved me from one, too," I said, finally calm enough to look at things rationally.

"What do you mean?"

We reached the top and exited the elevator into a low-lit observation room. "Let's go outside," I said. "The view is a little better."

What had been a gentle breeze down on the ground was a cold wind up top. I turned my coat collar up against it and tucked my hands into opposite cuffs, muff-style. We circled the unoccupied deck, me pointing out what landmarks and geographical features I could, and then stopped and leaned against the rail, where we had the best view of both amber-lit downtown and Elliott Bay, with the lights of a ferry crossing the black water to Bainbridge Island. A half-moon played hide-'n'-seek behind clouds drifting across the charcoal-blue sky.

"What did you mean about saving you from a terrible fate?" Ian asked again.

"Kevin. Hitting you. What kind of guy throws the first punch at a Christmas party?"

"He might have had too much to drink."

"I don't want to marry a violent drunk," I said.

"You don't have to marry him. Date him for a while. Give him a second chance; he didn't seem like that bad a sort. I'm rather glad he punched me. Shows protective instincts." He shrugged. "At least you could have fun with him."

"I don't know how to be like you, and just date for fun. I

don't know how to keep my heart from getting involved if I like someone, or how to have fun with a guy if I *don't* like him." I turned to face him. "How can you make love to someone if you don't love them? I don't think I could bear it."

"I always love the women I sleep with, in some way."

"But never enough to stay."

"Tessa," he said, taking my face between his two warm hands and looking into my eyes. "I want to take you to bed so badly it makes my balls ache."

I blinked in surprise. "But—"

"You have no idea how hard it was for me to stay away from you last night."

"But—"

His fingers slid back into my hair, his thumbs rubbing circles on the rims of my ears. "It was that call from Lauren. She reminded me of my promise not to touch you. Did you know I promised her that?" He went on without waiting for an answer. "She read me the riot act when she began to suspect what I'd been up to with you. She told me exactly what you've just told me: You're not the sort of woman who can be loved and left."

"What woman is?"

"You know what I mean. It's never fun and games for you. It means something. And if I'm not ready to give you what it means, then I have to keep my hands off."

"I don't want you to keep your hands off," I whispered.

He released me as if my skin burned him and stepped back. "Don't, Tessa. You don't know how close I am to forgetting my nobler instincts." He laughed, a short, dry cough of a laugh. "I don't have many noble instincts, and when one appears it has a hard time surviving amidst the weeds."

"I know you're leaving tomorrow," I said slowly, sorting out my own feelings as I spoke. All I was certain of was that I wanted him. Wanted him naked in my bed, making love to my body as no one had ever made love to it before. "I know we aren't going to have a relationship, even if we have sex a dozen times between now and when you leave. And I still want you to touch me."

He shook his head, but there was no conviction in it. "I promised. . . ."

I closed the distance between us, his wavering giving me a confidence I didn't know I had. "You didn't create that scene at the party in order to help push me and Kevin together." I laid my hands on his chest and leaned my lower body against him. "That wasn't the reason." I could feel the tension in his body, feel the rigidity of his stance. And I could feel something else that was rigid beneath the layers of cloth that separated us.

"I couldn't stand to see him with you," Ian admitted hoarsely.

"That was selfish of you." I slid my arms around his back and then down to his butt, squeezing gently and pulling him closer against me.

"I wasn't thinking."

I tilted my head up and spoke softly against the corner of his jaw, my lips brushing his skin. "Don't think now."

A tremor ran through him. "I *can't*," he whispered. "Please, God, Tessa, I *can't*. I swore I wouldn't. You'd regret this tomorrow."

"You made a promise that you wouldn't seduce me. There was no promise about allowing *me* to seduce *you*."

He brought his hands back up to my face, cupping it once again, but this time with a firmness that spoke of restraint more than tenderness. "Don't tempt me. I *will not* hurt you."

"I won't be hurt if you make one simple promise to me."

His thumb brushed over my lips. I drew it into my mouth for a moment and ran my tongue over it. "What promise?" he asked, his eyes half closing.

"Promise me that you'll never speak to me again after you leave. Never call me. Never e-mail me. Never ask Lauren how I'm doing. Promise that you'll never set eyes on me again."

His eyes opened wide. *"Why?"*

"Because if you promise me that, then I'll know that there is no hope of anything between us. You're not a stranger to me; I like you well enough to know that I would enjoy sleeping with you. But it's the hope for something more between us that would hurt me afterward. The hope that you would change your mind about me, or that you'd call and want to talk, or maybe visit again. Or ask me to visit you in London. It's the days I'd spend fantasizing about what our future together might be; that's what would hurt. Because it would never come true. So promise me that I'll never have contact with you again. Swear it on your mother's soul. And then the night is ours."

In the light and shadows atop the Space Needle I couldn't be sure, but I thought there was a crease of pain between his brows. And then his hands tightened on me so hard that it hurt. "I swear it," he said, and his mouth came down against mine. Hard. With a pressure that said I was no longer the seductress; I was instead the one who would be taken.

One arm went around my back and held me close, his other hand sliding back to cup my head. I abandoned my control to his, closing my eyes and letting him show me what it was to be desired beyond all reason. He backed me against the rail, his thigh parting mine and pressing intimately against me. I tilted against him, the wide, hard muscle of his thigh rubbing against my sex. A moan slipped out of my mouth and into his.

His mouth moved to the side of my neck, hungrily sucking and biting lightly, finding the tender places and sending shock waves through my body. I tilted my head back and opened my eyes, seeing the glow of the Christmas lights strung from the roof to the very top of the tower, then turned so that I could see the lights of the city.

He opened the neck of my coat and laid his moist mouth over my breast, sucking my nipple through the silk. His thigh was replaced by his hand pulling up my hem, and he laid his palm against my naked sex. He moved his whole hand lightly over it, grazing its folds as he sucked at my nipple, flicking the tip with his tongue. His hand moved deeper, the tip of one finger touching the slit of my opening, finding the moisture there and dragging it upward to wet the path for his caress.

I heard approaching voices, and Ian quickly dropped my skirt and closed the top of my coat. A group of revelers came around the curve of the deck, talking loudly.

"Let's go home," Ian said.

I didn't answer, grabbing his hand instead and dragging him with me to the elevator.

Chapter Eleven

The moment we stepped through my front door, a sense of awkwardness overtook me. The shadowed living room with its familiar battered futon and old rocking chair were reminders ōf daily life; the dining room beyond, with my desk and computer; the fluorescent light burning above the kitchen sink, the white glow stretching across the linoleum and spilling out into the dark dining area. It was all too real to me, even with the lights out, whereas the magic of night atop the Space Needle had been another world. An imaginary world, where there were no rules and no tomorrows.

Ian closed the door and came up behind me, his arms going around my waist. He pulled me back against him, bending his head down so it was next to mine. "Second thoughts?"

I laid my hands over his on my waist. "This feels unreal."

His arms tightened around me. "Tell me now if you've changed your mind."

I closed my eyes, feeling the warmth of his breath against my neck. The fine hairs at my nape stood up, a shivering tension washing across my scalp. He dusted butterfly kisses down the bend of my neck, then reached up and pulled my coat open, exposing my shoulder to his lips. "Tell me if you've changed your mind," he repeated.

"Don't ask me that," I said, my desire coming back full force. "I don't want to think. I just want to feel."

His answer was to unbutton my coat. His hand slipped inside and cupped my breast, thumb rubbing over my nipple. His other hand cupped my sex through my dress, the silk of that garment and my slip little barrier to the feel of his fingertips stroking up and down. His mouth moved up to the sensitive place behind my ear, tongue pressing in tight circles. Each touch upon me—neck, breast, sex—seemed to magnify the others, each demanding equal parts of my attention. Thought fled, my senses were overwhelmed, and I only dimly knew that I had thrown my head back against him and was rocking my hips to the rhythm of his hand.

"Tessa," he groaned against my neck.

"I don't want to wait," I gasped.

He kept his lips on me as he slid my coat off and tossed it aside. He lifted my hem and again found me, his fingertip dipping gently into my opening, finding the moisture and using it to paint the skin beside my entrance, the pad of his finger swirling against the smooth strip of flesh.

His other hand slipped the strap of my dress off my shoulder, letting it fall, half the bodice falling with it and exposing my breast. He traced his fingertips up my sternum, his palm grazing my breast; then he drew invisible circles on the flat space above my cleavage. Each time his touch neared the top of a breast, tingling anticipation washed over it and down to my nipples, and down farther still to where his other hand continued to torture me.

That other hand now had the palm pressed against my mound, moving gently up and down. The end of his longest finger eased into my opening, loitering in the entrance as his palm continued to massage me.

I raised my arms over my head, reaching back to touch his hair. "Ian," I breathed. "Please . . ."

His mouth traced up to my jaw, and I strained to turn so that he could find my lips. His hands left me and worked at his clothes as he kissed me.

A few moments later his hands were back, both of them on my breasts this time, caressing the fullness and then gently tweaking my nipples. "I'm covered," he whispered.

I nodded, having been half aware of his donning a condom that he'd taken from his jacket. "How do you want to—"

He interrupted by lightly biting the edge of my ear, holding me in place as his hands slid down my body, over my hips, and down the sides of my thighs. When they came up again, they brought the fabric with them. He slipped his erection between my thighs, the lubrication from the condom and myself letting it slide easily, parting my nether lips, the head nudging up against my clitoris and then past it. I reached down and felt the end of him, slightly protruding from under my mound.

He moved his hips, sliding back and forth, using his arousal to caress my most sensitive areas. His hand went back to my exposed breast, kneading it gently as I leaned forward and grasped the arm of the futon for support. We were half in front of the picture window to the street, but I didn't care. A passerby would have to look carefully to see us in the darkened room.

"Don't move," he said, and a moment later he was gone from between my thighs, his hand releasing my breast. I felt him shove my skirt up higher over my hips, exposing my buttocks even more.

I felt deliciously exposed standing there bent over, no clothing below my waist except for a pair of very high black heels. He nudged my legs apart, exposing me further, and then he knelt behind me on the floor.

I started to straighten, the intimacy of *this* much exposure more than I had expected.

"Don't move," he ordered again, and used one hand against my lower back to push me down.

I submitted, my heart beating with nervous anticipation, and waited for what he would do next.

His hands played lightly over the small of my back, teasing me, even while in my imagination I could feel his eyes looking at my sex. I turned my head, twisting to try to see him.

"Stay still," he said quietly.

My inner muscles clenched in pleasure. It felt as if my entire sex were swelling, heating, and moistening yet further, making itself as ready as it could for his penetration.

His hands moved down over my buttocks, massaging them and then moving down to their base and pushing the flesh out to either side. I could feel the cool air of the room against my hidden flesh, now uncovered and exposed. A piercing shyness ran through me, but my embarrassment seemed only to heighten my pleasure.

And then he licked me: a long, slow, delicate lave that went from as far down as his long tongue could reach, over the center of my parted folds, and ended at my entrance. He pressed his tongue inside me, the strength of it enough to part my flesh, but not enough, not nearly enough, to give me the satisfaction I wanted. I moaned, and pushed my hips back against him. I bent over further, my pelvis tilting to give him even more access.

He took my offering, putting his lips and tongue to tender work upon my nub, swirling his tongue around it and lapping delicately at the edges of my folds. He dipped his tongue again into my entrance, just long enough to remind me it was there in case I had forgotten.

I felt myself building toward climax. I wanted him inside me when I came; wanted to have his erection to clench my muscles against. I wanted to feel the fullness and stretching of having him buried deep inside me, thrusting. "Ian, please, now, I want you. . . ."

But he ignored me, continuing his mouthwork. I tried to straighten; tried to turn around so I could stop him and put the rest of his body to use; but he grasped my hips in an unrelenting grip and held me in place, forcing me to accept his ministrations.

"Please . . ." I said again, but my struggles subsided as my pleasure built, and I lost the will to correct what he was doing. I became a slave to his lips and tongue, the sensual excitement capturing my entire self and sweeping me away. He sensed my rising tension and quickened his pace, and then touched my entrance with the very tip of one finger.

I crested the wave, my entire body going taut as my inner world convulsed, pulsing to the release that seemed to go on and on and on. His mouth was still on me, but tender and gentle now, avoiding direct contact with my ultrasensitive nub.

I reached back and touched the side of his face. "Enough. Please, enough. Your turn."

"It is going to be *your* turn, every time," he said, then licked me once more and stood.

I straightened and let my dress drop back down. My legs were shaking, and I felt like I could happily lie down and let him take me six ways from Sunday. He could do what he would with me.

I turned around and saw the hard, thick branch of his erection, springing from his body like the appendage on a fertility statue. "Good God," I whispered.

He took my hand and pulled me a few steps over to the hefty rocking chair. He sat down on the edge of the seat, then turned me so my back was to him, lifted my dress again, and pulled me toward him, my legs forced to part as his knees went between them.

"What . . . ?"

"Trust me," he said.

I straddled him, my hands on his knees. He positioned me above the tip of his shaft, the head nudging inside me. With one hand he played again at my folds and my clitoris, reviving the fire that I had thought quenched.

"Oh, you can't mean . . ." I said, but even as I said it my

body knew what it wanted, and bit by bit I began to impale myself upon his thickness. His fingers worked at me, each gentle, skilled manipulation making my nether lips suck him inward, greedily swallowing him inch by inch. I moaned as he used a subtle movement of the chair to thrust in and out, the length of him still only half inside me.

He thrust and rocked, thrust and rocked, and the more of him I took in, the lower my body went and the wider my legs were forced to spread over his own thighs. Then at last he was fully inside me, and I could feel his loins against my buttocks, my body forced open wide to take him all in. He stroked his fingertips over me, and I whimpered in pleasure, feeling myself again on the brink.

His other hand pressed against my back, coaxing me to lean further forward. As I did so he rocked and thrust, and the change in angle made him press up against a delicious spot inside me. It was too much, and again I came, moaning incoherently.

Both his hands went to my hips, holding me as he began to thrust in earnest, riding my waves of contractions to his own conclusion. He was done quickly, his arms wrapping around me and pulling me back against him even as I was still experiencing the slowing of my own pleasure ride.

He held me that way for timeless moments, my legs still sprawled wide, his sex still deeply embedded within me, his arms around my waist and chest, one palm covering my bare breast as if sheltering it. I tilted my head back beside his, my skull resting uncomfortably against the hard wood of the rocker, but I didn't care about that discomfort. All I cared about was that I'd been taken as I'd never been taken before.

He kissed my ear, and in mutual understanding we untangled ourselves.

"To the shower?" he asked, one eyebrow going up wickedly. "We have about fourteen hours until I have to leave, but there are at least twenty different things I've thought of doing to you. Six of them can be done in the shower."

"I don't know if I have the energy for twenty," I said. "You've wrung me out already!"

He stepped close and kissed me lightly on the lips, no other part of his body touching me. It was a strangely tender thing to do, coming as it did after what we'd just shared. "We will never see each other again after these fourteen hours, but I will make you remember me, Tessa Shore. I'm going to give you such pleasure that you can never forget. I'll even spank you, if you want."

"Merry Christmas," I said, and smiled, refusing to think about the fifteenth hour, when I'd be alone again.

A girl could ask for worse than a Scotsman for Christmas.

Chapter Twelve

It was the end of the fourteenth hour when I looked disconsolately into the empty paper box, as if staring would refill it. "We should have ordered more spring rolls."

"There's a little *pad thai* left," Ian said, nudging a container toward me.

"No, thanks. You can finish it." We'd ordered Thai food delivered, our exertions through the night, morning, and afternoon having created a calorie debit that nothing in my kitchen could repay; not even the cookie dough ice cream in the freezer, the last of which had been devoured as sex fuel around ten A.M.

I glanced at the clock. Four P.M. The taxi we'd ordered should be here within fifteen minutes. "It's strange, but I don't feel as if you're really leaving."

He swallowed his mouthful of noodles and washed it down with a sip of pale ale. "I know I am, and I hate it."

I raised my brows in question.

He smiled wryly. "Part of my mind is already trying to check in at the airport, and worrying about whether I'll find a place to stow my carry-on luggage. What I'd rather be thinking about is whether or not I can muster the energy to do you one more time."

"Then thank heavens for carry-on luggage!" I laughed. "I think I'd have heart failure if we did it again. I think it's going to take my body a month to recover."

He smiled, although there was something sad in his eyes as he looked at me. "I think I'm going to miss you, Tessa."

"You sound surprised."

"Maybe I am."

But you won't miss me enough to make you want to stay. "Remember your promise."

"No phone calls," he said, and there was a wince of pain between his brows, there for a moment and then gone. "No e-mails. No asking Lauren how you are."

"And you will never see me again."

His lips tightened, and the rims of his eyes pinkened, a glossy sheen of moisture appearing. "Never."

I swallowed against the tightness in my own throat. *I will not think about him leaving,* I told myself. *Don't think, don't think, don't think!* But something inside me knew how to feel, even without the conscious thoughts. I bit the inside of my lip, forcing it to stop trembling.

"Tessa, I—"

A horn honked right in front of the house, making us both jump.

"He's early," I said, silently cursing the taxi driver. I went to the door and called out to him that Ian would be just a minute.

Ian put on his coat. His things were already stacked beside the door. I stood in front of him in my bare feet and jeans, my hair mussed from his lovemaking, the feel of him still aching in my loins. He himself needed a shave, and his hair was only slightly less mussed than my own. There was no polished perfection to him at this moment, and it made me want to slip into his arms and stay there forever.

"What were you going to say?" I asked.

"I . . . wanted to thank you," he said, and I knew it wasn't what he had been about to say at the kitchen table. "And I don't mean for last night, as much as enjoyed it. I mean, thank you for letting me into your life these past few days. You're unlike anyone I've ever met, and I will never forget you." He touched me lightly on the cheek and traced the shape of my jaw, his gaze following the movement of his fingertips as if trying to lock the lines of my face into his memory. "Whoever you marry someday, he's going to be a very lucky man."

I grasped his hand and turned his palm to my lips, kissing it tenderly. "I hope you find who you're looking for someday."

We hugged, and he kissed the top of my head. A moment later he was gone, jogging lightly down the front stairs, his luggage slung about him. I watched him load it into the trunk with the help of the driver, then turn around to smile at me and wave.

"Don't call me!" I said.

"I won't, I promise!"

The driver scowled at us and got back into his cab. Ian climbed in, the door shut, and the reflected gray light of the day made it impossible to see more than the dim shape of him behind the window. The cab pulled away from the curb, and I shut my front door.

I was alone.

I sat down at my computer to check my e-mail, hoping for something to distract me from the quietness of the house. I'd already cleaned up the kitchen and had a load of laundry running. I'd thought about scrubbing the bathroom, but then decided there were better ways to distract myself.

My e-mail program pinged with new messages. One of them was from the hostess of the Christmas party, and there was an attachment. The note was brief, explaining that she was sending everyone pictures of themselves that her hired photographer had taken. *I love the look on your face in this picture!* she wrote.

I winced and scrolled down, dreading my first view of the fight photo. But when the picture came up, it was not the fight scene at all. It was a picture I didn't even remember being taken, of Ian and me talking and laughing. I was looking up at him with blatant adoration in my eyes, and he had one hand on my shoulder, his head bent down to hear me. He looked as intent upon me as I had been upon him.

My eyes stung, and I quickly shut down my computer.

No, no, no, don't think about him!

How long had he been gone? I looked at the clock. Twenty minutes.

I put on my shoes and coat and went for a walk around Green Lake. It was dark, and Christmas Eve, but still there were dozens of strollers and joggers on the paved path around the lake. I forced my mind into distracting thoughts of tomorrow morning at my parents' house, and then looked across the lake at exactly the right point to see the Space Needle in the far distance, its Christmas lights aglow.

Dammit. The one bleedin' landmark you could never escape in Seattle was the Space Needle, and now the damn thing was going to make my heart ache every time I saw it. *Dammit, dammit, dammit!*

I stomped home and started throwing clothes and toiletries into a bag. I didn't want to be alone any longer tonight. I'd drive to Snohomish right now, and burrow under the covers of my childhood bed.

Bag packed, I ran upstairs to my sewing room to gather up the gifts I'd made. I stopped when I saw them, though: sitting on top of the pile of neatly folded garments was a small gift in gold paper, a red velvet bow tied round it. I approached slowly, heart thumping.

There was a card tucked under the ribbon. I pulled it out and opened it—it was one of my own Christmas cards that he'd swiped.

Dearest Tessa,

I've laughed more with you these three days than I can re-member doing since I was a young boy. You've made me look at myself with clearer eyes, and you've made me see that you yourself are far more than a beautiful face and sexy body. Not that you'd know I was thinking of anything more than that, given what we've been doing today.

You're a smart, funny, exciting, and kindhearted woman, Tessa. You deserve to be treated well, and to treat yourself well. Indulge in the silk panties once in a while.

You once said that you didn't deserve an antique garnet necklace. The truth is that you deserve more than a garnet necklace: You deserve every happiness that the world can bring.

With love,
Ian

P.S. You deserve better than Kevin, too!

I carefully tore open the gold paper and lifted the lid of the square cardboard box within.

It was the garnet locket. I turned it over, and behind the small pane of glass was a snippet of dark hair.

I slipped the necklace over my head, the heavy pendant falling perfectly into place halfway down my sternum. The weight of it against my skin reminded me of how Ian had touched me there, and I closed my eyes and cried.

Chapter Thirteen

"Oh, now, isn't this wonderful?" Mom said, opening the box with her new bathrobe inside.

"It's flannel on the inside, quilted on the outside," I said from amidst a pile of wrapping paper on the floor. "I dare you to get cold in it."

"It's just lovely!"

A piercing shriek echoed from the hallway, and then my four-year-old niece, Meggie, ran into the room, followed by her six-year-old brother, Jayden, both of them in the costumes I'd made them, both of them stuffed to the gills with sugar and excitement. Meggie threw herself on me. "Help me!" she cried, her small hands gouging into my skin with surprising strength.

"I will *kill* you!" Jayden growled, a plastic sword in hand. He took up a ninja stance in front of us and slashed the air, the blade coming dangerously close to my face.

I grabbed the blade mid-slash and locked eyes with him. "Bring this near me again and I'll throw it in the river."

He tugged at the hilt. "You can't do that!"

I kept hold of the blade. "Try me."

Something in my voice seemed to get through. "Okay, okay!" he said. I released the blade and he let the tip fall to the floor; then he kicked his sister. "Crybaby!" he shouted, and sprinted from the room and out of my reach.

Meggie scrambled off my lap and chased after him. "*You're* the crybaby!" she screamed. "You are! You are!"

Stern adult tones and strident child complaints drifted in from the kitchen as my brother sought to tame his wild off-spring. The back door banged open and then shut again. Even in cold weather, the kids zipped in and out of doors with more frequency than an incontinent schnauzer.

"Honey, are you all right?" Mom asked. "You seem down. And you were so quiet when you got here last night. Is everything okay?"

"It's nothing," I lied. If I told her even a little about Ian, she'd want to know more. And how could I tell more without telling her that I'd spent a long night with a man I'd known only a couple days, and whom I'd made promise never to speak to me again?

She'd think I was insane. Or a fool.

I was voting that I was a fool.

What lies I had told myself, saying it wouldn't hurt to give myself to Ian if I knew there was no hope for a future. I'd imagined that I'd be able to look at our time together as a naughty, exotic interlude in my otherwise tame life, and would keep it my own little secret, perhaps spilling it only forty or fifty years hence, when a granddaughter came to me for advice about her own love life.

Such lies I'd told myself.

I hurt. I hurt because I'd fallen in love with him, and then made sure I could never have him. I hurt because he'd made sure that I could never forget him.

He wasn't perfect. He had streaks of immaturity. He was a cynic and a sybarite. He was a womanizer.

But he had also made me feel beautiful, and funny, and fun to be around. He made me feel like his world revolved around me. He made me feel worth nice things, and worth being pampered and pleasured. He was generous and self-deprecating, and didn't care if he made a fool out of himself.

He wasn't perfect, but I thought he was perfect for me. I was happy when I was with him.

A door opened and slammed shut again, and then there were the running footsteps of children.

"Aunt Tessa!" Meggie shouted, skidding to a stop in the doorway, her cheeks red from the outdoors. "I have a present for you!"

"*I* have a present," Jayden said, coming up behind her and shoving her aside.

"Do not! *I* do!" Meggie gave him a good elbow to the gut and pushed him over.

I blinked in surprise. Strong girl.

"*I* get to say it," she said, kicking her brother while he was down. He groaned loudly and covered his head, curling into the fetal position. "*I* get to!" she repeated.

"Jeez, let up on him, will you?" I said, although I could see he was laughing and not truly hurt. "I think you made your point."

She kicked him once more for good measure, then planted her hands on her little hips. "*I* have a Christmas present for you. I found him outside."

"Oh?" Thoughts of earthworms and snails slithered across my mind.

"Will you come see?"

I shrugged and got up, then followed her to the front door, planning to go no farther than the front steps in my slippers and pajamas. She opened the door.

Ian stood on the other side, a look of cautious hope on his handsome face. "I finally thought of an appropriate song to sing." He brushed his hand through his hair and lowered his chin, looking up at me from under his brows. " '*Return to sender,*' " he started to sing in a bad impersonation of Elvis. " '*Bright and early next morning, it came right back to me . . .*' "

I stared, not believing it. "I'm not a fool; I'm insane," I whispered, and felt my knees start to buckle.

He swooped inside and caught me up in his arms. "Tessa!"

Meggie laughed and hit me on the rump. "He told me to say he was a present! And I did!"

"Ian? What are you doing here?" I asked, as I was dimly aware of my sister-in-law appearing and dragging Meggie away. "Did you miss your flight again?"

"I made my flight. I even found a place for my carry-on luggage. But then I realized that I was about to miss my one chance at something far more important: you."

"You got off your plane?" I asked, bewildered.

He nodded. "Rented a car. Went to your house, but you were gone. I waited outside for half the night before figuring out that you must have come here. I had a devil of a time finding this place. I wasn't even sure I had the right Shore residence until I saw your niece and nephew running around in those costumes you'd made."

"But . . . why?"

"Isn't it obvious?" he asked, running his fingers into my hair and tilting my face upward.

I shook my head.

He bent his head down and laid his lips close to my ear, whispering, "I've fallen in love with you."

I closed my eyes, the pain in my heart releasing in a flood of warmth.

"I realized that I didn't want to remember you: I wanted to be with you. My life suddenly felt false, like it was a poor copy of something that could have been much better. I realized I was never going to find someone who could make me feel as happy and alive as you do, Tessa. I was never going to find someone so real, so true. You challenge me. You surprise me. You make me laugh. And it feels so damn good when I see you smile."

I smiled.

"Do you think there might be a chance for the two of us?" he asked softly. "It would mean that one of us would have to relocate. I know that university teaching positions aren't easy to come by, so perhaps I could work from here."

"Are you sure your boss would go for that?"

He laughed, lifting his face. "Boss? I *am* the boss."

I blinked in confusion. "But you said you were a shop-keeper."

"Yes. But I'm not an employee. I *own* a chain of faux-luxury-goods shops. I came to the U.S. to see about expand-ing into this market."

"Oh." The information tried to sink into my stunned brain and failed. Not that it really made any difference, ex-cept that it gave him a certain amount of control over how he spent his time. "The fax you got, it was about that?"

He shook his head. "That was something unexpected. A major retail conglomerate has offered to buy my stores for a considerable sum, leaving me in place as president. At a hefty salary, of course."

"Just how many stores do you have?"

"Twenty-six."

"And the offer was for how much?"

He smiled. "Let's just say that I don't need to worry about being able to afford a wife and kids, if it should ever come to that. Might it, Tessa?"

I stood on tiptoe and kissed him softly. "It might."

"Do you think you might ever be able to love a scoundrel like myself?"

I laid my head on his shoulder and wrapped my arms around his waist. "I already do." His arms came around me and I closed my eyes, feeling truly home at last.

Epilogue

One Year Later

Dear Rachel,
  Merry Christmas!
  A lot happens in a year, doesn't it? This picture is of me and husband Ian in Bora Bora. Yes, husband! We eloped in October. I know, I know, you'd think that I of all people would have a huge wedding, if only so that I could have the fun of designing my own dress, but I've discovered that all those girlhood dreams of the big day don't mean so much once you've found the one. Being married is all that either of us cared about. We're planning on a smashing big reception and open house when the remodeling is done on the house we bought together in Seattle, though, so expect an invitation to be coming your way soon!

  Love,
  Tessa

The Single
Girl's Guide to
Christmas

by

JENNIFER ASHLEY

Being single at Christmas doesn't mean spending the holidays alone or lost in a crowd while you try to explain why you're not married. Create a Christmas to remember for one of the most important people in your life—you! Here are some simple ways to make Christmas this year extra special.

Indulge in a facial and manicure. . . .

"So tell us, *Angel*."

The famous bottle-blond, perky talk show host grinned, baring straight white teeth that must have cost her a fortune. "What happens when the single girl is alone in her apartment under the mistletoe?"

Penny McDermott, star of morning TV, was notoriously single, which was why my publicist had been able to wrangle me and my book a slot with her this close to Christmas. This was a live show, done every morning at ten in New York City, broadcasting to millions. I'd sell a ton of books, my publicist assured me.

Right now I wanted to hurl my hardback into Penny's lovely mouth and let the orthodontist sort it out.

For the last ten minutes Penny had disparaged me and my book in every possible way. Ten minutes had never seemed an eternity before.

"Have a facial?" she chirped. "Oh, come on, Angel. Don't mess with us. What you really do is stay at home, put on sad music, and shove a box of chocolates down your throat. Am I right?"

Her studio audience, mostly young girls with pretty hair and cherub faces, cheered.

"The point of the book is," I tried, "that you don't have to feel sorry for a woman who is alone during the holidays."

"No, of course not." Penny grinned, then she mouthed at the audience, *Losers!*

They screamed with laughter.

"You are a single woman," I countered. "No one feels sorry for you."

"Why should they?" she laughed. "I'm rich and success-ful. Honey, I'm Penny McDermott."

Her audience clapped again.

I would strangle my publicist, my editor, and every single person who told me that a shot on Penny McDermott's tor-ture hour would make my career.

Not exactly the career I'd had in mind. My book had come out of a series of columns I'd written when I'd looked around and seen lonely people facing the holidays—myself included—and decided that we deserved something better than pity and a warmed-up frozen turkey dinner.

So I gathered my courage and wrote a regimen for single women and the holidays. I covered everything from how to have Christmas dinner alone in your apartment to how to answer Aunt Sylvia at the family dinner when she asks for the fiftieth time why you aren't married.

The publisher that owned the woman's magazine I wrote for decided to publish the columns in book form, one col-umn per chapter.

The book made the *USA Today* top 150 and appeared for a week on the *Publishers Weekly* extended list for nonfiction.

Not bad, said the publisher. A little more publicity, and I'd be a household name.

Any more publicity like Penny McDermott's show, and I'd have to change my name, get plastic surgery, and move to Guatemala.

"And then when you're really lonely," Penny said, showing all her teeth, "you can call on Santa's helper." She waggled her eyebrows.

I stared at her, then realized, as her audience screamed with laughter, that she meant a vibrator. My face flamed.

Please can we have an earthquake? Can the stage fall in? Are there earthquakes in New York?

I gulped and tried to be witty. "I'm afraid I didn't include a chapter on that."

"Aw, too bad." The audience said, "Awwww," with her.

"Well, thank you Angie Suliman—"

"Uh, it's Sullivan. Angel Sullivan."

"—for talking with us today about *Christmas and the Single Girl*—"

"*The Single Girl's Guide to Christmas*," I said frantically.

Penny's smile turned hostile. "Whatever. *The Pathetic Woman's Guide to Not Getting Any at Christmas*."

The audience shouted and laughed. Over the chaos, Penny screamed, "I'm Penny McDermott, single and loving it! Don't go away. Next up is a guy who will teach us all kinds of fun stuff to do with whipped cream. It's not just for pumpkin pie anymore!"

The band started up, drowning out Penny, the audience, and my raging headache.

The cameramen stepped back, relaxing for the two minutes out, as the noise went on. Under cover of it, Penny dragged me up from the chair and gave me a big, insincere, perfumed hug. "That was fun, honey! You come back on my show anytime."

She shoved me toward her female assistant with a headset, who towed me off the stage.

That was it; I was done. No more lounge with coffee and

pastries, no women hovering over me with hairbrush and powder. Another assistant, a man this time, looked at me in a bored way, handed me my coat and purse, and led me down a back hall and out an unmarked door.

I found myself on a busy Manhattan street. Snow fell rapidly, covering the dirty half-melted snow from yesterday. Shoppers and tourists and businesspeople rushed past me, not even looking at me while I struggled to put up my umbrella.

There wasn't a cab in sight. Angel Sullivan, successful columnist and budding best seller, hefted her purse and trudged through slush to the nearest bus stop.

Take a long, hot bath scented with sandalwood oil and sip a glass of champagne. . . .

All I had in the fridge were two longneck Sam Adams winter brews. I drank one, sinking onto the sofa and propping my frozen feet on the coffee table.

Thank God the show had been live. That meant I didn't have to suffer through a tape-delayed broadcast later. The show was done, gone, history.

I lifted my cell phone from the table beside me and checked my messages. I had five. Three were from friends who'd seen me on the show.

"You were great, Angel! I was so excited I had a friend on television!"

"We had a party this morning, Angel, and watched you!"

"Hey, Angel, saw you on TV. Is your hair really that color? Maybe it was the lights."

I groaned and deleted them all.

Message four was from my publicist. "Angel? This is Barbie." She insisted on "Barbie," not Barbara or Barb. "That was terrific. I bet the book hurtles right up the lists."

Penny had never once gotten the name of the book right. Customers would pour into bookstores asking for *The Pathetic Woman's Guide to Not Getting Any at Christmas.* Yeah, I'd be a hit.

"I had my assistant tape the show," Barbie went on, as perky as Penny. "We can watch it together. And don't worry about your hair. It was the lights."

I deleted the message with trembling fingers.

Message five was from my mother. "Angel? It's Mom. We saw the show." A long pause. "We want you to come home for Christmas, sweetie. We didn't realize how hard it was for you during the holidays. So come home. All right?" Another pause. "Did you do something to your hair?"

I hung up and sat staring at the phone for a while. I hadn't had Christmas with my family back in Sonoma County in a long, long time.

I'd left home five years ago, over their loud protests. *You don't have to leave home to be happy, Angel. Look at your sisters. They found husbands and happiness right here.*

I loved my family, but they were large and smothering. I wanted to fly away, to see the world, to have adventures and a life of my own. I'd gotten myself a journalism degree from UCLA and accepted a job in Manhattan in hopes of launching a career. That and I was running from my first frightening taste of love, a wild encounter the last summer before I left California. No one knew about that but me.

We understand, my mother had said. She liked to say *we,* as though she were the spokesperson for the whole family (and she was). *You need to spread your wings.*

I flew all the way to Manhattan and my first glamour job in magazines. All right, my first job consisted of checking that Courteney Cox's name was spelled right and that four cups of sugar in a dozen brownies wasn't a typo, but the correct recipe. But from there I worked my way up to a position as columnist at a lead glossy, *Women of Today.*

Women of Today wrote about twenty-somethings and thirty-somethings who had made names for themselves, told single girls how to decorate their apartments without going broke, told women who worked all day how to throw cool and memorable parties, and—very important—we told them all about men.

About how to tell if he was Mr. Right—or Mr. Totally Wrong. What to do when you were attracted to your best friend's ex. Or attracted to your best friend's current catch. I wrote about how to break up. About how to console yourself when dumped. And about how to get out there and find another one.

I won awards for my columns. I garnered praise for my insight and received tons of mail from grateful young women. I had deliberately put love behind me, and I could write about it with cool detachment.

With the same cool detachment, I got myself engaged to a guy I'd convinced myself was Mr. Right.

I was wrong. He dumped me because he'd been dating my best friend behind my back.

Mark and Susan had read my column about being honest with your friend when you're poaching her mate. They felt guilty, so one night they took me out to dinner to my favorite Italian bistro, and they told me. Straight and honest, to my face.

While I sat there feeling like the minestrone had just been poured over my head, they announced that they were getting married. They watched me, eyes bright, as though they expected me to smile, praise them for their honesty, and then congratulate them.

I stood up, picked up my piping-hot plate of penne arrabiata, and plopped it into my ex-boyfriend's lap. I followed that with a glass of merlot. Then I straightened my hair, grabbed my purse, and walked out.

After that, I wrote columns called "How to Make It in Life without Men." And, "Men: Who Needs Them?" Or, "Don't Look for Mr. Right; Look for Mr. Right Now."

I heaved a sigh and took a swig of Sam Adams. Maybe next week I'd write the column, "How to Go 365 Days Without Sex."

Gah.

Now Mom called out of the blue and asked me to come home.

She'd disliked Mark, my ex, on sight (because she's smarter than me), but said she understood. When I had spent three Christmases with him and his family in Vermont, she'd again said that "we" understood.

Last year I hadn't told her that I'd gotten dumped, and she'd assumed that I'd gone to Vermont again. She'd wised up in the meantime, and now she was inviting me home.

Any other day I would have called and said no. A Christmas with my family meant not just my parents, not just my older sisters and their families, but my three aunts, four uncles, a dozen cousins, and Great-uncle Mike, if he managed to stay out of jail.

However, after being put through the meat grinder with Penny McDermott, I was tempted.

Very tempted.

Penny McDermott had managed to make Christmas with my family look like a fine treat.

As I sat there, lost in thought and Sam Adams, Barbie called me again. "Oh, I'm glad I caught you. I want you to see the show. You were great, but there were a couple of places—you need to brush up on a few interview techniques before I get you on more talk shows. How about Christmas Eve? It will be fun; we can watch the tape and get drunk on eggnog."

"Uh," I said. "Can't do it, Barbie. I'm going home for Christmas."

"Oh." She sounded baffled. "But I thought—"

"Nope. Going home." And maybe in the meantime someone would break into her house and burn all her videotapes. "I'll call when I get back."

Visit old friends; catch up on old times. . . .

I got on the Internet and bought the cheapest last-minute holiday fare I could find, and headed out on Christmas Eve.

On Crop Duster Airlines, I swear. We landed in every single town with an airport from New York to Ohio to Minnesota to Montana to Nevada and finally to California.

But wouldn't you know, that plane wouldn't stop anywhere near Sonoma, not even Oakland. I had to go to Sacramento and drive west in a rented car that smelled like something had crawled inside it and died.

I arrived at my family's home, an old winery renovated by my mother and father, at ten o'clock that night.

Because it was my family, the house was still lit up, and noise like a stadium during a football game poured out into the night.

Dad had gone nuts with the Christmas lights again. Every awning, every window, and every door of the house was decked out in bulbs that blinked white, yellow, blue, green, red, purple, and orange. Wire reindeer outlined in white lights with moving heads grazed on the lawn. On top of the house, a glowing Santa waved from an overstuffed sleigh that was pulled by not eight, but twelve large reindeer. Dad always thought eight wasn't enough.

Lights hung from every tree and outlined every bush. Three glowing plastic angels stood in the corner of the yard. They held songbooks in their glowing hands and burbled "Gloria in Excelsis Deo." Two giant plastic snowmen dominated the opposite corner of the yard.

I parked behind three SUVs and two PT Cruisers of different shades and dragged myself and my bags up the slick driveway to the front door. The door sported a huge green wreath decorated with lights and studded with apples.

I pushed the doorbell, because I'd left my key behind when I moved out and moved on. Voices filled the space inside, drowning out the feeble *ding-dong* of the bell. I waited. I pushed the bell again.

I heard a young voice scream, "It's Great-uncle Mike!" and the door slammed open.

A small person in a T-shirt that read, LITTLE DEVIL, hurtled into me. He stopped, looked up, and gaped. He had the Sullivan black hair and blue eyes, so I knew he belonged there.

He gave me the once-over, then yelled back into the living room, "It's some woman. I don't know who it is."

A girl came running. "Stupid! That's Angel." She flung her arms around my waist.

"Hi, Esmerelda," I said, returning the hug.

My cousin Ann had named her three daughters Tatiana, Katya, and Esmerelda. I guess she had gotten bored with "Ann." Cousin Ann herself came forward and shoved a martini into my hand. "Angel, so good to see you."

She didn't say anything about the TV show. I loved her.

I dropped my bag by the front door. Then I was passed from hugger to hugger. I hugged my sisters and their husbands—Brad and John, fine men who loved my sisters and didn't run off with their best friends.

I hugged their kids, Marta, Lisa, Devlin, and Tyler. I

hugged my dad, who'd had about ten eggnogs and could barely stand up. I hugged Aunt Elizabeth, Aunt Candy, Aunt Merline, Uncle Tad, Uncle Steve, Uncle Matt, and Uncle Chris.

I hugged their husbands and wives, I hugged their kids, and again hugged Tatiana, Katya, and Esmerelda, who'd come back for seconds:

I wondered where I was going to sleep.

"So what happened to Great-uncle Mike?" I asked as I finally got my breath back and had a chance to sip my martini.

"He's in jail!" came the chorus.

"He's with Sheriff Hanks tonight," my mother said, in her "we understand, but we disapprove" voice.

"What did he do?"

"He mooned the sheriff!" screamed the five-year-old who'd opened the door. His name was Theophile.

"Did he really?" I asked in dismay.

"Yes," said Aunt Candy. "Maybe he wanted some peace and quiet."

I looked around. Yep, a night in Sheriff Hanks's jail would be much quieter than this.

"Hey, Angel," my cousin Cherise sang out. "We need all single girls in this corner!"

She was standing across the living room by the fireplace, looking as weird as ever. Cherise was twenty-seven, the same age as me. She wore a tight black dress cut to reveal as much cleavage and thigh as possible without being obscene. Her nails were bright red, her face was white, her lips scarlet, and her eyes were outlined in black eyeliner.

Cherise prided herself on the fact that she went out with guys for sex alone. "Sweet-talk 'em, do 'em, dump 'em," was her motto. I remembered, cringing, that she always bought sex toys for everyone for Christmas.

In the past I'd given Cherise's gifts to Susan, who had liked such things. I realized now what my former best friend had done with them.

Cherise and I were the only two single women left in the

family, unless you counted the girls, all of whom were fourteen and under.

"Why?" I asked, clinging to the martini like it would keep me safe from her.

"We're going to play a game." Cherise smiled with her scarlet mouth.

I'd like to see Penny McDermott go one-on-one with Cherise. Penny would run away screaming. The thought cheered me up. "What kind of game?"

Marta and Tatiana, the two fourteen-year-olds, looked excited. "We're going to guess the name of the man we marry," Marta said.

Ah, fourteen, when you dream of being swept off your feet into a white dress and a honeymoon suite.

"I'm not getting married," I said. "I like being single."

The two stared at me as if I were crazy. "Why?" Tatiana demanded. "Don't you like guys?"

She looked astounded. But she was fourteen, and her hormones were just starting to rage. She probably had posters of Orlando Bloom and other movie hunks stuck up on her bedroom walls.

"I like them fine," I said. "I just don't want to marry them."

"Come on," Cherise urged. "It's only a game."

I drank down the last of the martini and popped the olive into my mouth. "Oh, what the hay. What do you want me to do?"

She smiled triumphantly and held out an apple. "Here."

I looked at it blankly. "What will this do?"

In her other hand Cherise held up a glinting, pointed kitchen knife. I took a step back.

"You peel your apple in one long strand with no breaks," she said. "Then you toss the peel over your left shoulder."

"I thought it was the right shoulder," Marta said.

"Doesn't matter. Whatever shape the apple peel falls in is the first initial of the man you'll marry."

She had a strange gleam in her eye. I wondered why on

earth she was doing this. Cherise, as far as I know, had never expressed interest in marrying. In fact, she went out of her way to avoid anything connected with matrimony. Why she suddenly wanted to play an old-fashioned "guess your husband" game was beyond me.

I figured she'd had too much eggnog, like my dad. Or she was teasing me to entertain herself. Either way, I was too tired to care. Let her tease me; it was Christmas.

I shrugged. "All right. I'll give it a shot."

"Great." She held out an apple and a knife. I set down my martini glass and took both. The apple was round and warm from her hand, the knife cool.

Cherise produced another apple and another knife and touched the tip of the blade to the red skin. "Ready, set, go."

"You have to say the magic words," Tatiana objected.

"I don't know them," I said. "You say them for me."

Tatiana and Marta looked astonished again; then they chanted a rhyme I'd never heard.

"Peel the apple 'round and 'round.
Throw the peel upon the ground.
His first initial will appear
The husband that you'll hold so dear."

"And then he'll ask you for a beer," seven-year-old Devlin finished, mocking their chant.

The two girls rolled their eyes. Cherise paid no attention. Her knife went carefully through the peel, so carefully that I'd swear she'd practiced. My knife slipped and slid, but I managed to keep the peel more or less intact. Juice oozed from the white apple flesh beneath, coating my fingers.

"Ready?" Cherise said.

"Yeah." I stuck the peeled apple between my teeth, then gingerly lifted my peel in both hands.

"One, two, three, toss!"

Cherise and I, at the same time, threw the peels over our left shoulders.

I turned around. I took the apple from my mouth, crunching a bite, and looked down at the peel.

"*S!*" Marta screamed. "Your husband's name will start with *S*."

The blob didn't much look like an *S*. More like a *P*. Actually, it looked mostly like a lump of red-and-white peel.

"Cherise's is *S* too," Tatiana said.

"You're both going to marry the same guy?" Devlin asked, puzzled.

"Ooh, kinky." Cherise grinned.

"No," I said. "Lots of guys have names that start with *S*."

"Sam," said Marta. "Simon, Steve."

"Stan, Stewart," Tatiana said.

"Sheldon," my cousin Ann said, joining the group. "Skyler."

"Samuel," Devlin said.

"Stupid," Marta told him. "That's the same as Sam."

"I'm not stupid!"

"Devlin," my sister Janet called. "Marta. Stop fighting."

"So," Cherise asked me, "who do you think this mysterious *S* will be?"

I took another bite of the apple. They hadn't mentioned the one *S* I'd thought of. *Sean.* Sean Chase. Sean Chase, with whom I'd spent two glorious months five years ago, the summer before I'd gone to New York.

We'd met while I was interning at a newspaper in Los Angeles and he was checking out business clients for his family's winery. He was in town for a couple of months, and I planned to head off to New York to a new job as soon as I finished my internship.

We hit it off and had an intense, fun-filled fling. We spent every minute of time together that we weren't actually working. He took me to restaurants that bought his family's wine, and I took him to the movies, but most of the time we hung out at my apartment and ate take-out burgers in the nude.

It had been the most passionate sixty days of my entire life.

I'd fallen hopelessly in love, but I never dared tell him. At the end we went our separate ways with fond memories of our time together. It was over, that was all. Time to move on.

At least, that was what I pretended. He was the love I'd run from, and one of the reasons I'd hooked up with Mark. I'd wanted to forget Sean.

Many times, after I moved on to New York and my new life, both before and after I'd met Mark, I'd looked in the mirror and remembered what it felt like to be with Sean. Then I'd groan and put my hands over my face. *Stupid, stupid, stupid,* I'd say to my reflection. *Why'd you let him go?*

But it had been for the best, right? He had his life, I had mine, and those lives were headed in opposite directions. Or we were parallel lines, never destined to cross. That sounds poetic, anyway.

After dumping my pasta on Mark, I had toyed with the idea of calling Sean. What for, I don't know. Maybe to say, *Hi, I just broke up with a total loser; are you married yet?*

Sean never met my family, because we'd parted ways before I'd gotten the chance to introduce him. Not that I'd been in a big hurry. Los Angeles had been peaceful and quiet next to a Sullivan family gathering.

I said, "The peels can only fall in so many shapes. The most likely are *S* or *C.*"

"Well, it wasn't *C.* It was *S.*" Cherise's eyes glinted. "We'll see."

At that point my mother called me to the kitchen for hot soup, and I gladly went.

My mother's kitchen is homey and built to feed a lot of people. The refrigerator is one of those huge, restaurant-size ones with the aluminum doors. She had a six-burner range and two cavernous ovens. An island stood in the middle of the room with a chopping block in its top and slots for knives all around it. Two knives were missing, probably the ones Cherise had appropriated for the apple game.

Mom was ladling soup from a huge pot on the stove when

I walked in. She set the steaming bowl in front of me on the kitchen table. Matching place mats had been set all around the small table, with a centerpiece of pinecones and greens and oranges and cranberries in the middle.

The soup was Mom's famous "kitchen sink" concoction. The thick broth held potatoes, carrots, celery, chicken, bacon, onions, leeks, mushrooms, and cabbage. I dug into it hungrily. The soup was never the same twice, but it was always peppery and warm and delicious.

Mom set a plate of crusty white bread by my elbow. "So when were you going to tell me about it?"

"About what?" I answered, busily slurping soup.

"About breaking up with Mark."

"Oh, that." I tore off a hunk of bread and dunked it in the broth. "We broke up. He married Susan Howard. In July."

Her eyes narrowed. "I thought Susan Howard was one of your best New York friends."

"She was. Now she's married to Mark. End of story."

My mother was in her fifties and still quite pretty. She dyed her brown hair a shade lighter every year. This year she was nearly blond. She didn't have many lines on her face and liked to wear makeup.

But she was still my mom. "You should have told me."

I had long since given up crying about Mark, but tears welled up in my eyes now. "I didn't want to talk about it."

"You know you can always come to us about anything. We're your family. We want to help you."

She said *we*, but she really meant herself. Mom was the fixer of all problems.

I stirred my soup. "I know. But I was the big shot running off to New York and getting a great job and a great boyfriend. And then he dumps me for my closest friend. I didn't want to admit how stupid I'd been."

My mother sat down across from me and put her elbows on the table. "That's not your fault, and you know it. We're all stupid about people sometimes."

"You picked Dad right off," I reminded her.

"I picked your dad when he was fifteen and I was four-teen."

They'd gotten married when they'd graduated from college, and they'd been married thirty years now.

"Do you ever regret being with the same person for so long?" I asked. "I mean, it was never anyone but him."

My mom smiled, a warm light in her eyes. "Nope. Never."

I hid a sigh of envy and went back to my meal. They'd met so young and known it was right. Not everyone was so lucky. Take me, for instance.

The doorbell rang. It was eleven now, and still the family gathering raged on. I barely heard the bell. Theophile heard it, though.

"It's Great-uncle Mike!" he screamed again, and I heard him yank open the door.

Mom got up. "If it is Mike, we have nowhere to put him. He'll have to go back to jail to find a bed."

I gave a short laugh. "Maybe I'll go with him. They might have a spare cell."

"Don't be silly. We'll put you in your old room."

I left my empty soup bowl and followed her. "No, stick me in one of the attic rooms. Don't rearrange everything."

"It's no trouble—"

She broke off as we entered the living room. Little Theophile was staring at someone who waited on the porch. "It isn't Great-uncle Mike," he announced at the top of his voice. "It's some guy. I've never seen him before."

My dad swept Theophile off his feet and onto his shoulders. "Howdy," he slurred. "Come in out of the cold."

"Thanks," a voice said. A deep, masculine, sexy voice. "I wanted to ask if I could use your phone."

My mouth went dry. Butterflies danced all over my stomach. Oh, my God. It couldn't be. Could it? No, the coincidence would be too much. Even Cherise couldn't wave a wand and bring him forward out of my past.

The man belonging to the voice stepped inside, and my world dropped out from under me.

It couldn't be him. I wouldn't let it be him. It must be Sean Chase's twin brother. Or his clone. Not Sean of the best two months of my life.

He hadn't seen me. Maybe I could sneak back into the kitchen, flee out the back door, jump into my rented car, and gun it all the way back to New York. So what if it would take four or five days and cost me a fortune in rental fees? Who cared, as long as I got away?

My feet wouldn't move. I stood there like a fool and stared at him hungrily.

Sean would be about twenty-nine now, a couple years older than me. He was still drop-dead gorgeous. He was tall and broad-shouldered, and even more good-looking than I remembered. He wore a black leather coat gleaming with drizzle. His hair was dark brown, and he turned the deepest, brownest, sexiest eyes in the world to my family. My entire family. He looked slightly alarmed.

"Of course," my dad said. "Our house is your house on this cold winter's night."

Sean started to give him an answer; then his gaze lighted on me. He stilled.

I gazed silently back at him. I mean, what do you say to an old flame who just crashed your family reunion? *Hi! Fancy meeting you here! Remember the time we had sex in the closet?*

Cherise pushed herself around me and, to my surprise, started for him, her hips waggling. "Oh, hi, Sean," she said. "Do you remember me? We met at Archie's in Oakland."

"Uh," said Sean.

She grabbed his arm, red painted claws sinking into his leather coat. "How wonderful to see you again." She turned to the interested group of my aunts, uncles, cousins, and assorted kids. "Everyone, this is Sean."

She looked at me, her eyes gleaming. "Sean, spelled with an *S*."

Treat yourself to eggnog, rich and creamy, with just a touch of rum.

"So, Sean spelled with an *S*," my father said. "What are you doing in this neck of the woods?"

We were all in the kitchen, me and Mom and Dad and Cherise and Tatiana and Aunt Candy and Cousin Ann. The ladies, except me and Cherise, were preparing pancake batter for breakfast the next morning. Cherise and I and my father and Sean sat at the kitchen table.

Sean had divested himself of his fine leather coat. Underneath he wore a black sweatshirt and jeans. He pushed up his sleeves to reveal a pair of strong, sinewy forearms.

I'd always been interested in forearms. I always say you can tell if a man is strong by his wrists. The muscle that ran from Sean's thumb across his arm to his elbow was especially attractive. I'd always liked it.

I jerked my gaze away. Sean hadn't said a word to me or my family about the two of us knowing each other or about having had a knock-down, drag-out, wild relationship. I figured he was being discreet and didn't want to embarrass me—or himself. I'd obviously told no one about him, because none of the family asked whether he was interested in getting back with me. Don't think they wouldn't.

And then I had a terrible thought. What if Sean didn't remember me at all? What if I was eating my heart out, and he was only trying to recall my name?

Was he sitting across the table thinking, *You know, she looks familiar. What was her name? Zephronia?*

I didn't care, did I? I was no longer interested in Sean. I mean, look at him. Wavy brown hair mussed by the wind and his attempt to finger-comb it. Long dark lashes framing soulful dark eyes. Muscular chest and shoulders filling out his sweatshirt. Tight jeans over a nice backside. A smile that could melt ice. Who needed it?

He answered my dad in his low, rumbling voice that made me think of warm blankets and hot buttered rum. "I was trying to get north, to Clearlake. My friend Archie told me it was a shortcut."

My dad snorted. "A shortcut to nowhere. This is the end of this road. You have to go back down to Sonoma and pick up the interstate."

Sean turned his cup in his fingers. "That's a heck of a drive."

"And too long to make in the middle of the night," my mother said from where she stirred batter. "Stay here. You can call your folks and tell them you'll be there tomorrow."

He smiled, lighting the room like summer sunshine. "I'm not on my way to see my folks. They're in England."

"Really?" Cherise chirped. "Why is that?"

"We have family there. My mother's gone to trace her roots. I plan to join them in January, but I had to finish up a job. Friends in Clearlake invited me to spend Christmas Eve with them, but it's too late now. I'll just go back home."

"Don't be silly," my mother said. "You can't spend Christmas alone because you took a wrong turn. You'll stay here."

He still smiled but shot a sideways look at me. "No, I couldn't."

"Of course you can," my mother said. "You are Cherise's friend, and we're her family. We can fit you in. You'll have to stay the night anyway. The weather's turning nasty."

He could not deny that. It rarely snowed in this neck of the woods, as my father called it, but we could get drizzle and freezing rain.

"Why did you need to use our phone?" I asked abruptly.

Everyone looked at me. The room grew silent. Aunt Candy froze in the act of cracking an egg.

Sean's gaze flicked to mine, and my heart thudded until I felt sick.

"I want to tell my friends I'm lost?" he offered.

"I mean why did you have to stop? Why not use your cell phone?" I pointed to the device hanging from his belt.

He unhooked the phone and laid it on the table. "I didn't charge it up. The battery's dead."

"You could charge it with your cigarette lighter in your car."

I didn't mean to sound like an interrogator. I was simply suspicious about why he'd turned up out of the blue. Or the black. The fact that he knew Cherise was a mite too convenient. I would not put it past her to have told him to come here and say he was lost, and *Oh, goodness,* Cherise would chirp, *where is he going to sleep? He can have my bed,* snicker, snicker.

Sean's cheeks reddened. "I'm a vintner, not an engineer. I lost that cord as soon as I bought the phone."

"I did that with mine, too," my dad said, all sympathy.

"Angel's a writer," Cousin Ann said, apropos of . . . well, absolutely nothing. "She has a best-selling book out."

"Cool," Sean said, interest in his eyes. "What's it called?"

"The Single Girl's Guide to Christmas," I said faintly.

He gave me an odd look. "I see."

"She was on Penny McDermott's show," Ann went on. "She was great. Did you see it?"

"Penny McDermott," Sean said. "That's impressive. No, I missed it."

Cherise picked up his cell phone and started running her fingers over it. "Angel was great."

"Actually, she humiliated me," I said.

"No, no," my mother said. "She was trying to be funny. That's her way."

"I wasn't laughing," I muttered.

"I know, let's watch it," Aunt Candy said. "I taped it. Your hair looks a little weird; otherwise, it's great."

"No," I said in alarm.

"Oh, come on," Cherise said, fingers roving over the cell phone. The number three button must be in ecstasy by now. "It's Angel on national television. How cool is that?"

I hated modern technology. A live show, which should have dissolved into the airwaves, or at least been relegated to an obscure drawer in a film archive, had been preserved for my pleasure by Aunt Candy's VCR.

"No, really," I said desperately. "Sean has better things to do than watch me and Penny McDermott."

"You were only on fifteen minutes," Aunt Candy said. "I have the tape with me. I'll go set up the VCR in the living room."

"No one has VCRs anymore, do they?" I bleated. "It's all DVDs and TiVo now."

"We still have ours," my dad said. "We have a lot of tapes, plus all our camcorder stuff."

Even the twenty-first century wasn't going to save me. Unless I could get to the tape before Aunt Candy did, rip it from its case, and pour eggnog all over it.

I leaped from my chair. Aunt Candy was already gliding into the living room. I tried to overtake her. Cousin Ann pushed past me, calling to her mother that the tape was in the red bag. She got in my way. I couldn't really wrestle her to the ground, much as I wanted to. I trotted out behind her just as Aunt Candy made it to the red bag and rummaged through it.

"Here it is." She pulled out a tape and held the black rectangle up triumphantly. "Turn that off, guys. We're watching your cousin Angel."

The large TV in the corner played the black and white version of *It's a Wonderful Life*.

I tried. "Oh, no, Aunt Candy, you can't turn off Clarence and Jimmy Stewart."

Aunt Candy did anyway, cutting off poor Jimmy mid-word. "We have our own angel," she said with a happy grin. "TBS is playing *It's a Wonderful Life* continuously for twenty-four hours, anyway. Besides, I have it on DVD."

Sure, now technology caught up to me.

Candy cleared out the young cousins, slid the tape into the player, and pushed rewind.

The rest of the clan trooped out and arranged themselves in front of the television. Cherise led Sean from the kitchen. Well, *led* wasn't the word. She had her hand firmly around his biceps, and she pushed him along, her bosom digging into his side.

Sean did not look extremely thrilled with her, which pleased me. Why some guys liked women with their breasts so obviously hanging out, I didn't know. Why didn't they go for nice girls in turtlenecks? There was my next column, "How to Have a Love Life without Big Breasts."

Uncle Tad had fallen asleep in a chair. He snored on, oblivious to the family clamoring around the television. I moved to the back of the crowd, ready to make a quick get-away.

I thought about positioning myself to tackle Sean and send him flying into the kitchen so he wouldn't see the tape. I knew it wouldn't work. Aunt Candy would simply hit pause and wait until Sean recovered.

Besides, Cherise had a firm hold of Sean. They stood against the wall, her head almost resting on his shoulder. I folded my arms and tried to fight off a chill.

The perky music of Penny's show filled the room. The speakers boomed the cheering of her fans and the sharp sound of applause.

"Welcome back!" Penny shouted. "Next up we have good news for single girls. You don't have to spend Christmas by yourself pathetic and all alone." She stopped and her audience cooed, "Awwwww."

"Angie Solomon has written a great book called *Christmas for Singles*. It's chock-full of advice on how to be alone and love it. But let's face it, folks"—here she leaned confidentially toward the camera—"that's no fun. Let's get her to write a book called *How a Single Girl Can Get Some at Christmas*." Her audience screamed and laughed and clapped. "Here she is, Angela Suttingham!"

The assistant backstage gave me a push. I tripped over a cable and nearly lost my shoe.

I'd hoped that had happened out of shot, but no. There I was, my ankle twisting in my high heel, my swingy short skirt flying upward. I righted myself and limped a little toward the chair to which Penny waved me.

She clapped long and hard, her hands held high and out from her body, as if demonstrating to her fans how it was done. As soon as she stopped, her audience abruptly did too, like well-trained monkeys.

Penny started her interview, every horrible moment of it. She bared her teeth and made snide comments, while I strove to be professional and clear.

But I barely heard Penny, or me, this time, because I was too busy staring at my hair. It was purple.

My hair is normally dark brown, and I wear it in a simple cut that hangs a little past my jaw. The hairdresser backstage had rubbed huge handfuls of mousse through it, making it plump out from my cheeks and stand up on my head. It looked a little like a button mushroom. Then she'd sprayed it with three or four coats of shiny hair spray. Onstage, Penny sat me down right underneath where a red gel light met a blue. The result glimmered off my sleek helmet hair in glossy, shining purple.

"Oh, my God," I groaned.

"Shhh."

While my hair threw out purple laser lights, I reminded Penny again and again that my name was Angel Sullivan.

She kept calling me Angie and Angela, until I was ready to believe that maybe my name really was Angie. Or Angela.

The torture continued. Penny held up the book, but she held it the wrong way, or upside down, so that either my cute pixie face showed on the back, or the red-and-green fancy lettering was indecipherable.

"So tell me, Angie," Penny said. "Why are you single? Do you embrace that lifestyle, or have you had a hard time meeting someone and making a real relationship work?"

I couldn't take any more. Quickly and quietly, I slipped out of the room, through the kitchen, and out the door to the back porch.

The cold darkness felt good after the overheated, noisy living room. Our back porch was deep, a veranda where we sat on wicker in the summer and drank lemonade and tea and chilled wine.

The rain fell harder. I folded my arms and hunkered into the wall while I waited to compose myself.

The back door opened, throwing out a bright rectangle of light. Someone fumbled at the latch of the screen door, and then Sean stepped out.

He carried his leather coat. "Hey," he said. "You all right?"

I swallowed hard. Why couldn't he have turned paunchy and ugly? I could have taken seeing him again if he'd gone to seed. "What," I said, like I didn't care how cute he was, "you didn't want to stay for more laughs?"

"No." He closed the door. "I never liked that show."

"The rest of America does."

Sean shrugged, muscles rippling in the way that had always made me wilt. "She makes her name ripping people to shreds. I can't respect that."

"Respect. Wow."

He shot me a look out of his beautiful dark eyes. "It's cold out here."

"I noticed."

He lifted his coat, leather rustling, and laid it around my shoulders.

The coat held heat and smelled warm and musky. I started melting. "You'll be cold now," I said.

"Not really."

"I'm sorry."

"Why?" He smiled, the corner of his mouth folding into a dimple that I used to kiss. "Because I'm not cold?"

"No. Because you got stuck here. I bet it was no accident. I'm thinking Cherise got you stranded at the end of this road on purpose."

"Maybe. She seemed pretty determined when I met her last month."

"She's not a typical Sullivan, you know. The rest of us aren't dominatrixes."

"I noticed." He glanced into the lighted kitchen window. "I also notice there's a lot of you."

"Oh, yeah, it's a Sullivan family gathering. They're always like this."

"I like it."

I stared at him. "Your brains must be frozen."

"You remember, I come from a small family. Just me and my mom and dad. Big families to me are fun."

"That's because you're not in them," I said darkly.

"They seem to really care about you."

"If they cared, they wouldn't have played that tape."

"They're excited because you were on TV. Most people get excited about that."

I grimaced. "I have to admit that I was, too, before I got to the studio. Then it was hell. I mean, look what they did to my hair."

"You have nice hair." He reached out and touched a strand.

His finger didn't even connect with skin. And yet an electric spark shot through me. I got hot all over. I had no business getting hot all over. I was finished with Sean. Right?

His hand dropped, but my temperature didn't. "It's great to see you again," he said softly.

"I'm surprised you remembered me."

"Are you kidding? That was the best two months of my life."

I wanted to say, *Mine too*, but my tongue was stuck to the roof of my mouth.

"Can I have a kiss?" he asked me.

"Huh?" I brushed my hair back from my ear.

"A kiss. For Christmas."

"All right." I didn't move. "Are you married?"

"No. Are you?"

"No."

He moved closer.

"Are you engaged?" I squeaked.

"No." He touched my face. "Are you?"

"No," I said. "Are you seeing someone?"

"No." He leaned down, his warmth covering me. "Are you?"

I ran out of words. He closed the inch of space between us and kissed me.

I expected an instant flashback to the times he'd kissed me in my apartment, or held me close at the movies, or awoken me with breakfast in bed (bagels and coffee—he couldn't cook).

Nope. Nothing. All I felt was his warmth cutting the chill of the December night and the soft brush of his lips on mine, his fingers points of heat on my face.

He stepped back, but I stayed where I was with my eyes closed and my lips pursed. Beyond the porch, the angels sang "Gloria in Excelsis Deo" over and over. It sounded like their CD was stuck.

"You all right?" he asked.

I popped my eyes open. "Sure. Fine." I gulped. "Fine."

He smiled again and stepped back. "Good. I'm fine, too."

Quiet fell between us except for the stupid angels and their stupid Gloria.

What had just happened? I'd kissed him, and I'd liked it. Me, who had walked away from him and from love. I wanted to kiss him again.

I studied his lips. ~~Smooth and dry, thin but not too thin. A~~ mouth that knew how to kiss. I wet my own lips.

"So," Sean broke in, "you're a writer now."

"Huh?" I dragged my gaze from his kissable mouth. "Right. A writer. Although after that show, I might be a street sweeper."

"Hey, street sweepers make a good living."

"Thanks a lot."

He held up his hands. "I was kidding. You know I'm a kidder. You used to, anyway. You probably don't remember that much about me. It's been five years."

"I remember everything about you," I blurted.

I wanted to slap my hand over my mouth. I was not exactly playing hard to get.

His eyes glowed with interest. "Do you?"

"Well, sure. Um, are you still in the wine business?"

Well, duh, of course he was. He'd sat at our kitchen table fifteen minutes ago saying he was a vintner.

"Yes," he said. "Still working with my dad. Running the place myself so he could go to England. Nothing's really changed for me. You?"

"Well, you know, New York City, work at a women's magazine, best-selling book, dated a creep who dumped me for my best friend, humiliated on a talk show. The usual."

He laughed. "I'm proud of you. I've seen your column in *Women of Today*. You went after your dreams." He paused. "Well, except for the creep and the talk show."

"What about you? Did you have dreams?"

He shrugged. "I like my work. I like the land and living in the country. So I guess I'd say I was happy."

"No wife, huh?"

"Not yet." His eyes sparked with warmth.

Now, why did I suddenly hope he was glad he hadn't found the right one yet? I really needed to get my head out of my butt.

Or I could ask him to kiss me again.

The idea hit me out of the blue. I tried to get a hold of myself. Then I thought, *Why shouldn't I kiss him?* We were alone, it was dark, and it wasn't like we were complete strangers. Almost strangers, but not complete ones.

Wasn't that supposed to be half the fun of being a single girl? You could kiss cute guys when the mood struck you. Surely there wasn't any harm in a little Christmas cuddling.

"Glooooooo-oooooooo-ooooooooria," sang the angels.

Words stuck in my throat. He stood close to me, bathing me in his handsome good looks and his masculine warmth.

"Would you . . . uh . . ." I started.

He leaned closer. "Hmm?"

Closer, closer. Any minute now, any second now, and our lips would meet again.

"*There* you are!"

Cherise's voice rang out into the night, drowning out the chorusing angels. "We've been looking all over for you."

She clicked across the porch and sank her fingers into Sean's arm. She blithely ignored the fact that Sean and I stood close together and I was wearing Sean's jacket.

"We're done with that stupid show, Angel. Your mom told me to find you and finalize the sleeping arrangements." She glanced coyly at Sean. "I'll show you where your bed is."

Sean sent me an ironic look. "Sounds great," he said.

Cherise more or less dragged him back into the house. I followed slowly. Once we reached the kitchen, I slid his warm coat from my shoulders and draped it over a chair. It hung there, its arms empty and dangling, and I abandoned it.

Put on some soft Christmas tunes, lie back on a pillow-strewn bed, drink hot tea laced with lemon and brandy, and soak up the warmth and cheer. . . .

Mom had given me a tiny attic room in the tower. They'd recently converted it into a guest room, and it had an old-fashioned high four-poster bed covered with quilts my grandmother had made. The space was large enough to hold only a bed, a small dresser, and a ladder-back chair from a dinette set of long ago. The window took up one entire wall, and the door could just open all the way. The door had a hundred-year-old lock, but someone had lost the key seventy-five years ago, and Mom and Dad had never bothered replacing it. No matter; I didn't expect company.

When I was a kid, I'd always thought this little tower room was haunted. Stories I heard told of a Victorian girl who'd died of grief in this room after her fiancé was killed in an accident the night before their wedding. I half believed it as a child, and the occasional rustling I heard up here scared me. As I grew older, I realized that the rustlings were

144

probably mice, because no one would dare haunt the house without my mother's permission.

Now I got to test the theory. Ghosts or mice? Or maybe Mom and Dad had gotten rid of all the mice and the spooks.

I was exhausted. I'd traveled a long way, I'd had the shock of seeing Sean again, it was the middle of the night, and I was still functioning on East Coast time. You'd think I would have thrown myself onto the bed and started snoring. But no. I thunked my suitcase to the floor, sat on the bed, and stared glumly at the freshly painted wall.

My parents had chosen a kind of pinky-peach for the walls and a small blue-and-pink rug for the board floor. The rug was cute and picked up the peach and blue in the quilt.

The cozy room was a complete contrast to my New York apartment. There, even seventeen floors up, I could hear the rush and roar of traffic, the wail of sirens, the honking of horns when someone waited a split second too long after a light turned green. Here, I could hear the fine rain on the roof and a tree branch scraping the windows. Instead of angry drivers and alarming sirens, I heard my nieces and nephews and cousins running up and down the stairs laughing.

Back in New York, I had my career, my friends, my publicist, my ex. People thought of me as a success, or at least heading that way. Here, I was just Angel, my mom and dad's youngest daughter.

In New York, I had a failed relationship to rise above. Sitting here, it was like my years with Mark did not even exist. I had catapulted back in time to the girl who'd fallen madly in love one summer with Sean Chase and thought it tragically romantic that we had to part and go our separate ways.

Not that I regretted running off to the biggest city in the U.S. and pursuing my dreams. I made good decisions regarding my career—at least before I'd agreed to be interviewed by Penny McDermott. But my love life?

In decisions regarding my love life, I absolutely sucked.

I sighed and heaved myself off the bed. Tomorrow was

Christmas morning, and I needed to unpack the presents I'd brought with me.

I plopped the soft bag on the bed and started pulling out packages. I'd bought small things, but many of them, and they'd taken up nearly my entire suitcase. I barely had enough room left for my underwear and clothes. That's what I got for insisting on only carry-on luggage. But airlines had the habit of losing my suitcases, and I didn't want to risk showing up here with no presents and no toothbrush.

I arranged the gifts on the little dresser. The bows had gotten squished on the plane, so I took a few minutes to plump them up.

As I tried to straighten paper that had weathered a couple thousand miles of travel, my mind wandered to Sean and kissing him on the porch.

I closed my eyes and drew a long, even breath. Could he kiss, or could he kiss? I remembered everything about his kisses, every lip press, every caress, every touch.

After I'd left for New York, I'd pushed those memories to the back of my mind, but seeing him again brought them all rushing at me. Every single skin-tickling, blood-heating, lip-bruising, drool-making kiss came back to me as I opened my eyes and stared at the presents on the dresser.

I wondered why Sean had suddenly sprung back into my life. Was it Christmas magic? Or something more mundane? While I strongly suspected Cherise had lured him here deliberately, I knew he wasn't Cherise's type. He was *my* type.

Was he still? He'd seemed happy to see me, and even wanted to kiss me, but I didn't sense anything from him but maybe old friends catching up on good times.

Was that all I wanted?

I picked up the present for Cherise, a copy of my book. The wrapping paper had torn, so I yanked it the rest of the way off. I smiled at myself from the back cover, my hair not purple, thank you very much.

I touched the lettering on the front, remembering how excited I'd been when I'd seen the first copy. I'd had many articles printed, but this was different. This wasn't me simply working for a magazine. This was a child of my own.

I opened the book. The introduction espoused my ideas that women were not worthless simply because they were not attached to a man. Women in the past had needed men—more specifically, husbands—in order to survive. The Victorian ghost of this room had probably died of grief because she wouldn't have someone to put food on the table and leave her a hefty life-insurance policy.

The world was different now. *Contemporary women are darned lucky,* I had written. *We can stay single if we wish, or we can look for a soul mate. The choice is ours.*

I sounded so positive in the book. But me, Angel, sitting in my parents made-over attic bedroom, having kicked out a ghost for the privilege . . . I felt suddenly alone and vulnerable.

I wasn't certain that my feelings for Sean were entirely gone.

I closed the book and put it in my drawer. I rummaged through my stash of small, just-in-case gifts until I found a jar of bath salts I could give Cherise instead of the book. She was a "men are only good for sex" kind of woman, and she wouldn't appreciate my saying that a good man could be a nice addition to her life.

I worried a little about Cherise's intentions toward Sean. He didn't deserve to be chewed up and spit out, which was Cherise's usual modus operandi.

Sean's being here caused another problem besides the destruction of my life. We couldn't very well give out gifts to one another tomorrow and leave him sitting there watching. And somehow I didn't think he'd like scented candles or bubble bath.

I put away my gifts, put on my knitted bootie slippers, and headed off to my old bedroom to fetch something I'd left there five years ago.

My former room lay on the second floor, near the big bathroom. I had always liked that bedroom, because not only did it have a nice view over the vineyards to the north, but on winter mornings I could rush into the bathroom and turn on the hot light before I had a chance to get cold. I would always beat my sisters, Emma and Janet, and they'd pound on the door and shout while I took my time with the hot water.

When I reached the door to the bedroom, I heard the voices of my nephews from inside. Mom told me she'd bunked the smaller boys in there together.

Devlin's voice rose. "And then the evil elf crawled out of the sled and slithered down the chimney. He hadn't eaten in three days, and he was hungry. He found the kids who were all sleeping together, and he grabbed the leg of the first one he saw." Here a child squealed, and I assumed his leg had been duly grabbed. "He said, 'I'm hungry,' and he sucked its brains out!"

"Nuh-uh," said a smaller voice. "Elves don't do that. They make toys for Santa."

"But this one's an evil elf. He sucked everyone's brains out; then he went downstairs and sucked Santa Claus's brains out, too. Left him all dry and corpsified on the living room floor. The mom and dad tripped over him the next morning. And the evil elf sucked their brains out, too."

I interrupted this gruesome catalog by opening the door.

All of the boys screamed out loud. I stood on the threshold, silhouetted by the light behind me, and let them think I was an evil elf.

"Oh, man," someone finally said. "It's Aunt Angel."

I snapped on the light. "If you don't go to sleep, Christmas will never come."

This was greeted with derisive stares and a "Yeah, right."

I stepped over small bodies to get to the dresser. "I came down to get something. This used to be my room."

"We got put in a girl's room?" five-year-old Theophile asked plaintively.

"There's nothing wrong with girls," I said calmly, opening the drawer.

"I'll say," said Tyler, who'd just turned eleven.

The boys had at least left my things alone. The drawers were mainly empty; most of my personal things were now in my apartment in New York.

But not this. I drew out a locked wooden box. I hadn't opened it in five years. I had no idea where the key was, but I wasn't worried.

"Go to sleep, guys," I said as I stepped over them on my way out. "Don't let any elves eat you."

Theophile whimpered. The others said, "Good night, Aunt Angel."

I went back upstairs. I wondered where Mom had put Sean, but I wasn't about to wander the house looking. If he was with Cherise . . .

I didn't really think he was with Cherise. My mom wouldn't stand for Cherise's antics at a family gathering. Cherise was out of luck.

Sitting cross-legged on the bed, I pried the box open. The lock broke easily, being a simple aluminum catch. I pulled out what I wanted. It was small. I put it into a little box, wrapped it in spare wrapping paper I'd brought with me, and tied a bow around it.

The gift brought memories of Sean and our glorious summer flooding back to me. I took off my clothes, put on my nightshirt, and crawled under the covers. The memories kept me awake until the window turned light gray; then I fell asleep to the sound of excited children rushing downstairs to the tree.

I guessed none of them had gotten eaten by evil elves.

On Christmas morning, indulge in a Belgian waffle and a cup of steaming latte....

By the time I showered and dressed and got downstairs, the pancakes were history. I rubbed my sandy eyes and rummaged in the refrigerator to find only a half-eaten container of yogurt.

"Good morning, sleepyhead," my mother said. "Did you rest all right?"

"Yeah, it wasn't bad. Shower was cold, though." I looked around surreptitiously for Sean. The kitchen was filled with uncles and aunts and sisters and cousins sitting or standing, drinking coffee, or helping Aunt Candy clean up the dishes. Sean was nowhere in sight. He wasn't in the living room either.

"Cherise and Sean went out for a walk," Aunt Candy said. "We'll do presents when they get back."

"You mean the kids waited for me?" I asked, surprised. "No way."

"No, they didn't. We let them go ahead. The adults will open their gifts when we're all inside again."

I finished the last of the yogurt and threw the container away. I went back upstairs for the presents and dragged them all down. To recover, I poured myself the last dregs of a bottle of orange juice. As I lifted the glass to my lips, Cherise came waltzing in with Sean.

He'd found his leather coat again, I guess, because he was wearing it. Cherise wore leather, too. Her tight leather jacket emphasized her white leather push-up bustier and her tight leather pants. Not to mention her ankle-high leather boots. I could imagine all the cows in the county holding up protest signs when she walked by.

Sean, oblivious to all the leather goods, smiled at me. Suddenly the sun came out. A beam shone directly on my forehead.

"Morning, Angel," he said.

I stood there like a stunned bird. His dark eyes held me. I think I said, "Erk."

"Angel, you're dripping orange juice down the front of your blouse," Aunt Candy said.

My gaze, locked with Sean's, never wavered.

"Angel!" My mother waved her hand in front of my face. "Orange juice. A white blouse. They don't mix."

I looked down. "Crap." A rivulet of orange creased my nice white silk blouse that I'd put on especially for Sean.

"Go change," my mother said kindly. "We'll wait for you."

"We're having cranberries at dinner," Cherise said with a smirk, "so maybe you should wear red."

I rolled my eyes, clapped my hand over the sticky stain, and bolted from the room.

Upstairs I put on a green Christmas sweater with a big reindeer on it and went back down. I caught sight of myself in a mirror in the hall. The bulky sweater obscured my form, making me look like a Christmas stocking. I thought of Cherise's curvaceous form covered by tight leather. But

Aunt Merline had knitted this for me last year, and I thought I'd make her happy by wearing it.

Sean was sipping coffee in the kitchen when I arrived again. Cherise sat next to him, her legs crossed to show them off. She rested her hand close to his on the table.

"Hi," he said.

"Nice sweater," Cherise chirped.

Sean caught my eye. He grinned. His smile would have warmed me if Cherise hadn't run her hand up his leather-clad arm.

Hey, there was nothing between me and Sean. Cherise could chase him all she wanted. I couldn't care less if he slanted an amused glance at her, if she smiled at him with her full red mouth. All that had nothing to do with me.

"So," I said brightly. "Let's open presents."

My dad got to his feet. I envied the man. He'd drunk a ton of rum-laced eggnog last night, and this morning his eyes were clear and he moved with a bounce in his step. Some people never suffered like the rest of us mortals.

We trooped into the living room. The fire in the hearth roared. Mom had lit up the Christmas tree. Blue and red and green lights blinked from its seven foot summit, and the angel on the top, with the cloud-white hair, smiled down as she had for more than twenty-seven years. As a kid, I'd thought the angel had been named after me.

Torn blue and gold and red paper and bows of all sizes and shapes carpeted the living room, evidence of the kids' Christmas orgy earlier that morning. The adult presents lay in a neat heap on the other side of the tree. I'd placed the gifts I'd brought among them.

I shoved aside used paper and sank to the sofa. Sean, unbelievably, sat next to me. Cherise sat on his other side, very close to him.

While my mother and father passed out gifts, our tradition, I tried not to enjoy the warmth of Sean's shoulder near mine or the scent of soap and shaving cream that clung to him. He'd removed his coat and sat in a black sweatshirt and jeans that stretched over well-muscled thighs. His strong hands dangled between his legs as he rested his elbows on his knees. I tried not to trace the sinews of his hands and wrists with my gaze.

Suddenly several brightly colored packages landed in my lap. I jumped about a foot.

"Angel, these are for you." My mother beamed down at me. She set another bundle of packages and gift bags at Sean's feet. "These aren't much," she told him. "But we didn't want you to be left out."

"Oh, hey, you didn't have to do that." Sean looked touched and grateful.

"Yes, we did. It was fun." She gave him a smile that crinkled the corners of her eyes, and moved on to Cherise.

While Cherise eagerly tore into her gifts, I slipped the small package I'd wrapped for Sean into his hand. He glanced at me sideways, his brow creased. I pretended to ignore him and started opening my presents.

I got another Christmas sweater from Aunt Merline, this one bright red with dancing elves on it. I got the usual gifts, like candles and chocolate and bath stuff from the cousins and the kids, although Devlin had drawn a picture of a very tall me standing among the buildings of New York City. I got a nice pair of earrings from my mom, some warm slippers and a robe from my dad, an art book from one of my uncles. I identified Cherise's present by its black wrapping and black bows. The package was long and narrow. I set it aside, already knowing what it was and not wanting to open it in front of everyone.

I glanced over to see Sean open the present I'd given him. I froze, my fingers caught in the act of untying a ribbon on another gift.

Sean set the wrapping paper aside and opened the box. He stopped.

On the cotton inside lay a bottle cap. It came from a beer we'd shared at a sports bar after a Dodgers game during our summer of love. We'd run short of cash and could afford only one bottle of beer, so we'd shared it. Sean had handed me the bottle cap and said, "Here's something to remember me by." Then he'd kissed me, draped his arm around me, and sipped the beer.

I'd kept the bottle cap to this day.

Sean's eyes met mine. I saw a spark buried deep. I was afraid it would ignite and melt me, but then again, I wanted it to.

Five years had only made him better-looking. Dark whiskers dusted his square jaw, and his eyelashes were black and thick. I couldn't even find fault with his nose, which was narrow and not too long. His dark hair curled around his ears, the lobes of which I wanted to nibble.

He looked down at the bottle cap, then at me again. "Angel."

"It's stupid," I babbled. "I kept it for some reason. I thought you'd think it was funny."

He obviously didn't. His mouth remained a straight line. He touched the bottle cap with blunt fingers.

I remembered his touch on my face and his kiss tasting of tangy malt. I wondered if he remembered, too, or if he'd put all that behind him. I thought of our kiss on the porch last night. His mouth had been warm, deliciously so. I wanted to drag him from the couch and out onto the porch and show him how much I liked to taste him.

"Interesting gift, Angel," Cherise said, leaning over to look at the box. "I don't think he can return it to the store, either. Here, open mine."

She thrust a black-wrapped package at him, displacing the bottle cap and box. The box fell to the floor and the cap skittered out of sight under some wrappings.

I nearly dove after it, then pretended I was too dignified. I did slide my foot over to the paper to mark the place I should start looking.

Sean, a polite expression on his face, opened Cherise's package. A black satin bag rested on the wrapping. Mystified, he unzipped it and pulled out what was inside.

He held up a very small, bright red spandex men's thong. His face went as red as the underwear. "Uh, gee, Cherise, I don't know what to say."

Cherise giggled. "Like it? Try it on and see if it fits."

Sean went red all the way down his neck. "Um. Maybe later."

"Promise?" Cherise licked her lips.

I sprang from the sofa. My foot landed squarely on the bottle cap under the paper. "Thank you all so much for your gifts," I babbled. "I'm going to the kitchen for more coffee. Anybody want some?"

Before anyone could answer, I strode away from the sofa, past my dad, who was staring in bafflement at the furry handcuffs Cherise had given him, and marched back into the kitchen.

Take a walk and enjoy the winter wonderland of sparkling lights and crisp, cold air. . . .

Winter wonderland in northern California doesn't always mean snow. Closer to the Sierras, in the gold rush towns like Placerville and Grass Valley, snow falls in December. Closer to the coast, we can get it, but what we mostly get in winter is rain.

However, today had dawned sunny and clear, and as soon as the kids dressed, they tumbled out of the house to play with their new toys and to judge who had made out the best in number and worth of presents. All wore various shapes and sizes of Aunt Merline's Christmas sweaters.

I would have stayed in the house helping my mom and aunts make dinner, but my sisters, Janet and Emma, had dragged their husbands out for a walk, and the husbands had invited Sean along. He'd seemed happy to escape the horde of boys who wanted to show him remote-control cars and planes, scooters, bikes, light sabers, footballs, and soccer balls, or drag him off to play the latest computer game. A quiet, non-tech walk must have seemed the safer bet.

Like I said, I would have stayed at the house and let Sean enjoy himself talking to my voluble sisters and their husbands, but Cherise decided to glom onto the group. When I watched her snatch up her little leather jacket and walk out, clinging to Sean's arm, my hand reached for my coat, and my feet made to follow them.

Cherise glanced over her shoulder as we hiked away from the house, smiling like she knew what I was doing. The fact that Sean didn't try very hard to lose her shouldn't have made me mad, but it did. He could at least pretend to be flattered that I had kept the bottle cap all this time.

Maybe Cherise was right; it wasn't a very smart gift.

We walked to the north of the house, down a dirt road that led to the hills around the vineyards. My family wasn't in the grape business; my father had bought the house from a vintner who had thrown in the towel after a few bad harvests. The vintner had sold the vineyards to neighboring wineries, and my father had purchased the house and a little of the land around it. We were far enough from the cities of the Bay Area not to have problems with traffic and pollution, but close enough that we could run in to San Francisco when the mood took us.

The vines that climbed the hills around us lay mostly bare. The latest grapes that produced the sweetest wine had already been picked. The vines waited for spring and warm rains to begin their cycle again.

I didn't really know why my sisters were eager to show Sean grapevines, since he was in the wine business. But he hiked along without complaint. The view was spectacular, in any case.

We stood on top of a hill, looking back down at the white frame house and all my father's angels, snowmen, Santas, and reindeer. On the other side of the hill, the country turned wild where the vineyards had been let go. The vines crawled down to a wood that followed a wide, shallow stream.

My sisters and their husbands turned to climb down the far side. They laughed and teased one another, and Janet stopped to twine her arms around her husband Brad's neck and kiss him. Yes, they were Brad and Janet.

I realized they were enjoying their freedom. With my father and mother and uncles and aunts to watch over their kids, Janet and Emma and Brad and John took the time to find romance again.

Cherise wanted to find romance and more, if I were any judge. Sean laughed at her jokes and let her hang on him, as he had done with me when we'd been together five years ago.

When they were halfway down the hill, me trailing behind, Sean stopped. "Hang on, I have rocks in my shoes."

Unbelievably, Cherise let go of his arm. "Well, hurry up. I'll wait for you at the bottom."

She ran on, her tight bustier looking ridiculous on her, not to mention her high-heeled boots. How she had walked this far in them, I had no idea.

Sean leaned against a boulder, took off his sneaker, and emptied it.

He straightened up as I approached. The wind caught his dark brown hair, letting sunlight dapple it. I got lost looking at him. His strong, wide shoulders filled out his coat. His waist was flat, his jean-clad hips narrow. The cold stained the tip of his nose red, but that could not detract from his chiseled good looks.

"What I can't figure out," he said as I gawked at him, "is whether you're happy to see me or you wish I'd fall off the face of the earth."

I stopped. He was talking like he remembered everything and wanted to remember everything. I gave a little shrug in answer to his question, because I didn't really know, either.

"I mean, you gave me this." He dipped his hand into his coat pocket and held out the bottle cap, only a little dented from where I'd stepped on it. "I can't tell if it was special to you or if you think it's funny."

"What is it to you?" I asked. I sounded calm for a woman with nervous energy zinging through her body.

"A reminder of the best summer of my life." He held the cap between his fingers. "You kept this. You make me hope that it was the best summer of your life, too."

"I threw it in a box. I haven't looked in that box in five years."

His mouth thinned. "All right. If it's not that important . . ." He drew back his arm like he would hurl it into the dying vines.

I leaped for him. "No."

He lowered his arm. "Then it is important to you."

"All right, it is. Maybe. If you don't want it, I'll take it back."

"I never said I didn't want it." He tossed the bottle cap in the air, caught it, and dropped it into his pocket. He stepped close enough to me that the heat of his body cut the wind. "You know, Angel, I always regretted letting you go."

"Did you?" I wheezed a short laugh. "You never called or e-mailed or anything. How was I supposed to know?"

"I thought you didn't regret letting *me* go."

"I regretted it," I said. "Why wouldn't I regret it?"

He put his hands on my shoulders. I felt them through the coat, warm and heavy. "I started this all wrong. I'm trying to say that when you left for New York, I didn't want you to go."

"You never said." My legs wobbled. Any minute now I'd topple over like a dead grapevine.

"You had big dreams. I didn't want to demand you give up your dreams for me." He circled his thumbs on my collarbone. "I had this fantasy that you'd achieve your dreams, then call me to come out and celebrate with you."

"You never said," I repeated.

"I know. I should have." His hands slid over my shoulders to my back, strong and sure. "I thought about finding you lots of times. I wanted to call your magazine and talk to you; I wanted to track you down and see you again."

"Why didn't you?"

He looked thoughtful. "I almost did, several times. But I was still a little pissed that you wanted to end it. Then I figured, why chase you if you didn't want to be chased?" His fingers pressed my back. "Those were your exact words when you left. You didn't want to be chased. You made a pun, because my last name is Chase."

Had I said that? Was I insane? "So what do you want to do now?" I babbled. "Be friends? Remember, we said we'd always be friends?"

"Believe me, I remember every single thing you said to me when you gave me the heave-ho."

He was too close to me. He filled my vision, his eyes dark and liquid and stern.

"What do you mean, I gave you the heave-ho?" I spluttered. "It was a mutual breakup. We agreed."

"*You* agreed. I went along with it because I knew you wouldn't change your mind. Not for me."

"You make it sound like I used you and dumped you."

"Didn't you?"

I stepped away, or tried to. His hands remained on my back, holding me too close. "Of course not. It was a summer romance. You know, a romance we'd always look back on with a happy memory. The last fling of our youth, stuff like that."

He looked at me like I was crazy. "What are you talking about?"

"That's what it was to you, right?"

"No. I was in love with you. I'd never met anyone like you."

My throat went dry. "In love with me?"

"That's what I said. But you had stars in your eyes about New York, and I didn't have the heart to keep you here. And when you said we should break it off clean, I figured you didn't return what I felt."

My mouth hung open during his entire speech. I popped it shut. "You're making this up."

"No. Why should I?"

"I don't know. Maybe you and Cherise decided to make fun of me."

"You have a wild imagination."

I smiled suddenly and sent him a coy look. "No, you did."

He actually blushed. "Hey, I was young and limber."

I blushed too. I was thinking of a particular night in the bathtub. I remembered Sean's bare, wet body against mine, how his hands had roved over me, how he'd slid his tongue down the inside of my arm. . . .

I think my eyes glazed. I snapped to the present. "So what about now? I take it you're not in love anymore?"

He released me. "I fell out of love when I read you were engaged, only six short months after we split up."

A spark of anger lingered in his eyes, but it was old and faded. I gathered that he no longer cared.

"When I met Mark, I thought he was the one," I tried to explain. "He was already successful, and I was starting to be. I thought we'd live in a lavish apartment and go to fabulous parties and give fabulous parties and know everyone. It was stupid."

His expression softened. "It wasn't stupid. It's what you wanted."

"No. Trust me, having my best friend walk off with my fiancé was not what I wanted."

It still hurt. Even standing next to gorgeous Sean and having him confess he'd been in love with me five years ago didn't take the sting out of it. Mark had humiliated me.

"He shouldn't have done that," Sean said. The angry spark was sharper this time.

"No duh. I guess you think I deserve it, right? I get my heart broken after I break yours."

He smiled, like the sun breaking through clouds. "I didn't say you broke my heart. I said I regretted letting you go."

"Oh," I said.

"Don't sound so disappointed."

"I'm not. Or . . . I don't know. I thought you said you were madly in love with me."

"I was madly in love with you," he said. "But I also had a life."

"Oh."

"There you go again."

I grimaced. "I don't want to break your heart. I just want to think that maybe I could."

He laughed. "You're so cute."

"I'm not cute. I'm an award-winning journalist with a best-selling self-help book."

"That's so cute."

"Shut up."

Abruptly, he wrapped his arms around me and lifted me off my feet. "You know what we should do?"

"What?" *Throw off all our clothes and make wild love on the grass?*

No, it was too cold. We could sneak back to the house and shut ourselves in my closet of a room. It was warm up there, and the bed had lots of quilts. The ghost would just have to give us space.

"We should talk," he said.

"Talk?" This time I really did sound disappointed. Sean was gorgeous. Sean was built. Sean was sexy. I wanted his naked body under a quilt, and I wasn't ashamed of wanting that. Alarmed, yes. Ashamed, no.

"Yes, talk," he repeated. "We should remember everything about that summer. Then we should catch up on everything that happened after that. Kind of get it out of our systems."

If getting it out of our systems meant reenacting some of the more interesting nights we'd spent together, I was all for it.

"Once we do that," Sean went on, "we can decide if we made the right decision five years ago. Or if we still want to just be friends and go our separate ways."

I bit my lip. I had started regretting letting Sean go in a big way. He'd been in love with me? I'd really thought he was having a fling, an exciting summer. He hadn't fought very hard to change my mind.

But what did I know about guys? Apparently, nothing. They didn't throw their arms around you and scream, "Don't go! Don't go!" Or if they did, you sent them to therapy. No, they got stoic and calm and said, "Well, all right, if that's what you want." Either that or, "Angel, Susan and I are in love. We thought you'd be happy for us."

How could any of us figure men out?

Sean sounded so logical. Sure, we could sit down and talk it all out and discuss everything rationally. Or, at least, he could while I remembered the taste of his mouth and how good it felt to snuggle up next to him in bed.

Why were these memories haunting me now? I had put Sean firmly behind me as soon as I'd boarded the plane to New York.

I realized now that I'd made myself simply not think about him. Then when Mark came along, I focused on him so that I'd never think about Sean. I had decided that Sean was a fun fling, and I forced him and what we had into that mold.

What if I'd been totally wrong? What if Mark was the learning experience and Sean was the right one?

How was any woman supposed to know when the right one came along? The guy you thought was Mr. Right could really be Mr. Pain in the Ass, and the guy you thought was a geek and a nuisance could turn out to be the one. It's a crazy world, romance.

"All right?" Sean asked.

"Huh? Sorry. What did you say?"

His eyes flickered. "I give up."

"I'm sorry, I was—"

He snaked his hand behind my head, pulled me against him, and kissed me.

My confusion died in a wash of feeling. His lips were warm and moved across mine with confidence. His tongue swiped past my parted lips, giving me a brief, heady taste of him.

I made a noise in my throat, grabbed his shoulders, and pulled him closer. He tasted warm and spicy, like hot

Christmas cider. This was no mistletoe kiss, no "hi, how've you been" kiss on the back porch. This kiss was serious business.

I must have been strangling him. He responded by running his hands gently down my back to cradle me against him. He smelled like cool leather and aftershave.

I could go on kissing him all day. Who needed turkey dinner and pumpkin pie with whipped cream when you had a man like this to keep your mouth occupied? Take back the presents and the lights and the lattes and the warm baths and candles. Give me this man on top of a cold windy hill.

Sean slanted his mouth first one way, then the other, then finally he slowed the kiss and eased himself from me.

"That's more like it," he said.

"Yep," I gasped.

He brushed his thumb across my lips. "So what do you think of my idea?"

"What idea?"

"That we get it out of our systems."

"Oh. That idea." I still had my arms around his neck. I fingered a strand of his hair. "Can we do more like this? I mean really get it out of our systems. I can think of other ways, too."

He gently pulled my hands away. "This is getting dangerous."

"I'd say it was already dangerous." I was hot all over. Little tingles ran from my neck all the way to my fingers and toes. *Yum, yum, yum.*

"We both know that after the holiday, I'll be going back home to my business, and you'll fly back to New York. Anything we start now will be as dead as it was that summer."

"Will it?"

"A clean break is better, don't you think?" he asked.

Sure, I'd thought so until he started kissing me. Now I

164

wanted everything to be complicated and long-lasting. I wanted to explore him, to get to know him, to find out what I'd been missing all these years.

"Clean break. Right." I drew a breath. "Well, actually, no."

"No, what?"

"There is no such thing as a clean break. We can't have a conversation and everything wrong is put right. Especially when you start with the kissing."

"I'm trying to make it easier."

I grew angry. "Easier for who? For you? Do you want a clean break so you can run after my cousin? She looks more than willing."

"You mean Cherise?" He lifted his hands in a surrendering gesture. "No. I mean, she's your family and all, but no. The whole kinky, leather, femme-dom thing is not for me."

"She's a man-eater," I said.

"No duh."

I softened. "The thong she gave you was cute, though. Are you going to wear it?"

"It looks uncomfortable."

"Oh, come on, I bet you'd look gorgeous in it." The sudden vision of him wearing nothing but the red spandex thong swam into my head. I nearly fell over. He'd be all muscle and bare bod with not much covering his privates.

I was about to drool on myself.

"You didn't open your present from her," he pointed out.

"I know."

His eyes twinkled. "Why not? Don't you want to know what she got you?"

"I already know what she got me. She gets me the same thing every year."

"It can't be worse than her giving a man she barely knows a boulder sack."

"Yes, it can." I sighed.

"What is it? Don't keep me in suspense."

I bit my lip and flushed. "Penny McDermott would call it a Santa's helper."

He looked confused. "What does that mean?"

"It's what you give a woman when she's all alone and has no way of being . . . uh . . . fulfilled."

He thought a moment longer; then his brow cleared. "Oh." He fixed his gaze on me and his eyes became sharp. "Oh."

"She gives me one every year. She thinks I wear them out."

"Now, this is getting *very* dangerous."

"Why?" I demanded. "Because you want a clean break? If you want one so bad, why are you confusing me and teasing me and kissing me? Did you think, 'Hey, there's Angel. Why don't I torture her'?"

"Torture you? What—"

"You show up here all gorgeous and leather-coaty and start kissing me and making me think about you in your thong and smeared with pumpkin pie and whipped cream."

His eyes widened. "Whoa. Where'd that come from?"

"And then you start talking about clean breaks and putting it behind us, and here I am all ready to have my Christmas pie. And then you start *kissing* me again. What am I supposed to think?"

"I don't know, but I'm getting confused."

"See?" I jabbed a finger at him. "Torture Angel. Go on, go ahead. Penny McDermott tortured me on television, made me a laughingstock in front of the entire country. Now you're torturing me, making me hope that I can go back and fix what I did, and then telling me I can't. *You* are the evil elf."

He held his hand up. "I really, really wish I could follow this conversation."

"Never mind." I glared at him. "Go on. Go find Cherise, and maybe she'll let you play Santa's helper."

He looked angry now. "Angel."

If I stayed any longer, my mouth would keep talking, and I'd make a bigger fool of myself than I ever had. Or I'd grab him and start kissing him again.

I screamed between my teeth. I turned on my heel and marched away down the hill after the others, my boots sinking ankle-deep into Christmas mud.

Sometimes the holidays can be lonely for others. Be there to help a friend or family member in need . . .

"So where's Sean?" Cherise asked when I rejoined the group. She craned her head, looking past me with eager eyes.

"I don't know. He's admiring dead vines or something."

She gave me a narrow look. "What's wrong with you?"

"Nothing. Why should anything be wrong with me?"

"I don't know, but it sure seems like it."

I folded my arms. My sisters and their spouses had walked on into the woods. Only Cherise waited, smirking at me.

"You brought him here on purpose, didn't you?" I accused her. "Don't deny it."

She opened her eyes wide. "Me? Why should I bring him here?"

"Because he's absolutely gorgeous. And you can't keep your hands off him. You arranged for him to get 'lost' and have to come here for help. And, of course, Mom and Dad wouldn't let him leave to spend Christmas alone."

Her red lips curved. "So? If he's so adorable, what's the problem?"

"The problem—" I broke off and glanced around. Sean was still up the hill. Janet and Brad and Emma and John had already disappeared. I lowered my voice. "I used to have a thing with him."

"Really?"

Did I hear interest perk?

"Yes, really. Don't tell anyone."

"Why not?"

"Because . . . because we broke it off. I don't want anyone grilling us about it or trying to get us back together or anything."

She shrugged. "Well, all right. Does that mean you're done with him?"

"Yes." I hesitated. "When you met him in Oakland, did you mention I was your cousin?"

She looked blank. "No. I don't think it came up."

Why did I feel a dart of disappointment? Maybe Sean was right. A clean break. Better that than these lingering feelings of jealousy and anger and regretting what might have been.

"Fine," I said in a hard voice. "You can have him. Enjoy yourself."

"Gee, you're generous."

"It's Christmas. 'Tis the season to be giving. But I don't want to see it, I don't want to hear it, I don't want to know about it. All right?"

Cherise gave me another blank look. "All right."

I started to explain that over really meant over, when a rustle in the overgrown vines caught my attention. It could have been a rabbit, or a bird, but it started making an awful lot of noise.

"Is that a dog?" I asked hopefully, trying to peer into the leaves. If it was a stray, I could walk it home, putting a big distance between me and Sean and Cherise.

Suddenly, Cherise screamed, "Angel, look out!"

A man sprang up from the grapevines and flung both

arms around me. He was very dirty and very smelly, and I screamed very loud.

"Angel?" I heard Janet's voice. "Cherise? What's wrong?"

One of the husbands shouted, Brad or John, I couldn't tell. The man's skinny arms tightened about me.

Then I heard Sean come barreling down the hill. He grabbed the man by the neck and twisted him away from me. Just like that, one-handed.

Panting and shaking, I backed away toward Cherise and Janet and Brad, who'd come running.

The man hung in Sean's strong grip. "Help," he said pathetically.

Sean held him tight. "Someone want to call nine-one-one?"

The man gasped. He jerked himself away from Sean and leaped into the vines. Sean sprinted after him. So did Brad and John. I ran along behind, hearing the faint cries of my sisters and Cherise as they struggled to keep up.

The man led us on a long chase through the old vineyards. Dead branches snagged my clothes and scraped my skin. I sank into mud and almost lost my boot pulling myself out. Leaves plastered my hair and coat.

I broke out of the vines in time to see Sean tackle my attacker and send him to the ground. I caught up, panting. The man struggled, strong and spry for a little guy. Sean dragged him to his feet.

"Stop!" I screamed. I leaped forward between my startled brothers-in-law and ran at Sean.

Sean looked at me in amazement. The man grinned. "Hi, Angel."

"Don't hurt him." I put my hands on my knees, trying to catch my breath. "That's Great-uncle Mike."

"Hiya," Great-uncle Mike said. His smile was so big I swore I could see all his teeth. "Thought I'd come home for some Christmas dinner."

Christmas dinner for one can be a simple, elegant affair. Start with steaming pumpkin soup. . . .

"You broke out of jail?" Devlin said. "Co-oo-ol."

Great-uncle Mike accepted a steaming cup of coffee from my mother. He grinned up at her, and she gave him a narrow look.

When we'd brought great-uncle Mike back to the house, my mother had given him what-for up one side and down the other. Mike had looked a little ashamed, but not guilty. And he certainly wasn't going back to jail.

Mom had shooed him upstairs to take a shower. She made Uncle Tad lend him some clothes, Uncle Tad being the closest to Great-uncle Mike in size. Great-uncle Mike had come downstairs again, dressed in jeans and a flannel shirt and socks, to sit in the kitchen and regale the kids with his daring jailbreak.

"Remind me again why we aren't calling the sheriff?" my sister Janet said. She didn't approve of Great-uncle Mike. But then, Janet was married to a yuppie from Chula Vista.

171

Having a great uncle who'd once been to prison embarrassed her.

Mike had gone to prison because he'd been the fall guy in an attempted robbery, left behind when the plan had gone wrong. Mike had done three years, because he refused to rat on his friends. That was in the 1960s. After that he got arrested for petty theft from time to time, but he mostly calmed down.

He enjoyed his rivalry with Sheriff Hanks, though. He'd do stupid things, like mooning people or trespassing or camping without a permit, to see if the sheriff would arrest him. He'd spend a night or two in jail, catch up on gossip with the sheriff, have a meal and a good night's sleep, then trudge back home when he was released.

The two of them exchanged Christmas and birthday cards and had attended each other's weddings. Sheriff Hanks had sent the biggest wreath when Great-uncle Mike's wife passed away, and Mike had taken the sheriff out for consolatory beers when Sheriff and Mrs. Hanks split up. Many friends weren't as close as Mike and Sheriff Hanks.

Great-uncle Mike's big jailbreak last night hadn't been that big, because Sheriff Hanks hadn't bothered to lock the door.

"I waited until he'd gone for more coffee," Great-uncle Mike went on. "I knew he'd be a while, because it's only him there today, and we'd drunk the whole pot." He took a swig from the mug in his hand, as though he couldn't get enough caffeine. "So I opened the door, real slow and soft, because I know it squeaks. Then I tiptoed out, down the stairs, and slipped out the door while he was running water into the coffeemaker."

"You think he'll come after you," I said.

Mike gave me an innocent look over the rim of his mug. "Why do you say that?"

"Because you were hiding in the bushes," Janet said, still annoyed.

"Nah. He'll figure I went home."

172

"Then why hide in the bushes?"

He looked guilty. "All right, maybe he's already looked for me at home. I figured I'd lie low for a while. He'll want to eat his Christmas dinner and give up soon."

My mom rolled her eyes. "No, that means he'll be here soon."

"Ah." Great-uncle Mike calmly took another swallow of coffee and set down the mug. "I'll be going, then."

"No, you won't," my mother said.

"I'll lurk in the woods. Send me out some turkey and pie, Angel. I like gravy on my mashed potatoes, too."

My mother put a hand on his shoulder. Mike was my father's uncle, and she, like Janet, had never approved of him. "You are staying right here. If you are stupid enough to moon the sheriff on Christmas Eve, you deserve what you get."

"Aw, Mary, have a heart."

"I do. I'm letting you stay here until Sheriff Hanks shows up."

He started to get up again. "No, I think I've had enough bad coffee at the jail. See you all later."

"Sit!"

Great-uncle Mike plopped back down. Then he looked chagrined. "You can't keep me here."

"Yes, I can. Brian."

My father stepped forward. He'd been watching the proceedings with an indulgent smile. "What?"

"Handcuffs."

My father stared at her. My mother held her hand out, her five-foot-two stature unrelenting.

My father unhooked the furry handcuffs Cherise had given him from his belt and handed them over. My mother quickly pulled Great-uncle Mike's hands behind his back and snapped the cuffs around them.

"Hey," Mike protested. "How'm I gonna eat my Christmas dinner?"

My mother rolled her eyes and walked away.

Help out in a kitchen, giving the gift of time to others. . . .

Sean joined the men (except Great-uncle Mike) to do manly things, meaning watching the sports channel and drinking longnecks in the living room. That left the kitchen dominated by women, except for Brad, who made a mean three-bean salad. Brad stayed manly by shouting into the living room with his opinion on whatever football, basketball, or hockey player was up for discussion.

Cherise, whom no one trusted with food preparation, flitted back and forth to flirt with Sean and torture me.

"What happened to the mistletoe?" she asked, hands on hips, while she stared up at the empty door frame. "I put mistletoe in every doorway. Did you throw it away, Angel?"

"I didn't touch it." I peeled potatoes, a glamorous job. The peeler was dull, so potato chunks flew out and landed in random piles around me.

"I want mistletoe everywhere," she announced. "There needs to be more sex in this family."

"There are twelve children here, Cherise," my mother said,

stirring up a pungent mixture of pumpkin, ginger, cloves, and cream.

"I didn't mean that. I want to see some kissing and touching like you all love one another."

"You only want an excuse to kiss Sean," Marta pointed out as she tore lettuce for the salad. "He's the only guy here you're not related to."

"Hey, I don't need an excuse to kiss Sean." Cherise waggled her eyebrows. "I.crook my finger, that boy's mine."

Potato peels flew around me like fleas from a dog. "He won't be your slave."

Cherise licked her lips. "Slave. Now that's an interesting idea."

"He's not a doormat," I snapped.

"What's wrong, Angel? You jealous? You told me outside I could have him."

"I told you I didn't want to hear about it."

My mother, Aunt Candy, and Janet watched me closely. They exchanged looks. I plied the potato peeler harder.

Devlin, who was pretending to help his father make three-bean salad, said, "I saw Angel kissing Sean out on the hill."

I froze. My mother, aunts, sisters, nieces, cousins, great-uncle in handcuffs, and brother-in-law all stared at me.

I never remembered seeing a small figure in a too-tight *Lord of the Rings* T-shirt out in the vineyards. "You couldn't have," I began.

"Did too. Through my new binoculars. I could see you from the bedroom upstairs. You and Sean were standing on the hill *kissin'*." He snickered.

Devlin was a good name for him. He should grow horns and a tail.

I stood there, potato peeler in one hand, dripping, half-bare potato in the other. My mother said, "Angel?"

Cherise smiled as though she'd done something clever. "So if you told me I can have him, why were you kissing him?"

I shot a frozen glance to the door to the living room.

Thank God my dad liked to listen to the sports channel with the volume all the way up. Plus he liked to talk over the commentators. Sean was safe behind a wall of sound.

"None of your business, Cherise," I said.

"Either you're finished with a guy, or you're not," she persisted. She giggled. "Unless you want to share."

"Cherise," my mother said sharply.

Cherise stopped. "What?"

"Go down to the basement and get some more potatoes. We don't have enough. Janet, take over this pie. Angel, I want to talk to you."

I felt as if I were fifteen. "*Mom.*"

"Don't 'Mom' me. We're going up to your room and having a talk."

"I have to peel potatoes."

"Brad can do it. He's almost done with his salad."

Brad opened his mouth to protest, then snapped it shut again when my mother glared at him. He didn't actually say "Yes, ma'am," but I saw the words form on his lips.

I dropped the half-peeled potato back into its bowl of water and wiped my hands on a towel. Brad picked up the peeler and flashed me a sympathetic glance. As I left the kitchen, Janet dragged a finished pie out of the oven and set it on the stove.

I followed my mom through the living room. The guys were watching Stanley Cup reruns. My dad said, every play, "That was great. I remember that."

Sean stood up and moved to me. "Everything all right?"

"Everything's fine," I said. "Why don't you go help Cherise lug potatoes out of the basement?"

He gave me a "huh?" look. I turned my back on him and marched to the front hall after my mother.

For two flights, my mother said nothing. She led me up the stairs into the tower and my little room under the eaves. I shut the door and stood uncertainly in front of it.

Mom perched herself on the ladder-back chair. She folded her hands on her lap and looked at me expectantly.

"What do you want me to tell you?" I asked.

"Everything."

"What do you mean, everything?"

She took on a patient, understanding expression. "Your family loves you, Angel. No matter what happens in New York, no matter what that tramp Penny McDermott says about you on television, we love you. She isn't single, by the way."

"She's not?" I didn't really care about Penny McDermott right now.

"No. She's gay. She has a partner who lives in Connecticut. Very hush-hush."

"Then how do you know about it?" Such news would be all over the tabloids, wouldn't it?

"My friend told me. She and her husband own a restaurant there, and Penny and her girlfriend come in all the time."

"Wow," I said.

"So let her make fun of you all she wants. She has worse skeletons in her closet than you ever will." Mom tapped her knee. "Speaking of which—spill."

"Spill what?" I said dully.

"Tell me about Sean. About the last five years of your life. Honey, you were going through so much, and you never talked to me. I can help you, Angel. That's what mothers are for."

I ran my hands through my hair. "I didn't want to talk. My life is fine. I have a career and friends and my own place in the world. Is that so bad?"

"No. It's wonderful. We're very proud of you. I know why you want independence from this family. It can be overwhelming. But independence doesn't mean going it alone. You don't have to prove anything to us."

I heaved a sigh and leaned against the high mattress. "Maybe I have to prove something to myself."

"That you're smart? We've always told you that."

"You told me that because I'm your daughter." A frustrated laugh escaped me. "Of course you tell me I'm smart and beautiful. It's your job. That doesn't mean you're right."

"Angel."

"If I'm so smart and beautiful, why did Mark decide my best friend was the answer to his dreams instead of me?"

Tears pricked my eyes. I swallowed them angrily. I had finished crying over Mark a year ago. I had moved on. I was stronger for the experience.

All right, maybe I was brittle and bitter for the experience. But the point is, I'd finished with it. Put it behind me. Forever. Like I'd put Sean behind me.

I was tired of putting things behind me.

My mother shook her head. "You can be smart and beautiful and still not right for someone. That doesn't make what Mark did right. He never should have led you on and cheated on you. But you're better off without that kind of man. Trust me."

Tears beaded on my lashes. "What if I really am a loser? What if I wrote that book to prove I wasn't a loser, because I really am?"

My mother sat silently, watching my tears fall. She used to do that when I was a kid and had the usual teenage problems. She'd let me cry it out, without hugs or lectures, then she'd offer comfort.

I wiped my wet eyes with my thumbs and sniffled.

"You wrote a fine book that spoke to young women just like yourself," my mother said. "Many people bought it because they needed to learn what you told them. It's all about *not* being a loser. It's about finding out who you are and liking yourself. It's about learning to be alone with yourself, and learning that being alone does not make you weak."

"That's not what it's about," I protested. "I should know. I wrote it."

"You know what you wrote down. Not what it's really all about. It's about not needing anyone but yourself to be complete."

I sniffled. "Maybe."

"Don't be stubborn. You know I'm right."

I smiled a little. "You always are."

"Of course I am. I have to keep track of your father and your sisters and your father's brothers and your great-uncle Mike. I don't have time to debate whether I'm right or wrong. I just have to be right."

I'd always envied my mother's self-assurance. Maybe if I lived long enough, I'd inherit it.

"Now," she said. "About Sean."

My panic returned. "What about him?"

"Why were you kissing him? Are you toying with him? Or is he toying with you?"

"Neither."

"Sure about that? Don't let Cherise push you into doing something you don't want to."

"What do you mean?"

"Don't let Cherise win," she said firmly. "Either decide you like this Sean, or turn your back on him and Cherise. She's goading you."

"I know."

"Do you like him?"

I laid my arm across my head. "I don't know. Yes. I guess."

"Well, I hope you don't dislike him, if you were kissing him. That wouldn't be fair to either of you."

"Of course I like him." I gave her a goofy grin. "He's cute."

"Looks aren't everything. But I admit, he is cute. Nice butt."

"Uh-huh," I agreed. Despite my agitation, I started imagining Sean's tight buns in the thong Cherise had given him.

"So what is between you?"

"What?" I forced my attention from the delightful picture in my mind. "Nothing, I said."

"I know you, Angel. You wouldn't start kissing a man you just met. You aren't Cherise, who would have had him in bed three times by now if he'd been willing and not such a polite young man. So what is between you?"

The trouble with my mother is that she's too smart.

"I knew him in L.A. five years ago," I confessed.

She did not look terribly surprised. "Why didn't you say? Is it such a secret?"

"The way this family demands to know every last detail? Yes, it's a secret."

"Not from me." She gave me a wise mother look. "What happened?"

I caved in. I gave her the whole story. I explained how I'd met Sean at a party the owners of the newspaper I'd interned with had thrown. One of Sean's clients had been invited and brought Sean. We'd met when I'd almost fallen into the pool in all my clothes, and Sean had caught me. I'd turned it into a joke to save myself embarrassment, and we'd got to talking.

We'd left the party and gone to a wine bar and then back to my tiny, airless apartment. No, not to have sex. To talk. I had never met a guy I could talk to as much as I could to Sean. He'd talked to me, too. By the end of the night we were both half-asleep and talked out, but in a contented kind of way.

He took me out the next night, and that was when we had the crazy sex.

Sean had been the second more-than-kisses relationship in my life. As an undergraduate, I'd lost my virginity with a guy I'd known from high school, but the encounter had been vaguely disappointing. Looking back, I realized our inexperience and lack of passion for each other was to blame. The guy had never talked to me again (probably from embarrassment). I'd gone on with my life, thinking sex wasn't all it was hyped to be.

Then Sean kissed me and cupped my face in his hands, and I changed my mind in a hurry. This was real. This was love.

"Were you afraid?" Mom asked me. "Of him staying around forever, I mean?"

I rested my head in my hands. "I don't know. I think I was afraid for myself. I mean, what if I fell madly in love with him and wanted to give my whole life to him, and he broke my heart? I couldn't stand that."

"You let Mark do it."

"But I wasn't afraid with Mark. I just . . ." I made vague motions with my hands. "I let things happen like they'd happen."

"Uh-huh."

"What, 'uh-huh'? What do you mean, 'uh-huh'?"

"I mean, you were never in love with Mark."

"Are you kidding?" I remembered the searing pain when he'd told me he was marrying Susan. I really hoped the hot pasta burned him where he needed to be burned.

"You ran away from Sean because you were afraid of your feelings," my mother said. "That means you actually had feelings. If you weren't so worried about them, you'd have stayed in touch with him. Sean seems like the kind of young man who'd be a good friend. You let Mark drift away because deep down, you didn't care about Mark."

My eyes widened. "What are you talking about, not caring? I was in pain."

"You weren't in that much pain."

"I was. I'm telling you, I was."

"You didn't run home and cry to me. You didn't run off to a tropical island and drink mai tais until you couldn't remember your name. You held your head up and kept going."

"It was my way of dealing with the pain," I said, offended.

"I'm not saying you weren't hurt. Of course it hurt. But you didn't grieve."

I stared at her. "You're saying I never loved Mark."

"Bingo."

"I didn't love Mark because I still wasn't over Sean."

"That's right."

"This is crazy."

"Love's like that," my mother said.

"What, you're saying I'm still in love with Sean? After all this time? I haven't thought about him in years."

"Haven't you?"

I stopped. "All right. I might have thought about finding him again after Mark dumped me."

She gave me a triumphant smile. "See?"

"That doesn't prove anything," I protested.

My mother stood up. "Oh, I think I've proved enough."

She hugged me. Now that she'd dissected me, she could comfort me.

I hugged her back. She smelled like nutmeg and pumpkin.

Someone knocked on the door. Mom opened it while I wiped my streaming eyes. Sean himself stood on the threshold. "Everything all right?"

"Yes." I sniffled.

"Angel and I were having a heart-to-heart," my mom said. "Everything all right with you?"

He glanced from me to my mom. "I'm not sure."

"Don't say anything more," I advised him. "She'll make you tell your whole life story."

Mom gave me a look. "Only if he wants to tell it."

Sean walked into the room and closed the door. His presence filled the space, crowding the rest of us against the furniture.

I gazed at him like an enraptured schoolgirl. I imagined even the Victorian ghost admiring his body while he worked himself up to say what he'd come to say. His eyes were so sexy. Deep and brown and . . . sexy.

"I'm causing a lot of tension here," he said quietly. "So I'll go."

"No," my mother and I said together.

"You can't rush off before you have dinner," Mom went on. "That wouldn't be right. I'll make Cherise behave herself."

Sean gave me a heart-melting look. "I shouldn't be here at all. I didn't realize that Angel lived here when I stopped."

I folded my arms. "If you had known, would you have turned around and gone back?"

He regarded me steadily. "Probably."

That hurt. "Thanks a lot."

"Because seeing you again—" He broke off. "This isn't only hard on you."

"Oh?"

"No."

We studied each other. My mother studied us.

"Maybe he'll stay if you ask him to, Angel."

I flushed. Sean remained still, frowning a little. He was adorable when he frowned.

Having him in the house did strange things to my emotions. Heck, having him in my bedroom did terrible things to my emotions. But I didn't have the heart to send him off into the cold winter afternoon to have Christmas dinner all alone. Did I?

"No," I forced myself to say. "I want you to stay."

And then I really did want him to stay.

He held my gaze. "I'd like to," he said. "But only if you really want me to. Are you sure?"

I nodded.

"Then I'll stay."

My mother breathed a sigh of relief. "Good. That's settled. Back to the kitchen with you, Angel. I need those potatoes done." She moved past Sean, opened the door, and walked out.

Sean and I looked at each other. I wanted, right now, to talk it out, like he suggested, but mom wasn't giving us the time. I wanted to think about what she'd told me about my own feelings. I wanted to explore them, and maybe kiss Sean while I was at it.

"You mean it?" he murmured into my ear as we went down the stairs.

His warm breath nearly melted me. "Yes."

"Good."

His eyes held promise. I gulped and hurried after my mother.

Whether you cook for yourself or for friends, keep it simple. . . .

The kitchen was chaos. Janet shoveled pies into and out of the oven. Cherise argued with Brad, waving potatoes in his face. Aunt Candy bent over the stove, frantically basting three huge turkeys.

Cherise finished piling a huge mound of potatoes where I'd been peeling them. I went back to them with a sigh of resignation.

"Hey," Great-uncle Mike said. "I'm losing the feeling in my fingers. And I want a cigarette."

"No smoking in my house," my mother snapped, then dove into the chaos and went back to work.

I picked up a potato and started scraping off its skin. A strong hand grabbed another one.

"You don't have to help," I said breathlessly.

Sean's dark gaze roved over me. "Yes, I do. I'm eating the food; I should do something for it."

"You're a guest."

"Uninvited and not exactly wanted."

"I want you."

The corners of his mouth twitched. "Glad to hear it." He leaned toward me. "I've been horny since I saw you last night."

"That's not what I meant," I hissed.

"Yeah, but I mean it."

I couldn't breathe right. His gaze was electric. I remembered how he'd looked at me upstairs, and my body tingled in anticipation.

No, no, no, this couldn't happen. I could not simply fling myself at him, especially not with my family hovering around.

He reached over and touched my hand.

His skin was wet with dripping potato. Didn't matter; I still went hot all over.

"Erm." I threw my peeled potato into the pot and whirled toward the stove. "I'll get the water boiling."

He smiled at me, knowing he made me nervous. I turned on a burner and hurried back to grab the pot. It was way too heavy, and water sloshed over the side. Sean caught it before I dropped it. "Get a second one," he advised.

I rummaged in the cupboard below until I found another pot. Sean and I plunked potatoes into it; then I dragged it to the sink.

Just as I turned off the water, a huge explosion rent the air.

My sister and all the kids screamed. Brad said, "What the hell?"

I swung around, water and potatoes flying all over the floor.

Hot pumpkin filling sprayed the room, followed by the smell of scorching crust. Janet shrieked and covered her eyes. Devlin burst into maniacal laughter.

"Help!" Great-uncle Mike shouted. "Help! Help!"

I stared at the stove in horror. I'd turned on the wrong burner by accident. Instead of the left rear, I'd switched on the left front. Janet's last pumpkin pie rested right on it, where she'd set it to cool. The electric coils had grown red-hot, and the glass pie plate had heated and heated until—boom. Janet's pie was now a molten mass of glass and pumpkin.

My mother hurried forward and clicked off the burner.

"Janet, stop screaming."

"My pies!" my sister wailed.

"One pie. Who turned on the burner?"

All eyes swiveled to me as I slowly raised my hand. "Sorry," I said.

Mom looked exasperated, but she shook her head. "Never mind. We have enough without it. Janet, you shouldn't have left the pie on the burner. And Angel, you should pay more attention."

"Yes, Mom," we said together.

"What's going on in there?" a voice from the back door demanded. A large man peered through the glass on the top half of the door. He held his hands in a tense grip around a very large revolver, its barrel pointed upward.

Devlin roared, "He's got a gun!"

Marta screamed, dropped a casserole of macaroni and cheese, and dove under the table.

My mother marched to the door and opened it. Great-uncle Mike smiled feebly. "Hi, Sheriff."

Sheriff Hanks was a large man, muscle running to fat, with a shock of white hair spilling from under his sheriff's hat. He glanced around the kitchen, then holstered his pistol, nodded to my mother, and came inside.

"Thought I heard a shot."

"No," I said. "A pie."

He stared at the globs of pumpkin and glass on the floor around the stove. "Oh."

"Have you come to take me away?" Great-uncle Mike said hopefully.

"You know I got to hold you for a hearing tomorrow, Mike," Sheriff Hanks said. He peered at Great-uncle Mike's wrists. "What have you folks got him tied up with?"

"Furry handcuffs," Cherise purred.

Sheriff Hanks knew all about Cherise. He raised his eyebrows but said nothing.

My mother stepped up to him. "At least let Mike have Christmas dinner with his family. He can't make a getaway here."

Mike sent the sheriff a pleading look. I think he wanted rescue more than he wanted his Christmas dinner. Whether Sheriff Hanks understood or not, he only nodded. He certainly was not about to defy my mother. "I suppose I can make an exception. You're the only lockup I have today, Mike. So have your dinner; then I'll come back for you."

Great-uncle Mike looked crestfallen.

"You'll stay too, of course," my mother told the sheriff.

Sheriff Hanks brightened. He removed his hat. "Don't mind if I do, ma'am. I'll just go pay my respects to your husband."

He ducked through the kitchen door, escaping the chaos.

"How'd he find me so fast?" Great-uncle Mike asked plaintively.

"I called him," my mother said in her no-nonsense tone. "Now, Angel, I cleaned off the burner. Get those potatoes on or we'll not have any for supper."

Good friends and family are the best Christmas gifts in the world. . . .

Dinner actually got served without anything else exploding. We had one less pumpkin pie and no macaroni and cheese, but no one grumbled. There were endless amounts of food, including a couple of mince pies that mom had made yesterday, not to mention mountains of mashed potatoes.

My mother had turned the dining room and sleeping porch into one big cafeteria. We got our plates and moved through the line to pile turkey, dressing, mashed potatoes and gravy, three-bean salad, yams, cranberries, greens, and bread onto our plates. We grabbed seats as we found them at the four long tables my mom and dad had set up.

Great-uncle Mike waited at one of the tables, one wrist handcuffed to his chair. I brought him a plate of food. "Thanks, Angel." He winked at me. "Guess you already got your Christmas wish. There wasn't an inch of space between you two out on that hill. When's the wedding?"

I rolled my eyes and stalked away. I heard him chuckling.

Sheriff Hanks sat next to him, his plate piled with all kinds of food. They started talking about the Christmas when his Marge had cooked a big dinner for them and brought it down to the jail. Those were good times.

I took a seat at the next table with my dad. I tried not to look for Sean, but suddenly he stopped at the chair next to mine. He smiled, his eyes warm. "Mind if I sit here?"

My heart missed a beat. "Yes. I mean no. I mean, yes, sit down."

His grin widened. He deposited his plate on one of my mother's favorite place mats and seated himself.

My sister Emma started to slide into the chair on his other side. Cherise appeared out of nowhere and shoved Emma out of the way with her elbow. Emma glared at her, then snatched up her plate and moved to the next table.

"Hi, Seanie," Cherise said, snuggling down next to him. "Great mashed potatoes, Angel."

"I only peeled and boiled them," I said, trying not to sound grumpy.

"Whatever. Try the yams, Sean. I made those."

Sort of. She'd stirred the butter and cinnamon into them before my mom popped them into the oven.

My father looked pained. "You didn't put an aphrodisiac in them, did you?"

Cherise laughed. "What an imagination. Though it's not a bad idea. Anyone bring any oysters?"

"Someone throw water on her," my dad advised.

I ground my teeth. Sean said nothing.

Dinner progressed without Cherise getting drenched, although I wanted to douse her repeatedly. She made a habit of touching Sean every chance she could. She'd "accidentally" brush his arm, then trace his muscles with her bright red nails. Every so often she'd coo, "Oh, Seanie, this is good; try it," and feed bits of things to him from her fork.

He didn't stop her, although he looked annoyed. He was trying to be polite. I wanted to tell him not to bother.

Cherise kept touching him under the table, too. I knew this because he'd jump every so often and clench his jaw. She'd smile, her red-lipsticked mouth moist.

Once she must have groped him in a private place, because he made a strangled noise and his butt bounced off the seat. He came down and started coughing into his napkin.

I couldn't take any more. I sprang to my feet. "Do you want more pie, Sean?"

"What? Uh, pie, yeah." He tossed down the napkin and scrambled from the chair. "You sit down. I'll get it. What kind do you want?"

I shot him a sympathetic look. "Pumpkin, if there is any more."

"Great." He held the chair for me while I seated myself. "I'll be right back."

He escaped. I leaned over his chair, still warm from his backside, and said, "Leave him alone, Cherise."

She gave me a pitying smile. "Honey, he's the most delicious thing in this room. I'm going for it."

I grew angry. "He doesn't like you all over him. Stop it."

Cherise tittered. "Men always pretend they don't like aggressive women. They're lying. They want women to tie them down and have their way with them." She looked thoughtful. "I wonder if Great-uncle Mike would lend me the handcuffs."

I thumped back into my chair, wondering what was wrong with me. Cherise's pursuit of men had never angered me like this before. I usually rolled my eyes and ignored her. This time she made me furious. How dared she run after Sean as though he were fair game?

Cherise was pretty, and many men found her alluring. More than one had let her have her way with him. Sean had protested that she wasn't his type, but you never knew.

Sean returned to the table. I sensed him next to me, his warm thigh in tight jeans nearly touching my shoulder. I swallowed.

He set a neat slice of pie in front of me, the pumpkin decorated with a dollop of cream. I wanted to plop the cream on the back of his sinewy hand and lick it off.

"Here you go," he said. "Hope you wanted whipped cream."

"Mmm, whipped cream," Cherise said dreamily. "Sounds fun."

My temper finally splintered.

"Cherise, would you shut up!"

My voice rang across the room in a sudden lull. Conversation died. Heads turned. Sheriff Hanks looked like he might go for his gun again.

"Ooh," Cherise said, but without her usual gusto. "Sounds like someone needs an eggnog."

Sean very quietly slid back into his place. Under the table, he gave my leg a warm squeeze.

"Angel's mad," little Devlin said loudly. "It's 'cause she was kissing Sean and she doesn't want Cherise kissing him."

"Devlin," Janet said in her weary mother voice.

I wanted to fall forward right into my pumpkin pie. The only thing that kept me upright was Sean's fine, strong fingers on my knee.

He saved my life. The conversation rose in a sudden crescendo. I sat in silence, reveling in the calming heat of his hand.

I picked up my fork and cut off a bit of pie. He winked at me as I took a bite. He kept his hand on my leg until I'd chewed and swallowed.

Then he smiled at me, picked up his own fork, and attacked his pie.

Go to bed Christmas night with a mug of hot chocolate (with marshmallows), a good book, and happy thoughts of your Christmas Day. . . .

I curled up in the high bed in my nightshirt and started scribbling longhand, working on a column due the week after Christmas. It would run in the July or August issue of our magazine. Bundled up in my flannel pajama top with quilts over my feet, listening to heat rattle through the vents, I brainstormed ways for twenty-somethings to meet guys in the hottest beachside bars in San Diego.

I wasn't into it.

My mind kept replaying the events of the evening. After dinner we'd tried to drag ourselves to the kitchen to clean up. Mom wouldn't let us. She insisted that everyone ignore the mess; the dishes would still be there in the morning, she said.

She wanted us to sing Christmas carols in the living room—no TV tonight. The kids groaned at first, but after we sang a few songs, they started having fun with it. Great-uncle Mike and the sheriff even sang a duet of "Good King Wenceslas," before Sheriff Hanks at last said they had to go and hauled Great-uncle Mike off to jail. Mom made them take mincemeat pie and a whole bunch of mashed potatoes with them.

Cherise quickly cut me out with Sean. I swear, it was like watching a horse single out a calf from a herd. I ended up next to the piano and my dad. Cherise pushed Sean to the far end of the room, squishing herself and her obvious breasts against him. I could tell he was not thrilled, but he didn't move away.

I gave up and stalked to the kitchen. The pile of dishes was no hardship compared to watching Cherise melt all over Sean. Let her have him. What did I care? I was single and loving it.

Great, now I was quoting Penny McDermott again. Who wasn't really single, the big faker. I wondered if Barbie knew that. I wondered if Barbie could use Mom's information to get me a better interview or even an endorsement for the book.

I finished the dishes, wiped down the counters, threw the towels into the washing machine, and sneaked away upstairs to the relative peace of my bedroom.

The bedroom was restful, I had to admit, perched high and away from everyone else. Even the ghost was peaceful, as long as it didn't look like Cherise.

I scribbled in my notebook, *Stay cool at Mission Beach's new Hooligan's Hideaway, a short roller-skate journey from the beach.*

I threw down my pen and buried my face in my hands. My messy hair tickled my fingers. Who was I kidding? I couldn't care less about Hooligan's Hideaway. They'd overcharge for the drinks and probably be closed a month before the magazine came out. Maybe it was time for me to move on to something new. Maybe I could be a travel writer and journey around the world to cushy hotels, far, far away from my screwed-up love life and my cousin Cherise.

I heard soft footsteps on the stairs leading to my door. I

groaned. I was not up for another visit from my mom, who'd have more theories on what was wrong with me. Maybe it was one of the kids wanting to play evil elf in the tower room. Or maybe, I thought hopefully, it was the ghost.

The footsteps, firm and very unghostlike, came closer.

Cherise's voice suddenly rang out from somewhere downstairs. "Sean? Where *are* you, sweetie? Are you going to bed?"

My door swung open. I jerked my head up. Sean paused on the threshold, his breathing rapid, his dark eyes wide.

I opened my mouth to ask him what he was doing, but he frantically signaled me to silence.

"Cherise?" I whispered.

He eased the door closed without a sound. "Can I hide in here?"

I shrugged. "Sure. No one's here but me and the ghosts."

"What?"

"Back in the Victorian days—"

I broke off. His demeanor had changed, and I realized he was looking at my body. My nightshirt hung loose from my shoulders, and I didn't have on much underneath.

His attention lingered on the gaping opening of the nightshirt, then traveled slowly down my bare legs. His look was appreciative. His eyes met mine, and my skin began to prickle.

"Sean, are you up there?" Cherise shouted.

Sean's expression turned hunted. "Doesn't she ever give up?"

"No," I said.

We heard her footsteps on the stairs. She was on her way, determined.

"Under," I hissed, jabbing my finger at the side of the bed.

Sean didn't argue. He dove to the board floor and slid himself under the high bed. Just in time. Cherise's spike-heeled boots clicked rapidly on the stairs; then she yanked open the door.

She hesitated in the doorway, trying to catch her breath.

Her sleek hair was mussed. "Hey, Angel. Have you seen Sean?"

"You could knock," I pointed out.

She rapped loudly on the open door. "There. Have you seen Sean?"

"No."

"I don't believe you."

I slammed my notebook closed and dumped it on the nightstand. I sat back against the pillows and folded my arms. "Fine. While you're not believing me, will you close the door? You're making a draft. Oh, and turn off the light. I want to get some sleep."

She craned her head to glance around the room, but she did not spot Sean. She studied the bedstead thoughtfully, but even Cherise would not crawl under a bed hunting for a man.

I hoped.

At last, she heaved a sigh that nearly spilled her out of her leather bustier. "Well, if you see him, tell him I'm looking for him." She licked her finger suggestively.

"I'll be sure to do that."

Instead of leaving, Cherise leaned against the door frame, resting her long red nails on the jamb. "What's wrong, Angel?" she asked. "First you say I can have Sean; next you're furiously jealous of me. You can't have it both ways."

I winced, thinking about my behavior downstairs. "I'm not jealous," I tried. "I'm . . . disgusted."

"No, honey. You're jealous. When I'm like this with any other guy, you ignore me. This time, you're taking it personally."

My face heated. I couldn't exactly tell her the truth with Sean under the bed, but I knew I couldn't fob her off with lies.

"I really don't want to talk about it," I said.

"Why not?"

"Because I don't."

"You said you had a thing with him before. Was it serious?"

My face heated. "I guess."

"Were you in love with him?"

My mouth went dry. I imagined Sean lying under the bed, dark eyes glistening, while he listened to every word. "I said I really don't want to talk about it."

"So you *are* in love with him."

"*Was.* It was a long time ago."

She gave me a deprecating look. "Oh, come on, Angel. You got all huffy at me at dinner. I saw your face when he reached down and squeezed your leg. Yes, I saw that. You turned red, like now, but you looked pleased. Happy, even."

I hugged my arms across my chest. "So? I do like him. He's always been a nice guy. Will you go away now?"

"You don't just *like* him." She came closer, resting her clawed hands on my bed. "You're really into him. If I wasn't around, you'd be chasing him to his bedroom."

I flushed, wanting to say that no, she'd chased him to mine. "I'm not going to chase him."

"Why not? He's gorgeous. You think he's gorgeous, right?"

I sprang up on my knees. The bed rocked. I winced, hoping I hadn't just smacked Sean in the face with the springs.

"Yes, all right," I said fiercely. "He's gorgeous. I like him. I get happy when he touches me. Now, will you please go away?"

Cherise's dark eyes widened. "Don't get all hysterical. I'm only saying you'd chase him around if you had the chance. It's your own fault, you know. You said I could have him."

I sank back on my heels. "Cherise, will you please just go?"

She straightened up, shrugging. "All right. But if you see him . . ."

"Yes, yes, I know. I'll tell him you're looking for him."

Cherise sauntered to the door. "Good night, then." She snapped off the light. The glow from the stairwell silhouetted her like a curvaceous paper doll. "Merry Christmas, Angel."

"Merry Christmas, Cherise," I said neutrally.

Finally, finally, she closed the door and left me alone. I sat in the darkness listening as her high-heeled boots clicked away down the stairs.

"All right," I whispered. "I think she's gone."

I heard nothing from under the bed.

"Sean?"

No answer.

Oh, great, had I knocked him out when I bounced on the bed? I leaned over the side, hanging on to the mattress, and peered underneath.

Sean lay on his back, swiping at a dust bunny stuck to his chest. "Yuck," he said.

He slid out from under the mattress, bringing the dust bunny with him. I still hung on to the bed, watching him. He sat up, muttering curses as he shook the ball of dust away.

The room was dark, but the light from under the door and from the large moon outside touched the planes of his face and his midnight hair. He was the most beautiful man in the whole wide world.

"Don't go yet," I said.

He raked one hand through his hair, letting more dust fly. "Yeah, I think we need to talk."

"I didn't mean that. I mean she's probably lying in wait for you at the bottom of the stairs."

Sean shot a panicked look at the door. "Would she?"

"I know Cherise. She never gives up."

"Damn. You have a hell of a family, Angel."

"They're not so bad," I said defensively.

He opened his mouth to tell me that no, they were insane, but suddenly he grinned. "You're right; I like them. Your mom is great. She keeps the whole clan in line, doesn't she?"

I rolled my eyes. "More than we like her to, sometimes."

"You have good people. I'm glad I met them."

"Except Cherise?"

"Well . . ."

He hoisted himself to his feet and took a seat on the ladder-back chair. He leaned forward, elbows on knees, and gave me an intense look. "I'm not wrong. We really do need to talk."

My heart thumped. "About what?"

"About what you said to Cherise," he said quietly. "About being in love with me."

I gulped. "*Was* in love. Was. Past tense." Right?

"I was in love with you, too."

"That's what you said out on the hill."

"It's true." He laced his fingers together, moonlight casting white bands across his arms. "I would have done anything for you. But I guess being in love isn't enough."

"No, it isn't," I agreed. "There's the rest of life to get through."

He looked up. "Oh, bullshit."

"What? You just said—"

"I meant, that's what *you* thought. You thought love would get in the way of whatever you wanted, so you dumped me."

"I did not dump you," I said hotly.

His eyes glittered. "Really? I remember the day we broke up. You sat on the bed in my apartment, like you are now, and explained that life was already too complicated for the added complication of a relationship. 'A clean break,' you said. 'Let's just be friends.'"

"I thought that's what you wanted."

"Why?" he asked impatiently. "Did you ever hear me say that?"

"No. But you're a guy. Guys always want that."

He stood up and turned his sexy body toward me. "You know all about guys, do you? I read that column of yours. You have no idea what you're talking about."

"Of course I do," I protested. "I do research."

"No, you don't. You talk to *women* about men. I never notice you asking guys what they think."

"What, you want me to interview you?"

"That's not a bad idea. A guy telling women what guys are really like. Or don't they want to know the truth?"

I glared at him. "Oh, we know the truth."

"No. You don't."

I got to my knees, my skin hot. "Well, what do you know about being a woman? A single woman? The women who read my magazine have to wade through guys who are interested only in sex or someone who'll do their laundry. Men don't want women to have lives; they want them to stand around and tell men how great they are."

He raked his hands through his hair, making it stand on end. He looked really cute like that. "I don't remember any of this from our summer together. I remember taking turns with laundry and me being proud of you and encouraging you. And, all right, great sex. Which you wanted as much as I did."

"I'm not talking about our relationship," I said desperately. "I'm talking about men."

His mouth turned down. "We aren't arguing about men and women, Angel; we're arguing about you and me."

"Every relationship is about the differences between men and women."

"Geez, could you put away the pop psychology already? Real life isn't some researcher's statistics. We weren't doing a relationship experiment, or a survey for a magazine. It was real, with real feelings."

"I know that."

"You wanted to break up with me, Angel. *You* wanted it. Not me."

I balled my fists. "Of course you wanted it."

"I never did. I never wanted you to go."

I sprang from the bed and faced him, breathing hard. "I don't remember you arguing with me at the time. I remember you saying it was all right, we didn't need to see each other any longer."

"You were halfway out the door. I was trying to save my dignity."

"You could have tried harder to stop me."

He gave me an incredulous look. "You lectured me for half an hour on why you wanted to leave. I thought that's what you needed. Sure, I wanted to haul you back and say, 'You my woman. You no go.' But I was trying to be cool."

I watched him, throat tight, tears burning my eyes. "You can't tell me it wasn't for the best."

"You never gave me the chance to tell you what I thought. I was ready to go with you to New York, to watch you bloom. There's plenty for me to do there—it's not like they don't have restaurants I could sell wine to."

I started to lose fire. "You never said that. You never once mentioned coming to New York with me."

"You never gave me the opportunity." He stopped and held up his hands, his voice quieting. "And all right, I probably didn't try very hard to tell you what I wanted. I was mad at you, and you hurt my pride. Plus I was young and stupid."

"It was only five years ago," I pointed out.

"I've grown up a lot since then. Mostly because I let you get away. I should have grabbed on tight and not let you go."

We faced each other in silence. He stood near enough that I felt his warmth through my nightshirt. I wanted him to grab on tight right now and say, "I'm never letting you go again, Angel."

I hugged my arms about my chest. "Your plan isn't working, is it? We are supposed to catch up on old times and then go our separate ways."

Sean went silent. His gaze roved me, as warm as his touch. Even in my anguish, I couldn't help noticing how gorgeous he was. His dark hair was mussed where he'd shoved his hands through it, and his body held a pent-up energy that threatened to ignite us both.

He closed the distance between us. I stood right against the bed and couldn't back away, not that I wanted to.

He cupped my shoulders, his fingers hot through my nightshirt. "I've changed my mind."

He lowered his head as though he would kiss me. I held myself back. "This might be a mistake."

"It's a huge mistake," he said softly. "But I want to make it."

His mouth met mine. I held myself rigid, trying to resist the heat that leaked through my body, but I lost the battle mighty quickly. His kisses could make the world go away.

He dipped his tongue between my parted lips. He tasted like champagne. He tasted like pumpkin pie and whipped cream. He tasted like Sean. I itched for him and hoped we would accidentally topple onto the bed.

Before something that exciting could happen, he eased the kiss to its end. He brushed his thumbs over the corners of my mouth, his lips nearly touching mine.

"Was what you told Cherise true?" he whispered. "That you're happy when I touch you?"

"Um," I breathed.

His eyes narrowed. "Was that a yes?"

"I think so."

"Good."

He traced the opening of my nightshirt and then, joy of joys, he slid his hand inside. Did his touch make me happy? I'd say yes, very, very, very, very happy.

He leaned to kiss me again. I met his mouth eagerly. He cupped my breast as our lips tangled, the kiss a little more heated this time.

It all came back to me now. I remembered lying with him in my stuffy apartment while the faulty air-conditioning wheezed and churned, trying to cool our sweating bodies. I remembered the way he'd draw his lazy hand across my waist and kiss me slowly. I remembered how he'd murmur my name and smile when he did it.

I remembered us laughing together over some corny movie or having stupid little arguments about nothing, which would end in frantic kissing. I'm sure everyone who saw us together thought we were appallingly cute.

Best of all was simply lying next to him while he slept and thinking how utterly at peace I was.

No, I have to be honest. The best part was the sex. Wild, screaming, funny, slippery, happy, delicious sex. It had been *fun*.

I'd left this man behind. Was I insane? He liked me, me with my pixie face and brown hair and less-than-perfect figure. Cherise's curves, her red lipstick, and her body-hugging leather weren't for him. He wanted my pale lips and unendowed chest. He wanted *me*.

And yet I'd walked away, so sure I knew everything about everything.

Stupid, stupid Angel.

I wrapped my arms around him and kissed him with everything I had. Who cared if every single person I was related to was downstairs? Up in my snug bedroom in the moonlight, there was only the ghost. And me, kissing the most gorgeous guy in the world.

His lips were warm and smooth, spicy and skilled. In a few minutes he might agree that our breakup was for the best. He might end the kiss, walk out the door, go downstairs, and drive away, and I'd never see him again.

So why not grab all I could tonight? Heck, it was Christmas.

Something Cherise said before she left nagged at me, but I pushed it aside. I had better things to concentrate on than Cherise.

I ran my hands over his abdomen, tracing the tight muscles under his sweatshirt. He pulled me closer. His tongue roved my mouth.

Had he always tasted this good? I drew my hands up his spine, loving the way his muscles moved as he pressed against me, his hard body to my pliant one.

I wanted to grab him, drag him up on the bed and strip him naked. I wanted him to strip me naked. Whatever it took, I wanted us both naked.

Sean broke the kiss at last. He rested his forehead against mine, his breath ragged. "Do you want me to go back to my room?" he asked.

"No." I clung to him. "I want you to stay here and hide from Cherise."

He pretended to be calm, but his voice shook. "I might want to go to bed. It's been a long day."

I gave him a small smile. "I think going to bed is a fine idea."

"You might be right." His slow, firm touch moved down my sides to the hem of my nightshirt. "In that case, we should get rid of this."

"If you want," I said, pretending to be nonchalant.

He scooted my nightshirt upward. I raised my arms and he slid the flannel top over my head and tossed it aside.

I stood before him, bare except for my bikini briefs. I was suddenly glad it was dark, because I couldn't stand it if he were disappointed.

He didn't look disappointed. He rested his warm hands on my waist and studied me with dark eyes. "You're beautiful," he murmured. "I missed you so much."

"You should have told me."

"I'm telling you now."

His hands warmed my skin. I felt wild and wicked pressed against him while he was still fully dressed. I liked the feeling. I hadn't been this uninhibited since . . . well, since my summer with Sean five years ago.

It struck me, as he bent to kiss me again, that my mother was right. For two months of a spectacular summer, I'd lost myself in Sean and in joy. I'd been crazy and happy and madly in love.

I'd enjoyed every minute of it, and at the same time, our love had scared me. That summer had been my last before I launched myself into the real world. I thought I had to give up the wild joys of love and life in order to be a serious career girl. So I'd run away from the man who'd made me feel like this.

I couldn't explain that to Sean. He'd think I was crazy.

I *was* crazy. I'd had this man, and I had let him go.

He raised his head. His breathing came fast, and his eyes were dark. "Get on the bed," he ordered.

Was I going to resist? No way.

"Sure, no problem."

I scrambled to the top of the quilts. My knees sank into pillows. Then, lucky me, I got to watch him undress.

He kicked off his shoes at the same time that he pulled off his sweatshirt. Moonlight traced the hard muscles of his chest and shoulders. I watched the play of sinews in his arms as he lifted his foot to pull off his sock.

The sock stuck. He hopped and tugged at it. I prayed no one heard downstairs and came to investigate.

He pulled and pulled on the sock that wanted to adhere to his foot. I giggled.

"Thanks a lot," he said, but he grinned.

The sock gave way, and Sean sat down hard on the chair. I pressed my hands over my mouth to stifle my laughter. He stripped off the other sock, then stood up and popped open the button of his pants.

I stopped laughing. He stripped off the pants and tossed them aside. Instead of the red thong that Cherise had given him, he wore a pair of black bikini briefs. His legs were strong, his backside tight. He was raw strength. He probably worked out on machines, but I guessed a lot of his strength came from walking around his vineyards with his dad. He was built, but not a show-off. A modest man with a bod to die for was so damn sexy.

I'd made myself not think about this gorgeous hunk for five years. Where was my brain?

He put his hands on his hips and looked at me.

"Aren't you going to join me?" I asked shyly.

"I'm admiring you," he said, running his gaze in a flattering way over my body. "But yeah, I'm going to join you."

He vaulted onto the bed. He miscalculated and landed on my legs. We went down in a tangle of limbs. He stopped my laughter by kissing me. I sank into the warmth and softness of the bed as his hard arms came around me.

His fingers slid beneath the waistband of my underwear. He caressed my backside, his touch strong and warm.

His breath heated my skin. He left off kissing me to nibble my ear. I traced the muscles of his arms and shoulders while I returned the nibbles on his earlobe.

He kissed me, his mouth hot; then he licked his way down my throat. I made a noise of pleasure as he scooted down the bed, caressing my bare skin with his lips as he went.

When his mouth closed on my breast, I whimpered in delight. I wove my hands through his hair while he nipped and licked and drove me insane. He touched me all over while his mouth continued to work its magic.

He moved down to press kisses to my belly; then he licked my navel.

The quilts pressed into my back, and this wonderful man pressed against my front. I drew my foot along his leg, reveling in his strength and his sexy excitement.

God, I had missed him. I'd missed him every day of every week of every year, even when I'd been with Mark. I realized now that throughout my relationship with Mark, I'd been a little disappointed that I'd never felt the sparks or those moments of joy I'd experienced every day with Sean.

Maybe I'd never truly connected with Mark because part of me was still kicking myself for leaving Sean.

Now Sean was with me, and the sparks rained. It was like those old movies where they show the hero and heroine kissing in bed, then pan to a shot of fireworks. I swore I saw fireworks out of the window, red and green and gold sparkles against the night sky.

Later, I learned I hadn't been imagining things. One of the angels had shorted out and exploded, popping its head off and pouring blazing embers all over the damp yard.

Maybe the electricity flooding my room had something to do with the angels overheating. Maybe not, but it felt like fire filled the room. As the sparks hissed outside, they flared inside.

Sean slid down my bikini briefs, and I wriggled out of them. Wicked, uninhibited Angel didn't struggle while Sean put his mouth right over my wanting opening. I crammed a pillow to my mouth, letting it stifle my cries of pleasure.

Too long, too long I'd loved this man. I loved how he made me feel. I loved his handsome good looks, his deep, sexy voice, his dark, beautiful eyes, his charming smile. I loved him, and I loved what he did to me.

I lay there and let him pleasure me. He licked me and kissed me, swirling his tongue in a maddening pattern.

Just before I climaxed, Sean pulled away. I nearly cried

out in disappointment. But then, happy day, he slithered out of his underwear and dropped them to the floor. He lay down on me, his blunt hardness brushing my thigh.

Yes, yes, yes! I tossed the pillow aside and reached for him. And then, all of a sudden, he was gone.

"What?" I groped for him, my hands connecting with empty air.

"Condoms," he said.

My heart sank. "Oh, no," I moaned. "I don't have any."

"I do." He bent over—a nice sight—and rummaged in the pocket of his jeans. "Courtesy of Cherise. She gave me a couple after dinner."

"What? Oh, I don't believe her."

He peeled a wrapper. "I'm happy she did. By the way, they glow in the dark."

I started laughing.

He wrestled with the wrapper, then the condom, and finally slid it onto himself. He struck a pose. "There. How do I look?"

His hardness stood out from his body, as long and lovely as I remembered. Except now it was glow-in-the-dark translucent red.

"She gave me a green one, too," he said. "Christmas colors, I guess."

I lay back and laughed until the tears streamed down my face.

He laughed with me; then he said, "You know, that reaction can kill a guy's confidence."

"You're beautiful," I said wiping my eyes. "You're perfect."

"That's more like it."

He leaped onto the bed double-quick, no more miscalculation. He pressed me down into the quilts and pillows. "I'm ready to have my way with you, woman."

"Good." I wrapped my arms around him.

He parted my legs and slid straight into me, then stopped. I closed my eyes in pleasure.

This felt so right, I thought, he and I together, tucked up in my high tower room. He brushed soft kisses on my hair and lips while we lay quietly and allowed our bodies to grow accustomed to each other's once again.

"I missed you," he murmured. "I never forgot what it felt like to be with you."

"Likewise," I said.

He raised up on his hands, his face flushed, his smile devilish. "I'm ready to remember some more."

"All right."

He began to move inside me, slowly at first, then building to a smooth, maddening rhythm. I laid my head back and enjoyed the feeling of the heat at my opening and his length inside me. I was naughty. I was beyond naughty. I didn't care.

Sean kissed my ear. "You're beautiful, Angel. I never stopped loving you."

"Never?" I asked.

"Never."

I wanted to believe him. For that moment, I did believe him. I pulled him deep into me, our breathing ragged. The bedstead creaked. Outside, the angels sang "Gloooooo . . ." and fizzled out.

Then my world exploded, just like the angels and the overheated pumpkin pie. I swirled away in delicious, dark feeling while Sean murmured my name and kissed me, his skin slick with sweat. I might have told him that I loved him; I have no idea what I said. I knew only that I loved this feeling, and I loved being with him.

As wave after wave of delight washed over me, his breath grew hoarse and his eyes lost focus. "God, Angel, I love you."

He thrust hard one last time; then he collapsed onto me and was still.

I held him in the sudden silence that descended on the room. Eyes heavy, he let his fingers drift across my skin.

"You feel nice," he whispered.

"So do you."

We lay in silence for a few moments, our limbs relaxing together.

"I meant what I said," he murmured.

"Mmm?" I was warm and drowsy and happy.

"I love you."

He laid his head on my shoulder and closed his eyes.

I lay still, uncertain what to answer. It was one thing to have him say it while we were having rollicking sex, another to have him say it while we settled down for the night.

Afterglow. It must be. He was basking in afterglow, like a drunk man. Come to think of it, he'd had a lot of champagne downstairs. He'd likely lie here with me for a while, then get embarrassed, grab his clothes, and hurry back to his own bed.

It would be over. Again.

I knew with all my heart I didn't want it to be over again. This time I did not want to close the door on him when I returned to New York and my life there. I'd run from Sean five years ago, because I thought having a relationship would mean no career. I thought I had to prove to my family I could make it on my own. I thought I couldn't do that while melting all over Sean. A clean break and a romantic memory— that was what I'd wanted.

Now I was older, and, oh, God, so much wiser. This time I did not want to run away. I did not want to end all possibilities with Sean. I did not want to draw lines, with him on one side, me on the other. I wanted to let the lines be fluid, and for what was meant to happen, happen.

A soft snore told me that Sean hadn't waited for my reply. He'd said what he needed to say and left me to deal with it.

I brushed a lock of hair from his forehead. His face relaxed into heavy sleep and contentment. I felt the same contentment, and always would with this man.

I closed my eyes and slid into slumber.

* * *

A crash woke me. Broad daylight streamed in through the window. The door stood wide open.

My nephew Devlin stood in the doorway, staring at us in surprise. The door had struck the wall where he'd banged it open.

Beside me, Sean jumped awake. "Crap," he hissed. He scrambled to pull covers over us.

"Hey," Devlin shouted at the top of his adorable little voice. "How come Sean's sleeping in Angel's bed? If I'd known Sean was in Angel's bed, I'd've taken his."

Spend some Christmas time with children. They know how to put the joy into the holiday, no matter what. . . .

I wanted to strangle the kid. He stared at us, his big blue eyes taking in everything.

Of course, his shouting brought people running. My mother came first. Piling up behind her on the stairs were Aunt Candy, my sister Janet, my nieces Tatiana and Marta, and my cousin Cherise.

They stared into the room, openmouthed, while I held the quilt over my bare breasts. Sean rose up on his elbow and looked back at them.

Only my mother did not look surprised. And, weirdly, neither did Cherise.

Devlin yelled, "So, Mom, can I have Sean's room?"

"Janet," my mother said, her voice quiet and strained. "Take Devlin back downstairs. Everyone else, go with them."

As one, my sister and aunt and cousins turned stiffly away, like robots following orders.

"You too, Cherise," Mom said severely.

Cherise grinned in at us. She didn't look angry or even surprised. She looked like we had given her the best entertainment she could possibly have this Christmas. Under my mother's glare, she turned away and disappeared, snickering.

"Well," my mother said to us after she had gone. "I'm sorry about Devlin, but what's done is done. You two will have to come downstairs and face the music."

Sean pushed his gorgeous dark hair from his eyes. He didn't look one bit ashamed or even worried. "There won't be any music," he said. "I plan to marry Angel. I was going to ask her this morning."

I lost my hold on the quilts. Sean grabbed them just in time.

My mother raised her brows but looked a little bit smug. "Glad to hear it. Come on down to breakfast. I'll save some waffles for you."

She left the room and closed the door with a little thump. We heard her humming as she descended the stairs, her step light.

Sean moved his arm and the quilts fell from my breasts. His dark eyes started to sparkle. "Not exactly how I'd planned it," he said. "But, oh, well."

I gaped at him. "Planned? You planned this?"

"Not our being found in bed together. Or even *being* in bed together. But the asking-you-to-marry-me part I planned as soon as I saw you. I didn't want to let you get away again."

He leaned to kiss me. I scooted to the edge of the bed. "Now hang on a darned minute. I'm willing to leave things open between us, but marriage?" I put my hand to my head. "Husband-and-wife marriage? Geez, Louise."

"Your family will expect something. What are we going to tell them, that we're not in love? That we just decided to get our rocks off?"

I sprang out of bed, dragging a quilt to cover my body. Unfortunately, said quilt had covered Sean, and now he lay there, naked. He looked really good naked.

My voice cracked. "This isn't a Victorian novel. You don't have to marry me to save my reputation. Lots of couples have sex nowadays."

"At least you're calling us a couple."

I ran my hand through my already messy hair. "That's because last night you were kissing me and touching me and making me feel . . ."

"Feel what?" He circled his bent knee with his arm and gave me an intense look. "What did you feel, Angel?"

"Great. Happy." I waved my arm and the quilt slipped. I grabbed it. "Loved."

"So what's the problem?"

"I want to try again with you, but I thought we'd take things slow. And now you're here, all gorgeous and muscley and turning me on, and my mother knows I'm sleeping with you. Heck, the whole family knows, and someone is probably calling Great-uncle Mike in jail by now to pass on the news."

"What does it matter if they know?" he asked.

"Because I have to go downstairs and face them. So do you. Why aren't you worried?"

He reached for my hand and clasped warm fingers around mine. "Because I'm not ashamed to tell them that I love you. I want to be with you." He tried a grin. "Now, if I'd been caught with Cherise, *then* I'd be embarrassed."

"It isn't funny," I said.

"Yes, it is. They'll laugh at us, but I'd rather have them laughing than angry. I love you, Angel. Let them laugh."

"Do you have any idea how hard it is to go down there and tell them they were *right?*"

He frowned. "Right about what?"

"Everything. I was so proud when I waltzed out of here. I was going to do everything right—perfect career, then perfect marriage. I didn't need them anymore. And then everything started going wrong, and I was afraid to tell them. I got dumped, badly, and then Penny McDermott made me and my book a laughingstock."

"Don't let what Penny McDermott says control your life,"

he said. "She's an irritating woman who'll be history in a few years. You will still be you."

I swiped at my nose. "She isn't even single."

"She's not?"

"No, she's gay. My mother told me."

He stopped a moment. "Does your mother know everything in the universe?"

"I think so."

"She's a very wise woman."

"Because she thinks we should get married?"

"Yes." He smiled at me. "So how about it?"

I screamed through my teeth. "*Men.* I can't stand them."

"Since when?"

I shook off his grasp. "Do you still plan to uproot yourself and follow me to New York? It's not fair to you. You have a life here."

"I told you, I want you to work at your magazine and write your books. You obviously love it. The winery has clients in New York already, and we should go after some more. Opening a small East Coast office is a good idea. I'd run it, and my dad would run the winery in California, once he's back from England. I'd have to travel a little, but so what?"

I fell forward onto the bed, burying my face in pillows that were warm with his heat. "You make it sound so simple."

"It is simple." He stroked my hair. "Trust me."

"It's scary," I said. "I really want to be with you, but it's scary to start all over again."

He traced my cheekbone, his finger warm. "Take all the time you need, Angel. Really. I love you. But don't shut me out. Don't decide you would rather put it all behind you again. I can't take that a second time."

I couldn't take it a second time, either. I wanted to stand in this cold room and feel Sean touch me forever. I wanted to trust.

It was not easy for me. I was scared, and I'd been burned.

"While I'm deciding, can I get back in bed with you?" I asked. "I'm cold."

He grinned and moved the quilts aside. "We're supposed to be getting dressed. Your mom is saving waffles for us."

"They can wait." I scrambled into the bed, enjoying the warmth from his body.

He slid his arm around my back. I melted into his side, my head sinking to his shoulder. "Why do you smell so good?" I murmured.

"I don't know. I bathe?"

"Whatever you do, keep doing it."

He nuzzled my cheek. "Don't you want waffles?"

"We can go out for breakfast." I turned and wrapped my arms around him. "Right now I want you to teach me to trust you."

"And how should I go about doing that?"

I kissed the corner of his mouth. "I'm sure you'll think of something."

"Sounds good to me."

He pressed me down into the bed. I knew one thing—I liked having his warm weight on top of me. It was exciting and, at the same time, comforting.

He started kissing me, his hot mouth sliding over mine. I closed my eyes and threaded my fingers through his hair, putting my fears aside for a while.

He made love like wildfire. I lay back, letting him have his wicked way with me. When he was done, he collapsed beside me. I held him, stroking my fingers over the hard planes of his body.

I remembered how we'd done this all that long summer, not only lain together, but talked and laughed and shared hopes and dreams.

Life hadn't exactly worked out as I thought, and here he was, offering me the chance to start over again. Would I take it?

I'd left home in the first place because my mom and family had tried so hard to persuade me to stay. *Happiness is here*, they'd implied. *You don't have to fly away to find it.*

They were right, and they were wrong. I liked what I

found in New York, despite Mark, despite Penny: a life of my own making, and a job I was actually good at.

But maybe I'd been in too much of a hurry to cut the ties to this kind of happiness, too: home and family and simple joys. Could I have both? Many people implied that you could not, but lying here with Sean, I saw a glimmer of hope that perhaps I could.

I sighed. First, I had to, as my mother said, "face the music."

The best Christmas gifts are the ones that take you by surprise . . .

Sean and I took turns showering in the tiny bathroom at the bottom of the stairs; then we went downstairs together.

One ragged waffle lay in the waffle iron next to an empty batter bowl. My mother gave me a disapproving look. "I tried."

I went to her and kissed her cheek. "I know. Sean and I are going out to breakfast."

"Are you going to take him up on his offer?"

"I'll tell him when we get there."

If Sean heard, he made no indication. He picked up his leather coat, opened the door for me, and led me outside.

We crunched down the drive through a cold, clear world. Whatever rain had fallen had dried up, and our breath hung heavy in the chill air. The hills lay stark against the blue sky, marching to mountains in the distance.

I slid my hand into Sean's. He said nothing, only held my fingers tight.

We walked past the various and sundry cars. Aunt Merline and Uncle Tad were packing their car. They stopped to give me a farewell hug and kiss and shake Sean's hand and throw us knowing grins.

Sean's black SUV waited at the end of the line of vehicles, right behind my rented car. As we passed the angels, one of them headless, Cherise bounded out from behind them and planted herself in our path.

"Hey, Angel," she said. "I see you got lucky."

Today she wore a buttoned-up red leather coat, a short black leather skirt, and knee-high boots. Her cropped hair touched her cheeks, and a pretty butterfly tattoo showed at her collarbone.

Sean actually smiled at her. "I'm the one who's lucky," he said, lifting my hand for a kiss.

Cherise raised her penciled eyebrows. "Did she say yes?"

"Not yet, but I'm working on it."

Cherise smirked. "I know what that means." She gave me a sly glance. "So, Angel, did you like what I got you for Christmas?"

Sean looked puzzled. "She never opened it." He turned to me. "Did you?"

I started to tell Cherise what she could do with her useless Christmas gifts, but something about the way she smiled struck me.

"Sean," I said, untwining my hand from his. "Will you give me a minute?"

"Sure." He didn't know what was going on, but he was fine with leaving Cherise behind. "I'll warm up the truck."

He kissed my cheek, his soft coat brushing my chin, then he turned and walked away. "See ya, Cherise."

"Anytime," Cherise said brightly. She waved.

We watched Sean unlock the door of his SUV, swing himself into the driver's seat, and crank the engine to life.

I swung on Cherise. "What do you mean, what you got me for Christmas?"

Cherise tried to look innocent. "Well, I know you don't

like the vibrators. Considering how uptight you usually are, I bet you never use them."

"Never mind about the stupid vibrators. Tell me what you meant."

"I meant that I got you something else." She glanced at Sean, who had leaned over to look for something in the glove compartment. "Do you like it?"

Lights swam before my eyes. "Wait a minute. Don't try to tell me you brought Sean here for me. You've been chasing him around like a maniac this whole time."

She touched her finger to the side of her mouth. "Worked, didn't it?"

I stared. "I don't understand you."

"You were always a slow learner. When I met Sean in Oakland, he found out my last name was Sullivan, and he asked if I knew you. He had such a forlorn puppy dog look on his face."

"Wait," I said. "You told me he hadn't talked about me."

She gave me a weary look. "I lied. He told me he'd met you in L.A., but knew you were from up here in wine country. He got this sweet smile on his face when he talked about what a great summer you'd had together. I was surprised you'd kept your relationship a secret from us, especially when the guy seemed so cute and into you. Later, I heard from your mom that you were coming home for Christmas this year. So I called up Sean's friend and arranged for him to send Sean down the wrong road. And here he is."

I listened, openmouthed. "But you wanted him for yourself."

"Nah. He's too tame for me. He doesn't even have any tattoos; can you believe that? I knew he'd be perfect for you. You're both a little uptight, but you look so adorable together. I followed him around so he'd get sick of me and run to you."

She smiled, mentally patting herself on the back for being so clever.

I cleared my dry throat. "I still think you're making this up. Why not simply invite him? Why the goose chase and getting him lost?"

Cherise rolled her eyes. "Oh, please. If I'd invited him, would you have had anything to do with him? He probably wouldn't have come, anyway, if I hadn't tricked him. You'd have turned your back and ignored him, and you know it. But I made you a little bit jealous, and nature took its course." Her mouth curved. "I think it's sweet."

I growled. "I think it's the most interfering, underhanded, low-down trick you could have ever played on me."

"Oh, yeah?"

"Yeah—" I broke off. I looked over at the SUV, which sent white exhaust into the cold, dry air. Sean wasn't looking at me. He had spread a map across his steering wheel and was studying it, head bent. I gazed at the curve of his face, his blunt, bare fingers, and his dark hair, still a little mussed from the shower.

I could look at him every day for the rest of my life if I wanted to. All courtesy of my crazy cousin Cherise.

He was gorgeous, he understood my life, and he loved me.

Indignation died on my lips. I thought over the past forty-eight hours—how Cherise had suggested the stupid apple game, how Sean had appeared out of nowhere, how Cherise had leered at him until I'd been ready to strangle her, how she'd hunted him and driven him to hide in my bedroom.

She really was crazy.

I wondered if my mother knew what Cherise had been up to. I wouldn't put it past Mom to have guessed, or even to have conspired with Cherise.

I wanted to groan. Sean and I were a pair of idiots, and they had played us.

But you know, maybe that was what it took.

I looked at Cherise, who smiled at me just as she'd smiled at me when we were both ten and she'd told me that a boy who was eleven wanted to kiss me.

"Why?" I asked. "Why would you do this?"

" 'Cause you're family, and I love you. Besides, you're no fun when you're all mopey."

I burst out laughing. It felt so good. I flung my arms around her and squeezed her, patchouli-scented leather and all. "You are the best cousin in the whole world."

Cherise hugged me back; then she disentangled herself from me. "I know. You go be happy, honey. I'm heading back to San Francisco and a great New Year's Eve party. I met these two guys, and they want to—"

I held up my hands. "Don't tell me. Please, don't ever tell me."

She laughed. "Merry Christmas, Angel."

She walked past me with a grin on her face, her high heels clicking, her hips swaying in her tight skirt.

"Merry Christmas, Cherise," I said.

She waved her long-fingered hand and kept walking.

I watched her go, then strolled to the SUV. Sean leaped out, throwing his map in the back. Like an old-fashioned gentleman, he opened the passenger door for me and handed me inside.

"Everything all right?" he asked as he returned to the driver's seat.

"Everything is just fine."

He gave me a puzzled look, but didn't ask. He turned the SUV around and drove silently down our rutted private drive to the main road into town.

Apple Grove was a small community that thrived on wine growing and tourism. No small town in America had as many wine bars and bed-and-breakfasts as we did. The main street was lined with a row of Victorian houses and shops preserved by artsy people who'd saved the town from its fallen-down, after-the-gold-rush decay.

Because it was the day after Christmas, the place was jumping with after-Christmas sales and people released from being cooped up with too much family for too long.

Apple Grove had a dozen wine bars, but only one breakfast restaurant other than the B-and-Bs. Sean parked in front of it, a little café that made fantastic apple babies and mile-high pancakes.

We went inside and sat across from each other in a booth. We ordered from a waitress who was friends with Great-uncle Mike; then Sean reached over and rested his hands on mine. "So, what did you and Cherise talk about?" he asked. "Furry handcuffs?"

"Not exactly."

I decided to tell him. He'd been a dupe as much as I had, and he deserved to know.

His expression turned incredulous as I told the story. Then he relaxed, becoming reflective. "You know, I thought she was being too obvious. No woman has ever chased me like that before. I mean, she was running after me waving a sprig of mistletoe. That's why I hid in your room."

"It worked out," I said.

"Yes, I'd say hiding there was one of my better ideas." He stroked his finger along the curve of my thumb. "But why should she go to all the trouble?"

"She wanted to give me a Christmas present, she said. She's always been a little strange."

"This time, I don't mind." He leaned over the table and kissed me.

I savored the kiss, warm and strong and melting. I was fully aware that I sat in the window of the café and everyone in town knew my parents and that I was giving them an eyeful. I didn't care.

Sean sat back. "I'm glad she chased me. I might not have pushed myself all the way if she hadn't given me a shove."

"Me either," I admitted.

"I wonder why we wouldn't have," he mused. "What stopped us?"

"Fear. Hurt."

"I'll concede both of those." His hands tightened on mine. "You haven't given me your answer. I'm afraid of what it will be, but I have to know. Will you marry me? Or will you shatter my heart in a million pieces, and I'll lose all will to be a human being and end up riding boxcars from one end of the country to another, trying to forget the woman who brought me low?"

"Oh, hey, no pressure."

"No." He gave me a serious look, his dark eyes watchful. "No pressure, Angel. Really. If you say no, I'll go back to my vineyard and keep on bottling grapes. I'll be a broken and empty husk of a man, but I'll be all right."

"Stop telling me I'll break your heart. You're scaring me."

"Sorry. I'm teasing. I do that when I'm nervous."

"I'm the one who's nervous." I swallowed. "What's to say you won't run off with my best friend?"

"I don't know your best friend. And anyway, didn't she already run off with your last boyfriend?"

I grimaced. "Don't remind me."

He squeezed my fingers. "I'm not a jerk, Angel. I don't know how to prove that I'm not. But I will prove it—every day if I have to. The last thing in the world I want to do is hurt you."

"I don't want to hurt you either."

He withdrew his hands and gripped the edge of the table. "I hear a 'but.' That's never good."

I shook my head. "No buts. I ran away from you because I didn't know what I wanted. I thought I wanted complete independence from my family. Then I thought I wanted a man who'd look good on my résumé. Well, complete independence can be lonely. I shut my family out because . . . well, because they always try to smother me—but they're good people. Even Great-uncle Mike. He wants someone to think him important, even if it's only Sheriff Hanks." I touched Sean's fingers. "There was so much love in that house these last few days, you could taste it. I think it rubbed off on us."

"In a good way." He winked.

"I know." I thought of how he'd made love to me this morning, and I shivered. "I ran away from them, and I ran away from you because I was afraid of what I felt. Independence to me didn't mean making it on my own or having a good career; it meant not feeling anything. So now I have a good career and decent money, but I want more. I want to feel again."

He watched me. "Is this all working around to your running off to a colony of boy toys with Cherise?"

I laughed. "No, this is working around to asking you to go to New York with me. To shack up. To get married if that's what you want."

His body relaxed, and his eyes took on a sparkle that sent excitement through me. "Yes, that's pretty much what I want."

"Then I guess my answer is yes."

I expected Sean to give me a sexy look and a kiss, but instead, he whooped and threw his hands up in the air. "She said yes!" he screamed.

The entire restaurant heard him. Heads turned; conversations halted. The waitress, marching toward us with a huge tray of waffles and pancakes, set it down and started clapping. The rest of the breakfasters spontaneously picked up the applause and began cheering. Sean stood up and took a bow. I buried my face in my hands.

He slid into the booth beside me and put his arms around me. His strength enfolded me. "Angel, you make me so happy."

I kissed him. "You make me happy too."

"All right," said the waitress, thunking down plates. "That's the blueberry pancakes for the handsome man, and the short stack for the Christmas Angel."

She slid the pancakes, already oozing syrup, before us. "And one giant cinnamon roll, on the house." She set down a dinner plate–sized roll glistening with butter and cinnamon and dripping with white icing.

My eyes widened. "I'll never be able to eat that."

Sean grinned. "We'll take it to the kids."

The waitress winked. "Congratulations, Angel. So how's your great-uncle Mike? Still cute?"

She was about the same age as Great-uncle Mike, robust, and eager-eyed.

I nodded. "Still cute. Ask him about his furry handcuffs."

The waitress's eyes went wide; then she chuckled. "That I will," she said, and sashayed away.

"Love is in the air," Sean said.

"Yes."

He kissed my cheek. "So what does your book say about a single girl meeting someone at Christmas?"

I smiled, put my hands on his shoulders, and gave him a long, hot kiss. "It says, 'Go for it, honey.'"

O Little Town
of Kettlebean

by

NAOMI NEALE

Chapter One

His was the voice that had thrilled three generations of theater patrons. The silky tones of his youthful Romeo had made thousands of maiden hearts flutter, and the Cyrano of his middle age had evoked countless tears. His mature Lear had riveted audiences to their seats a decade ago. It was in that last award-winning lion's roar that Harrison Carew, Broadway's living treasure, now uttered his declaration. "'At Christmas,'" he boomed, every syllable atremble, "'I no more desire a rose than wish a snow in May's new-fangled mirth.'" His hand raised up to the heavens, and his famed instrument dropped to a whisper. "'But like of each thing that in season grows.'"

The speech would have been more convincing had he not punctuated it with a belch raspy enough to peel paint. Trust me. It was ripe. "Verrrrrry nice," I drawled, not amused by the widening eyes of the two mechanics listening to our star's little road show. Capping the pen I'd used to scrawl a postcard to my old college roommate—*Beautiful Kettlebean, New York!*—I glanced over the counter. "Angel, tell him to put a sock in it, would you?"

Our wardrobe master sat in a folding chair near our van's open back doors, one leg crossed over the other as he peered through a pair of reading glasses, intent upon the tiny stitches he was making despite the garage's poor and distant overhead light. For a moment I thought he was ignoring me. Finally, his voice sounding as weary as mine, he said something I couldn't quite hear. "What was that?" I asked.

Angel DeCasseres was not a small man. His six-foot-four frame was covered in layers of dark-skinned muscle; with his shaved head and thick, glowering eyebrows, he resembled an angry professional wrestler, or nightclub bouncer, or someone you might not want to run into from *The Matrix*. With a needle in his hand, however, and when he spoke in his softest tones, he was no more threatening than Hello Kitty dressed as a sumo wrestler. "I said," he repeated with infinite patience, pausing to nip off a length of thread with his front teeth, "what's the point?"

"Shakespeare!" declaimed our star. *"Love's Labours Lost."* He expelled another blast of pent-up intestinal distress. This time, however, it didn't come from his mouth. The sickening explosion ended with a wet mini-coda that nearly made my stomach flip. Men passing gas wasn't exactly a shrouded mystery to me. After all, I'd grown up with four older brothers and had endured a thousand games of pull-my-finger when they passed through adolescence. A girl has limits, however. My new job title was less than three weeks old. I badly wanted my first Broadway show as a full-fledged stage manager to succeed, but I'd be damned before I changed the star's soiled boxers.

"Angel?" I'd hoped my unspoken question, complete with raised schoolmarm eyebrows, might guilt him into action—that'd he'd leap to his feet and do something about the stinking mess of vapors and fluids and BO that had been occupying an air mattress on the van's floor for the last three and a half hours.

The wardrobe master regarded me over his half-moon

spectacles, tightening a stitch. "Yes, Riley?" He didn't want to be here any more than I.

"Hey!" The older of the two mechanics stopped by the van's rear doors. He was trying to wipe his hands on a rag that seemed more old oil than actual cloth, seemingly unaware he was fighting a losing battle. I guessed that he was the senior Mendez of the MENDEZ & SON logo painted on the side of the tow truck. He shook a grubby forefinger at Harrison's supine form. "I know him!"

"Here we go," Angel mumbled, returning to his seam.

"I know him!" Mr. Mendez sported a thick gray handlebar of a mustache that quivered like a cat's whiskers when he leaned in further, probably sensitive to the stink. "Leo!" he called to the mechanic I'd been eyeballing every chance I got, who had been investigating whatever mechanical horrors lurked under the ancient vehicle's hood. "Leo! You know this guy! Come look!"

"Dad?" When Leo Mendez stepped around the van, I couldn't help but compare him with his father. In profile, their noses protruded in exactly the same way, sharp as a drafting triangle, but somehow not at all displeasing to the eye. They had the same bow-shaped lips, the same paintbrush slashes of eyebrows. They even wore identical dark blue coveralls. Yet where MENDEZ was short and bulgy in figure, & SON was tall and bulged in the right places. Judging by the curly ends that stuck out from under the woolen cap Leo still wore, his hair was dark and long. His father's brush cut had long ago gone white. Better, the cloth on which the younger Mendez wiped his long fingers was actually stain-free. "I could use a little actual help?"

I needed to stop ogling the guy. Mechanics went for long-legged girls on pinup calendars, right? Not a short, sensible girl like me, with what I liked to think of as a swimmer's build and my plain brown hair in a braid. The apologetic smiles he cast in my direction made me shiver. Not that they were Hannibal Lecter, fava beans-and-Chianti leers, by any means. Any woman with an ounce of good taste would have appreciated that Colgate-quality, gleaming array of teeth. No, I shivered at the memory of the first time I'd seen that smile an hour before, when out in the middle of nowhere Leo Mendez had pulled up to our broken-down van in that battered old tow truck, rolled down his window, and said, "You look like you're in trouble."

He hadn't known the half of it. If we didn't get back to the city . . . Well, that wasn't going to happen. If I had to throw Harrison Carew's stinking carcass over my shoulders and walk to Manhattan, I'd do it.

Mr. Mendez snapped his fingers several times in a row, trying to dislodge the association stuck in his brain. "You know this guy! He was on TV." *Oh, no.* This conversation was heading nowhere good. "He was on that show. You know, that show we watched."

Uh-oh. Mr. Mendez was walking on delicate territory here. So long as he stuck to one of Harrison's past guest appearances on the classier nighttime dramas like *Hill Street Blues,* or his recurring character on *Frasier,* we'd be okay. If he was one of the ten people nationwide who'd seen one of the two episodes of the sticky-sweet and swiftly canceled Fox sitcom Harrison had made after winning his Tony, playing the uptight (and vaguely English) single grandfather to three wild (and thoroughly Californian) preteens . . . well, that might prove a little trickier. Harrison was still touchy about that particular project. The younger Mendez, in the meantime, was shaking his head. "What show?"

"You know! Oh, I got it. I got it now!" While I stared at him from behind the counter and, while Angel watched him over his mending, Mendez Senior stepped back and held his arms open wide, then said in hammy British vowels derived more from *Are You Being Served?* than *Masterpiece Theatre,* "Why, suh! It's a meat poy as big as yer 'ead!"

Oh, hell. He hadn't resurrected the Michaelson's Heat-'n'-Eat Meat Pies butler! I barely remembered the ads, myself— they'd been in heavy rotation during my college years, when I had holed myself up in the theater department's scene shop, much to the detriment of my other classes—but they'd all been the same. A pair of different doofuses, sometimes football players, sometimes elderly women, sometimes construction workers, would be debating exactly how big their microwaveable meat pies were. Then, magically, Harrison Carew, as a splendidly attired butler, would appear to deliver the punch line.

When the cast of *Square Root* had moved out of their rehearsal space and onto the stage of the Claibe Richardson Theater a week and a half ago, word on our set was that the Michaelson's commercials had marked the beginning of Harrison's decline. He'd reputedly been living on the residuals ever since. Our director, Grant Foster, had forbidden anyone to mention them or, God forbid, utter the tagline in the presence of our star. None of us connected with the show wanted anything to interfere with what was probably Harrison's last shot at a comeback. Though tempting, meat-pie jokes weren't worth the risk when our employment and reputations hung on the line.

At the sound of arguably his most widely witnessed performance, our fading star lurched upright. When Angel and I had snatched him, commando-style, from a lakeside love nest earlier, he'd been wearing only a robe. It fell open, exposing more leathery skin and colorless chest hair than a girl really needed to see in a lifetime. "Meat pie!" he sputtered. Wait a second. Was that a *woman's* robe? Somehow, in our SWAT-team kidnapping, neither Angel nor I had noticed we'd hustled the guy from bed wearing a woman's terry cloth robe with pink piping and our producer's wife's name embroidered on the pocket: DANI. I quickly made a mental note to make sure we burned that damning piece of evidence once we got back to the city. Meanwhile, Harrison was working himself into a dignified outrage. As dignified as one could be, anyway, clutching a bathrobe several sizes too small to one's chest. "Meat . . . !"

His eyes rolled back in his head. Then, with a thud, he fell straight back onto the mattress. I think we all winced at how close he came to cracking his skull open, me most of all. I hated other people's injuries; I always had. The sight of someone with a cut finger reduced me to a puddle. When someone in the scene shop had an accident with a tool or— I winced merely thinking about it—a nail gun, I was reduced to such sympathetic agonies that when the first-aid kit came out, the rescuers inevitably ran to me instead of the real victim. I cringed and covered my head with my hands, opening my eyes only when I didn't hear anyone screaming for me to call 911. Both of the mechanics, shaking their heads, had returned to the van's innards around front. "What was that?" I asked Angel. "Is he dead? He can't be dead. Please tell me he's not dead."

"Riley, haven't you ever seen anyone drunk before?" Angel wanted to know. He didn't even look up from his sewing.

"Of course I have." He raised an eyebrow, clearly doubting me. "I've seen people drink!"

"Have you?" Whenever Angel used this particular tone, it sounded like a reprimand. "How many shows have we worked on together?" I conceded it was a few. "And how many of the cast parties have you attended?"

I pretended the question was irrelevant. "I'm not the innocent you think." Nor was I a good actor. I'd barely squeaked through the required classes in school. I left that particular craft to the hams and the attention hogs; my particular talents were better suited for behind the scenes. It was plain that Angel wasn't buying what I wanted to sell.

So maybe I'd never seen anyone really drunk before. There were better things to do with my life. Right? Like work? And getting my career in order? Well, those were the same thing, really. Instead of drinking, I'd been keeping the theater in running condition. If I hadn't been on top of that, I would never have redeemed years of obscurity as assistant stage manager by becoming the youngest full stage manager the Claibe Richardson Theater had seen. Admittedly, there'd been only three full-time people in that position since the Thirty-ninth Street venue had been renovated from the former porno palace it used to be, but it was still an accomplishment. *My* accomplishment.

But I'd seen stuff! For years I'd known all the transvestite hookers that hung out behind the theater. That was stuff! So were all the cast and crew affairs I pretended not to notice, married or single. With a few of the actors there'd been drugs I hadn't seen but was sure were on their persons. For the love of Pete, I'd spent the last eight of my twenty-nine years working in the *theater*, not a convent! Day after day I'd seen people steal ideas and claim them for their own. I'd seen bad actors upstage and sabotage good ones, and watched meek, shy little mice turn into the biggest backstabbers and gossips the minute the curtain fell.

During a show, the theater is like any of the planets or moons circling the sun—there's a side where the actors and the costumes and sets bask in bright light, while the rest of the world and the backstage people like me sit in darkness. Those of us in the dark half of our little world see everything.

"There's no way you can call me sheltered." If I could have stepped out from behind that counter, I would have, but Angel and his sewing kit had me quite literally by the seat of my pants. My overalls had met an untimely fate during the long wait by the side of the road when my bladder overfilled and I'd squatted down in a ditch to do what had to be done. Barbed wire. Who knew? I kept my voice down to the growl that had gotten a lot of use since my promotion earlier that month. "And you know what? Now that I've spent an entire Friday driving over three hundred miles from midtown Manhattan to the farthest reaches of upstate New York's Wayne County in a blinding snowstorm, because of our director's nervous breakdown after getting a drunken long-distance phone call from Harrison saying he was going to miss rehearsal—and not just any rehearsal, mind you, but the final rehearsal before the preview that begins the day after Christmas—so we could yank our star out of the producer's bed he was sharing with several bottles of the producer's Jack Daniel's and the producer's trophy wife—*Dani*, for chrissakes!—only to end up stranded without my pants somewhere off the 104 in the director's broken-down van, never, *never* again suggest I'm sheltered, okay?"

My bluff didn't work. Angel was one and a half times older than I, and had seen more of the dark side of our little moon. "All I'm saying is that you could come to one or two crew parties now and again."

"Ma'am?" Angel and I had been so busy exchanging glares that for a moment Leo Mendez's voice didn't register. Then, with what felt like a stomach suddenly weighted with concrete, I realized he was talking to me. "Ma'am?" he repeated. I could only stare. I know, I know, I *know* that these days *ma'am* is a generic kind of address for any female adult, and that its use is not deliberately intended to imply that I'm a shriveled-up old hag with liver spots, support hose for my varicose veins, and a blue rinse. But still, I was too young to be a *ma'am*, especially when the person ma'aming me was my own age! I'd warmed up a few minutes before, but that single word was enough to do what three solid hours stranded by the side of the road earlier, while snow inched up around us, hadn't: completely and utterly freeze my brain. When I didn't respond right away, the mechanic cleared his throat, raised his eyebrows, and said, "We can discuss your problem if you'd like."

He was clearly waiting for me to follow him, and for a brief, thoughtless moment, I nearly did. "I-I can't," I stammered at the last moment. "I don't have any clothes on. Well, pants." I still wore my mock turtleneck, fortunately.

"Oh." I couldn't really blame him when his eyes flickered down to the general vicinity of my thong. Hundreds of thousands of years of hunting for shelter from impending glaciers and searching for technological innovations and trying to figure out Page Six blind items in the *Post* has left the human brain naturally inquisitive, so when a girl announces she's pantless, a man's first reaction is not, *Well, gee, I'd better not look!*, but instead, *Oh, yeah? Lemme see.* It's not as if he could catch a glimpse of anything, anyway, with a counter concealing my lower half. "Okay," he said slowly, studiously looking at the garage's ceiling, once he'd remembered his manners. "How much do you know about auto mechanics?"

"Quick answer? Not a thing." Leo Mendez had the kind of face that most people would call *amiable*—apple-round cheekbones to anchor his broad smile, chocolate-brown eyes, light brown skin speckled with a day's growth of stubble. I wanted to step from behind the counter to talk to him, but my natural modesty prevented me. A thong is not the most practical underwear for abducting Tony Award–winning icons of the stage, but I'd expected to spend my day running over the cue list, not driving to Boofoo, Egypt, and back again. For a moment I was actually tempted to pretend nothing was wrong with walking around and letting my cheeks swing wild and free, but my middle-class, Episcopal upbringing gave me pause. "Is it that bad? On a scale of one to ten . . . ?" He winced. That couldn't be good. I tried another tack. "Okay, if you were a surgeon, would this be, like, a tonsillectomy with ice cream after? Or an emergency appendectomy? Or . . . ?"

"If I were a mortician, I'd recommend cremation," he said without breaking stride. When I cracked a grin at what I thought was his little joke, he shook his head. "No, seriously. We have a technical term for this particular type of car that you might have heard: *piece of crap?*"

Back home, I would've muttered obscenities. Everyone backstage had heard me swear at some point. I didn't want to compound the PR damage our star had already done, though, so I kept it to a quiet, "Damn." At that moment, Angel finally rose from the folding chair and held out my mended overalls. I grabbed them and immediately began to stuff my feet through the legs. "How long is it going to take? An hour?"

His laughter caught me off guard. When I stumbled out

from behind the counter, sneakers in hand, he looked back over his shoulder as he ambled over to the van. "If you want to fix this up for the long term . . . well, I think we'd have a better chance of fixing up the hillbillies' truck in *The Grapes of Wrath*." A Steinbeck reference, out here in the middle of nowhere? Ordinarily my heart might have thumped a little at the recognition of a kindred spirit, but I was too busy scowling at the grimy van. "If you're only after getting back to Manhattan, we can probably get by with replacing the fuel pump that left you stranded. We don't have a replacement in stock for this old a van, though. I'm going to have to drive to Newark tomorrow to get one."

"Newark, *New Jersey?*" I nearly shrieked, hauling up my shoulder straps. What irony that would have been, soiling my pants literally the moment I put them on. "Wait a minute." Once my sphincter kicked in, I came up with a clever idea. "That could work. You could drop us off in the city in your tow truck on your way."

Lady Luck wasn't on my side that evening. Apparently she'd taken one look at me and fled. "Newark, New York," he said, wearing the look of a businessman who knew he shouldn't laugh at the customer, but could barely help himself. Behind a closed fist, he pretended to clear his throat. "It's about thirty minutes down 88."

Mr. Mendez, still moving grease around on his fingers with the dirty rag, peeked around the car. "Looks like you folks will have to sit tight for tonight until we can get the parts tomorrow. Anyway, you don't want to be driving in weather like this, do you? We're supposed to get another half foot or more of the white stuff overnight."

"Is there a car rental place in town?" They shook their heads. "A train? Anything?"

"There's a train station," said Mr. Mendez. My heart leaped at the sound of that sweet, sweet news. "But you'd still have to stay the night, since the only city-bound train passes through in the morning."

My distress must have been evident in the way that my

jaw hung slack and my lungs produced nothing but word-less whimpers. "Don't worry about the train. When we get the part, you'll be back on the road tomorrow," the younger Mendez assured me. Whatever amusement he'd felt over my geographical ignorance a moment before had vanished. My sheer panic was obvious enough to arouse the chival-rous instinct residing beneath the surface of his dirty blue uniform. "Do you need some water? Are you okay? Do you need to sit down? Dad, get Ms. McIntyre a chair."

Angel was already leaping up to offer me his seat, but I waved him away. I merely needed air. Big gulps of it. And an oxygen mask. "Listen," I told Leo. "This is vital. We have *got* to get back—"

"Are all of you show folk?" the senior Mendez wanted to know. "Are you two famous actors, too?"

"*No!*" Angel and I both protested too loudly and at the same time. "We're not actors," I continued to explain. "I'm a stage manager. Angel takes care of costumes."

"Takes amazing care of costumes," prompted the patron saint of self-promotion.

"Takes amazing care of . . ." I said automatically, before realizing what I'd done. I shot Angel a dirty look. "Mr. Carew is in a show called *Square Root* that's going into pre-views the day after Christmas. On Broadway. That's Tues-day. It's *essential* we get back there as soon as possible!"

That should have been simple enough for them. Mr. Mendez beamed from ear to ear, finished wiping his hands on his uniform, and said, "Everyone will be real excited when they find out show folk are in town, won't they, Leo? Especially when they find out it's the meat-pie guy. No of-fense to you two, but he's the famous one, right? Hey," he said, some big idea obviously occurring to him. "We're put-ting on a pageant Christmas Eve, down at the church. You folks should stay for that! You'd love it, and everybody would get a kick out of seeing the meat-pie butler!"

"Dad," said the younger Mendez, face pained. He shook his head.

The suggestion flustered me on too many levels. "We *can't*—and he hates it when people bring up his ads. He's quite—"

"Oh, he's shy?" asked Mr. Mendez, nodding.

I started to nod along with him. Various other finishes to that sentence had occurred to me. Like, *sloshed* or *a has-been* or even *litigious. Shy* would do.

"Dad, they won't stick around for that," said Leo Mendez. "They're professionals. They don't want to see an amateur church Christmas pageant."

The younger Mendez had been so nice to us that I immediately felt bad about coming off as the big, mean Broadway bitch. "It's not that. . . ."

"Amateur! He's being modest," boomed the father. "He's made the best sets this side of Broadway!"

Leo grimaced. The poor guy was embarrassed. What was there to do for a Christmas pageant save throw some hay on the floor, put up a hitching post for the cardboard camel, and call it a day? "Is there another garage in town? Maybe they might have what you need?"

"We're it, little lady." Honestly, Mr. Mendez's voice landed like a baseball bat swung by a bodybuilder. Either that, or I was oversensitive from the headache I was developing. "Kettlebean's not that big a town, you know."

I much preferred getting my bad news from someone easier on the eyes. "You'll get the part tomorrow?" I asked the younger Mendez.

He nodded. "It'll be okay. I promise." I felt better knowing that Leo Mendez would be on the job. Ever since he'd appeared in the snowstorm that afternoon, he gave me the impression of being competent. And in my book, there weren't any better adjectives than that.

"And exactly where are we going to sleep tonight?" Angel asked from across the room. Good point. I'd rather share quarters with all the animals of the manger than the back of the van with Harrison Carew.

I appealed to the father and son. "Is there a motel in town

or something?" How much money did I have on me, anyway? And how much was available on my credit card? The ATM in my head whirred and whizzed and came up with a discouraging answer to both: not much. Angel might have more cash on him. Scratch that. He had three kids at various SUNY campuses. I was surprised he could afford clothing of his own. "Somewhere cheap?" I caught another whiff of Harrison from the back of the van, and tried not to reel away. "Somewhere with showers?"

Father and son exchanged glances. "There's the Ontario Motor Lodge," said the elder.

"It closed three years ago," said the younger.

"I was going to say that. But there's the Kettlebean Inn. It's a little bit older—dates back to the days this used to be more of a fishing town. You fish?" the father asked Angel, who shook his head. "There's ice fishing. You ever been ice fishing?" When Angel stared at him the way he might at a raving madman, Mr. Mendez clucked. "Nothing like ice fishing. Six-pack, sports on the radio, out on the lake, hoping you don't crash through. It's beautiful. You should go tomorrow."

Tomorrow was when they'd better goddamn well be working on that van; that's what tomorrow had better be, I thought. Leo was shaking his head at his father, letting him know that he was being a little too garrulous. "Mamie's gone to Boca Raton to visit her son, remember? So the inn's closed."

My headache was intensifying by the second. Not much in the way of funds. No wheels. No place to stay in this godforsaken town. Harrison Carew all to ourselves. What in the world could make this day worse? "Hey, now," said Mr. Mendez, his hands on his hips. "Why don't you folks stay with me and the missus for the night?"

Oh, yes. That would do the job nicely.

"Dad."

"Leo, you don't live with your mama and papa anymore. We can give the men your old room with the bunk beds, and Ms. McIntyre here can sleep in Dora's room; Dora can stay with Nick for a night. Easy! You'll be our guests! Don't listen to Leo. My kids are always criticizing everything I do! 'Dad, you're too friendly; Dad, you're too trusting; Dad, your clothes look awful.'" I glanced down at the Cirque du Grease on his uniform and tried to figure out where they got that one. "But it's Christmas, you look like good folk, and how many times do we have the meat—Sorry." His voice dropped to a whisper. "How many times do we get the meat-pie butler in Kettlebean?"

"Dad." Leo Mendez shook his head.

His father ignored him. "C'mon. What do you say?"

I looked at Angel. Angel looked at me over his spectacles, eyebrows raised. I took a deep breath, sighed, and tried to spread a smile across my face. After all, if we were Mr. Mendez's guests, he wouldn't charge us, right? We might even get a doughnut or two out of it in the morning. What did I say? "Sure," was what I said. "We'd like that very much."

Leo was still shaking his head when he led me in the direction of the open hood. "Hey, mister," I heard the elder Mendez say to Angel from the back of van. "Did you guys fall into a snowdrift? Your buddy's pants are all wet." I closed my eyes and sighed, wishing that of all the days in my career, I'd made this the first in my eight full years of work that I'd called in sick. Being reliable got a girl into too much trouble. "Oh. That's not snow, is it now?"

I closed my eyes and winced hard. Why was it that I'd wanted to go into the theater, again?

Chapter Two

When I was twelve—hard to believe that was a whopping seventeen years ago, but time flies when you're working six days a week, fifty-one weeks a year—my parents took me to see *The Nutcracker* at the New York City Ballet. It's one of those Christmastime traditions that's inevitable among the middle class; a fate that, much like one's first period, is utterly unavoidable and not much more pleasant. With my jaw set, I sat in the hard seats of Lincoln Center and watched in utter disbelief while sugarplum fairies and delicate flowers minced their way across the boards. And those were just the male dancers! By the time I'd been inundated with marzipan shepherdesses and dancing candy canes, I was slumped down in my seat between my poor parents, resenting every moment spent away from my then-current obsession. Which, to my eternal shame, had been New Kids on the Block.

Afterward, though, when we stopped off in the gift shop to buy a program to commemorate that endless Sunday afternoon, I wandered off to a quiet corner away from the crowd and found myself entranced by the most breathtaking, beautiful, and captivating object I'd ever seen in my life:

241

a miniature three-dimensional theater made out of cardboard. Its proscenium was printed to resemble an old Victorian stage, with actual working teasers and tormentors that could be adjusted to frame the interchangeable sets at the back. There were little figures from *The Nutcracker* that could be perched within, but I couldn't have cared less about those. I knew at that moment I wanted to spend the rest of my life in that miniature little world.

When my parents wouldn't buy me the glorious little toy theater, and since I'd spent all my allowance on oversize posters of Jordan Knight, I decided to make my own. So with some balsa wood I'd appropriated from my older brothers' hobby bench, I tried to fashion my own miniature stages. The first few fell to bits like houses of cards, but I was a determined little girl. The more library books I borrowed to copy from, and the finer the paintbrushes I snitched from my brothers, the more passable my diminutive little worlds became. In my later teen years, I'd cadged show tickets from my relatives for my birthday or Christmas—*The Magic Flute, Cats, The Phantom of the Opera, Rent*—and then I'd run home and try to re-create what I'd seen. I loved those long afternoons in the quiet of my room, door shut, humming to myself. It was my own peaceful, secret place, a private acre away from my parents and noisy brothers. I wandered that acre dreaming of the day I'd graduate from my toy theaters to the glamorous world of the real Broadway stage, with all its excitement and fascination and glamour.

I'd never once imagined that part of the glamour would include sitting at a kitchen table in a robe and slippers belonging to the dead mother of my hostess, while her family stared at me like I was some traveling exhibit at the zoo. Elena Mendez, a round woman with a cheerful face that after twenty-odd years of marriage had grown to resemble her husband's, minus the mustache, beamed across the table. "So good to see that robe get some use," she said for what had to be the fourth time. "I bought it for my mother's birthday, but she passed before she could open it. Eighty-two, she would have been." She closed her eyes in an impromptu prayer for a moment, then said brightly, "You can keep it if you want."

"Oh, I couldn't!" Mrs. Mendez was a kind woman. She had to be, didn't she, to shelter without warning three strangers who showed up at her back door at ten o'clock at night, and then to offer them clothing as well? But I honestly couldn't. For one thing, Grandmother Mendez must have been one enormous dame, because I could have fit three of my slim frames inside the voluminous folds of cloth and still had enough left over to make curtains. When I walked, the hem swept the ground like some kind of Elizabethan court train.

Again we fell into one of those awkward silences. I felt awkward, anyway; Angel sat across the table sipping at his coffee with one leg crossed over the other and his spectacles perched at the tip of his nose while he scrutinized the paper. Mrs. Mendez blinked, worked her lips into a potential question, thought the better of it, and smiled. Meanwhile, fourteen year-old Dora, who had spent the previous ten minutes stirring Frosted Flakes around a bowl until they'd dissolved into mush, rested her head on her hand and stared at anything that wasn't her mother or her two guests. I'd been fourteen once. I didn't like it much. Dora didn't seem to, either. I cleared my throat. "Thank you for letting me use your bed last night!" I tried to sound enthusiastic. For all the response I got, I could've been the Invisible Man's more invisible sister. "You've got a great collection of *Little House* books," I ventured. I was rewarded with a large and exaggerated roll of the girl's eyes.

"Dora? She loves to read." Mrs. Mendez seemed grateful for any tidbit of conversation.

Dora stared at her mother with the same insolence I imagined Lizzie Borden graced her parents with right before she gave up her amateur standing in ax-grinding and went pro. "Not *baby* books." Ah, adolescence. I remembered it well. Between the mood swings, the zits, the massive amount of hormones, and the even more massive amount of self-doubt, it was such an enchanting time for everyone involved.

"What do you read, then?" I asked, trying to sound like I wasn't twice her age. I wasn't the girl's mother, though. She didn't have to respond to me. Dora picked up her spoon and let the frosted mucilage drip from her spoon, obviously trying to pretend I wasn't there.

Oookay. I knew when to leave well enough alone. Somewhere between "gosh, your daughter's a charmer" irony and "sorry you've got four to ten more years of this ahead of you" sympathy I managed to pluck a facial expression that I hoped conveyed to my hostess, "I'm sure she's an absolute sweetheart." It must have worked, because Mrs. Mendez pulled her lips to their widest and once again studied the bottom of her coffee cup, while silence fell over the room.

Angel appeared oblivious to my desperate attention in his direction. He flipped the paper over to study the Wayne County obituaries page. Was I really one of those people who couldn't take a little bit of awkward silence? Apparently so. I was used to being onstage, headset in my ear, while people barked instructions at me, or spending my time working with all the various professionals butting heads over how a show should be put together. My ears were accustomed to the yells and shouts of Manhattan at all hours of the day. Even when I was home alone in my cramped little Chelsea walk-up, I played the radio or TV to drown out the little sounds that so easily made me feel like a future assault victim who probably had some binocular-pointing stalker from the high-rise opposite, simply because I hadn't had time in four years to buy or make a pair of curtains. "You have a lovely home," I ventured, for the sake of some noise.

It was a white lie. With its vinyl wallpaper in lurid yet patriotic hues of red, white, and blue that depicted scenes from the Revolutionary War, its unsteady kitchen table with plastic wood grain laminate, its harvest-gold appliances, and its ancient linoleum stamped to resemble some sort of

Pompeiian tessellate with glitter in the cracks, the kitchen looked like something my half-blind grandfather might have designed by sticking a pin at random in the pages of a Sears Roebuck home-design Sunday supplement, circa 1978. I'd seen the living room only briefly, on the way in the night before, but my impression had been of enormous hanging lamps, white furniture, and a hundred glass figurines purchased from whatever circle of hell in which eBay ran its Web servers. Beggars, however, couldn't be choosers, and Angel and I were practically sitting by the on-ramp to the expressway, cups in one hand, WILL WORK FOR FOOD signs in the other.

I was about to say something inane about the snow that hadn't quit falling all night when from the stairwell we heard the sound of footsteps. "That'll be Nicolas," said Mrs. Mendez, at last sitting up straight. She looked almost relieved. "You haven't met him yet. He's our darling baby boy."

I grimaced. Oh, but I had met the younger Mendez boy less than an hour before. And not under the best of circumstances, either. I clutched my robe and prayed that the subject didn't come up. Even Angel had finally torn his attention away from the newspaper at the sound. "Oh," said the cereal mixer, suddenly coming to life. "*He's* your darling. *I* see."

"Dora!" Mrs. Mendez's voice was full of reproach. "I love all my babies the sa—"

"What*ever*." Despite the dismissal, Dora was obviously a grudge-hound on a hot scent, and she intended to follow it to the source. "*I'm* the youngest, but *he's* your baby."

"Dora!"

"Whatever!"

Mrs. Mendez gave the two of us a panicky sideways glance. "Why don't you eat your cereal and we can talk about this later?" The words *when these weird theater people aren't around* were left plainly hanging in the air. Before her daughter could offer another *whatever* as benediction, Mrs. Mendez rose from her seat and held out her hands to the boy slumping into the kitchen. "Nick!" she said with an enthusiasm that narrowed Dora's eyes. "Baby, I want you to meet your father's guests. This is Mr. Angel. . . ."

"DeCasseres, actually," said Angel, at his most regal. He tilted his head forward to get a good look at the boy. "Pleased to meet you, young man."

Though it was all of six scanty degrees outside, Nick Mendez wore a basketball jersey that exposed arms ropy with muscle, and a pair of long matching shorts. Beneath his thick, sculpted brows, his lids were deliberately droopy— the sort of postadolescent bedroom eyes that, when I had been eighteen or nineteen like him, would have had me giving him second or third looks. His hair was as dark as his brows and even more dense; it poked out from under the edges of the do-rag he'd fashioned from an old blue bandanna. "There's some old drunk guy in Leo's bed," he announced.

Angel and I silently conferred with each other, lips compressed. Aflutter with nervous laughter, Mrs. Mendez tried to shoo her son in the direction of the cereal boxes she'd set out onto the Formica counter. "Don't be rude, Nick," she said. "I'm sure he's only sleeping!"

"Okay, whatever." Apparently the middle Mendez child had attended the same school as his sister when it came to arguing. "But I bet that fifth of bourbon he's got his hand wrapped around is better than a sleeping pill."

I mouthed one word to Angel: *Shit!* He looked as alarmed as I, shaking his head in my direction to let me know he didn't know anything about it. Where in the world had Harrison managed to find a fifth of bourbon? He hadn't . . . my eyes slid past the harvest gold refrigerator to a cabinet in the dining room, a faux-antique in high Colonial style. The glasses on its top sparkled with light reflected from the snowy landscape in the window opposite; a neat and even row of liquor bottles had been spaced out on the shelves underneath. Even, that is, save for one empty space where a bottle was obviously missing.

"You know, Mr. Carew is really . . ." I tried to search for words while my mind frantically rifled through what I'd have to do to smooth this over, once I got back to the city. Perhaps I could get Grant to spring for a gift basket for the Mendezes.

"Eccentric," Angel supplied for me. I hoped he could see the gratitude on my face. From upstairs, I heard the sound of something falling to the floor—nothing glass, luckily. "Quite eccentric."

A very large gift basket. And flowers.

Over the sneers and snarls Nick and Dora were exchanging across the table from each other, Mrs. Mendez smiled uneasily. "Eccentric. Of course." Her eyes flickered up toward the second floor. It took a moment for her to fully regain her composure, but she seemed determined to be as polite as possible. A change of topic was just the thing. "Anyway, back to our guests. Nick was working late at the church hall on the pageant last night, weren't you, sweetheart? That's why he didn't get to meet you when you came in," she explained to us as she pulled off the makeshift do-rag and smoothed her son's lank, dark hair with her fingers. I froze in my seat. A return to that particular topic wasn't at all what I'd hoped for, after the . . . *encounter*, shall we say . . . that Nick and I'd already had in the bathroom.

"Kissing up on Maria, you mean," Dora muttered to her cereal.

"Shut up!" Nick bounced in his seat at the accusation.

"You were."

"Shut up!"

"Well, you *were*."

Angel, whose own kids had already survived through adolescence, seemed happy to ignore the bickering. Mrs. Mendez sailed on through as if she didn't hear her children at each other's throats. At least it didn't seem like news to her that there was a girlfriend to be kissed up on. I don't think I could have dealt with a parental inquisition into the suitability of this . . . what was her name? Maria with a long *i*, as in what they called the wind, in the song from *Paint Your Wagon*.

"Nick, sweetheart, Mr. Angel is a costume designer. From New York City." For a moment, Angel looked prepared to contest both his name and his profession, but in the end he shut his mouth and returned to reading the scanty county newspaper. "And you haven't met Miss McIntyre, either. She's a stagehand. On Broadway!"

The *Miss* I could overlook, though sadly there was a technical truth to it. Stagehand, though? I thought not. "Stage manager, actually." I could sense Angel raising his eyebrows at my correction, but damn it, he'd been wardrobe master at one theater or another for close to two decades. I'd worked hard for my new title, and until I'd had the luxury of growing into it, I intended to protect it. "Nice to meet you, Nick," I said, trying to sound pleasant. I still couldn't look him in the eyes.

"We met." No mythical beast could have turned me to stone more swiftly than Nick's flat statement. Before I could brace myself for the impact, he added, "Upstairs. Remember?"

Was that a smirk on those peach-fuzzed little lips? I wanted to completely hide inside the folds of my robe and melt away into the ground, like the Wicked Witch after a quick pail bath. "I . . . I . . ."

"She showed him her boobs," Dora informed her mother.

Mrs. Mendez had done an admirable job so far of managing her own little one-ring circus, but upon being informed that one of her guests was some kind of son-molesting nympho, she lost a little of her composure. Nick slid down in his seat and covered his face with his hands. At least he had the slight decency to be ashamed of it! "It was an accident," I tried explaining, using a perfectly reasonable tone of voice to try to erase from my hostess's face that awful look of shock and betrayal. Were her fingers twitching because she wanted to dial 911? "Embarrassing, really. I was getting out of the shower when Nick opened the bathroom door and . . . he didn't really *see* anything."

"Yes, I did." That little perv wasn't ashamed. He was *laughing* at me behind those hands!

"You told me you didn't!" He answered me with another round of muffled sniggering.

"She *showed* him her *boobs*, Mom." Dora apparently had a bright future ahead of her as the person who drove home the last nails in coffins.

"I'm sure it was an accident?"

Mrs. Mendez seemed desperate for any kind of confirmation from me—confirmation I was only too glad to give. "Absolutely!" Treating it like a bad joke would allay her fears. "He didn't know I was in there, I'm sure. Besides, it was all so quick. He couldn't have seen much."

In an undertone, Dora added her own footnote. "That's because he said there wasn't much to see." Brother and sister both broke out into laughter. It was positively the most cheerful I'd seen Dora all morning. One of my hands protectively clawed its way across my chest, covering what I apparently lacked in the cleavage department. "Don't be showin' 'em to me!" Dora said, misinterpreting the motion. "I don't want to go all blind!"

"I'm not!"

"She took off her pants at the garage, you know," Dora said, my lashes whipping up a wild sirocco of outrage as I blinked rapidly. Dora smirked. "That's *disgusting*."

Thank goodness Mrs. Mendez seemed to think Dora was exaggerating. Still, I couldn't summon words. "I didn't . . . It wasn't . . . you're . . ." High school taunts were beneath me, I reminded myself. I shut my mouth, drew my robe tight, and rose from my seat. A dignified exit, stage right, would be best for everyone concerned at this point. I could sulk upstairs in my temporary bedroom until my overalls were out of the dryer. "Mr. Angel" could fend for himself.

A blast of cold air from the back door arrested my flight.

Although there was a screened-in porch beyond, Mr. Mendez carried enough fresh snow on his heavy winter jacket for the wind to cover the table and floor with a fine, cold spray. "What're we sitting around for?" he asked, more jovial than the Macy's Santa. "You should be down at the church hall!"

"Hector!" Mrs. M. cocked her head.

"There's rehearsal! Have you forgotten? You're playing Shepherd Number Three!" he exclaimed to his wife. "Dora's handing out props! Your own son is playing Joseph! Important roles!"

"Leo's playing Joseph?" I tried to picture the mechanic in the role and couldn't quite manage. Maybe it was that I'd always pictured the earthly father of the baby Jesus to be something of a homely nebbish who couldn't get his girl bride a room for the night, not a looker who was really handy with a pneumatic drill.

"Not Leo. Nick!" Mr. Mendez thrust out his thick fingers in his younger son's direction. Nick sank down lower in his seat and rubbed his would-be fuzzy face, embarrassed. Oh, yeah, I could picture him as Joseph. A particularly lecherous sleazeball of a Joseph who concocted the no-room-at-the-inn lie to cover up that he'd already lost his last few shekels at the ram's-knuckle craps table of a Bethlehem casino. "He's a great Joseph. Ain't ya, Nick?" When his father suddenly mussed his hair with a vigorous shake, Nick jerked his head away lazily and rolled his eyes.

"He's only doing it so he can kiss up on the Virgin Mary," Dora sneered. When Nick sat up in his seat again, she said, "Well, it's *true.*"

"Shut up!"

"Make me."

"Shut up!"

"I can't help it if you have a fat girlfriend!"

"She ain't fat!" To reply, Dora puffed out her cheeks until her face looked rotund, and held out her hands to mime an imaginary enormous waistline. She rolled around in her seat like a children's Weeble. "You're dead meat," he announced, not seeming particularly inclined to follow up on the threat with any kind of action.

"Kids!" said Hector Mendez to Angel, shaking his head. "You got any?"

"I did," said Angel, regarding our host over his half-glasses. In his dry voice, he commented, "Then I misplaced them at the airport and never did fill out that lost luggage form."

"Hah! Hah!" Mr. Mendez wheezed out a paroxysm of laughter. Once he recovered, his hand dove in for another touchdown on his son's head, which Nick avoided at the very last moment by diving to the side. It land on Nick's shoulder, instead. "Come on, *muchacho*," he said. "Maria's already down at the hall. She was asking about you. . . ."

"Fine. Whatever." Nick's sloppy posture might have been saying, *I'm only doing it because you told me to,* but the way he suddenly sprinted up the stairs, taking them three at a time, spoke volumes. He actually was sweet on this Maria girl.

"Come on, Shepherd. You've got sheep to tend! Chop-chop!" Mr. Mendez clapped his hands together. "You. Scoot," he commanded Dora, who rose from the table as if dragged down by a larger planet's gravity. She slumped upstairs, shooting me hateful expressions.

Shepherd Number Three looked a little put out. "But Hector! I thought with our guests—"

"Oh, you can all go on ahead!" I assured her. That suited me fine. Angel and I could kick back in our robes, relax for a while, stay out of the snow, clean up whatever mess Harrison had made upstairs, and then get back on the road once Leo, trusty Leo, finished with our van. "We don't mind!"

The mechanic's mustache bristled. "You're coming too."

The announcement hit me like a water balloon filled with frozen Jell-O. "No, really."

"Really!" Mr. Mendez seemed to think it a foregone conclusion. "You'll love it! It's right up your alley!"

My mind desperately searched for an out. "But my

clothes are in the dryer," I said. We could hear the metal catches of my straps hitting the tumbling drum from where we sat. At that moment, right as if I'd cued the Claibe Richardson sound guys with my own headset, we also heard the buzzer. The appliance powered down to a halt. "And Angel hasn't had a shower." That was scraping the barrel for excuses, but it was nonetheless true.

"What's he need a shower for? He's got no hair to wash!" Deprived of his son's hair to riffle, Mr. Mendez ran a palm over Angel's head.

Angel stared straight ahead, like a patient old Labrador enduring a too-enthusiastic petting from a toddler. "Thank you for noticing," he said at last, pushing his reading glasses farther up his nose.

"Plus we really should be getting to the garage," I continued, smoothly pretending none of the preceding had happened.

"Leo's not back yet," said Mr. Mendez. "I've told him that when he's done with the pump, he's to come get you at the church!" He intended this last argument as his *coup de grâce*, and beamed at us both. "Sounds like a plan, right?"

"It does to me." Angel folded the newspaper and set it on the table, letting his glasses hang on the chain around his neck. "I think the pageant sounds enchanting, particularly after all your gracious hospitality, Mr. Mendez."

"Call me Hector! We're practically family now, right? There's the Christmas spirit!" Mr. Mendez could have given a post–Zuzu's petals George Bailey a run for the money in a competition for manic cheer. He looked at me expectantly.

I knew when we were sunk. Angel's last comment had been intended primarily for my benefit, to counteract all the *buts!* filling my brain like popping corn. *But! We need to be back on the road!*, for example. Or, *But! Our show opens in three more days!* Or, *But! Grant is probably going crazy right now!* Every atom of my body wanted to be far away from this rinky-dink town as soon as possible. But . . . it wouldn't happen until Leo came back. "Yes," I said, gulping down resentiment like the bitterest of coffees and trying to sound as pleasant as possible. "For your hospitality, it's the least we could do, Hector." I saw Angel give me an approving, paternal nod.

While Mrs. Mendez stood up and began to collect dishes from the table, her husband clapped his hands together in sheer happiness. "Marvelous! Marvelous!" he practically yodeled. "You'll have fun. Perhaps you can give us a few tips, eh? Eh?" Angel smiled and nodded, laughing along with our host. I tried to, too, but mentally I was trying to map out possible timetables of how quickly we could get back to the city. "Besides, Mrs. Robinson will be there."

"Mrs. Robinson?" I asked, visions of Anne Bancroft dancing in my head.

"Oh, Mrs. Robinson will be there?" asked Mrs. Mendez, suddenly sounding anxious to go. She abandoned the dishes for later and beetled off for the bedroom. "I'll get dressed."

"Everybody loves Mrs. Robinson," promised Hector, following in his wife's wake. "I'm going to get my camera."

Finally Angel and I were alone. "I'm not trying to be ungracious," I said, jumping right to the heart of the argument we were going to have at some point anyway. "It's just coming out that way!"

"Go to the rehearsal, Riley."

"I'm going! We're going! I didn't say we weren't!" I dropped my voice to a fierce whisper, so it wouldn't be overheard. "Forgive me if I'm concerned about a show that could mean a year or more of gainful employment and steady box office receipts. Though more likely it'll turn out to be the biggest bomb since *Carrie: The Musical* if we don't get our star back home to sober up before our producer figures out something fishy's been going on right beneath his nose."

"All work and no play . . ." said Angel, singsong.

"Don't." If I had a dollar for every time someone had said that to me! I'd heard it from earnest young boys in college who didn't understand why I wouldn't go to the frat house beer busts. I'd heard it from old Roger, the stage manager before me at the Claibe, who always thought I worked too much. I'd heard it from actors who thought they could sweet-talk me into a little flirtation while I was on duty and they were lounging around waiting for cues, and from girl-friends and old roommates who didn't understand why I didn't go out and enjoy myself once in a while.

None of them understood—I did enjoy myself. I adored my work. Wasn't spending a lifetime doing what you loved what most people wanted out of a career, but never achieved? Sure, there were parts of the job that I would rather have behind me, this particular excursion being first and foremost. But among the people I knew outside the theater, I was one of the few who could crawl into bed each night and actually look forward to the next day's work. Didn't that count for something? "Don't go there," I warned Angel.

"Maybe Mrs. Robinson will cheer you up, little Riley," he teased. "Everyone loves Mrs. Robinson."

"I bet," I said darkly. "She's probably the town prostitute." At Angel's rolled eyes I riffed on. "Seriously. I bet she's got the biggest bosoms in the town and that every father takes his son to her boudoir on his sixteenth birthday to learn how to be a man. I bet she has a mole on her cheek with a hair growing from it and wears too much lipstick and mascara and too many gold chains. And smells like an ashtray. She probably has half-off coupons for ice-fishing season."

"Working yourself into a better mood, I see," said Angel, rising from his chair so that we could both go change. "That's the Riley I know."

"Darned tootin'," I caroled, standing up. "Here's to you, Mrs. Robinson, you nasty old whore!"

Chapter Three

"And this dear, sweet, beautiful girl is my newest great-granddaughter, Tallulah. My grandson says she looks like me!" Wallet-size photos lay spread across my lap, a plastic accordion documenting decades of winsome dimpled chins, excruciatingly cute smiles with missing baby teeth, and school photographs of various Robinsons near and far. Yeah, I could totally see the resemblance. I mean, the baby in the photograph had the beautiful, round bald head of a newborn, and the woman in the wheelchair wore the lined and spotted mask of immense age that represented the ultimate nightmare of my more moisturizer-conscious friends. Yet there was a certain sweetness to the curves of both their cheeks, and a definite similarity in their robin's egg-blue eyes that was absolutely undeniable. Mrs. Robinson even vaguely smelled of baby shampoo and powder.

"If you mean that you're both absolute peaches, I'm afraid, ma'am, that I must agree." Angel, sitting on the elderly woman's other side, slid the photo wallet a little closer to him. At Mrs. Robinson's delighted, wordless denial, he nodded. "Raised in the sunshine and ripened to perfection."

"Oh, you charmer!" Mrs. Robinson dabbed a hand in Angel's general direction. Her bones were so delicate, so bird-like, that the most gentle of motions had me worried that she might accidentally break something. "Isn't he charming, Beryl?"

I'd gathered that the woman in question, a practically dressed matron manning the back of the wheelchair, was one of the old woman's daughters or daughters-in-law. She pulled a bundle of wadded tissues from the top pocket of her cardigan and applied them to the area below her nostrils. "Don't wear yourself out, Mother," she warned, then explained to us, "She gets tired so easily, because of the chemo."

I tried not to wince with sympathy, because through spectacles so thick that on the woman's shrunken face they looked like oversize props from a comedy sketch, Mrs. Robinson fixed her eyes on me and graced me with a smile. "They asked me if I really wanted to go through with all those *chemicals* when I was diagnosed with leukemia last autumn, right after my cherry pie receipt won a blue ribbon in the county fair!" Not since my own late grandmother had I heard anyone use the word *receipt* for *recipe*. It made me go all gooey and soft inside, though the most I let show was a sympathetic nod.

"They didn't think she could fight it," said Beryl, dabbing at her nose again.

"Of course I plan to fight it! There's moxie in the old girl yet!" The little rallying fist that Mrs. Robinson waved in the air was so valiant that across from me, Angel immediately thrust one of his clenched hands against his mouth. Many times during affecting scenes I'd seen him do the same thing backstage. He was the one heterosexual man I'd known who'd been deeply moved by a night-off outing to *The Vagina Monologues.* "My only wish . . ."

"You're tiring," complained Beryl. "We should get you home."

"One moment more." Mrs. Robinson had enough command in her to arrest her daughter's hands on the wheelchair handles. We all leaned in a little closer to hear her weakening voice. "My only wish . . . I suppose it's selfish, really. But I'll say it. I started the tradition, and I wish I could have directed my fiftieth Christmas pageant." Her lower lip aquiver, Mrs. Robinson lifted her chin. Like falling leaves on a drowsy autumn afternoon, her hands tenderly descended upon Mrs. Mendez's own. "But it's all in good hands with your husband, dear."

I didn't have to see our hostess's face to know her eyes were wet with tears. I could hear them in her voice. "I'm sure he'll do you proud. I'm sure he'll . . ." Like Angel, her hand flew to her mouth.

For a moment our little tableau seemed like a scene from one of those Spanish-language soaps I would occasionally see as I flipped my way through the channels—the kind where everyone's wailing and beating their breasts over the deathbed of the dearly departed, though none of us were nearly as well dressed or coiffed and there wasn't a glowering, disreputable hunk in the background making eyes at the married-but-wavering heroine. Okay, save for the big sanctuary crucifix hanging at the church's front, maybe there wasn't much similarity at all. "I'm sure he will," said Mrs. Robinson. "I can't wait until Christmas Eve to see it. I think . . . I think I'm getting tired," she said to her daughter. "Maybe we should go home." Beryl nodded in agreement, and smiled briefly at the rest of us before lurching the wheelchair into a practiced circular path.

Beryl pushed the wheelchair up the red-carpeted center aisle, in the direction of the narthex. I wasn't at all surprised when the twenty-five or thirty people who'd showed up to rehearsal that snowy morning crowded down the church's center aisle to follow it. And I mean *everybody* trailed behind—even Dora and some similar-looking jaded teenagers smiled and waved good-bye to her at the door. Sometime very recently, the church had been decorated with two tall fir trees that flanked the altar area; berried wreaths with candles hung upon each of the windows. Over the scent of evergreen, I seemed to smell something fainter and sweeter—the vitality of Mrs. Robinson herself. A legacy of gumdrops and hard candies and sugar cookies reduced to an essential oil, sweet and lingering.

Mrs. Mendez clutched hard to my wrist when the old woman gave one last, fragile wave, and allowed her daughter to wheel her out. "And to think that in October she made her famous popcorn balls for the children."

"No!" said Angel, shaking his head. "You hear that, Riley?" he asked, wearing the simper of an innocent man instead of the sadistic torturer he really was. "Popcorn balls!" His arm went around my shoulder as he murmured into my ear, never losing that smile, "How's that for your nasty old whore?"

"I know, I know," I muttered back, feeling lower than the lowest for prematurely maligning Kettlebean's answer to Mother Teresa. "I'm going straight to hell, do not pass Go, do not collect two hundred dollars."

"I bet she showed Nick how to be a man, all right. Can't you picture it?" Now that Mrs. Robinson had been wheeled out, a lot of the pageant participants, their heads wrapped in white towels and belts for a biblical look straight out of Bethlehem's own Bed Bath & Beyond, were refocusing their attention on us. Angel kept his expression cheerful, as if he were whispering in my ear words of inspiration. "Her, him, a pickup truck . . ."

"Shut your trap." I tried to seem jovial, too, despite the fact that my words were being forced through more of a grimace than a grin. I mean, hell, after all those terrible things that had come out of my mouth, if I saw myself coming, I'd cross the street to get away from me.

"A twelve-pack of malt liquor . . ."

"When we get back to the city," I said, my vowels distorting around the rictus of my bared teeth, "I am going to sneak into the wardrobe room and pour an entire package of scarlet Rit dye into your washer, so that the first time you launder one of your precious costumes—"

"Damn." Angel whistled, nodding at a small group of towel-headed cast members—shepherds? people of Bethlehem?—as they walked by and greeted us. "You are *cold*."

"You all right, honey?" Mr. Mendez had come up behind his wife and stretched an arm behind her; she settled her head quite naturally on his shoulder. It was such a loving and intimate gesture that I averted my eyes. Somehow I didn't need the reminder that I hadn't allowed myself to rest my head on anyone's shoulder in a very long time. "She gets emotional."

Still relying heavily on a plastic travel pack of Kleenex to which several other community members had already helped themselves, Mrs. Mendez sniffled and dabbed away at her eyes, then checked the tissue for evidence of running mascara. "I wouldn't talk! He's an old softy himself."

"That's why you married me." Mr. Mendez gave his wife a big, big smile that could have melted snow in a good portion of the Bronx. Obviously embarrassed at all the affection he was showing her in front of strangers, Mrs. Mendez wiped away the last of her tears and playfully swatted her husband away. With a clap of his hands, he became all business again. "All right, folks! We've got professionals in the house! Let's show them what we can do!" This whole last twenty-four hours had been a nightmare of major proportions, but I could appreciate the signs of someone anxious to get down to business. "People of Bethlehem, you know where to go. Harve, you stay on stage. No, you stay . . . yes, in the chair. Cherubim and seraphim! In the balcony! Dora, you need to get to the props table." Her fingers probing her mouth in search of whatever candy she sucked on, the youngest Mendez shot her father a look of odium nearly strong enough to make me promise myself that if the time ever came when I had a teenage daughter of my own, I wanted either her or me on sedatives during the entire adolescence thing. "Let's go! And you two," he said, suddenly turning to us. "Sit in the front row!" Hector Mendez pushed us forward, then skittered to the side aisle to attend to something.

"All rightie," said Angel. I tried to resist, but he dug his fingernails into my shoulder and dragged me forward down the aisle.

"I don't want to," I growled, dimly aware that in my reluctance I didn't sound that much older than Dora.

"It's Christmastime," he said.

"Yeah, ho-ho-ho, bah, humbug, and you can deck my ass with a big, fat bough of . . . Hello again, Mr. Mendez!" I said, dropping the attitude. "What've you got there?"

My super-duper chirpy tone fit me about as well as Mary Poppins's duds on a particularly neurasthenic Woody Allen. If Mr. Mendez seemed taken aback at my transformation, at least he didn't show it. "I thought you might want to take notes during the rehearsal," he said. "You know. Anything that will help us improve. Anything." I looked down at the packets of paper he pushed into our hands, which seemed to be some kind of attendance registers he'd plucked from behind a couple of the hymnals, along with tiny pencils that looked as if they came out of my childhood game of Clue. "No matter how small. Because . . ."

"Because we're all doing this for Mrs. Robinson." From the mass of pageanteers, a middle-aged woman had detached herself and floated over. She was one of those statuesque matrons that I associated with the church of my Syosset youth, deftly ladling out scalloped potatoes in the basement for St. Bede's Episcopal Wednesday night dinners one moment, then turning around and leading the handbell choir the next. Everything about her seemed optimized for practical church duty, from the gray cropped-at-the-neck bob, to the stretchy turtleneck and sweater she'd layered herself with to ward off the sanctuary's Saturday chill, to the reading glasses on a gold-and-pearl chain, to the pocket New Testament conspicuously peeking from her cardigan pocket. "There is no *I* in *theater*."

"No, but there is a *t-h-r-e-a-t*," I commented. Her comment was the kind of vaguely inspirational platitude I'd heard often enough in my years backstage that my response came automatically popping out; I honestly hadn't meant to take her aback.

Yet the patient smile on her face made it pretty plain that I was back in sixth-grade Sunday school on Long Island, trying to explain to Mrs. Rossi that I hadn't *meant* to get paint on the picture hanging on the art room wall of Jesus showing a little boy how to steer a ship through what looked like the Galilean *Perfect Storm* in the background, but that my brush had simply slipped. Across the boy's face. In the exact form of a mustache. "*So* pleased to meet you," she said, apparently willing enough to overlook my indiscretion that she offered me a hand. "Mrs. Henry R. Andersson. You can call me Anneke. I've been asked to step in as Our Narrator." The hand I'd moments before shaken fluttered up to her sternum, denoting modesty, but at the same time, from the loving way her voice caressed the title, I could practically hear the capital letters. "Such an important role. I hope I can do it justice. For Mrs. Robinson, of course . . . that poor, sweet, dear old darling."

Angel, whose expression was so serene and constant that he could have posed for a dictionary illustration of the word *genial*, reached out his own hand. "So pleased to meet you, Mrs. Andersson. I'm—"

"Oh, no need! No need!" Our Narrator's smile was apologetic, as if sorry to make Angel bother. "We all know who *you* are, Mr. DeCasseres. And you, Ms. McIntyre. Such a great honor, truly. Though I was given to understand that you had another . . . compatriot of the stage with you?" Although she must have already stood nearly six feet tall, she elevated herself on the toes of her practical flats and looked around the room with expectation. "Mr. Carew? *Harrison* Carew?" She let the *R*s roll longingly on her tongue.

Angel and I looked at each other mutely. In the back of my mind, I'd thought the extent of our participation might be sitting in the back of the church exchanging snarky comments. We hadn't thought to prepare a story. "Uh," I began, exhibiting the same loquaciousness I'd displayed during the Jesus-painting-mustache incident.

"You see," said Angel, extemporizing.

Thank God for Mr. Mendez, who'd allowed his attention to be diverted for only a few brief seconds to attend to a question. "Mr. Carew is back at the house, sleeping." Angel and I both sighed in audible relief that he hadn't added the final two words of that sentence: *it off*.

Mrs. Andersson pouted slightly. "Such a shame. I'm a big admirer. I hoped I might get a few autographs." From the satchel slung over her shoulder, she dug out no less than five copies of *Playbill*, obviously held at the ready. I recognized the topmost from the staging of *Lear* that had netted Harrison the Tony. Another bore the logo of the production of the Kelsey Grammer *My Fair Lady*, into which Harrison stepped for a month as a favor to the star. After playing the role drunk one too many times, he'd promptly been replaced with Eric McCormack.

"Later, Anneke, later," promised Mr. Mendez, his hands on our backs as he pushed us forward. "We're rehearsing now," he reminded her.

"Oh. Yes." The *Playbill*s disappeared back into her satchel, and Mrs. Andersson drew herself back up to her full height. "Of course." As if her particular church-lady model had been built with silent wheels in her robot feet, she glided in the direction of the lectern.

"Stop looking at your watch. It's rude," Angel growled at me a moment later, after Mr. Mendez had fussed over us, given us hymnals to write on, and double-checked to see if our pencils were sharp enough. Had our host seen my sign of impatience? From where he stood over at the side, excitedly talking to a number of the company, I doubted it.

"I know." Every cell in my body protested my crabbiness. I liked thinking of myself as hardworking, good-natured Riley McIntyre, not this surly impostor who'd stepped into my overalls the previous afternoon. "What the heck's wrong with me, Angel? I'm not usually like this."

To my utter relief, my friend didn't contradict that statement. In fact, he said, "No, you're not. Maybe it's being so far away from the city, so close to the holiday. I mean, I'm anxious to get home and spend it with my own family. . . ."

"But I don't do anything special for Christmas," I told him. "I mean, I drive out to Long Island and spend the day with my parents and brothers." Which got more difficult year after year, as with every new child and mortgage and Little League team, my four brothers became more firmly entrenched in their married lives. Their families would show up in small battalions, noisy, bursting with vigor, and clamoring for attention. Then there I'd be, sitting on a stool somewhere in the background. Not forgotten, exactly, but no more in the spotlight than I would have been during a show's run. "I don't really look forward to that. I'd rather stay home with the stereo on and cook myself something nice."

"So stay home this year. Treat yourself. It's your holiday, too."

"Have you *met* my parents?" I asked wryly, knowing full well that the last time my mom had come to one of my shows, she'd cornered Angel for a full hour afterward and milked his wallet dry for donations to the various animal shelters she worked for. "Only dire illness would get me out of it."

"Call in sick."

We both looked up as, overhead, someone switched out the giant hanging lamps. Judging by the creaky floorboards, the narrow and uncomfortable pews, and the massive beams holding up the plaster, the church must have been at least a century old. "Won't work. They'll know I'm calling in single."

We had been speaking softly before, but as the sanctuary grew quieter, Angel's voice lowered to a whisper. "Believe it or not, I do have a point. If you don't chill, you're going to have a heart attack by the time you're thirty. Accept that there are things you cannot change about this situation. You can't get the mechanic back with that part by sheer will, forceful as yours might be. You cannot make him fix that van any faster."

"Not even through bribery?" I asked. "Can you put pay-offs on a Discover card?"

He glossed right over my objections. "Be wise enough to know that we are going to be stuck in Kettlebean for a few more hours. While we're here, we might as well be gracious about it."

"You sound like an AA meeting," I grumped, though I knew he was right.

"Twenty-two and a half years sober and counting, thank you very much," he murmured.

Ouch. Too conveniently, I'd forgotten that particular chunk of his past. "Sorry."

"Repay me in patience, if you truly feel the need."

I owed him. Angel had been a good friend to me over the years, and at the very least, I needed to make good my careless AA comment. "I will," I promised. "But we're not going to get involved in this whole amateur-pageant thing. Right?"

"There's a difference between being polite and getting involved. I don't want to get mired down here any more than you do, Riley."

"All right then." I raised my eyebrows to make the point. "I'll remember you said that."

Mrs. Andersson had discovered the switch on the microphone. "Ahem." The noise that she made from the lectern wasn't so much a clearing of the throat as it was the actual word *ahem* decorated with a slight cough. When I looked up from my confab, I realized she was glowering right in our direction. Amazing how a single little affectation reminded me of all the reasons I'd stopped going to church the minute I graduated from high school. "Are we ready? Yes? Well, then. Quiet, everyone." Meaning us. Angel and I settled ourselves, hymnals and pads in our laps, and simulated attentiveness. I'm not graced with much of a butt, so I knew that on the hard wooden benches, I was in for something of a long haul. "Good evening, members and guests of the First United Methodist Church of Kettlebean."

"Is this town really big enough to have another Methodist church?" I muttered. When Angel's eyes sidled over to glare at me, I sighed. "Patience. I know, I know."

Meanwhile, Mrs. Andersson wasn't so much speaking into the microphone as seemingly offering to give it a little Monica Lewinsky–type tongue action. She looked down at the clipboard in front of her and began to read in a stilted voice. "As chair of KFUM's United Methodist Women, acting chair of the administrative board, and president of the church choir, I would like to welcome you this evening and thank you for joining us for the fiftieth anniversary of the First United Methodist Church of Kettlebean's annual Christmas pageant. Smile at audience." For a moment, she panicked. "Oh. I wasn't supposed to say that."

I slumped down in my seat, feeling the pain. Out of respect for Angel, though, I kept my mouth shut.

More or less deftly recovering her composure, Our Narrator continued. "Let us begin this most holy of evenings with that most beautiful and reverent of songs, 'O Holy Night,' performed by myself, Mrs. Henry R. Andersson." A hunched-over woman at the piano began to pound out slow triplets.

I found myself suddenly wishing I was a character in an Ibsen play. Good old Ibsen. You could always count on those Norwegian playwrights to stow a gun in a drawer for that moment when life was too much to bear. But then, right as I and my ears were at my most despairing, two men in towel headdresses stepped out and approached a long, tall rectangle of plywood that rested against the railing where ordinarily the altar stood. Until they began unfastening hooks at the top corners, I'd actually kind of assumed that the wood, which had been painted with gorgeous red and gold paints in a pattern that reminded me of old wrapping paper, or of an embroidered gown, had been part of the holiday decorations.

When it eased down on a hinge, I realized it was intended to be the pageant's backdrop. From another flat of plywood the same size as the first, a three-dimensional outline of a city's distant silhouette unfolded, casting shadows against a night sky painted the deepest of blues. The backdrop was very much like one of my childhood pop-up books, in which cardboard cutouts sprang from between the pages to amaze and delight me. The construction was so intricate, yet surprisingly simple in concept. For a moment I was totally able to forget my multiple annoyances—the singing, the personalities, even the broken-down van—as I was transported back to those moments on my little childhood acre of privacy. I was able to suspend everything else going on in my head, for a second, at the sight of an oversize pop-up book that whisked me to a desert far outside the Bethlehem city limits, two thousand years before. "Oh, my gosh," I murmured to Angel. "That's really nice!"

At the conclusion of Mrs. Andersson's song, a group of men wearing dirty jeans, work boots, sweatshirts, and the inevitable towels over their heads, hopped out from the room to the right of the altar area. They seemed to have horses's heads protruding from their groins; it took me a moment to realize they straddled stick horses. "Prithee, gentle wanderer," said the first to another man, "but which way lay . . . lays . . . lies Bethlehem? For our Emperor . . . um, our Emperor . . . Oh, shit."

"Augustus," prompted one of the others in a stage whisper.

"For Emperor Augustus hath . . ." The first guy looked around in confusion.

Mrs. Andersson fellated the microphone, booming, "Decreed."

That was too much for the fellow. "Ah, hell. I can't get this crap." On the lectern, Mrs. Andersson put her fingers over her delicate ears and made a moue of disapproval.

"Cut!" Mr. Mendez made a sudden appearance in the aisle behind us, startling me. "Let's start from the beginning, folks. And get it right this time."

Despite her blocked ears, Mrs. Andersson heard that one, all right. That klieg-light display of molars was aimed right in our direction. Ten times as loud as anyone else, Our Narrator said into the microphone, "I'll start from the second verse of my song, shall I?" Angel's pencil made scribbling noises as it skittered across the page.

At least I managed not to growl as I slunk lower into my seat. Patience, I reminded myself. I needed lots of patience. It was going to be a long, long morning.

Chapter Four

Angel clutched the sides of his head and opened his mouth to say something. Changing his mind, he instead ran the flat of a palm over his face, as if the stress had accumulated like salt spray from the ocean and he could simply wipe it away. Finally, following his own advice about exercising patience, he let out a heavy sigh and quite slowly said, "But the University of Pennsylvania wasn't *founded* in the year B.C. It would be *highly unlikely* that the Virgin Mary would wear a sweatshirt advertising its presence on the night she gave birth to the Son of God."

Maria Elliman didn't crack a smile. For the last several minutes, she'd resisted all Angel's attempts to make her look a little less like the night janitor down at the Tastee Freez and a little more like the Blessed Virgin she was supposed to portray. The poor girl crouched over in the front pew, her shoulders and posture defensive to the last. She really was quite pretty, especially her slightly slanted, heavily lashed dark eyes that most any model would pay her weight in MAC makeup to have. Yet she seemed morbidly embarrassed by her weight, which was a damned shame. I'd no ticed it during the rehearsal; in almost every scene in which she wasn't hiding behind Nick, a big bundle of swaddling clothes, or a semicircle of cherubim, she seemed to shrink away, frightened at the notion that someone might be looking at her—let's face it—ample middle. "But they told me I could wear this," she said, frightened.

"But honey." Though they'd been around this circle before, the wardrobe master remained gentle. "It's not period."

"Angel?" From where I stood at the altar rail, I jerked my head for him to join me. My heart went out to the girl. I knew of "serious" actresses who'd paid big bucks for such ample breasts, but Maria had hidden hers behind layers and layers of turtlenecks and sweatshirts and an enormous cardigan sweater. Presumably she hoped to hide her natural curves, but all the layers made her resemble an orange woolly mammoth. It was a shame. While Angel shambled over to me, disappointed at not having made any headway in the conversation, I watched Nick take his girlfriend's hand and pat it. Something about the sweetness of the gesture floored me, coming from the kid who had slouched and eye-rolled his way through breakfast not four hours earlier. His silent support made me almost a little envious. I'd never had a boyfriend like that when I was fresh out of high school. "She's embarrassed about her weight," I explained softly. "Can't you see how she's covering up what she thinks are her problem areas?"

I was grateful he didn't immediately crane his neck around to stare at the girl. "I am aware of that, Riley," he said, arms crossed. "If I had a nickel for every female actor who felt compelled to blame the tightness of her costume on shrinking material instead of on her own expanding waistline, my kids could have gone to Harvard. I've been trying to show her that draped fabric would be both more authentic and more flattering to her shape."

I folded my own arms and leaned in, professional to professional. "The actors we encounter are used to having these conversations in front of all the backstage staff. We're invisible to them. This is an ordinary girl. Find somewhere private. And take Nick, too. He seems to keep her calm."

"He's a decent kid." Angel shot them a sidewise glance. "At least he was, until you started flashing your mammaries at him."

Why dignify that kind of thing with an answer? "And what happened to your promise?" The height of his eyebrows betrayed how clueless he was. "Your promise that we wouldn't get involved?"

"Oh, stop," he said, looking pained. "This isn't *involved*. A bolt of fabric, a simple tunic for her, a quick burnoose for him . . . Maybe I could show some of the mothers how to make angel wings for the cherubim and seraphim. . . ."

"You swore," I chided, stabbing a finger at him. Not, alas, my middle one. "Don't make me flash you."

With all the mock horror of a silent-film star, he cringed. "Girl, I'm blind enough as it is! Now, let me at least fix up our Virgin before we go," he mused, taking his leave of me. Already he hummed to himself through his fingers while he wandered back to Maria and Nick, trying to figure out what mixture of flattery and appeal might get her into one of his improvised creations.

When I turned, Mrs. Andersson and her five *Playbills* were making a beeline for me from the far side of the sanctuary. As casually as possible, I began scuttling up the aisle in the direction of the narthex, pretending to be suddenly parched for water. I waved my hand in the general area of my throat until I realized I was giving various shepherds and cherubim the distinct impression that I was trying to soothe a mysterious neck rash. I switched to clearing my throat while beetling into the lobby in as speedy a getaway as possible. Scarcely had I passed through the wooden doors with their panes of seeded glass than I ran into Mr. Mendez. "There you are!" he said, his round face plainly happy to see me fall into his lap, almost literally.

My brain played a lightning round of "The Church Lady or the Tiger?" and decided I was much better off with my host. "Here I am!" I said brightly, grabbing hold of his arm and keeping my quick pace so that, basically, I was dragging him beside me. Behind us, the sanctuary doors swung open, but I didn't dare turn to see if Mrs. Andersson had followed. "How's the van?"

"I was coming to tell you!" he said. "I got off the phone with Leo just now, and he's—"

"Done?" Oh, by all that was holy in this church, I prayed, let it be done.

"No. He's still got a while to go. But he's back from Newark! Say, tell me what you thought of the—"

"Yes, about the pageant." The church was old and poor enough that it had grown in fits and starts, the original building acquiring a warren of hallways seemingly thrown together at random, some of them leading nowhere in particular, as if Kettlebean's Methodists had intended it to be the ecclesiastical equivalent to the Winchester Mystery House. At the end of one passage, however, I spied some kind of church parlor furnished with ancient leather chairs and deep pile carpet. I pulled him in and let the door swing shut, instantly plopping into one of the high-backed chairs and motioning him to follow. My hope was that we might not be visible through the little glass panel if Mrs. Andersson had been set on stalking me; there was something unsettling about her grim jaw and her church-approved smile. Not to mention her vibrato, wide enough to drive a circus caravan through. "Lose the stick horses, for one thing."

"Oh." I'd never seen Mr. Mendez look crestfallen before. His mustache drooped to a new depth. "I thought that was cute."

"It's not cute," I assured him. Almost instantly I worried that I'd taken the wrong tack. Most people, when they ask for a critique, don't really want the unvarnished truth. They want a nodding head and a bright smile and someone to tell them all the best secret things about themselves they'd hoped were true. I'd learned that from years and years of watching directors interact with their actors and artists;

271

maybe I should have tempered my tongue accordingly. "Well, it's not *bad*," I told him, then watched his mustache curve back into its usual genial shape with my next pronouncement. "For a children's pageant, stick horses would actually be quite cute! But you know, for Mrs. Robinson . . . maybe you should have the visitors to Bethlehem arrive on foot."

He nodded, instantly understanding. "It has to be special."

"Yes," I agreed. "It has to be special." From where I sat, I watched several shadows cross the wall opposite the door. A few quick outlined figures passed by as well, but no Mrs. Andersson. I began to relax a little. "Don't you have costumes and props from previous productions?"

"Not enough to go around. Used to be that we had only seven, eight people in the pageant each year. Plenty of costumes for everyone. This year, everyone who's ever done it in the past wants to be there for Mrs. Robinson. How do you pick and choose who gets to wear the good stuff?" While that sank in, he leaned forward without warning. "Say." His mouth quirked. His eyes sparkled with mischief as he obviously tried to hold back a delightful secret. "Want to see something?"

"I don't know. Do I?" I asked, loath to leave the comfort of my armchair. But he was up and crossing the cavernous interior of the parlor, the floorboards beneath the carpet snapping with every new step. I didn't have much choice but to follow him into a kitchen furnished with Formica-topped tables and chairs edged in chrome, straight from some mid-century dinette set. The western-facing windows were covered with wind-driven snow, making the little room somber. Mr. Mendez beckoned me, then raised his eyebrows, as mysterious as any Lewis Carroll character. *Curiouser and curiouser*. Pressing a finger against his lips, he let out a shushing sound, then opened the door of an upright chest freezer older than probably even Angel. Yellow light streamed from around the uniform green boxes filling its interior, illuminating both our faces from underneath as we stared in rapt attention. We probably looked like some undiscovered masterpiece of Georges de la Tour: *The Adoration of the Frozen Foods.*

Mr. Mendez, in the meantime, seemed proud as could be. "How about that? Huh? Huh?" he wanted to know.

It really was hard to know how to react. "It's a whole bunch of frozen meat pies," I said, winning for my reward an enthusiastic nod. Was he some kind of microwave meal fetishist? Was he going to ask me to fondle his Hot Pockets and not leggo his Eggo? Suddenly, and with a rush of personal relief, I got the significance. "Oh. Those are Michaelson's Meat Pies, aren't they?"

"Yeah!" Mr. Mendez's half-moon of a mustache spread wide as he beamed, "I got both Original and Country Cottage flavors. You think that'll be okay?" When he shut the fridge door, the room immediately grew darker and gloomier.

"Okay for . . . ?" What was he going to do? Have Harrison autograph all those boxes? There had to have been at least thirty.

"Dinner tonight." I could only blink. If I had dinner that night, it was going to be a cheeseburger and fries from the bottom of a fast-food bag in the driver's seat of that van, on the highway back to Manhattan. When I didn't respond immediately, Mr. Mendez threw out his chubby hands. "It's a party! Everyone in the pageant's coming to meet your Mr. Carew!"

"Oh, no," I stammered. "No. No, no, no. We've got to be on the road, for one thing."

"You can stay until dinner! No problem!"

"Problem! Hello!" Mr. Mendez apparently didn't want to hear my objections, for he walked off in the direction of the parlor once again. Annoyance kept my feet fleet, however; I skidded across the floor on my sneakers' rubber soles and tried to keep up as his little legs propelled him ahead. "No offense—I'm sure they're fantastic meat pies; I really wouldn't know—but the three of us definitely have to get on the road this evening, once Leo finishes the. . . ."

"Aw, Leo!" Over his shoulder, Mr. Mendez made a dismissive motion. "I told you, he won't be done for a while."

"A while?" I squawked. "How long is a while?"

But he was through the parlor's double doors and back out into the hallway, where in the distance I could hear the echoing sounds of conversation from the sanctuary. "Don't worry!" he said, keeping up his brisk pace. "You'll have time for dinner."

"I . . . You . . . !" I didn't like the sound of that, but what could I do? Frustrated, I stopped dead in the middle of the flagstone floor and let my head loll back. I was never going to get out of Kettlebean. I was going to spend the rest of my life in Kettlebean eating Michaelson's Heat-'n'-Eat Meat Pies from the First United Methodist Church of Kettlebean freezer, and after I'd stood all I could stand of Kettlebean and thrown myself from Kettlebean's highest point, the top of Kettlebean's picturesque clock tower atop the Kettlebean town hall, I'd be buried in the Kettlebean cemetery. Seriously. What was supposed to be a short stay here was fated never, ever to end. "Crap!"

There's a Sartre play called *No Exit* in which three ordinary people are escorted into a perfectly normal room. Then they realize they're dead, and in hell, and that they're doomed to spend eternity tap-dancing on one another's last nerves. Maybe I was in that play. I was in the middle of squeezing my wrist to make certain I still had a pulse when, from around the corner, Angel appeared, the fluorescent lights making his head shiny. "There you are," he said. He looked back in the direction he'd come, then lowered his voice. "We have trouble."

"So you heard?" I asked, briskly walking to his side. We started heading back in the direction of the sanctuary.

"Heard! I saw it for myself. Big and round as life."

Okay, now I was confused. "Wait a minute. You saw the van?"

"Van?" he halted, his reading glasses swinging from the chain on his neck. "What are you talking about?"

"What are *you* talking about?" I asked. "I just heard from our host that we're expected for dinner tonight. A big church dinner. *With* Harrison, I might add."

"With Harrison?" He sounded as horrified as I felt.

"Yeah, like I'm going to let that happen. Worst PR move ever. I'm going to walk to the garage now, in fact, to see what's happening. But what are you talking about?"

"Hmmm." He regarded me for a moment, then jerked his head for me to follow him down one of the side corridors. Farther down the hall Nick Mendez lounged, hands stuffed in the pockets of his hoodie. At the sight of us, the boy lurched away from the wall and approached. There was something defensive in his eyes; that much I could tell immediately. Nothing remained of the sleepy lethargy he'd affected earlier. "You said you weren't going nowhere," he accused Angel. To me he gave a frank scowl.

"Young man," Angel said, at his most quietly assertive, "step aside. Ms. McIntyre is qualified to see this sort of thing."

Huh? I couldn't ask what I might be qualified to see, after that. I pulled the corners of my mouth wide in a semblance of a confident smile.

"Maria . . . she's—" Nick started to say, silenced when Angel laid a hand on his shoulder. "I've got to look out for her. She's got nobody else on her side."

"I know, son." Angel nodded. Maybe when my head had been in the freezer with the meat pies, it had frozen, because I wasn't following any of this conversation. "We won't be long. Why don't you go wait in the sanctuary?"

After considering for a moment, Nick gave silent assent. He walked away from in front of the door, on which rested a plate that read, HENRY R. ANDERSSON, MUSICAL DIRECTOR AND ORGANIST. *Fantastic*, I thought to myself, recognizing the name almost immediately. No wonder his wife assigned herself all the solos. "What *is* this all about?" I murmured, once Nick was at the end of the hall and out of earshot. "If it's a weight issue, lots of young women have problems, and making her feel self-conscious about it—"

"Riley." Angel paused, his hand resting on the doorknob. "It's not a weight issue."

I blinked. What in the world was it, then? Did she have some kind of tumor? Was this one of those feminine hygiene things he thought I'd be better equipped to handle? Because frankly, after high school gym and four years of sharing a communal shower with other women in a dormitory, I'd sworn off involving myself in anything involving other women's smells, undergarments, and bodily fluids. He would have to—"Oh, my God!" I stared at the girl, suddenly understanding all the cloak-and-dagger antics.

Somehow Angel had coaxed Maria to remove her sweaters and sweatshirt, leaving her clad in only an extremely tight T-shirt and jeans. Seated among the stacks of sheet music, the metronomes and batons, and the piles of CDs nearby, and with her hair pulled back to expose the tough, determined line of her jaw, she seemed younger than she had at the front of the church during rehearsal. Scarcely had the words come out of my mouth than she began to cover herself, hands reaching for the exposed flesh of her arms, elbows crossing to protect her breasts and bulging midsection. Though proud, her eyes looked hurt and vulnerable. I instantly regretted saying anything. "You'd better not tell." Her words were a challenge.

"Of course. Oh, of course," I said, trying to sound reassuring, shocked though I was at the sight of her. "Angel? Can we . . . ?"

I didn't know if I'd be able to restrain myself until we went back out into the hallway, but I managed to give Maria a reassuring, woman-to-woman smile before we left. Poor thing. She needed some kind of reassurance, I knew. "You see what I mean?" Angel asked, once the door was closed again.

Finally I was able to say it. "She's got to be in her second trimester! *Well* into it!" He nodded in agreement. "That poor girl. It's got to be like living a nightmare, day in and day out. No one knows?"

"Nick does. It's his."

"Well, *obviously.*"

"So what do we do?"

I couldn't believe he was asking that question. "What do we *do?*" I repeated, making sure I'd actually heard those words. "How about nothing?"

"We can't abandon—"

"We can! We're going to!" I could tell I'd upset Angel by the way he placed his thick-framed glasses onto his nose and peered at me through them, like someone studying the stinking black lump that had somehow invaded his baked potato. "We're leaving as soon as Leo gets that fuel pump thing back in! We're not getting involved."

Angel added crossed arms to his arsenal of displeasure, then capped it off with a tilt of his head. "These kids are neck-deep in trouble." Talk about pointing out the obvious. "If they were my children—"

"They're not. We're not getting inv—"

"Don't say that word," he begged. "Any other word but that one, Riley."

"Fine. Enmeshed, then."

Whether he'd given up on saving the youth of Kettlebean, or whether he was simply humoring me, I couldn't tell. But Angel pressed together his lips, sighed, and, after a very long silence, said, "Fine. No enmeshing."

"Good boy," I told him.

For a second I thought our dismount from the tricky situation had stuck, until he spoke up again. "She hasn't had a prenatal exam." In response to my raised finger, he closed his lips once more. "Not that it's our business. No enmeshment. I've promised."

I knew Angel too well. "You're going to get involved anyway, aren't you?" I asked, sighing. No matter how old his kids might be, Angel took the Ward Cleaver role too much to heart. I could tell from his noncommittal face that he'd be up to something the moment I left. "Fine, let it be on your head when you disclose to Mr. Mendez that his Holy Virgin is anything but."

"I don't know if I'm going that far." Angel puffed out his cheeks and let out a stream of air. "Keeping this a secret isn't doing anyone any favors. Someone's got to talk some sense into that girl, though. Or the Mendez boy, at the very least."

I knew exactly what he meant. I had a Mendez boy of my very own to talk some sense into.

Chapter Five

Leo Mendez was a singer. Not only that, but he was also something of a dancer, judging by the way his feet tapped and swayed side to side from underneath the van, keeping beat with the tinny music pouring from the van's AM radio. "We are something," he warbled, slightly off-pitch. "Heartache to heartache, we something. Something, something, no demands. Something something. Love is a . . ." I waited for him to finish the lyric, but instead, from underneath the van I heard something metal clatter to the ground. "Hey, buddy-boy, can you bring me some rags?"

At the sudden address, I froze. I hadn't realized Leo knew someone else was in the garage with him, much less that he had seen me. "Yeah, you, you little buttwipe," he continued. "I can see your feet, ya dope. What're you standing there for? Get some rags already." Oddly, the word *buttwipe* didn't offend me. For years I'd been so used to backstage fetching and carrying that I'd automatically started surveying the room for rags to bring him. "Not that way. Quit goofing around!" he barked out, when I started off to investigate the shelves at the back of the garage.

After that false start, I noticed a big roll of paper towels sitting on a bench nearby. To retrieve it took a few quick steps; I knelt down and thrust it bottom-end first beneath the van. "What the . . . ? That clueless act doesn't fly with me, dipshit," he called. "Bring me some real rags!"

When I leaned over to look underneath, my braid swung down and brushed the floor. "I'm sorry," I apologized. "But I don't know where you keep them."

His legs flew up into the air, followed by the sound of rollers against the pavement. Only at the last moment did he regain his balance before he fell off the dolly on which he lay, and then it was with such a thud against the undercarriage that I was nearly certain he'd concussed himself. "Oh, crap," he swore.

"Are you okay? Did you hurt . . . ?"

He wheeled himself out, emerging inch by slow inch of his dark blue coveralls, the broad planes of his handsome face the last to appear. I reached out instinctively to help—it wouldn't have been the first time I'd been called on to perform first aid because of a work-related accident—but I couldn't see any bumps or cuts or abrasions. "No, I'm fine," he said, sitting up. I'd suspected his hair was long, but free of its cap it hung in thick waves that curled right below his ears. As if aware it was something of a glorious mess, he self-consciously ran his fingers through the mop. Dirty fingers, yes, but somehow that didn't detract from its tousled appeal. "I thought you were my brother. I called you a dipshit, didn't I?"

"Uh-huh." I couldn't stand the stricken look in his eyes. I suppose it made perfect sense that he'd mistaken me for someone else. And to be honest, I'd more or less developed an immunity to that whole macho-locker-room-talk thing, after living both with my brothers and the largely male fraternity of those who worked backstage. "But I've been called a lot worse." I realized that perhaps I wasn't exactly taking the right approach to reassure him I was a reasonable individual, and attempted to explain. "Only by family, I mean. And coworkers." Worse and worse. His eyebrows rose. Probably best to make a joke of it. "And, you know, now that I'm getting it from complete strangers, I guess I've more or less covered all the bases, save for church dignitaries and the Arts and Entertainment writers for *The New York Times*. So, where are those rags?"

"Don't," he said, looking at his hands and realizing how grimy and oily they were. He made an attempt to wipe off the worst of it on the legs of his uniform, seeming almost embarrassed about the grunge. But hey, I wasn't exactly Mrs. Clean in my profession, either. I even kept spare pants at work in case of rips, spills, tears, or small fires. Stuff happens when you use your hands for a living. "I'll get them."

"You stay put," I told him, standing up. "Want to know something about us McIntyres? We have an actual motto. Oh, yeah, an actual motto, taken from the family crest."

"You have a family crest?" His eyebrows shot up, but he remained sitting cross-legged on his dolly.

"Of course. Mint flavored. We all share the same tube." He opened his mouth to protest my sorry joke, but I stopped him with a grin. "Okay, so we don't have a crest, but we do have a family motto, honed to a sharp edge after many years of debate and compromise, and I think it applies here perfectly."

"Okay," he said. Now he was resting his forearms on bent knees, watching me in fascination. Either that, or he finally realized he was dealing with a desperate crazy lady. "I'll bite. What's your family motto?"

I raised my hands to some distant, invisible horizon and emphasized the words as I spoke, as if each were embroidered on some flying banner. "Put up," I intoned, "or shut up. So, keeping that in mind, what can I do to help you, Le— Mr. Mendez? Seriously. I have to get on the road. You and your family want us out of your collective hair. If you want rags, I'll get you rags. If you want me to hand you wrenches like some kind of attendant in the ER, I'll hand you wrenches. If you want me to lift up the front end of the van . . ."

"It's Leo. Mr. Mendez is my pop. I think I get your point," he said gently. "We keep a supply of rags over there," he said, pointing to a room at the garage's far end, where I could see a mop and rolling bucket, as well as a couple of different wastebaskets and some winter boots surrounded by a puddle of water.

"Rag girl it is, then!" I said, turning and flouncing off.

"I wouldn't normally suggest this," he added, arresting me in midstep. "But if you're offering help, I mean, with my pop off doing his thing . . ."

"Oh, yeah. Oh, heck, yeah!" My enthusiasm wasn't in the least feigned; part of me was totally elated at the thought of helping out. I mean, it wasn't as if I possessed even a rudimentary knowledge about fixing up a broken-down van. When I'd had a choice years ago in middle school between a short auto mechanics elective or a class in woodworking, for eight weeks I'd inflicted wooden checkerboards and birdhouses on my poor family. I don't sit on the sidelines very easily, though, not without a task to perform. Waiting for these repairs had been driving me absolutely bonkers. Actually being able to help get Grant's damned van back on the road, no matter how piddling a contribution, made me feel less out of control.

"Nothing major," he promised. "But it'd save some time if you could set out parts as I hand them to you." I nodded to let him know I could handle setting out. Whether it was scripts for the actors, or props on the prop table, or cue diagrams, setting things out in an orderly fashion was a job skill I exercised daily. "And it's kind of dirty," he added. "You might want to change."

"Change out of these expensive duds, you mean?" I said, gesturing to the faded denim of my overalls. "Because it would really be a shame for this haute couture to get dirty."

Sometimes I worry that guys will mistake my playful

facetiousness as some kind of commentary on their intellect—as if they might think I'm meeting stupidity with sarcasm. Luckily, Leo Mendez seemed to realize the comment was more a jibe at my own practical, if sloppy, taste in clothing than on anything he'd said. "At the far end of the break room there's another uniform hanging from the last peg. It's clean. Should fit you, too. You can be another 'and Son' for a little bit, if you want."

One cue was plenty for me. The dark blue uniform hung exactly where Leo said it would on the last peg, underneath a broken umbrella and a pair of baseball caps. It wasn't simply clean; it seemed new. The pants portion of the coveralls still boasted an out-of-the-bag crease, and unlike either Leo's or Mr. Mendez's uniform, it had none of the wear and tear of laundering or everyday use. The embroidered patch over the left jacket pocket bore Nick's name.

"I'm kind of guessing that your brother isn't as active in the family business as you," I announced, once I'd donned the outfit and loaded my arms with clean rags from a hamper. Even the tag at the back of my neck still had its sharp, original edges. "I found towels."

"You'd be right on the Nick thing." Beneath the van, Leo's voice echoed oddly, as if the baritone syllables had to wend their way through the maze of shafts and pipes and gears before finding their way to me. Digging his booted heels against the concrete, he used his legs to pull himself out from under again. "He's the family's black sheep. Well," his voice sounded normal as his head emerged from the car's underside and he began to sit upright, "more like the gray sheep. Charcoal gray. Whoa." At the sight of me, he stopped talking, though he did keep wiping the grime from one of his hands. "Whoa," he repeated, eyes big behind his safety goggles.

"What?" He definitely wasn't looking at the baseball cap I'd borrowed, or in the vicinity of my face. I looked down at the rest of my body and only saw blue fabric. "What?"

"Nothing." There was no way I was buying that answer. A girl hears a *whoa*, and naturally she wants to know what's at the other end of the reins. He met my upraised eyebrows with a sheepish expression. "You look a lot better in that thing than Nicky ever could, that's all." As if thinking better of his frank statement, he added a pained, "Sorry."

I'm not built like a man, even of the nineteen-year old variety, and I'd found that the uniform was a little roomy around my midsection. So I'd taken the cloth belt from my own overalls and tied it around my waist. I hadn't really realized it would create a more formfitting effect. The idea that Leo might think I'd done it deliberately mortified me. "Anyway," I mumbled, feeling horribly self-conscious. I mean, what kind of person tries to tart up a pair of neck-to-ankle coveralls to show off her waist? Aside from Ellie Mae Clampett? "Rags," I reminded him, pointing to the cart where I'd stacked them.

"Yeah. Rags." Dragging his eyes away from me seemed to be something of an effort, which made me feel more . . . I don't know. Embarrassment was at the forefront of it, but at the same time, I wasn't going to deny that the novelty of a guy actually looking in my direction didn't . . . well, please me. And not some effete, on-the-make actor who primped in every mirror and smoked to keep his weight down, either. "All right," Leo finally said, lying back down on his dolly. "Let me . . . yeah. So anyway, I don't think Nick's worn that before. Dad got it for him on his seventeenth birthday. I think he kind of hoped Nick would want to join us, but he was always up to other things. Here, take this, would you?"

As of a half hour before, I knew exactly what Nick had been up to, and it wasn't PlayStation. I couldn't help but wonder if Nick's ovine hue would darken further in the Mendezes' eyes if they knew what he'd done—but it was really none of my business, and I intended to make certain it didn't become so. I took the twisted what's-it that Leo proffered to my ankles and set it to the side. If that was going to be my job for the next few minutes, I realized it might be better to lower my center of gravity. I settled onto the floor. "You did get the gas pump? Fuel pump?"

"You can calm down. It was in the break room. You probably didn't notice it while you were in there." Leo's voice was so calmly reassuring that I immediately felt a little guilty for asking. He oozed professionalism. It was obvious I should trust him.

"Was it in a red-and-white box?" I asked. At his grunt of assent, I added with a note of triumph, "I did so notice. Should I get it?"

"Not right yet. I won't need it for a little bit. Could you wipe this down?"

I'd risen onto my haunches, ready to spring, but I settled back down again, ready to clean off some kind of brace-looking thing with one of the rags. The tag at the back of my neck was really beginning to drive me nuts; every time I turned my head, there it was, scratching my skin. In fact, the entire unwashed cotton-poly-something blend was beginning to give me the creepy-crawlies. I should've kept on the mock turtleneck I'd been wearing beneath my own overalls. "So if your brother's the troublemaker, does that make you the good one?" I wanted to know.

I had to wait for a few seconds for an answer, while Leo concentrated on something that, from the racket of it, required a considerable amount of attack from a power tool. "Nick's never really been a bad kid," he finally said. "He kind of flirts with trouble, but never gets into bed with it." My mouth automatically opened to contradict that unfortunate choice of words, but at the last second I shut it. "The folks would kill him if he did anything serious."

"Kill him, huh?" A dandy reason not to say anything, handed to me on a plate. I was glad we'd be well out of town by the time any of this went down. I preferred my drama on the stage, where I knew exactly how it would end at every performance.

"It's a rebellious phase. We all went through one of those,

285

didn't we? I remember when I was Nicky's age, I saved up for a motorcycle. . . ." Leo paused, shuffled some tools around, then started right where he'd left off. "Then I bought the darned thing without asking my folks' permission. Just showed up one afternoon in front of the house, grin on my face. All I can say is that it was a good thing I was wearing a helmet, because the way my mother tried to beat me . . . I could hear your eyes widen from underneath here, you know."

"If they were wide, it was from trying to picture you on a chopper," I joked. Leo really didn't seem the Harley type.

"Chopper? Hardly. It wasn't a good motorcycle. Not a big ol' manly hog. Some cheap little foreign number, but to my eyes it was pretty sweet." Even with several tons of van between us, I could still hear his little sigh. "I had to return it, of course. And what about you? What'd you do to rebel?"

I took another grimy part from him and began to wipe it off as best I could. Considering how corroded it was, however, I was afraid of rubbing it into dust. Wrinkling my nose, I replied, "I wasn't much in the rebel department."

"Well, if you don't want to say . . ."

"No, it's not that." I figured the guy was asking me about my life because he needed company after driving to Newark and back all morning, and with his family still practicing the pageant down at the church, I'd be asking a perfect stranger questions, too. "I had multiple older brothers growing up. They used up all the creative ways to rebel long before I ever got to adolescence. Funny hair, inappropriate dates, cross-dressing . . ."

"Really!"

"Once. For Halloween," I hastened to explain. "Let's see. One of them ran away from home, but only for three hours, so we didn't have time to notice. Marshall—he's the oldest—did the drug and booze experimentation thing in college and got put on academic probation, Jed wrecked my grandmother's car—"

"Ooooch."

Something clattered to the cement. I was hesitant to ask if Leo's outcry had been for the sorry state of the van, or for poor Jed. I decided to assume it was the latter. "Yeah. After all that, Chaz managed to squeeze out a few drops from the old throwing-a-huge-forbidden-party-while-the-'rents-were-celebrating-their-anniversary-in-the-city scheme. By the time my teens came around, all the normal forms of rebellion seemed kind of clichéd."

Leo wheeled himself out once more, but he didn't seem to want any of the parts I'd dutifully wiped off and set in a neat row. "Now that," he said, looking me right in the eyes, "is a shame. Seriously. Everyone needs a good old-fashioned rebellion once in a while."

He was poking fun at my boring history, I gathered. "I'll be okay. Thanks for your concern." Despite my demurral, he continued staring at me as if we were sharing some kind of joke. Yet one of us wasn't getting it. "What?" I finally asked, uncomfortable and wanting to laugh at the same time.

"You've *never* done anything rebellious."

I shrugged at his flat statement. "Not really."

"Not as an adult? You've never stayed out late partying when you knew you had to go to work the next day? Called in sick so you could enjoy the spring weather? Wore inappropriate clothing to a holiday dinner?" The smile on my face grew wryer with each question. Apparently he thought I was joshing him. "Ate hot dogs with extra chili? Accidentally belched in public and tried to pretend one of your friends did it? Cut class? Played with matches? Made out with a guy you hardly knew?"

I'd been laughing at the barrage, but the last one caught me off guard, making me part my lips in wordless surprise. Maybe he hadn't meant for it to sound the way it nearly did; maybe he was afraid I'd interpret it in an entirely different way from how he'd intended. Maybe he'd already construed my hesitation as some kind of serious consideration, that I'd interpreted his innocent question as an invitation, because without another word, he lay back down on the dolly and propelled himself back into the shadowy world beneath the van. "I'm not the chili type," I told him. When he didn't reply, I added, "Go ahead; you can say it."

"Say what?" He was back at work again, peppering the silence with short bursts of power tool noise.

"What most of my friends say. Like, 'You need to live a little,' or, 'Loosen up already,' or the one that starts, 'All work and no play . . .'"

"If you've got your friends telling you that, there's no need for me to join in."

"I like to work. I take my job seriously." The old justifications sprang to my lips readily. "Throwing all that away for a night of partying doesn't really appeal." He grunted, not sounding surprised. Should I have told him how much I was tempted to call in sick some nice spring day for the first time ever? After all this unending lake-effect snow, Central Park in May sounded tempting, if I knew someone who'd spend the day with me. "If I sound boring, I'm sorry, but that's me. Plain, dull, boring, tedious, old—"

"Don't do that," he said, interrupting me. "Don't put yourself down for my sake. I bet you wouldn't say negative stuff about yourself if you were interviewing for a new position somewhere." He was right. I wouldn't, but was I interviewing for something here? "Don't do it for me. So this Carew guy who came with you. He's famous?"

"Famous enough that your dad wants to throw a dinner for him at the church tonight. But honestly? Was famous, past tense." The transition from my self-deprecation to Harrison Carew was jarring enough to give me whiplash. Maybe he thought I'd been fishing for compliments. Why in the heck was I speculating about what he thought of me? I'd never been one of those girls who gave a flip about what others thought of her—except in the professional world, of course. That was the only place where other people's opinions mattered. I clutched at my neck again, where the tag was chewing away at my nape, and then let my hand inch around inside the uniform to scratch at my collarbone. "Big theater star, starting during the sixties," I explained. "Made his stage debut as Romeo at seventeen . . . he was supposed to be the next Laurence Olivier."

"That's impressive."

"Solid work in serious plays until he landed a Tony a little over a decade ago. Then, *phffft*. He dried up. Alcohol, bad career choices, the usual *E! True Hollywood Story* stuff." I hesitated. I'd already said more than I should. Even to what friends I had back in Manhattan, I didn't often gossip about the actors appearing on the Claibe Richardson stage; it wasn't good form. Leo, though, had already seen Harrison at his worst, sprawled out in the back of the very van under which he labored. Trying to gloss over the obvious wouldn't fly. "This play that's opening Tuesday, *Square Root*, is supposed to be his big, serious comeback. The show's basically his—it's a philosophical two-man play set in the sixties. There's a mathematician who helped theorize and build the hydrogen bomb in the forties, and his son, this hippie kind of rebel guy. It's not my cup of tea, to be honest, but it really could jump-start Harrison's career again if it caught on. And here I am, chasing after him."

"What are all of you doing up here, anyway? We're not on anyone's tryout route."

It was a natural question. An innocent question that I found myself not able to answer completely honestly. "He kind of . . . ran away."

Admitting that Harrison was a bit of a mess was one thing. Telling the whole sordid tale of how he'd ended up bedding the producer's wife was entirely another. Either Leo rightly interpreted my silence as reluctance, or else he didn't really much care about the answer, because he kept right on talking. "Just up and left you in the lurch, huh?"

"Something like that," I replied, grateful for the out.

"Harper Lee never published another book after *To Kill a Mockingbird*, you know. She kind of retreated into private life and hasn't been seen much since." We were discussing literature, now? I could hardly contain my surprise at the change of topic. What kind of guy was Leo Mendez, anyway? Between the occasional pauses and grunts as he tinkered with the van's innards, he continued. "I can understand how it would be, to win a Pulitzer for a book I'd written and have it made into a movie that everyone loved, and to have it read by, you know, generations of high school kids everywhere. How do you follow that up? To me, it sounds like your actor is scared."

"Scared?"

"I know it's the worst kind of pop psychology, but yeah, scared. Scared of having to duplicate that level of success again. You know how it is—you're always supposed to be moving upward and onward, in most people's eyes." Pop psychology or not, Leo had a point. I didn't know whether he could hear my grunt of concurrence from where he lay, but he added, "Maybe it was easier for him to run away than face having to outdo himself, after getting a big award like that."

I accepted another rusted part from his hand. This was all making some kind of weird sense to me. "To do the rebellious stuff a theatrical legend shouldn't?" Every time I'd addressed him, I realized, I'd been more or less talking to the intersection of his spread legs. While it might be true that a good 70 percent of the men I worked with talked out of their asses on a regular basis, Leo didn't seem to be one of them. I averted my eyes.

He inched a little bit farther beneath the van. "There's a world of difference between letting off a little steam and committing career suicide."

I didn't know. I wasn't entirely convinced. "Don't you think . . . ?" I hesitated. I wanted to ask if he thought whether the line between the two was thinner than onionskin paper. It had always worried me that they might be.

"What?"

No, I couldn't say what I thought without sounding like the stupid, single-minded nerd that deep in my heart I feared I might have become. I tried to cover up my doubts by changing the topic a little. "Don't you think this conversation is a little weird? I mean, I don't have talks like this with my friends."

Apparently what I'd said was enough to intrigue him into sliding out again. He angled himself so that I could see the entire right side of his body below the van's running board. "What kind of conversations do you have, then?"

In a word? Shallow. "Well, my girlfriends all tend to be interested in shopping, or their guys, or their kids." Because, you know, rubbing my childless state in my face is the favorite pastime of my married friends from college. "Movies sometimes, but not film, if you know what I mean. Television. Gossip. I think I get invited to their lunches and parties because they know I can get free tickets for them."

"What about your boyfriends?"

"I don't have time to see anyone," I stated flatly, bristling at the implication. "Certainly not multiple someones."

"What about your boy, comma, platonic, comma, man friends? Of the male gender?" he repeated patiently, like I was some kind of special needs student.

My hands flew to my face to cool my cheeks, suddenly hot as coals. "Oh, jeez," I grumbled, mortified. "Do me a favor and turn on the van. I feel this sudden urge to suck on the exhaust pipe until I pass out." He shook his head, not letting me get away with feeling bad over my stupidity. I let my hand scratch once more around my neck and shoulders while I tried to think of what male friends I actually had. "Well, Angel and I go way back. . . . We talk about work, mostly, or what's going on with his family. I have a couple of other work friends. But I guess it's kind of the same thing. Work, mostly." Gee, I sounded lame. Fifteen minutes with this guy, and suddenly I had my life laid bare in front of me; he had to see me as a lonely, anal-retentive, dateless old maid who some day would end up in a tiny apartment filled with illegal cats, clutching a handful of *Playbills* that meant something only to me. Like Anneke Andersson. Except worse. Mrs. Andersson had a husband, and I couldn't envision her letting a cat shed a single hair near one of her practical ensembles. "So what's *your* story?" I asked, feeling vaguely depressed.

Although he'd remained visible for the last part of the discussion about my sorry personal life, without warning he grabbed hold of something under the van and swung back beneath. "What about it?" he asked, amending quickly with, "There's nothing interesting about me."

"Yeah, nothing interesting at all," I said. I ticked off my thumb and first finger. "Except that you're conversant with *The Grapes of Wrath* and *To Kill a Mockingbird*, you're funny and smart, you made some set backdrops that were so stunning they made my teeth hurt, and you live here in a backwater of a town, no offense, with your folks. Again, no offense. So I ask again, what's up with that?"

"I live in the apartment over the garage, not with my parents."

Was there defensiveness in that statement? It certainly sounded like it. "What about the rest?"

"I like the ice fishing."

I waited for a less smart-alecky answer, but apparently one wasn't coming. "You made the backdrops, right? All three of them? Did you find the designs on, like, the Internet or somewhere? The manger one was so delicate—I can't imagine how much time it took to put that together." You know, most people recognized the cues contained in normal conversation. Not Leo. Either he didn't hear me, despite having heeded perfectly everything that had gone on before between us, or else he didn't want to talk. Had I somehow offended him by implying he still lived with his family? I could see a guy of nearly thirty being upset at that. "I didn't mean—"

"The designs are mine." His words were so flat that immediately I felt chagrined at having implied otherwise. That wasn't the entire reason for his silence, though. He'd clammed up on me before I'd made the Internet comment.

What was I supposed to do? "Well, they're really, really great," I finally allowed myself to say.

Did it sound condescending? I feared so. Even worse, it was a period of several moments before he spoke again. "Why don't you go get the fuel pump, if you don't mind?"

"Yeah. Fine." I didn't know what had changed our garrulous conversation into something more silent than Grant's Tomb. Some typical macho-guy bullshit, maybe. God knew I'd seen enough of it with three older brothers. "I'm going to take a minute to put on my shirt under this uniform thing, if you don't mind. The itching is driving me absolutely bonkers."

"No rush," he said. "I've still got a little while to go under here."

To me it sounded as if he were trying to get rid of me and my nosy questions, but I tried not to take it too personally. Not exactly the easiest task in the world, when you'd been having an interesting conversation with an even more interesting guy and suddenly you found his lips stitched. In another hour, though, it would be a moot point, once the three of us were back on I-90. I had to remind myself of the day's motto, as I crossed the garage: I simply wasn't going to get involved.

Once safely in the seclusion of the break room, I groaned with relief. I unfastened the uniform's buttons to my navel and let its top half hang around my waist so I could soothe the tender portions of my poor, raw neck and detach the bothersome tag. Amazing how something so small could create so much discomfort! When I took a moment to examine the sore spot in a mirror over the sink to see how red it was, and whether or not it was my imagination making it feel like raw steak after a good fork tenderizing, my heart sank for a moment. "Crap," I said aloud at the sight of my back; the various auto parts I'd wiped off had been so dirty that apparently I'd gotten more of the grunge on my fingers than on the rags—and every time I'd reached back to rub at my shoulders or neck, I'd left dark streaks on my skin. Parts of me looked like I'd lain down in a coal bin and, like a resentful dog trying to eradicate all traces of its fresh bath, rolled around with abandon. It wasn't limited to my back, either; my shoulders and the front of me were incredibly grungy. Somehow I'd managed to transfer a lot of smudge prints to my bra as well.

Thinking about what that sooty grunge was made of made my skin crawl—the first things to come to mind were road salt and ordinary dust, followed quickly by visions of expectoration, dog pee, drunk pee, homeless pee, chemicals, sewage, and roadkill. "Ew, ew, ew!" I said, sotto voce, so that Leo wouldn't hear me shrieking like a girly-girl confronted with a centipede and come running.

Luckily, there was something I could do about it. Though I knew that unhooking my bra would get the material dirty, it had to be done. Once the straps were loosened, I let them fall from my shoulders and dropped the bra onto the nearby hook where I'd hung my clothes. One arm instinctively covered my breasts, although I knew I was alone in the little room. A roll of paper towels hung near the microwave. Under the faucet I wet a few of them with lukewarm water, and started rubbing at the grime. The plastic bottle of hand soap nearby held but a trace of orange-pink fluid, but after a considerable amount of pumping, I was able to get a small amount of suds onto my poor shoulders.

Seeing the white towels turn charcoal where I scrubbed them against my soiled skin made a neatnik like me feel a little bit ill, but it didn't take me long to erase the worst of the mess. With the top half of the MENDEZ & SON uniform still hanging around my waist, I used the last of the paper towels to dab off the leftover moisture. Had I been too long? I hadn't heard Leo calling impatiently for the fuel pump, so I probably had a couple of minutes before I was needed again. I turned around, intent on getting my turtleneck from its hook.

There in the doorway stood Nick. He stared at me with wide-open eyes, first at my blank face, then squarely at my breasts. Panicked, I realized they weren't at all covered, but jerking my arm in front of them again was probably too late an afterthought; he'd seen the goods again, for the second time that day. It was a strange moment, and reminded me of nothing more than one of those occasional early spring mornings at my parents' house in Syosset, when I'd stepped out to get the morning paper and come face to face with a rabbit or a raccoon or some other untamed animal. We all knew in theory that there was wild animal life on Long Island, but none of us actually expected ever to encounter it.

As might a rabbit and morning paper scooper-upper, we simply stood there, eyes wide and wary, staring at each other, making not a sound. Then like the skittish bunny, Nick was off—there one second, gone the next on scampering legs that took him from the break room and left cool air in his wake.

In the seconds after he vanished, I had to ask myself: had that really just happened? And exactly whom upstairs in the heaven department had I pissed off? What kind of bad behavior had landed me the gig of appearing topless for Kettlebean's junior Casanova at every turn? Was it all those times I refused to let guys get their hands under my bra in high school?

Whatever it was, I had absolutely no intention of discussing it with anyone else. When I finally stepped out from the break room, much more comfortable with a layer of much-washed cotton protecting me from the uniform's seams, though, I was still a little dazed. "What's wrong?" Leo was getting to his feet on the other side of the room; his dolly still rolled slightly. I shook my head and put my hands on my hips, unable to say anything coherent. My mouth worked, and I wanted to say something, but what? That his little brother had seen more of my breasts than anyone in years, outside of my ob-gyn? I ended up shaking my head again. "You look like you've got to get something off your chest."

After a gawped protest, I narrowed my eyes and stared at him. "What did you mean by *that*?"

"Well, you looked like you were going to say something, that's all." Believe me, if there'd been the slightest sign of that oily smugness guys get when they're trying not to snigger at a smutty joke, or that terrible sexist, condescending manner some of them adopt when they think they're one up on you, I would've seen it. Though I waited for a puff of hard-to-suppress laughter, or the slightest twitch of the lips, Leo had only a kind of naive innocence to him. Which made sense. Nick had vanished so quickly that unless he'd bent over and shouted, *I saw the van lady's boobies!* on the way out, Leo shouldn't necessarily know anything. Good. "How about the part?"

My arms flew up across my chest. "What parts? What part?" I corrected myself.

"The fuel pump?" He raised his eyebrows. "You were going to get the fuel pump."

"Oh." A rush of realization seemed to revitalize every nerve ending in my body, bringing me back to aching life. "Oh! I don't think . . ." Weird. I had a memory of the red-and-white box sitting on the counter when I'd been grabbing for the paper towels, but after that? "I don't think it was there." Immediately I swiveled and returned to the little room. No, the carton wasn't on the counter. Had I moved it, maybe? Picked it up and put it elsewhere, in absent-minded confusion? My eyes traveled over all the places it might be, but I didn't see it anywhere. I certainly didn't remember handling it. Leo had followed me into the room and stood staring at the counter, exactly where I thought it had been. His uniform was covered with the same grime I'd cleaned from my back a few minutes before, but he'd managed not to get any of it on his face. For a brief moment, in the good light of the break room, I almost wished he had, so I'd have an excuse to lick a tissue like my great-aunt Patty and clean away the dirt. "Maybe I was thinking of a different box."

"No, it was right there," he said, pointing. "Did you move it?"

"I already thought of that, but no. Did you come get it, maybe?" I winced at that. Having both the Mendez brothers catch me *en dishabille* was a little too much to contemplate.

"It couldn't walk away on its own," he muttered, looking all over the room. There weren't that many places to look, though he did open the cabinets above the counter. They held the usual assortment of coffee filters, grounds, and mustard packets one typically finds in finer frat house kitchens. Without another word, he walked out into the garage, presumably to continue his search there.

"Then it's got to be somewhere around here, right?" Barely had the words left my lips when I answered my own question: *Not if someone else walked off with it. Or sneaked off. Or fled like a frightened rabbit who'd been caught contemplating the melon patch.* But why? I didn't have time to think why. I ran out into the garage, where Leo was investigating every flat surface that could possibly hold a carton. "Nick!" I shouted. He straightened up and stared at me, his brows knitted together from fretting, but obviously had no clue what I was talking about. "Nick took it!"

"Why in the world would Nick take a fuel pump?" Leo asked. "He doesn't have an old van that could use it. He doesn't own a car."

I could tell from his tone that he thought I was some kind of crazy woman. It didn't help that I blurted out, "Because he saw my breasts!"

The words were enough to make Leo focus on an entirely new zone of my body, but I was too certain of my hypothesis to care. "What does a fuel pump have to do with your breasts?"

"My breasts don't need a pump!" Again, worse and

worse. "Strike that." Shock had turned to anger. That little devious . . . He hadn't been spying on me at all, hoping for another glance at the goods. He'd deliberately come to steal that fuel pump for some mysterious reason! I started to pace back and forth as I fumed. "I know he took it!"

"You're not making any sense. What would Nick want with a fuel pump? You can't bribe that kid to lift up the hood of a car."

That was the kicker. Why in the world had he done it? None of it made sense. The sole thing to be accomplished from the trick would be to annoy the hell out of me. Or to keep me from getting on the road. No, to keep *all of us* from getting on the road. I snapped my fingers and knew I had the answer. "Because he wants me to go to dinner!" Leo had put his fingers over his mouth as he regarded me solemnly. They twitched, as if he wanted to call the men who would come to put me in the nice white jacket with long arms and take me away to a pretty little padded room. "I'm not crazy! I know that's why he did it! It still doesn't make sense, though. Why would your brother want me to go to dinner? No!" In a lightning flash of inspiration, I had the solution. "It's your dad!"

"My dad stole the fuel pump?" Leo narrowed his eyes.

"No, Nick stole it *for* your dad."

"Because my dad wants you to go to dinner?" I nodded with vigor. Suddenly his eyes open wide again. "Oh. My dad wants you and Angel and *Harrison* to go to dinner."

"Tonight," I said.

"At the church." He shook his head again, pressed his lips together in thought, and finally said, "You're not as much of a lunatic as I thought."

Considering the circumstances, I decided to take it as a compliment.

Chapter Six

"It's colder out there than a bottle of beer after a Hungarian potluck, isn't it!" Mr. Henry R. Andersson, musical director and organist of the Kettlebean First United Methodist Church, had positioned his face close enough to mine to make every fat pore on his red nose appear big enough to cozy an egg. "I bet it's nothing like this down south!"

Were the cold and snow here a source of local pride? I didn't really have the heart to inform the guy that we Manhattanites had to deal with pretty stiff winds, and that once they'd been shepherded through all those tall buildings, they cut through our thick coats like the Grim Reaper's sickle. "It's pretty chilly," I admitted, trying not to let the man block my view of the doorway. It was futile, though. There were too many people milling around the parlor, where a half dozen church ladies busily spread plastic cloths over the long banquet tables the men had moments before finished setting up. I knew this drill since childhood, only the church of my youth had been much bigger, much richer, and the dessert table had contained three times as many Jell-O molds. "Have you seen your brother?" I murmured to Leo, who sat on the little love seat next to me.

"No, and I've been all over this church," he told me in subdued tones.

Mr. Andersson, however, wasn't in the mood to allow private conversations. He'd pulled a chair across from me for what I considered an invasion of personal space, and what he had called "a nice visit." Yeah, if he intended on visiting my uvula. "Stop me if you've heard this one before," he said with a wink, "but there was a military cook, a hairdresser, and a female lion tamer who all were in a lifeboat, and—"

"Henry!" Anneke Andersson reminded me of the mysterious white lint that suddenly appeared all over my clothes whenever I wore something black; I never really noticed either until it had sneaked up on me, and then I could never get rid of the stuff. In a chair next to her husband's, she clutched at a little silver charm around her neck that I fancifully wished were a goat's head sporting an inverted pentacle, but that was more likely a little cross sporting the Methodist flame. "Not in polite company!" She fanned herself with a *Playbill*.

"Wives!" Mr. Andersson winked at both of us. "There was a man who was engaged to be married to the most beautiful girl in the world. 'What's mine is yours,' he said to her. The next week, she sold his car and moved to Rio with the guy who bought it!" His considerable midsection convulsed with laughter. He should have been a joke archeologist, excavating moldy chestnuts from dusty, forgotten tombs of yore. "I bet he was lonelier than a ham sandwich at a Jewish wedding!"

"Henry." Mrs. Andersson's scowl was something to behold. In classical times, she could have worked as a stand-in for a gorgon if it ever wanted to take off an afternoon for a spa treatment. "Please. And I hope you'll be more in control of your humor when Mr. Carew appears!"

"Carew? If he was captain of a ship, would you be one of

his Carewmen?" Another fit of laughter. I don't need to say it wasn't mine.

"Maybe I should go see where Mr. Carew might be," I said, standing up. It seemed a little bit of a dodge to leave Leo in the lurch with the Anderssons, but he was going to be stuck with them in the long run, once the three of us had blown this ditchwater town. Besides, I couldn't stand so close a view of Mr. Andersson's winter-reddened face. "Do you know where . . . ?" I added to Leo.

Though he was still on the alert for either his father or brother, both of whom had been AWOL since we'd returned to the church, Leo actually looked fairly comfortable. "They're in the main office."

Anneke began rising, her face nobly bearing the regal mien of a Scandinavian monarch. "I could escort you," she suggested. "Our hallways are tricky."

"I wouldn't dream of it!" I scoffed. "I know exactly where it is!" And if I didn't, the multiple signs sporting arrows and reading MAIN OFFICE would certainly help. I hadn't really been trying to make Mrs. Andersson pout. But it was a bonus. "Will you . . . ?" To Leo I waved my hands about in a vague gesture meant to imply, *Will you keep an eye out for your peeping Tom brother and that insane father from whose loins you sprang?*

Apparently he got it. "You bet," he said. "I'll come get you."

Leo was a nice guy. A handsome, patient, nice guy. Why didn't they make guys like him in the city? I smiled at him as a thank-you, and slithered between the churchgoers assembling for the special meal. Out in the hall I passed a number of cherubs running around with wings they certainly hadn't been wearing at the earlier dress rehearsal; Angel had been working a little costume magic with wire and draped lengths of gauzy material. Outside the first floor choir room, a pair of women sat with a pile of metal clothes hangers and a pair of needle-nosed pliers, one of them patiently bending wire into harplike shapes. They smiled at me as I walked by.

"There you are." After he opened the locked office door to

let me in, Angel spoke with the weary voice of a father whose three-year-old has been on a several hours-long sugar high. Almost immediately, he sat back down in a chair along the wall and picked up a sewing project. "You told me you'd be here a half hour ago."

"And I was here about a half hour ago, before I got waylaid by the church ladies anxious for a sighting of . . ." I gestured at Harrison, rather than saying his name. For all the fatigue in his words, Angel certainly didn't appear to be overexerting himself. Admittedly, he'd apparently spent the entire afternoon clothing little cherubim using materials salvaged from the choir room robe closet and somebody's forgotten wedding veil, but while Leo and I had been driving around and visiting the places Nick was most likely to haunt—which consisted of the Mendez house, Vic's Pic 'N' Shop CD and Video Game Exchange, Maria's house, the bleachers behind a high school deserted for the holiday break, and the church itself—both he and our star had been cooling their heels in that cozy office. Harrison sat behind the desk. Both his hands were clenched into fists that supported a head that appeared to be heavier than the rest of his body. "Where did you get his clothes?" I asked, lowering my voice. Harrison's jacket and shirt weren't the nicest or the newest, but they were at least clean and didn't look at all rumpled and stained with bodily fluids and booze, like the crumpled set we'd rescued from his illicit love nest and thrown in the van's rear. He'd even acquired a conservative tie. Somehow Angel had managed to find clothes that made Harrison look vaguely respectable, vaguely tweedy. Given a choice between that and the disheveled-hair/lipstick-smeared-face/women's-robe-couture look, it was very much how an ordinary person might think an acclaimed stage actor should appear.

"There's a bin in the basement filled with used-clothing donations," Angel told me. "I managed to find a few less objectionable pieces in approximately his size."

"You took clothes from the *homeless?*" I had been about to add, *for that loser?* or something similarly insulting to my statement, but I'd stopped myself. Odd, how for this entire trip I seemed to have assumed that Harrison couldn't actually hear the things I'd said in front of him.

For the first time since I'd entered the room, Harrison spoke up, his voice pained. "My dear," he said, not looking up. When I glanced over, his eyes were squinted tight. "I appear to have the most enormous headache. Might you modulate your volume to the lower end of the spectrum?" After all the trouble I'd gone to for him in the past twenty-four hours, it was difficult not to stick out my tongue in his direction.

"Girl, look around." Angel's voice was as soothing as ever. There was no need for him to tone it down. "We are in the middle of Mayberry, RFD. There are no homeless people here. Those clothes were for the needy, and if there's anybody needier. . . ." Rather than drive home the point, he let it evaporate. "Besides, I've been scavenging from it all afternoon for scraps and dib-dabs to show these people how they can costume themselves to look like something other than ancient Bethlehem meets army-navy surplus."

"Is he . . . ?" There really was no universal sign language for *off the hooch*, so I risked a quick shake of my hand, thumb and pinkie extended, to signify *drunk*.

He shook his head in answer. Good. I couldn't have managed a drunk Harrison that night. "Grant called." Angel pulled a long stitch through what looked like an old purple Mexican throw he seemed to be attaching to a length of a canvas-like material. "He was wondering where we might be."

"Oh, God. You didn't talk to him, did you?" I couldn't help myself. The very thought that Angel might have told our director that we hadn't gotten a good hour away from Chez Dani gave me palpitations.

"Of course I talked to the man. Besides, he said he'd been leaving voice mails on your cell all afternoon." That was true enough. I'd ignored every one, and devised a cunning plan of claiming I'd been out of my service area, if asked about it. My palpitations were threatening to turn into an aneurysm when Angel added, "I explained to him our mechanical difficulties, and he seemed to understand. He was quite reasonable, actually."

Suddenly I could breathe again. "He's not pissed at us?"

Angel's arms crossed when he dropped his sewing and looked dead at me. "What is there to be pissed about? He's the one who insisted we make this trip and provided his unreliable vehicle. Neither of us sabotaged it deliberately." I hate it when people make perfect sense. It left me without adequate rebuttals. "I need to say something. You've got to get over this . . . this . . ."

"This what?" I asked, genuinely shocked. "I've got something so irritating that you can't even put words to it?" Thinking that Angel, one of my oldest friends, had been nursing some secret grudge against me made me feel as if I were in seventh grade and found that my best buddy had passed around a slam book devoted to cataloging my every fault. When he didn't answer immediately, I began to get more frightened. "Angel! What's going on? Do you hate me, or what?"

From the other corner, Harrison groaned at the desk. Angel looked from him to me, and said, "Riley. Calm down. I don't hate you. Far from it." The reassurance soothed my suddenly ragged nerves some, yet I was not so gullible that I couldn't see a big, fat *but* headed in my direction. "But." There it was, as ominous as it sounded. "You've gotten it into your head that your world is going to tumble to pieces if so much as a hair gets out of place."

"I haven't!" I protested. All it took was a raising of his left eyebrow to reduce me to a sullen silence. It lasted only a moment, however, and then everything I'd been feeling over the last day came spilling out. "All right, I have. Fine. I'm a control freak. I'm anal. It's my *job*. It's my duty to keep everyone on track so that performances don't get out of control. Don't," I told him, holding up a finger. He hadn't opened his mouth, but I knew what he was thinking. "You can tell me it's easy to keep things organized at work because the stage of the Claibe Richardson is teeny-tiny compared to the real world." Like my old toy theaters that I could loom over, godlike, controlling everything inside. "I know that I cloister myself in that teeny-tiny little world. I know that things can go wrong in that teeny-tiny little world, just like in the great big world outside. And that I have to cope. And I know that I'm not a stage manager twenty-four hours a day and that sometimes I have to go with the flow. And I know I'm bad at that. Everyone tells me I am." As I'd always said, I was not an actor. My little monologue was wearing me out. "So I've got my flaws, and I know what they are, and maybe one of these days I can work on them, but at the moment, we've got a play opening in a matter of days, and all three of us need to be back there for that to happen. Until that moment when we haul our asses through the stage entrance of that crusty old building we both love and adore, I'm on the clock. And I'm going to be my usual, anal, control-freak self."

Angel shook out his sewing. Somehow he had transformed a strip of blanket and a bundle of rough fabric into a passable covering from the B.C. era. It might have been a burnoose, for all I knew. "You know," he said, considering his handiwork, "if my own children had argued with themselves at such length and to such effect when they were growing up, I could have gotten in a lot more TV viewing." He began folding the costume into a neat square.

"These clothes aren't mine," Harrison said suddenly, investigating the insides of his jacket, then wincing at the volume of his own voice. I can't deny I didn't take a slight bit of retaliatory pleasure at the sight. It was a bit of a shock to hear the man whose dramatic oratory had thrilled legions of theatergoers reduced to wrinkling his nose and declaiming, "And they reek of *cabbage*."

"And you!" I said, suddenly whirling on our star with my index finger extended. "You are going to be on your best behavior tonight. There are people out there anxious to see you." Through the little glass panel in the office door I had seen the occasional face peek in. Every time, the curious on-looker would stare long enough to get a glimpse of Harrison, then dash off before he or she could be noticed. Even as I pointed, I spied a face there now. "They are all acquainted with you and your work," I said, using the bossy voice that had cajoled many an actor from his dressing room when he was throwing some kind of hissy fit with which the director didn't want to deal. I·deliberately didn't mention that they barely knew his award-winning Broadway roles, but loved the era when he'd prostituted his talent to the Madison Avenue ad boys. "So you *will* pull yourself together. And you *will* make an appearance at this dinner because it can't be avoided. And then, come hell or high water, we *will* be leaving this town and heading back to Manhattan. Oh, don't give me that look," I told him, reacting immediately to his huffs and puffs of outrage. *Scratch an actor and find a drama queen,* was my motto. "If you hadn't been hell-bent to be a bad boy, we wouldn't be in this mess. The way I see it, by the time I get you back home, I'm going to be nigh on un-fireable, no matter how much you dislike me. So get used to seeing my little face, mister." Harrison's mouth popped shut. From the corner of my eye I could still see the face peering in. "No matter how much they gawp, I want you smiling. Smile, damn it!" I commanded.

"I don't care for when they stare," he muttered. At the same time, however, the corners of his mouth inched upward—well, millimetered upward, anyway—and trans-formed his expression into something still macabre, but at least slightly less funereal.

The man at the little window tapped with one of his fin-gernails. "That's the price of fame. And I know this particu-lar guy is ruder than most of them, but regardless, you . . . Oh!" During my verbal spanking, I'd turned around to catch a good glimpse of the gawker. It was Leo, and he was looking more at me than anyone else. I rushed for the locked door and pulled it open. "Hi," I said.

"I was trying to get your attention," he apologized.

"I'm sorry."

"Without making a spectacle."

"You didn't." From his chair, Angel looked our mechanic up and down, his eyebrows raised in speculation. Once Angel noticed me observing him, his eyes glided back to his work. "What's up?" I asked Leo.

His eyes flickered past me to my companions. "Well," he hedged.

"Has our missing fuel pump resurfaced?" At Angel's question, Leo's face seemed to relax. Perhaps he hadn't been entirely certain how much I'd told them about our temporary holdup. "As I'm sure Riley has mentioned, much as we appreciate your family's hospitality, we really do have to return to the city."

I still wasn't used to the sight of Leo in street clothes that made him look like . . . well, the people I worked with on a day-to-day basis. He filled out his white sweater nicely. His lean hips shifted uncomfortably as he stuck his hands in the back pockets of his jeans. "I know," he said. "I'm sorry about that."

"Are you?"

No matter how frank he was with me, Angel was never a fan of the sharp rebuke; the tone of that question, however, brought both Leo and me up short. I gaped at him. "Of course I am," Leo said, mingling apology and surprise in a minimum number of words.

"Leo's not the one who took the pump," I said, defending the poor guy. Angel only raised his left eyebrow again. "He's not! That's so unlike you!"

"Anyway." Leo didn't seem anxious to argue the point. If there'd been any doubt in my mind about his involvement in the theft, it would have been allayed by the way he didn't bother to belabor his innocence. I had no doubts, however. Leo was about as upright as they came. I liked that about him. "I know where Nick is. You want to talk to him with me?"

"Oh!" The news was like a tonic. "Do I ever! Should I get my coat?" I wasn't looking forward to tramping around out in Winter Wonderland again, but at that point you could have slapped a harness on me and I would've pulled a sled in the Iditarod, if it helped me get the hell out of Kettlebean.

"No need. He's here. I'll take you to him if you want."

The invitation was obviously intended for Angel as well, if he cared to accompany us. He simply gave me a level look and smiled. "I'll keep a close eye on our star until it's time for his dinner appearance."

"Your choice," I told him. I didn't get the mixed signals he was shooting, but if he didn't mind babysitting Harrison Carew, I wasn't going to argue. I waited until Leo and I were out in the hallway with the office door latched behind us before saying anything more. "So where is he?"

"Someplace where he can't get away," was all that Leo would say.

That someplace turned out to be the nursery, a dank room in a corner of the building farthest from the sanctuary, painted with bright teddy bears and rainbows hovering over Noah's Ark. Playschool houses and plastic animals lay scattered on the floor between the cribs; through the large glass panels I could see Nick sitting on one of the primary school chairs, his knees almost up to his chin. Was it the toys that were keeping him there? No, a fellow I recognized as one of the Three Wise Men stood right inside the swinging doorway, his arms crossed, obviously keeping guard. At the sudden sight of us, Nick's brows folded into a scowl and his eyes rolled.

I was about to barge through the doors when I felt Leo's hand on my upper arm. "Hold up," he said, pulling me back. It was enough to stop my momentum. "I've got a question to ask."

For some reason, I automatically assumed the question had something to do with Nick and Maria. Automatically I began readying my innocent denials. Of *course* I didn't know a thing! How shocking! Thus I was surprised when

Leo murmured, his mouth close enough to my ear to arouse the hairs on my neck, "You don't think I had anything to do with the fuel pump going missing, do you?"

"No!" The denial was honest and immediate. "Listen, I don't know what's wrong with Angel. All those wings he's made today have gone to his head. Let's go in and clear up . . ."

Once again he held on to my arm. He had something else to say. It took a moment, though, for him to work out the words. "I have to know something else. When . . . when you asked me about those folding backdrops, and I told you they weren't . . . you know. From the Internet . . ."

I waited a few seconds for him to finish his thought, not exactly getting where he was leading. Then I wanted to kick myself. "Oh. Oh, Leo!" He had all but connected the dots for me, but there I stood, clueless to the last, not seeing the pattern. "Of course you didn't get those online. It was too good a design to get from some dumb Web site. Good God, don't listen to anything I say. Sometimes I open my big, fat mouth and the most appalling stuff pops out." Something else began to make sense now. "Is that why you clammed up on me this afternoon?"

His eyes shifted away from mine. Was he embarrassed? "Let's go talk to Nicky."

Now I was the one holding Leo back. Inside the room, Nick watched us from under heavy-lidded eyes, scissoring his knees nervously. "No, seriously. Was that the reason? Because you didn't think I believed you?" He'd caught that virus exclusive to the members of the human race with XY chromosomes that locked their jaws rigid when confronted with the truth, but I didn't care. I'd been the one who'd behaved more badly, implying that he hadn't been original. When I looked into his eyes, though they wouldn't meet mine for more than a few milliseconds at a time, I could see pride there, and stubbornness, and maybe a little fear. "Listen to me. I believe you."

"Thanks." He was still embarrassed and a little grim, as if

unused to praise. All the creative types I knew craved applause of one sort or another, but I knew a huge proportion of them never really believed they deserved it. Leo seemed to fall squarely into that camp, for he quickly changed the topic. "Maybe . . . we should go in, you know." Finally our eyes met. I smiled and nodded.

The nursery smelled of ammonia and graham crackers. "Okay, Bert." Leo nodded to the fellow who'd been keeping an eye on his brother, and waited until the moonlighting Wise Man had left before facing Nick, his arms crossed.

"Well, well, well," I said, stalking around the edge of the nursery, casually taking a squeezy duck from one of the bookcases and playing with it. "If it isn't little Nicky. Sweet, innocent little Nicky."

"What cop show you been watching?" he wanted to know, snorting.

"I don't like your attitude, mister!" I snarled, pointing the squeezy duck between his eyes. *Oh, crap.* He was right. I was the bastard offspring of the dark half of good cop/bad cop, by way of a hot one-nighter with the *Romper Room* lady.

"Nick, come off it already and tell us what you did with the pump." Leo seemed to be playing it bored, as if he was tired of games.

"I didn't take any pump." I'd seen more convincing performances from actresses who owed their entire careers to the casting couch.

"Listen, you," I growled. It would have been a more threatening moment if I hadn't still been gesturing with the duck.

"Come on, bro. If Dad told you to take it, say so and we'll take our questions to him and leave you alone."

Despite the length of his limbs, in the tiny, low chair, the younger Mendez brother looked impossibly juvenile. Sulkily, he said, "Dad didn't tell me to take nothing."

We weren't getting anywhere. "Leo, I want to talk to your brother alone," I said with sudden decision. Leo regarded me with surprise. "No, seriously. Let me have a couple of minutes, would you?"

After letting out a long sigh, Leo told me, "I don't think you're going to get anywhere with him, you know. He's pretty stubborn."

"Give me a chance?"

I didn't think he would do it, but Leo shrugged, turned, and shouldered his way out the swinging doors. I waited until he was all the way out in the hallway with his shoulders resting against the opposite wall before I turned back to his brother.

"What are *you* gonna do, rough me up?" he wanted to know.

With a foot I yanked out one of the tiny blue chairs and, in one swift motion, hefted my adult heinie into what precious little seat there was. "I might." When I slammed my fists on the table, the duck squeaked. I really needed to lose that particular prop. I threw it against the wall behind him, where it knocked against a jack-in-the-box, which sprang open with a recorded chuckle. The toys were conspiring against me. "I think we can come to terms, don't you?"

His head lolled back. "I don't know what you're talking about."

"I know you do, and you're going to tell me, or else I might have to let slip some information I have in my possession." Oh, that brought him to life, all right. He sat bolt upright and regarded me so warily that I couldn't resist rubbing it in a little more. "About you, your girlfriend, and a certain unplanned accident?" His lips twitched. I had the upper hand, baby, and lots of it!

After studying me for a moment, he shook his head and slumped back down. "Nah, you wouldn't."

Crap. He had me there. I wouldn't. I couldn't. I couldn't bear to be the one who made poor Mrs. Mendez's sweet face crumple into tears, or who reduced a stalwart mechanic to a disappointed, graying, pot-bellied man. But I sure could be the one to bluff about it. "Yeah, I would."

"Nah, you wouldn't."

"Yeah, I would!"

311

"Nah, you—"

I slapped the table so hard that it made both of us jump. "Don't try me!"

"Whatever." Nick crossed his arms. It was a move I dreaded seeing, because I could tell he'd thought up some kind of counterproposal. "You do that, and I'll tell my folks that you keep trying to jump me." *What!* I tried to squawk out a protest, but I'd lost all power of speech; I could only let the very bottom of my jaw dangle so low that it could have scraped the "Books of the Bible" wooden puzzle on the table. "You keep throwin' those boobies at me."

"I am *not*, repeat, *not* throwing my *boobies* at you!"

"Every time I turn around, there you are, jiggling them in my face."

I hated his smirk. "My boobies—my breasts—have happened to make *accidental* appearances that *coincide* with your . . . You know, I don't care. Tell them. They're not going to believe you."

"My mom already knows about this morning," he reminded me. "She might think that one was an accident, but what's she going to think when she hears you did it again?" He put his finger against his nose. "Yeah, you're going to get drummed out of town when she hears that."

If steam had started pouring from my ears accompanied by a whistle sound, like some Warner Brothers animated character, I wouldn't have been surprised. "I'm not going to get drummed out of town because I don't have a van to leave town in, thanks to you!" I said, three shades short of a shout. "That's it. I've had it."

After I'd managed to pull myself up to my feet again, I heard Nick's voice at my back. "You're not telling anybody anything!" It was all I could do not to throw another body part in his direction. Namely, my middle finger.

"What's the matter?" Leo asked, once I'd pushed through the doors so hard that one of them nearly crashed into the wall before rebounding. "You look like you could chew up an iron bar and spit nails."

"You got an iron bar handy?" I growled, flashing my teeth at him. "Your brother is the most annoying, *juvenile—*"

"Hey, hey, hey!" I heard from down the hall. Apparently my feelings of ill will in the house of the Lord had only brought down more punishment on my head, for Mr. Mendez was walking down the hallway in our direction, extending his hands. "It's time for dinner, you kids. Everyone's waiting. Chop-chop!"

"I'll chop-chop your—"

Leo interrupted my mutter before his father got too near. "Dad, do you know anything about the fuel pump that got taken from the garage? In the middle of my repairs?" Again, I'd seen hammy silent-film stars with more subtlety than Mr. Mendez's gamut of frowns, pouty lips, and fingers held to his mouth, all to connote doubt. "Dad. Seriously."

"No, no, is there something missing? The fuel pump? Really? After you drove all that way for it? Maybe you misplaced it? I'm sure it's somewhere around the garage, isn't it?" I narrowed my eyes, not buying a word of it. "You know how it is. You make a long trip, you're tired, you forget where you put something. And in a garage that size . . . it's easy to lose something, right? I do it all the time."

Apparently Leo wasn't any more pleased with the waffling than I was. "Are you saying it's still somewhere in the garage?" he asked, surprisingly stern. "Did you *hide* it?"

Someone should have notified NASA, because Mr. Mendez's eyebrows took a trip into the stratosphere. "I never said such a thing! Of course I didn't take the fuel pump! You're tired, son, and—"

"Where is it?" I'd had enough of the games. "Please. Just tell me where it is."

He held out his hands in a "nothing up my sleeves!" gesture. "Miss McIntyre, I really don't know, but once this pageant is over, Christmas Eve, I'm sure I could go over to the garage and give a good lookie-loo for it, because you never know where things might turn up in that place. A couple of

313

weeks ago, I set down a wrench—didn't I, Leo?—and when I turned around—"

"That's blackmail." House of the Lord or not. I was going to swear. I was sure He'd heard it all before. "You are fucking blackmailing me."

The bastard didn't appear fazed at all. In fact, he smiled broadly. "Young lady, that is not a very nice thing to say. Not very nice at all! I'm offering my assistance! After the pageant, of course. Now, let's go to dinner. Our guest is waiting." He turned and began to hurry down the hall. Leo and I glanced at each other, and followed in haste.

"You can't keep me here," I called out. "The three of us are taking that morning train into Manhattan tomorrow."

"Grand!" said Mr. Mendez without turning around. "It leaves at nine-thirty. You'll have time for a good breakfast. Best way to start the day!"

"You can't stop us from getting on that train!" I called out. It had no effect. Mr. Mendez was a man with a mission, and now that he'd managed to delay our departure for a few hours, I was nothing. He had bigger fish to fry.

And there was the big fish himself, sitting at the table in the church parlor nearest the fireplace, his back erect, his neck quivering, looking to all the world like an asthmatic set down in the midst of a hothouse, waiting for the inevitable sneezing to begin. Actually, the whole scene resembled that famous picture of the Last Supper, but with disciples of both sexes leaning toward the center of a table set with paper plates and cups, supplicating a savior clothed in a tweedy, ill-fitting jacket. Angel sat calmly on Harrison's right side, with Mrs. Mendez next to him; an adoring Mrs. Henry R. Andersson graced the actor's left. "Here we all are!" Mr. Mendez's voice broke through the low whispers. "Isn't this great?"

No one else at the long table could see it, but from where I stood in the parlor door, I could; Angel kicked Harrison beneath the table, forcing him to speak up. "A veritable feast of goodwill and good food, I am certain." The mere sound of his voice, so cultured, so nuanced, brought smiles to the faces of the good folk of Kettlebean. "Was it not the Bard of Avon himself who said, 'If music be the food of love' . . . er, yes." Another of Angel's prods brought that speech to a close. "If now we are all here, bring on the baked feast!"

"Bring it in!" called Mr. Mendez. "Bring it in, girls!"

From the kitchen, a plump church lady wheeled out a rickety metal cart, atop which sat a domed serving platter. I recognized the smell, and instantly felt a moment of dread. There was no way that Harrison would play along with this stunt. Even in the name of politeness, they were going to push him too far. When I looked at Leo, his face was blank. He didn't know what was coming. Mr. Mendez, however, wore an expression of pure glee. He had planned this entire venture from start to finish, never suspecting that with Harrison Carew involved, it could only end in certain disaster.

Too late. The platter had arrived at his table, and the woman had already positioned it in front of him. I held my breath when she grabbed hold of the dome's handle and lifted it up. Steaming from its sojourn in the church ovens, the concoction of pastry, potatoes, and beef sat blandly in front of Harrison, as it had for countless commercials during the dark years of his career.

The inheritor of Olivier's mantle, fork in one hand and knife in the other, stared at the lard-colored pastry for a moment, and then regarded Mr. Mendez. No twitch betrayed his emotions. He looked down at the pie again, and then around at all the people regarding him expectantly.

"Don't say it," I whispered to myself, so softly it was inaudible.

Mrs. Andersson leaned forward, reverence in her eyes. "Oh, do say it for us."

Harrison Carew cleared his throat, and then set down the fork and knife. Was he going to stand up and leave? No. He merely closed his eyes and took in a deep breath. "Why, sir!" he intoned lifelessly, affecting both a stiff upper lip and a British accent. "It's a meat pie as big as your head!"

The applause that followed was considerable, but I

couldn't listen to it. Much as I disliked Harrison after all he'd put me through, watching him demean himself for people who thought him famous solely for being the Michaelson's Meat Pies butler actually hurt. I'd been the one to lecture him earlier about playing nice, but he shouldn't have had to do that. It felt like it was all my fault. "Can we do something?" I said to Leo, suddenly tired of it all. He raised his eyebrows, curious. "Where do you go in this town when you want to get wild and crazy?"

"Wild and crazy? In Kettlebean?" he said, surprised. "I guess . . . I guess we could—"

"Surprise me," I told him, jerking my head in the direction of the door.

"But . . . do you want to leave Mr. Carew with your friend? Aren't you supposed to—"

"You know what? Angel told me I work too much. If he gets miffy over it, I'll tell him I'm clocking out for the day. How about it?"

"You're on." The grin he gave me was nothing compared to the one I wore simply at the thought of being free of the pageant for a couple of hours.

Chapter Seven

The wine we'd been drinking was a not-bad red. The lighting was subdued. The music a barely audible mix of hits from the nineties. The mood . . . well, the mood had been slightly marred when Leo had launched into a warbling falsetto imitation of Anneke Andersson, complete with that alarming vibrato, and as a result, my mouthful of wine nearly escaped through my nose.

All that made up for both the decor and the food. Though the sofa was comfortable enough, there wasn't much to recommend the knotty pine paneling on the walls, the basket of neglected laundry by the fireplace, or the frozen pizzas we'd half-finished a few minutes before. I didn't care. Getting away from all the noise in my head was enough. I lay back on the pillows and sighed, my belly still aching from the laughter. "When you said you knew someplace to go, I didn't know it was going to be your swinging bachelor pad, mister."

At some point in the previous hour, Leo had chosen to stretch out on the floor of the apartment over his dad's garage, using pillows to prop himself up while we talked.

He reached up and from the wooden coffee table took another slice. "Listen. You're expecting way too much of Kettlebean. If you want good food, you have to drive to Newark. The Newark in *New York*," he teased, reddening my face. "The one restaurant in town is the diner, and that's closed because the couple who run it are at the church eating pasties."

"What?"

"Pasties. Meat pies. Whatever you want to call them." He chewed contemplatively on the cardboard-like crust for a moment. "This isn't New York, you know. I bet you can walk out your front door and there's an all-night coffee shop, or a great little Italian restaurant nobody knows about."

"There's a coffee shop down the street," I admitted. Across the room, in the fireplace, logs popped and settled as they burned. I curled my toes and nestled comfortably among the cushions. "And the restaurant nobody knows about is Vietnamese, but it's still great. Ooh, but if we were home right now, you know where I'd take you? There's this little soup kitchen right near me that's open . . . Well, it's hard to say when it's open, because it doesn't have any hours posted. It's open pretty much whenever the fat Russian couple who run it feel like being there, which can mean that some days it's closed before midafternoon, and other days the lights are on until after midnight. They have the *best* homemade soups there. At least five or six at a time."

"Borscht?"

"They usually have borscht, though I don't like it. There's a chicken-and-dumpling soup that is to die for. And there's a mushroom barley that you have got to try. Seriously. It's the best." My voice trailed off. I really would have liked to take Leo to that weird little soup place to see how he liked it, I realized. It wasn't the wine making me think that, either; after spending most of the day with him, I'd genuinely come to feel comfortable around Leo. It seemed a little unfair that after my little crew left Kettlebean in our wake, I'd probably never see him again. "Have you ever been to New York?" Could he hear the wistfulness in my voice? I occupied myself with what was left of my wine, so he wouldn't be able to tell.

"A few times. Amazing place." He pulled himself up to an upright, cross-legged position, and studied his own glass, as I did mine.

"You should move there." After the suggestion left my mouth, I was horrified at myself. I barely knew this guy. What if he thought . . . Yet why did I worry so much about what he thought?

He had looked up at me when I spoke. After regarding me briefly, he held up both hands and looked around the apartment. "And give up all this? You've got to be crazy."

He'd made me laugh again, but I still felt residual guilt. I must have seemed awful to him, making fun of his hometown, deriding the pageant, mocking the people at his church. I was one of those personalities I hated most at work—the big-city girl who walked onto the stage and expected all the players and scenery to conform to her liking. "So what's there to do in Newark?" I asked, trying to shoo the spotlights in his direction.

"Not a lot." He grinned. "But it's bigger than here, and just down the road. I . . . There's a community theater there. I kind of work with them." This was more like it. I'd wanted to hear more about this side of Leo's life, but the day's craziness hadn't allowed us to explore it. I nodded encouragement. "Tech stuff, mostly. Building sets, some prop work . . ."

"Set design." He nodded, but didn't elaborate as I hoped he might. Why was it so difficult to get him to open up on this particular topic? "What shows have you designed for?"

He shrugged, taking more interest in the Cheetos we'd been sharing from a bowl, than in me. "A few."

"Did you study somewhere?"

"A couple of places."

Every question felt like I was prolonging an interrogation. "How long have you been doing it?" I swore to God, if he said *a while* and gave me the same offhanded attitude as a response, I was going to grind my teeth into nubs.

After a very long silence, during which I could have completely disassembled, oiled, and put back together a table saw, and still had time left over for a short round of canasta, he finally sighed. Leo's voice was extremely small when he admitted, "Since I was fifteen or sixteen."

For a moment I thought of bringing up all those miniature sets I'd made in my own teens. Maybe, though, that would be too personal. "Do you not want to talk about this?" I had to know. The conversation, so natural and easy before, had taken an almost painful turn. I'd tried giving it a shot, attempting to make up for my insensitivity of earlier in the afternoon, but perhaps it wasn't going to work. "Because I can change the topic. I thought, you know, because we had that aspect in common, it might be fun to talk about, but if not . . . well, we really don't have a lot more time to get to know each other. I intend to be on that nine-thirty train tomorrow morning, after all." A sudden, suspicious thought occurred to me. "It is a nine-thirty train, isn't it? Your dad didn't tell me the wrong time to throw me off?"

While I'd been speaking, Leo had wrapped his arms around his bent knees, upon which he'd rested his chin. He laughed a little. "No, it's a nine-thirty train. I've taken it myself when I've gone into the city. I don't think Dad would go that far."

"He's gone pretty far!" I growled. "But fine. I feel better about the train, anyway. Listen, we can flip on the TV or something if you want, and—"

"I studied from books," he said suddenly. Leo wore the shyest expression I'd ever seen. "There used to be these books at the Newark library, with all the best plays of each year, from the forties up until the seventies. There'd be a short version of the play, highlights, kind of. And photos of the sets. They were such bad photos," he said, shaking his head, lost in memory. "But I loved them." He cleared his throat. "Anyway. Then I found there were other books, some in color. And I studied those. Then in college . . . well, I threw myself in the theater program. Small as it was. But . . ." While he'd been talking, I couldn't shake the feeling that he'd been letting me have a glimpse into a confidential part of his life. I thought I'd lost him again when he slipped into silence. "This . . . this isn't easy to talk about."

"I'm sorry," I said softly.

"To you."

How was I not supposed to react to that? The verbal codicil felt like a slap in the face. After I'd been so encouraging? After I'd tried to draw it out of him, despite his being so frustratingly clammy-uppy and *male*? "Why?"

"Because you're so . . ." His hands flew up in the air as he searched for the right word. I already knew what he was going to say, and my heart ached at the certainty of it. *Difficult. Unapproachable. Aloof.* Finally his lips parted. "Important!"

I reeled. That was so not what I thought he was going to say. Practically hiding behind one of his sofa pillows, I said timidly, "What?"

"It's frustrating, Riley," he said, sounding almost as if he were trying not to yell. "You're a professional. You're no older than I am, yet you're at the top of your field. You've got success written all over everything you do. You're gorgeous, you're motivated, you make me laugh. You've got Harrison freakin' Carew riding shotgun with you. Why in the world would you give a good goddamn about . . . about the stupid designs of . . . of . . . a stupid—"

"Don't," I begged through a mouthful of pillow. "Don't you dare finish that sentence. You wouldn't let me put myself down, remember?"

"It's the way I feel. And that's why it isn't easy." He glowered at the sofa on which I sat as if it had personally insulted him. Without a word more, he folded the paper napkin in one of his hands and began straightening the coffee table, sliding my remaining frozen pizza onto his plate, then preparing to carry them into the kitchen to put or throw away. Classic male avoidance strategy.

Yet I couldn't blame him. Everyone cultivates a private, sacred acre where they build dreams and store those things that are most precious. I'd poked and prodded at the gateway to his, yet given no assurance that I wouldn't trample the grass or litter the grounds. "You're frightened," I said.

He stopped in the middle of collecting the plates. "I don't know about that."

"You are. Oh, come on, pop psychologist," I said, keeping my tone light. "You're afraid that the big old mean stage manager is going to think you're subpar. Me, the girl who's spent an entire career in the dark backstage, the one no audience member sees. The one whose bio never gets read in *Playbill*. Me, the one that all the cast and crew forget about the moment that curtain is down and they've gone on their way. I'm the big, bad boogeyman, all right."

"No one forgets you." Leo's thick, dark eyebrows were set into a frown. "I mean, jeez, the way you yell at people when you're on a tear . . . Yeah. You're right. That alone scares the pants off me."

He had me smiling now. "Okay, fine, smart-ass," I told him, leaping up and finally emerging from behind the safety of my pillow. "You know you're going to have to show me some of those sketches now. Don't even *try* to hold out on me. I'll beat them out of you if I have to!"

" 'Mechanic Found Dead from Blueprint Beating'?"

"Don't tease. It could happen!" But no, I couldn't joke forever. "Seriously," I told him, leaning forward so that we were at eye level. "I want to see." When he seemed to hesitate, I shook my head to let him know he didn't have an option. "I won't condescend. I won't lie to you. If it stinks, I'll say so."

"That's reassuring," he said, not looking entirely certain. At the same time, I was sure the words were what he wanted to hear. Finally, he made a decision. "Okay." He rolled his eyes, a bit self-conscious about how much of himself he'd revealed moments before. I didn't mind. I'd gotten to see a side of Leo that I suspected few of the other Mendezes had ever seen before, much less anyone outside the community theater where he volunteered his time. "But—"

"Oh, by all that's holy, enough of the *buts* already. Let's see!"

He vacillated for a moment, then finally rose to his feet and beckoned. We left the plain comfort of the worn rag rug around which most of the living room furniture sat and padded in our sock feet across the cold wooden floors. I regretted leaving the warmth of the fireplace almost immediately; the old garage building was drafty enough to leave a distinct chill on this wintry evening. I would have endured arctic temperatures, however, for this opportunity.

We walked through a doorway near the back of the living space. The switch that Leo flipped turned on a pair of table lights that flanked a bed near the door. When he kept walking, however, I realized that the room was much more than a place to sleep. Nearly three times the size of the little living room where we'd laughed and eaten bad pizza, it contained not only a small corner decorated to resemble a bedroom, but a much larger area where Leo had set up a drafting table and a tall workbench. He turned on goose-necked lamps attached to each; they lent the deep room a golden glow almost warmer than the fire we'd abandoned.

Sketches covered an entire wall on the room's far side, thumbtacked to the knotty pine. My eyes wandered among them while I staggered forward. There was some alcohol in my system, yes, but mostly I felt drunk on images: compelling shapes, deft and swiftly drawn, of landscapes and interiors that Leo had envisioned while dreaming of the theater. Most were impressionistic drafts, chiaroscuro patterns of light and dark, indistinct but not at all vague. On every single one of those sheets of paper, it was impossible to miss the artist's intentions, whether it be to support the actors by giving them broad planes on which to stand, or to overpower them with shapes and shadows. "Leo," I whispered.

He was beside me, looking at the wall as I did. "That was for a production of *As You Like It*," he said, pointing to one of the sketches. "The director wanted something that wasn't the traditional forest design, so I came up with an idea to use movable towers and gloom to . . ." Though he kept talking, I had to admit I wasn't paying full attention. It was his images that had grabbed me, and kept me moving. At sketch after sketch, he paused to explain when he had drafted them, and what he had intended. I didn't need the words. Like those of any good designer, Leo's drawings spoke for themselves.

How long did I stand there, entranced by that wall? I really had no way of knowing. Only when Leo touched me lightly on my arm did I tear my eyes away from those images of pencil and charcoal. "You haven't said a word," he said. In the warm light of the lamps, he looked boyish and uncertain. "It's kind of freaking me out."

"Oh. I'm sorry." It was too overwhelming, all this raw talent. "It's good. *Really* good. I mean, I've known high-paid professional designers who have churned out much less creative stuff. Leo, you're . . ." I didn't know how he'd take what I wanted to say. He'd already gone so far as to let me tiptoe on the outskirts of his private acre, the most guarded part of his imaginative life. I feared ruining its tranquillity with a misspoken word. "Why are you here? Why aren't you down in the city, making a go of it?"

What was that odd expression in his eyes? Had I gone too far? "I'm not anywhere near that talented," he said, trying to laugh off my suggestion.

"Yes," I insisted, "you are. Don't you think you owe yourself a shot at it? Come down for a few days. Stay with me. We can show some of these to Grant, my director. God knows he'll owe you a favor for putting up with us for a few days. He might know of someone who's looking for a fresh new designer, and—What are those?" In all my rapture over the wall of sketches, I hadn't noticed what sat upon his workbench until that moment: small boxes, intricate and beautiful. The one closest to me was constructed of dark wood set upon small feet, with hinged doors that opened. A Palladian temple facade graced its front, giving the box a cabinet-like appearance. Its outside had been painted with windows in the style of an old engraving. The words THE OLD VIC crossed the gap in the doors. I reached out to swing open the small panels. "Oh, that's a silly hobby of mine," he said. "You might think it's cute, though. I like making . . ."

"Toy theaters," I said, at the same time he did. Inside the doors was a perfect reproduction of a Victorian stage. The back of the box had been constructed and painted in exquisite detail to represent a proscenium arch and hanging velvet curtain, complete with royal crest. It surrounded a sylvan backdrop of water and trees. On either side of the stage, actual audience boxes angled out toward the box's front; two tiny rows of orchestra seating sat on the floor.

I couldn't move.

"You'll get a kick out of this," he said, walking around to the other side of the table. "I don't usually put them all on like this, because it's kind of a fire hazard with the wiring up here, but . . ." He fiddled with a number of extension cords, and flipped a toggle on a power strip. "Ta-da!" His voice was as exuberant as a kid's.

The theater had lit up. Each of the boxes, with their bowed, sculpted balconies, had its own little bulb in the ceiling, illuminating it from the inside. The stage was lit from three different color battens that brought the backdrop to vibrant life. And it wasn't the only stage to be bathed in light. To the left and right of the miniature Old Vic were more stages. Covent Garden. The Globe. The Savoy, where the back of a tiny conductor protruded from the orchestra pit as he presided over a production of *The Mikado*. All of them were entrancing, all of them beautiful. "Oh, Leo," I whispered.

I had always wanted such a theater of my very own. No—in my youth I'd always wished for the ability to envision and create such theaters, but my paltry cardboard-and-balsa contraptions were nothing like these. The sight of so much beauty, so much care and loving attention to detail, made a giant lump rise in my throat. Without knowing, I'd waited all my life for this moment. "What?" he asked. I shook my head. "Riley, what?"

I didn't think it would be possible for me to speak, but I forced out the words. "They're amazing. You're amazing. You really are." I took a deep breath, knowing that if I paused during the next speech, I might not be able to finish it. "Leo, you have to come to the city. You have to give all this, your dream, a chance. You'll never be able to live with yourself if you don't. Don't say no," I warned him, when I saw the terror begin to surface once more in his eyes. "Agree with me. I'll be there by your side the entire time, I promise. Say you will."

I was afraid he wouldn't. Maybe he'd been right about Harrison, about Harper Lee, just as I knew I was right about how scared he was, though he wouldn't admit to it. Just as I'd known Angel had been right about me earlier. Fear held us all back from doing the things we wanted. I could encourage him. I could offer him all the support in the world, but unless he risked stepping into the spotlight, he'd remain in the dark for the rest of his life. *Please*, I prayed. I didn't know to whom I thought that word, but I yearned for it to be heard. *Please*.

His lips worked, trying to summon up speech. "You didn't mean that about . . . me staying with you? If I came."

"I meant it," I assured him. We stood close together, near that row of toy theaters and their twinkling lights. Funny. My skin was in goose pimples, but I didn't notice the cold anymore. "Did . . . did you mean what you said earlier? About me being . . ." I was afraid to say the word in case it had been my imagination, but if he was being courageous, I had to match him fear for fear. "Gorgeous?"

At my embarrassed laughter, he smiled and lifted a hand to my face, letting the backs of his knuckles trace my ears, my cheeks, my chin, my neck. "I'd kind of privately decided you hadn't heard that part," he admitted.

I had, but when he'd said the word, I'd put it aside to consider later, when I could appreciate it more. Like now. "Believing that kind of thing always scares me," I admitted.

"Let me show you how beautiful I think you are," he said. His hand was on the back of my neck now, easing me closer. Our lips met and parted. The bristles covering his cheek and chin were rough against my skin. Still, I fell into the kiss as if it were the downiest of mattresses, sinking against his body and feeling the heat there, warmer than any fireplace.

"But I'm taking the train home tomorrow," I said, fearful I might want too much from him if I gave in.

"And you've invited me to visit the city," he said. "You still want me to come?" Oh, I did. I did. "Then let me show you." When I hesitated, holding on to his shoulders for support, he looked down at me. "Okay?"

How could I resist those gentle eyes? The first time I'd seen him, I recognized how kind they were. Making the decision was easy: I was going to let myself lose control for a while, and my world wouldn't crumble to pieces. "Yes," I said, as I let him lead me to the room's other side.

When he turned out the bedside lights, I could still see him in profile, illuminated by the hundreds of tiny, twinkling lights of the toy theaters, aglow over private acres we had long shared, yet until that moment never explored together.

Chapter Eight

"I thought I heard a train." Six pairs of eyes turned to where I stood on the landing of the kitchen stairs. Maybe I was something of a mess, in that robe tailored for Jabba the Hutt and with my hair flying every which way. The expression of wild, stark fear across my face helped lend me a certain madwoman-in-the-attic flavor, I'm sure. "Did you hear a train?" I asked Angel, who was spreading jam across an English muffin at the breakfast table.

"I did," he replied, calm as ever. He finished with the muffin half in his hand, placed it on a plate, and slid it in front of Harrison Carew, next to him. Though dressed in the same clothes as last night, Harrison blinked rapidly and repeatedly, as if not really sure where he was, or how he got there. A tall glass of still-fizzing Alka-Seltzers sat in front of him. "Drink," Angel instructed the actor.

"It's just the eight-twenty freight pulling through town, sunshine!" *Sunshine, hell.* Hector Mendez was the bright and cheerful one. He'd chomped most of the way through a breakfast of eggs and chorizo, hash browns, and a chocolate-iced doughnut. That much food this early in the

328

morning made my stomach roil. "You've still got plenty of time."

I disliked that smug, insincere smile on Mr. Mendez's face, but at the same time, at least I had the satisfaction of knowing that there was no way he and Nick could get away with crawling under the train engine and stealing parts. The clock over the stove read eight twenty-three. Another hour and seven minutes, and the three of us would be out of this town. "Breakfast?" Mrs. Mendez smiled at me broadly from where she stood at the stove, holding out a frying pan half-full of another round of sausage and eggs. I held up a hand to indicate a pass.

"Get enough sleep?" Mr. Mendez's question was loud enough to make me jump and clutch my robe a little more tightly.

"Why, yes, I did, thank you." Oddly, I felt more refreshed than I'd expected, even after waking so abruptly and catapulting myself downstairs.

"She didn't get in until after *one in the morning*," Dora announced with the hateful intensity of meaning that only a fourteen-year-old could bring to such a simple sentence. "*Leo* let her in." I was suddenly very, very glad that I hadn't had a younger sister when I had grown up, because if my current impulses were any indication, I would probably still be doing hard time for unrepentant sororicide.

Instead of lunging at the little brat's throat, however, I merely stepped down into the kitchen and pretended that my late arrival was no big deal. "I didn't have a key," I said.

"Uh-huh."

I shot Dora a quelling look. "Leo and I had been trying to find the fuel pump that *mysteriously* had gone missing," I said, pouring myself half a glass of milk. Part of me noted how closely Nick decided to study his cereal at that moment.

"Oh, really. Did he find it under your shirt?"

"Dora!" said Mrs. Mendez from the stove, without turning around.

I decided that a lofty response would be best. "I didn't

know you were up so late," I told the girl, smiling. "I would have waved to you if I'd known."

"With what? Your tongue? I don't know how, since it was already shoved down—"

"And how are you, Angel?" I asked briskly, moving on. Despite his seeming unconcern, he had been following our conversation with eager ears. I could tell by the way his mouth had pursed to the side that he was restraining himself from interrogating me. "All packed and ready to go?"

"You seem in a bright and cheerful mood," he said. Then, blandly, he looked at me over his reading glasses. "Am I to guess that the mechanic found the parts he wanted?"

There was a nasty double entendre somewhere in there that I didn't care to pursue. Not with Leo's parents hovering so close. "We didn't find the fuel pump, no."

"Ah. Pity."

"It's gotta be there somewhere!" said Mr. Mendez through a mouthful of doughnut. "If you want to skip the train and stay a few hours tonight after the pageant, Nick and I can help look over the—"

Oh, wouldn't he like that, if we did. "That's really so nice of you. But we'd hate to be any more of an imposition."

His wide mustache curved up at its farthest edges. "All righty, then!"

That was it? I'd expected more. More pleading. More begging. More outright dirty tricks, or the invocation of Mrs. Robinson, Kettlebean's home-brewed saint. None was forthcoming. *Well, then.* I cleared my throat. "Since I have a little time, I'm going to hop into the shower."

"Mmmfph." The strange sound came from Nick's mouth, a muted snort of amusement. Had I said something funny? Oh, wait. I knew. He was probably thinking about the eyeful he'd gotten about the same time yesterday morning. Yeah, that had to be it. Dora snickered too, her hand covering her mouth while her shoulders shook up and down. They both kept their heads low. Hard to believe that they and Leo had sprung from the same loins. Loins. Leo certainly had a good set of those. No, that line of thought wasn't going to get me clean. Regally, I rose from my perch against the counter and glided upstairs, dignified all the way.

I'd honestly thought that with the train arriving so relatively early, we'd have a hectic morning of it. Yet there I was, humming during my shower, smiling while I shook the wrinkles from my overalls and turtleneck in the steamy bathroom afterward, and feeling no ill will toward anyone—even Dora—as I dressed myself. Part of it was the afterglow of the night before, but mostly I was happy to be going home. The bedroom clock read eight fifty when finally I smoothed the bed down and did a quick check to make sure I hadn't forgotten anything. I had the little backpack I normally took to and from work, which contained my wallet, a notebook, pens, a collection of Tony Kushner plays I was trying to work through, and what precious few cosmetics I felt it necessary to haul around with me. I had my coat and gloves and woolly hat, my ChapStick, my watch. . . . No, I didn't have my watch. I could've sworn I'd tumbled into bed without taking it off, but there it was on Dora's desk. I must've been more tired than I'd thought.

I checked the watch against the bedroom clock. The train station was five Kettlebean blocks away, and Kettlebean blocks were nothing compared to Manhattan city blocks. We still had plenty of time.

I'm not exactly sure what I expected from the Mendezes when it actually came time to leave. Part of me thought that perhaps Mrs. Mendez might corner me or, more likely, Angel, the soft touch, and gently plead for us to stay. Another part of me definitely thought that Mr. Mendez, under the mistaken impression that I was bluffing about abandoning the van and returning to the city via rail, would suddenly relent and produce the stupid fuel pump. I'd dreamed of that moment since the night before, and of how he'd chase after the train, red-and-white box in hand, begging us to reconsider. Sometimes the dream concluded with a toss of my head and an evil little laugh courtesy of Cruella de Vil, which probably explains why acting was better left to people other than me.

And the last part of me definitely expected Dora to stand on the front porch and give us the finger when we left.

But there was no resistance from the Mendezes when, at five minutes after nine by the mantel clock, the three of us finally escaped the confines of that two-story, vinyl-sided Alcatraz. No pleading. No tears. No fingers. In fact, I was surprised that only the two adults were there to see us off, and, save for a couple of perfunctory handshakes from him and light hugs from her, neither of them seemed particularly sorrowful to see us go. Maybe they'd talked about it and decided we were more trouble than we were worth, because afterward they both sat down and gave each other a certain look. It was odd, that look, half guilty, half full of dread. Perhaps they were envisioning with alarm the day after the show's opening when one of us came back to reclaim Grant's van.

"Wasn't that a little anticlimactic?" I asked Angel, once the door had closed behind us and we'd crunched down the salted front steps. Not even Dora hovered in the upstairs window, spying on us.

"You really wanted more drama?" You would have thought that Angel was Harrison Carew's personal insurance carrier, the way he helped the guy navigate the icy walkway to the little picket fence leading to the side street.

"Good Lord, no. Come on, Harrison. Only a few more hours and we'll be home." At least the actor had recovered enough from his massive hangover of the day before that it didn't look like he was being dragged; he even managed to carry a pillowcase Mrs. Mendez had donated, full of what clothes we'd been able to salvage during our love-nest commando raid. Not much more than the bathrobe he'd been wearing and a T-shirt. I hoped Dani had the presence of mind to burn whatever we'd left behind. My one impression of the woman had been of her big doe eyes and her considerable implants.

The winter morning was so bright from the sun glancing off snow-covered surfaces that it was difficult to see. The county must have had a good fourteen to eighteen inches of snow in the past two days; the trees were almost completely hidden beneath thick blankets. I didn't care. I might have met someone special here—someone actually pretty wonderful—but he was coming to join me in the city soon. Besides, Kettlebean was quite literally hell frozen over, and I was glad to be leaving my last footprints across it.

The small town's train station could be described as a shed with a kerosene heater. "Penn Station, New York City, please," I told the round-faced man behind the ticket gate, brandishing cash I'd borrowed from Leo for the deed. "Three tickets on the next train."

"On the next train? Absolutely, ma'am." In his little office on the other side of the window, the station agent began processing my request almost immediately, though he took a second to glance over my shoulder to where Angel and Harrison were taking seats on the bench. "You know, it really was an honor to have Mr. Carew at the dinner last night." I smiled vaguely, recognizing the guy as one of the shepherds in the pageant. He'd been the one who'd been pushing his daughter's stuffed sheep around with his foot until Angel had taken it away from him, I believed. "His speech was really an inspiration, you know." There was a speech? An inspirational speech? From the man who, after we'd retrieved him Friday afternoon, had only produced perspiration? That was news to me. That morning, Harrison looked more like a Central Park flasher than the next Tony Robbins. "It must be wonderful working with him."

"You have no idea," I said through my teeth. It wasn't a lie, exactly.

"Tell me," said the man, collecting the tickets and pushing them across the counter, "is he like that all the time?"

What the heck had Harrison done after I'd left? Obviously it had been something fairly unbelievable. I didn't want to pooh-pooh this guy's experience; it would feel a little too much like sitting in the front row of church during a service and sighing audibly at the points of the sermon that everyone else enjoyed. Instead, I tilted my head, looked the man in the eyes, and with the utmost sincerity said, "I've dealt with him for only the couple of weeks his show's been rehearsing in the theater, but for the most part, he's always been a consummate professional."

That seemed to leave the man shiny-eyed and happy. Once I returned to the bench with our tickets safely tucked into my coat pocket, I sat down between the two men and looked at my watch. It was nine twenty-two. "Harrison made some kind of speech last night?"

"Oh, it was quite the show." Angel had picked up a few of the brochures from the tourist information display by the trackside door. As he casually browsed through them, I recognized the card on top—a green and pleasant photograph captioned BEAUTIFUL KETTLEBEAN, NEW YORK!, of what had to be the town's main street and clock tower when it wasn't under a foot and a half of snow—as the same complimentary postcard I'd picked up at the garage Friday night. "Lasted the better part of fifteen minutes. As best as I could tell, it was a mixture of monologues from Miller, Stoppard, Pinter, and a touch of Tennessee Williams, with several quotations from *Measure for Measure* thrown in for spice. Not altogether comprehensible, but it was certainly impressive."

"*All's Well That Ends Well.*" I'd been so accustomed to Harrison sitting on the sidelines that his sudden participation in the conversation startled me. "'I have forgiven and forgotten all, though my revenges were high bent upon him. . . . Let him not ask our pardon: The nature of his great offense is dead, and deeper than oblivion we do bury the incensing relics of it: let him approach, a stranger, no offender.'"

His voice had trailed off at the end of the little speech, sounding both melancholy and very old. "You know," I said to him, "whenever I hear Shakespeare spoken aloud, there's a slight time delay while my internal translator kicks in. So excuse me for asking, but was that an attempt at an apology?" If that was the case, Harrison wasn't planning to be any more forthcoming about it. He refused to look at me, instead letting the sun streaming through the eastern windows cast his profile in silent and stubborn silhouette. I found his silence maddening. "What is it with you?" I managed to modulate my tone so the words came out more as a humorous inquiry than laced with anger. "We're going to have to work together for the next few weeks at the very least, and maybe months or even years after that, if you get your act together. You and me, mister, relying on each other. We're going to be part of a team, like it or not. And what I want to know is, why've you been so anxious to shoot yourself in the foot?"

"Riley." Angel put down the brochures and cocked his head at me, disapproving.

"Angel, sweetie, you can mommy him all you want once we get back to the Claibe. That's your job, making sure the actors look their best. My job is to make sure they're on their marks and ready to go, and I really want to know something." I faced Harrison. From the way his chin jutted out, defensively and quivering slightly, I could tell he was conscious of every word I said. "I'm not trying to be mean. I'm really not. I need to know you're going to be serious about this show. We're going into previews day after tomorrow." Still he said nothing. "Are you one of those actors who just isn't *there* unless a spotlight's on him? Or are you a Harper Lee?"

"Harper Lee?" Angel mused behind me. "Sounds familiar. Is she one of those society girls, like Paris Hilton?"

"Are you going to be one of those people who has one shining, award-winning moment in the spotlight, then spends the rest of his life shying away from ever again living up to it? If that's the case, I wish you hadn't taken this play, because . . ." Way to go, Riley, I told myself. Tell the guy that the livelihoods of a lot of good people will be on the line if he doesn't get his act together! Send him into an even more catatonic state! "I guess I'm looking for some kind of sign—anything, Harrison, any sign at all—that I'm going to be able to count on you. I sincerely want to be able to." Still nothing. I hadn't gotten anywhere, and probably I never would. At last, I turned to Angel and sighed. "It's Christmas Eve. I'm due some kind of miracle, right?"

Angel smiled and patted me on the arm with one of his mittened hands. I'd said really all I could, hadn't I? Harrison wouldn't respond to me. I could envision how the show's run would be, with the strained addresses I'd have to make to him and the icy silences I'd receive in return. At best, I could claim to theater management that he was "difficult" and cling on to my position. Or maybe I could simply hope for the inevitable bad reviews and swift closure. The thing was, I'd seen him in *Square Root* rehearsals on the Claibe's stage, and he'd been *good*. I didn't care what kind of bum he might have been in his personal life. On the basis of his acting alone, he deserved better than this slow decline into obscurity, better than becoming the inevitable shrug of a shoulder to a *Trivial Pursuit* answer no one recognized.

Once more I looked at my watch. Nine twenty-seven. I stood up to look out the window, hoping that I'd be greeted with the happy sight of a train pulling into the tiny station. No such luck. "I'm going to make a phone call," I told Angel from where I stood near the door, enjoying a private tickle of delight at my little secret.

"Tell him I said hello."

"I'm not calling Grant," I told him, punching the call button on my cell phone.

"Oh, believe me, I know, dear." Angel accompanied his words with the blandest smile possible, but he knew he'd won a coup. "I know."

So much for my little secret. Still, I thrilled a little when Leo finally picked up at the garage. "Hey!" he said at my greeting. "How are you?"

What was I supposed to say? That I'd already gotten the best Christmas gift ever, the night before? That I wished I could pack him in that pillowcase of his mother's and take him back to Manhattan with me, instead of waiting a couple of weeks for his trip? That merely talking to him made me giddy? I wanted to say all that and so much more, but I settled for the short version. "I'm good." That seemed awfully inadequate. "I'm really, really, really good," I murmured. Apparently I was so good that I scared the station agent a little, because he pulled down a shutter on the inside of the booth, after giving me a frightened look. The fact that he was closing down before the train arrived seemed a little odd, but I didn't care. "Thank you for asking."

"Don't you go anywhere!" I heard Leo say in a sharp tone. "No, not you," he said to me once again. "My little brother's here. So are you on the train?"

"Not yet."

"Really? I thought you'd be a good chunk of the way through the state by now."

What had he thought I'd do, hijack the driver's seat and haul ass downstate? Cut a hole in the floor and run us home, Fred Flintstone–style? "The train's not here."

He huffed out his disbelief. "Sorry about that. Usually it's right on time."

I looked at my watch again. It was nine twenty-nine. Sweet of him to be worried. "We've still got one more minute before it's officially . . . Oh, crap." When finally the panic settled on me, it attacked first my shoulders and upper arms, then settled low in my back, as if I'd donned some kind of invisible electrified cape. "What time is it there?" I gabbled out.

He laughed. "The garage is a quarter mile from you, not in a different time zo—"

I was too busy wrenching the phone away from my ear to hear the rest of that sentence. My eyes focused on the numbers at the bottom of its little display: ten thirty. As I watched, it changed to ten thirty-one. "Oh!" I yelled, ripping out the tickets from inside my coat. "Oh, no!" Barely able to believe my eyes, I scanned the dates on all three. "Oh, no, he *didn't*!"

"Riley?" I heard from my phone's little speaker, where I held it to my shoulder. I couldn't answer; I had run outside onto the snow-packed sidewalk, where I held up my hand to my forehead and studied the clock tower in the distance. It was ten thirty. I clicked off the phone.

"Riley, what's going on?" Angel stood in the door, huddling his arms around his chest.

"December twenty-fifth!" I waved the tickets I still held in my hand. "I asked for the next train and he gave it to me. On Christmas day!" Angel stepped aside when I shoved my way halfway back into the station. "Grab your pillowcase, Carew," I shouted. "We're not clear of this place yet."

"I'm sure they'll let us on the train—"

Angel didn't get it. "We missed today's train," I told him. I'd been pretty loud after my realization, but I hadn't really felt any anger. At that moment, I knew why. "Don't you get it? It was a good one. It's funny. It's actually *funny!* We have been outscammed by the scammiest scamster ever. What time does your watch say?"

"Just after nine thirty."

"Right. So does my watch. So did every damned clock in the Mendez household, because *they set them all an hour back.* Every single clock in every single room. They even managed to get my wristwatch off in the middle of the night and change it, too. It was like the end of daylight saving time, two months late. Or ten months early, your pick. That train that woke me up? *That was our train!*"

Finally he understood. "Well, I'll be damned."

"Remember how weird the kids acted this morning? They were in on it. So was the ticket guy. I'm willing to bet the whole town wanted to guarantee we'd be stuck here through the pageant."

"They did this to us after all the help I gave them yesterday? I sewed more for them than I did for that Howard Crabtree costume revue I worked on, years ago. I don't think this is funny at all, Riley. I don't think this is funny at all."

"It's *because* you helped them. And because of . . ." I gestured at Harrison, who had obediently gathered his things and stood ready to go, though obviously he preferred to pretend I wasn't there.

"I have a family that I had planned to be with, Riley." His jaw was set and his hands lay on his hips as he lectured me. "My wife is an understanding and patient woman. She has to be, in our profession. She is used to my returning home in the small hours of the morning and having to work through her birthday, our anniversary, and Christmas Eve. She has been remarkably indulgent that our sojourn in Kettlebean has lasted longer than anticipated. Yet I can guarantee that the one thing that Melanie will *not* forgive is if I am not there tomorrow morning to preside over the festivities."

"Okay, okay." I tried to reassure him. "So it's not ha-ha funny. But you do kind of have to admire the ingenuity of it all." He wasn't buying it. "Listen, worse comes to worst, we get the stupid fuel pump back after the pageant. Leo installs it, we hop back in the van, and, barring any more breakdowns, we're back in Manhattan by what? Midnight? One in the morning? Nothing worse than a show night." Still he stared at me with the most hostility I'd seen on his face since a particular unpopular director had to his face dismissively called him a "seamstress." "It's going to be okay!"

"Of all the people in the world, I cannot believe that you, Ms. Riley McIntyre, are telling me that this will turn out all right."

I grinned. "The tables have turned, my friend."

"Hmpf." He shook his head. "Maybe it's because, as of last night, you have one less reason to want to leave this town?"

"Maybe." I couldn't resist the smile that crossed my lips right then, no matter how angry Angel might have been with me or the town or the situation. "Probably. But Angel, sweetie, that reason is our sole ally in this town now. Let's go talk to him, okay?"

After a moment, he nodded. "I intend to be home for Christmas tomorrow," he reminded me. "Or heads will roll."

We didn't pass a single townsperson on our walk. Considering Angel's black mood, that was probably a good thing. Nor did the sight of Leo outside the Mendez & Son garage bring him back to his usual unruffled self. Apparently we'd caught Leo just in time; he was stuffing his arms into his coat as if heading somewhere. Any other day before yesterday, I would have been intent solely on getting done what needed doing. That morning, though, I felt like jumping into the air, clicking my heels together, and humming a little song at the sight of him. I smiled and waited for the affectionate words he was no doubt preparing to greet me. His mouth opened. "Do you know what that little shit, my brother, did?"

Well, it wasn't exactly what I expected, but I could roll with it. Or maybe I couldn't, I realized, because I didn't exactly know which of the little shit's infractions Leo might mean. At the last possible moment, I decided to go with the least of them. "The thing with setting the clocks back?"

That was enough to stop him cold, one arm still unjacketed. "Oh . . . oh, don't even get me started on that stunt! Yes, I found out about that one, too." Too? So the original misdemeanor that Leo meant was . . . what, exactly? "I was coming to get you," he explained.

"Here we are," Angel pointed out. He still didn't sound happy. "Why don't we go inside?"

Any questions I might have had were instantly erased once I stepped into the garage, where both Leo and Maria sat in chairs dragged to the room's center. Their clasped hands hung limply between them. Oh. That. "So you knew," Leo said to both Angel and me. "They told me you knew."

I knew this might take a while. Since I doubted our star had a single coherent memory of the few hours we'd spent in here Friday evening, I pointed to the beat-up vinyl-covered sofa that sat near the register. "Harrison, why don't you have a seat . . ." His neck stiff, Harrison Carew stalked away before I could finish. Fine. I'd tried to be nice. I addressed Leo instead. "Angel found out . . . well, we both found out yesterday when Angel was trying to get her into a costume a little more Virgin Mary and a little less dowdy."

"Leo, this isn't none of their business, man," Nick complained, beginning to rise from his chair. He quickly sat down again when his brother wheeled around with both of his thick eyebrows raised high in the air. "This is for family."

Was this what it looked like when other people got stressed? I felt as if I were the one island of relative calm surrounded by crazy people. It was quite the novelty. "If this matter was for family, Nick, you would have come to me before today. *Before* everything got out of hand!" Leo thrust his fists into his pockets and paced back and forth. "I mean, Christ, there's the unprotected-sex issue, the pregnancy issue, but on top of that, you went and hid it for . . . I don't know how many months!" He turned to me. "Apparently Maria's sister called her at the grocery where she works to say their parents had found some book in her bedroom. *What You Expect* . . . I don't know. They were in hysterics."

"*What to Expect When You're Expecting*," said Maria, Angel, and I, in chorus. Both Leo and Nick regarded us all with surprise. It figured. I mean, Angel had been through four births. I'd endured the glow of pregnant friends. And Maria actually was expecting. She looked miserable, poor thing, as though she'd been on a long crying jag, and neither Mendez brother had thought to suggest a tissue or good cleanup. "It's my fault." She sniffled and wiped her eyes on the sleeve of her checkout-girl uniform. "They're going to kill us."

"If my folks don't kill the both of you first!" Leo reminded her.

Somehow I couldn't see either of the Mendezes running after these poor kids with a shotgun or a butcher knife. Though Dora might, just for sport. "They wouldn't. Would they?"

"Riley, you of all people should know my dad is crazy. *Loco.* Bugged-out insane. I mean, the clock stunt alone!" He paused. A corner of his lips twitched, and the anger in his eyes softened for a minute. "Though actually, no offense, that was kind of a good one."

"That's what I said!" I blurted out, pleased.

"If you two lovebirds would return to the matter at hand?" Angel had his coat off and his arms crossed, and his best displeased expression prominently on display over his half-glasses.

"Ew, you're in *love* with her?" Nick said, scowling. "That'll go away fast when you see her breasts."

"Hey!" protested both Leo and I. He turned to me and quirked an eyebrow. "Do I want to ask?"

"Not really."

"The point *is*," Angel emphasized, trying to keep everyone on track, "that we have a pair of young people in trouble. What are we going to do about it?"

We all looked at Maria and Nick, and then at one another. They looked so young and spectacularly helpless, slumped down in their chairs, covered by drab winter clothing. "I really don't know you anymore, Nicky," Leo said, shaking his head.

"I'm marrying her!" his brother protested. "I was planning to marry her all along! I was going to do the right thing. I didn't know when to say it, you know, so that people wouldn't get all cuckoo."

"It's not only that. It's the lying, the stealing."

"The breasts," I added.

"The bre—" Leo started to repeat, then reconsidered. "Yeah, maybe that's something I don't want to know. But Nicky, seriously, what is it that you are going to do?"

Nick spread his legs wide and looked down between his feet. Maria squeezed the hand she still held, and nodded. In a small voice, he said, "We talked about it. What we want is to go somewhere. Like, for the night. Then come back tomorrow and, you know, sit down and talk about it." He sighed. "With everybody. I mean, who's going to be upset about a baby on Christmas, right?" Leo nodded. I could tell he thought it was a reasonable idea. "So can I take your car?"

"I've got to be honest, bro." Leo shook his head. "No."

"I don't have my own car yet!"

"I don't know if I trust you with mine."

The brothers stared at each other for a few moments, utterly silent, both willing the impasse to end, but neither giving in. So stubborn, both of them. Especially when the solution was perfectly obvious. Was stepping in the right thing to do, though? I cleared my throat. "I'm usually the last person to get involved," I said, glancing over at Angel. When he nodded, not so much to agree as mutely to urge me on, I knew I was right. I walked over to the counter, where the van's keys still lay, and scooped them up. Back over to Nick I walked, letting the keyring dangle from my forefinger. I waved them before his eyes like a hypnotist. "Let's swap," I suggested. He didn't seem to follow, so I spelled it out for him. "My van for the night. You 'find' the fuel pump."

He understood that, all right. "Deal," he said, and without a word more, turned to Leo. "How long will it take to put that thing in?"

"You two can be on your way to Newark in an hour." He stopped and stabbed a finger at Nick. "But I don't want you overnighting in the vehicle. You've got—"

"I know, I know, I've got a future wife here, man, and the mother of my baby." Though her cheeks were tearstained, Maria lit up at the sound of those words. "I'm going to take care of her. We'll get a motel or something."

"Okay. Fine. Now go get the fuel pump." Leo turned to me as Nick leaped to his feet and immediately dashed into the back room, Maria following behind. "I knew they hid it somewhere in here! Hey, that was some sacrifice you made."

"Young man," Angel intoned, "that was no sacrifice. Because the moment that pageant is over, you personally are driving the three of us back to New York City. I have a wife and family of my own to take care of, and I intend to spend Christmas with them. Besides," he said, relenting a little. "It'll give the two of you a few more hours together."

Leo looked as if he didn't mind that proposition at all, and I was all the gladder for it. "We're staying for the pageant, then?" I asked.

Angel raised his eyebrows. "Child, thanks to you, the Kettlebean First United Methodist Church has lost both its Mary and its Joseph. And what is a pageant without a Mary or a Joseph?" While Leo and I regarded each other in sudden alarm, Angel smiled. "The girl who refuses to get involved is about to find herself waist-deep in it."

"Oh, no," I protested. "Oh, no!"

"Oh, yes," Angel said with finality. "And oh, by the way, young man." He clapped Leo on the shoulder. "Have I got a burnoose for you!"

Chapter Nine

The door to Mr. Henry R. Andersson's office opened a split second after I had removed both my poor dirty overalls and my turtleneck. I was clad only in my bare feet, thong, and bra, naturally. After all, why should Kettlebean let Riley McIntyre actually undress in solitude when everyone could have a gawk at her goods? Although my back was to the door, my arms flew across my chest. Then my butt. Then my chest again. "Nick," I said aloud. "If I find out that's you, you're not going to have to worry about fathering any other children."

"How about if it's me?" At the sound of Leo's voice, I turned and not-so-carefully picked my way through the office, knocking over a stack of sheet music from one of the chairs.

It was a little shyly that I tiptoed to give him a kiss. I wasn't exactly sure of the protocol of greeting someone you're mad about when he wore a burnoose and you were in day-old underwear. "That I don't mind in the least." Neither did I object when he grabbed me tightly and held me as if he'd never let me go. I didn't care that the Mexican blanket's fibers raked against my skin. And I certainly didn't protest his lips against mine. "What's going on out there?" I asked, as I left him briefly to clean up the music I'd spilled.

Leo made a show of thinking, but I could tell he was watching me prance around in practically nothing. "Hmmm. Let's see. We've got one set of parents blaming the Mendezes for all the ills of the world, from their daughter's pregnancy to population explosion to every disease known to mankind. Then there's another set of parents—mine— with a sobbing mother and a hyperactive father who keeps trying to reassure everyone that everything will work out. There's a missing Wise Man, a first-grade cherubim who's vomiting in the girls' room, a whole fleet of people with stage fright, a wardrobe master who keeps glaring at me like I've got designs on his favorite daughter, and, oh, yeah—the baby Jesus doll is missing his head." I peeked over the top of the desk at that one, eyebrows raised. "Apparently one of the children of Bethlehem was playing with him a few minutes ago, broke off the head, and won't tell anyone where it rolled. So watch where you step, pretty basically. I think that's it for scandal and drama."

"How about a music director with a bottle under his desk?" I asked, plopping a bottle of Bacardi 151 on the blotter. It had been hidden at the very back of the desk's leg recess, behind a pair of galoshes, where one of the sheets of music had fluttered. "Half-full. I guess that makes me an optimist, all of a sudden?"

Leo didn't seem surprised in the least. "Even a good teetotaling Methodist would be tempted to drink with Anneke Andersson as his wife. Come on, Mary. We're starting in, like, two minutes, and this show is nothing without a Virgin."

"I *hate* this," I muttered. Crap. I didn't have on my tunic yet. Luckily it was nothing more than the simplest of outfits—a potato sack with holes for my head and arms, basically. I fussed with the veil I draped over my braid more than I did the outfit itself, but in less than a minute, we both were out the door and down the hallway, on our way to the sanctuary. The flagstoned room was full of the pageant cast and a few ushers; at one end, an adult corralled the adorable cherubim with their new wings near the steps leading to the balcony, where they would sing carols at appropriate moments. The people of Bethlehem were trying to get themselves in order without making too much noise. And with a clipboard in his hand, Angel presided over the ragtag lot, making sure everyone was where they needed to be. Through the whispers, excitement was palpable in the air. I said a short swear word and brought us to an abrupt stop.

"It'll be okay," Leo reassured me. "I'm the one with lines!" he cleared his throat. " 'Have you any room at this inn tonight?' " he murmured softly.

I tried to ignore the fact that he was absolutely adorable, practicing his one line like that, and explained: "I didn't put that bottle back," I said in a low voice. "I don't want Mr. Andersson thinking I was going through his stuff, after he's been nice enough to lend me his office for my dressing room."

"We'll take care of it," he assured me, pointing to the choir loft behind the lectern. "Look, he's at the organ. Mrs. Andersson is doing her solo. He won't be going back to his office until after you've changed back into your regular clothes. Let's go."

I balked. No one told me there were going to be so many *people*. They crowded the pews of the small church, dressed in their Sunday finest. Families. Old men and women and couples with grown children come home for the holidays. I didn't know there were enough citizens in Kettlebean to fill all those seats, especially with so many in the actual pageant. But there they all were, listening to Anneke's vibrato-laden rendition of "O Holy Night," respectful and silent. "I can't do this," I whispered to him.

"You're going to have to," he said. I looked up. Mrs. Andersson had regained the lectern, and the first of the people of Bethlehem had taken steps down the main aisle. Where the altar normally sat, Leo's beautiful storybook cutouts provided the backdrop for the ancient world we'd be inhabiting for the next hour.

"Prithee, gentle wanderer," said one to another. "But which way lies Bethlehem? For our Emperor . . . for our Emperor Augustus . . ." All of us in the narthex held our breath. Would he get it? "For our Emperor Augustus hath decreed that we should return to the land of our fathers so that our names may be recorded in the census! Hey, I got it!" The audience laughed. A woman near me smiled my way and made a mime of wiping her brow with relief.

"Bethlehem is well crowded on this eve," said the other man, more confident in his lines. "It may well be that many travelers on this fair night may find themselves without shelter."

By now, more and more of the cast had wandered down the aisles. Angel approached us, clipboard in hand. "Very nice," he said, appraising his handiwork. "Very nice, you two."

"You're an evil man, and I'm going to have my revenge in New York, you know," I hissed at him.

"La-la-la, can't hear you," he lied, pretending to be writing something.

"Where's Harrison?"

He heard that one well enough. "He was in the way, so I sent him to the choir director's office a minute ago." Angel tilted his head, listening to the action. He didn't see my panicked jaw trying to work out the warning I needed to give him. "Okay, you're on."

"But—" That bottle of rum was in plain view!

"You're *on*," he repeated, pushing me from behind. I looked over at Leo for support, but he was practicing his line to himself, over and over.

I couldn't leave without warning Angel. "He's going to—"

"Shut up and look holy!" One mighty shove, and I found myself walking down the main aisle.

From the lectern, Mrs. Andersson's gray bob joggled up and down as she announced, "And from Nazareth, in Galilee, came Mary and Joseph to Bethlehem in Judea, for Joseph was of the lineage of David." Heads turned. People were looking at me. At *me!* That realization was enough to make me hold my hands prayerfully, as I'd been instructed, and to look down at my feet. I didn't feel at all holy with the murderous thoughts I was having. When Harrison got sloppy drunk off of that bottle of liquor . . .

And then, from above me, the cherubim began to sing in their sweet child trebles.

> *O little town of Bethlehem*
> *How still we see thee lie!*
> *Above thy deep and dreamless sleep*
> *The silent stars go by.*

Leo squeezed my hand right then. And suddenly it struck me: this pageant was very real. I'd derided it in my mind for days, thinking of it as some kind of stupid, cutesy-pie tradition that no one really cared about. Yet here I was, trembling, worried I wasn't good enough. Everything else in my life seemed to vanish at that moment—all the worries, the fears, the grudges. Let Harrison drink himself into a stupor. Barring ugly pit stops, it would make him more docile on the trip home. Forget Nick and Maria and Hector Mendez, and all the anxiety I'd been carrying around like a backpack of wet sand. The only things that mattered right at that moment were the pageant and the feeling of Leo's hand on mine, as he led me toward the holy city.

And Mrs. Robinson. Mrs. Robinson mattered, too. I could sense her shining eyes staring at the two of us as we passed where she sat next to her daughter, wheelchair positioned in front of the first row. Amazing that she had done this for forty-nine years on her own. It was a feat that made the most hectic production I'd ever worked look like a picnic.

How did actors cope when they were onstage? Did the action always fly by in a rush like this? From backstage, shows always proceeded uniformly and according to script. Yet here I was in the middle of it, and everything seemed to be speeding by. I was in the middle of some time-lapse effect, in which I stood stationary and the world rushed around me while I watched, only half comprehending. There were carols I barely remembered, and snippets of verse that sounded familiar from my youth. The plywood cover of the inn backdrop had closed at some point, and I found myself kneeling before Leo's beautiful pop-up construction of the Bethlehem stable, with its stylized white animals to either side. My own identity and sense of time seemed to vanish, with all those people's eyes on me. I'd always seen acting as simply another duty, a form of labor like any other. Yet there was great freedom in losing myself under the spotlight. I could finally see how actors found it addictive.

A whisper brought me crashing back down to earth. "Pssssssst." I turned my head, just as the congregation began singing "What Child Is This?" Dora Mendez gestured at me from behind the Christmas tree, a bundle in her arms.

"We're supposed to receive the baby Jesus now," Leo murmured, leading me up the stairs and behind the tall fir. Almost immediately, Dora handled me the holy infant, wrapped in swaddling clothes. "Did you find the head?" Leo whispered to his sister.

Why was she beaming? She didn't like me. She'd never liked me. And now she was granting me a beatific grin? "No," she admitted. "I found a substitute. Break a leg, Riley!"

She could have meant that literally, but I didn't have time to navigate the intricate maze that is the adolescent mind. We were back on. With my newborn baby in my arms, Joseph and I stepped back out into view. Trying to appear motherly, I pulled back the opening of the bundle and gently smiled down into the face of . . .

What the heck child *was* this? An infant holy, infant lowly, with a Michaelson's Heat-'n'-Eat Meat Pie for its head. Country Cottage flavor, by the smell of it.

So startled was I that I fumbled the bundle and caught it only at the last possible second, after several terrifying moments in which I envisioned the baby Jesus' meat-pie head bouncing from my arms and down the steps of the altar, finally to collapse in a greasy puddle at Mrs. Robinson's feet. When I looked over my shoulder, I saw Dora smirking my way. That little wench had done this deliberately, to throw me! With the shepherds approaching, however, there was really little I could do but gaze back down at the meat pie and pretend I'd given birth to the darned thing.

The hymn ended. We were surrounded by the shepherds of the field, each swathed in yards of rough burlap, thanks to Angel. All reverently bowed on bended knee to the newborn king in my arms. I recognized the guy from the train station immediately, but he wouldn't meet my eyes. Mrs. Mendez, however, shot her son a proud smile before gazing at my feet. A final shepherd straggled in behind the others, tall and slow-moving, his gait at once familiar, though I couldn't place him. Mrs. Andersson, at the lectern, resumed her narration. "And there were in the same country . . ."

Her voice trailed off and fell silent. Something was happening where I stood. The last of the shepherds hadn't bowed down with the others; instead he had wended his way through the prone forms and walked straight to me. For a moment I thought that perhaps I was missing one of my cues. I had a sudden sympathy for all the actors I'd ever prompted from the wings over the years, because I felt helpless and paralyzed. Was I supposed to be doing something? Why was the shepherd trying to take baby Jesus? I didn't remember any of this from the rehearsal!

And then the burlap fell from the shepherd's head to reveal his face. "Harrison," I whispered. What in the heck?

If there had been any justice in this world, I should have gotten rave reviews for the moment I instinctively helped Harrison cradle the baby's head, once it shifted from my arms to his. Yet I wasn't really trying for realism—I was still haunted by that image of the squashed Messiah's head in front of God and the entire Methodist congregation. His posture proud and erect, his exposed chin lifted high, Harrison turned to the audience. Did he smell of rum? I couldn't tell. I feared he must. Why else would he have interrupted the proceedings? We weren't going to leave this town after the performance. We were going to be sticked-and-stoned to death for messing it up.

He who had faced glittering opening-night audiences of New York's crème de la crème looked out at the citizens of Kettlebean, opened his mouth . . . and hesitated. He who had thrilled to tears men and women of all walks of life, froze. I waited for someone to realize that he wasn't supposed to be there, but no one moved. All attention was on Harrison Carew and the bundle he held in his arms. Mrs. Robinson, the veritable picture of frailty, held her hands together in rapture, as if the actor's unexpected presence were an unannounced surprise, especially for her.

Stalling for time, Harrison parted the cloth covering the infant's face, bent down his head, and gazed straight into the heart of darkness.

For several moments he stared at that meat pie, blinking. Then he looked at me, as if waiting for me to give him a cue. I couldn't do a thing. I wanted to improvise something, or to make him suddenly fade into the background, but it was too late. All I knew was that the last thing I wanted, the last thing that could possibly happen at this point of the pageant, would be for Harrison to utter the catchphrase that had brought him so much fame and residuals for the last ten years.

Slowly, inexorably, he lifted the bundled child out to the audience as would a butler proffer a tray of delectable viands to his master. I closed my eyes and waited, certain of what was coming.

" 'And there were in the same country shepherds abiding in the field, keeping watch over their flock by night.' " His voice was mellifluous and strong, reaching the upper rows of the balcony as effortlessly as if he were speaking to someone a few feet away. "And, lo, the angel of the Lord came upon them, and the glory of the Lord shone round about them; and they were sore afraid. And the angel said unto them, 'Fear not: for, behold, I bring you good tidings of great joy, for unto you is born this day in the city of David a Savior, which is Christ the Lord.'"

Through the tears in my eyes, I could see Angel at the very back of the sanctuary, standing in the door of the narthex all by himself. I wanted to pick up the skirt of my tunic, run to him, and give him a great big hug. He hadn't sent Harrison into that office to keep him out of the way. He'd decided at the last minute to put the man to work, and as a result, Harrison had stolen the show. The audience was eating from the palm of his hand, and he knew it. His voice grew stronger as he recited the next verse. "And suddenly there was with the angel a multitude of the heavenly host praising God, and saying, 'Glory to God in the highest! And on earth—peace and goodwill toward all!'"

The applause began before he'd uttered the last word. In the front row, Mrs. Robinson dabbed at her eyes with a tissue, the smile on her face so broad that it shone brighter than all the church's twinkling Christmas lights combined. From the back of the crowd, someone let loose with a whistle, and another quickly followed. Even Mrs. Andersson had stepped away from the microphone, though her quick claps thudded over the loudspeakers. I felt Leo's hand take mine. I turned to look up at his sweet, lovely face while he spoke loudly enough to be heard over the ovation. "They'll remember this for a long time to come, you know." He laughed. "You planned all this, didn't you?"

"I didn't, I swear!" At that moment, standing in front of that beautiful backdrop of his, I knew his laughter was something I'd want to hear for years to come. "It was all his own idea."

I turned back to find Harrison ignoring his acclaim so

that he could regard me. He carried baby Jesus as would an old man his own grandchild—with tenderness and delicacy, as if afraid of harming a hair on the baby's head. That moment was the first time in days that we had looked at each other, and for a moment I feared what he might have to say. When he spoke, however, it was with a certain timidity. "Do you think," he said, hesitating, "that you can work with me?"

I'd gotten the sign I'd asked for. "Yes, sir," I replied, nodding gravely. "I believe I can."

Members of the audience were on their feet now, still applauding as loudly as at any Broadway curtain call, as the organ began to sound the opening chords of a joyful carol. Harrison bowed in my direction once more. "May I ask you a question?"

I nodded, squeezing Leo's hand. "Anything."

"Am I utterly mistaken, or does the baby Jesus have a meat pie for his head?"

It was difficult not to break into laughter, but I managed to remain somber. "I'm afraid he does."

"Ah," he said, nodding as if that were perfectly reasonable. "I'm so glad. For a moment I thought I was hallucinating. Still. Very odd, that."

When he joined in with the hymn, it was not with the voice of a has-been who yearned for younger and better days, but the strong baritone of a man facing a new prime of his life. I placed my hand in the middle of his back to show my support, then opened my mouth to join. Leo placed his hands on my shoulders, his tenor mingling, and so did Angel, his deep, rumbling bass audible from the back of the church. We all sang that Christmas Eve, our voices raised in celebration of the season.

Hark! the herald angels sing, glory to the newborn king!

LISA KLEYPAS
LISA CACH * CLAUDIA DAIN
LYNSAY SANDS

Wish List

Dear St. Nicholas—
What we'd really like for Xmas this year is:

An Irish Estate
A Family
~~Mountains of Sugarplums~~ (Too fattening)
A Quiet Elopement
Someone to ~~burn~~ close down all the London clubs (like White's)!
Marriage to a Man who is Honest, Loving, Sexy, Handsome, and Titled.

But we know there aren't enough of those to go around...
are there?

—*Respectfully,*
Four Hopeful English Ladies

NAOMI NEALE
CALENDAR GIRL

Name: Nan Cloutier

Address: Follow the gang graffiti until you reach the decrepit bakery. See the rooms above that even a squatter wouldn't claim? That's my little Manhattan paradise.

Education: (Totally useless) Liberal Arts degree from an Ivy League university.

Employment History: Cheer Facilitator for Seasonal Staffers Inc. Responsible for spreading merriment and not throttling fellow employees or shoppers, as appropriate.

Career Goal: Is there a career track that will maybe, just maybe, help me attract the attention of the department store heir of my dreams?

No way. That's a full-time job in itself!

- -

The Care & Feeding of Pirates

Jennifer Ashley

Lovely Shoshana was ripped from the arms of her Apache people to be raised as a white woman. But when she returns to the Arizona Territory, a perplexing dream begins to haunt her; a vision of a golden eagle carrying her mother to safety and beckoning her home. Whether her mother is still alive or not, Shoshana knows she must answer the mysterious call. Ignoring her adoptive father's warnings, she sets out to explore the place of her birth. But will she find her mother, a scalper, or the legendary warrior whose honor is admired even in Fort Chance, and whose bronzed good looks are surpassed only by his...

Dream of Me
LISA CACH

Theron, undying creature of the Night World, knows everything about making love. But though he's an incubus, a bringer of carnal dreams to sleeping maids, he has grander ambition. He plots to step into the mortal world and rule as king.

The beautiful Lucia is imprisoned in a fortress atop a mountain. Her betrothed, Prince Vlad of Wallachia, wants her purity intact; but when the prince breaks his vow, nothing can keep her safe. In the name of vengeance, Lucia will be subjected to Theron's seduction; she will learn all his lips might teach.

A demon of lust and a sheltered princess: each dreams of what they've never had. They're about to get everything they wish…and more.

Kate Moore

SEXY LEXY

In fleeing to Drake's Point, California, and buying an inn, Lexy Clark stretches the truth. Her bestseller—*Workout Sex, A Girl's Guide to Home Fitness*—was written for active women with busy lives. Its publicity campaign has led to Lexy's days being filled with men who want her to spend her fifteen minutes of fame in compromising positions. Changing her name and moving to a remote little town seemed the best escape.

Until she meets Sam Worth. Lexy can't imagine a better partner for "home fitness"—and maybe more. But Sam is too smart to buy Lexy's innkeeper disguise for long. She is willing to let him uncover everything about her—except the truth. For when fame catches up with her, will Sam still want Sexy Lexy?